MW00574290

CHRISTMAS
AND OTHER
HORRORS

Also edited by Ellen Datlow and available from Titan Books

When Things Get Dark: Stories Inspired by Shirley Jackson

CHRISTMAS
AND OTHER
HORRORS

EDITED BY ELLEN DATLOW

TITAN BOOKS

Christmas and Other Horrors
Print edition ISBN: 9781803363264
E-book edition ISBN: 9781803363271

Published by Titan Books
A division of Titan Publishing Group Ltd
144 Southwark Street, London SE1 0UP
www.titanbooks.com

First edition: October 2023
10 9 8 7 6 5 4 3

This is a work of fiction. All of the characters, organizations, and events portrayed in this novel are either products of the author's imagination or are used fictitiously. Any resemblance to actual persons, living or dead (except for satirical purposes), is entirely coincidental.

Introduction © Ellen Datlow 2023
The Importance of a Tidy Home © Christopher Golden 2023
The Ones He Takes © Benjamin Percy 2023
His Castle © Alma Katsu 2023
The Mawkin Field © Terry Dowling 2023
The Blessing of the Waters © Nick Mamatas 2023
Dry and Ready © Glen Hirshberg 2023
Last Drinks at Bondi Beach © Garth Nix 2023
Return to Bear Creek Lodge © Tananarive Due 2023
The Ghost of Christmases Past © Richard Kadrey 2023
Our Recent Unpleasantness © Stephen Graham Jones 2023
All the Pretty People © Nadia Bulkin 2023
Löyly Sow-na © Josh Malerman 2023
Cold © Cassandra Khaw 2023
Gravé of Small Birds © Kaaron Warren 2023
The Visitation © Jeffrey Ford 2023
The Lord of Misrule © M. Rickert 2023
No Light, No Light © Gemma Files 2023
After Words © John Langan 2023

CONTENTS

INTRODUCTION

WHAT do *you* think of when you think of the celebrations focused around the winter solstice? Gift-giving, eating and drinking with friends and family around a fire?

But what if someone in your family wanted to kill you? What if the jolly, gift-giving Santa Claus got pretty damned angry if he didn't get what he considered *his* due? What if you discovered that your friends lied to you? What if the rituals you've honored over the decades are broached—just one time?

Even though many celebrate the winter solstice as a time of joy, there is a darker tradition of ghost tales and horror stories taking place around the time of the winter solstice. The stories in this anthology embrace that dark tradition by presenting the unholy, the dangerous, the horrific aspects of a time when families and friends come together—for better and worse.

Here you'll find the Celtic Mari Lwyd; wood demons of Finnish mythology; the Schnabelperchten—creatures from

Austrian mythology that will punish you if your house isn't up to their standards of cleanliness during their annual visit; the Lord of Misrule, whose origin dates back to Roman times and who was appointed a master of revels; a Santa Claus who is not the nice guy we like to believe he is; a carnivorous witch; young gods overthrowing older gods; a time tripping nightmare on the shortest day of the year, and other strange horrors.

I hope these stories will amuse you while causing that cold finger of dread to creep up your neck.

THE IMPORTANCE OF A TIDY HOME

Christopher Golden

I F anyone had told Freddy he would one day be elbow deep in a garbage bin behind a third-rate restaurant in Salzburg, searching for a late dinner, he would have scoffed at them. Haughtily, of course, the way professors are meant to scoff. That had been his occupation—both vocation and avocation—until 1957, when addiction to morphine had led first to petty crimes and then to a psychiatric hospital. This was before Austria had begun to approach drug addiction as a problem requiring treatment instead of punishment, and so there had been a bit of time in prison as well.

Prison had helped.

Freddy knew that wasn't the case for many who had been in his position, but for him, prison had been a time of clarity. Without drugs, without alcohol, without distraction. He had learned that the mania he had always experienced, the way his skull felt like a hive of agitated bees, could be survived. And if that meant he sometimes saw things that weren't there, or said things that others interpreted as either a bit mad or wildly inappropriate, well, that was the eccentricity of a professor.

Of course, once he had been released, no one wanted him as a professor anymore. Or anything else, for that matter.

By that night, the fifth of January, 1973, he had been living without a home for nine years, during which time he had never diluted his brain with a single ounce of alcohol, nor the use of any illegal substance. But since the polite society of his city had finished with him, Freddy had finished with it. He lived in its parks and haunted its alleys, he accepted the offerings of strangers but never met their eyes, he forged a life from their castoffs, from food and clothing discarded and forgotten just as he had been.

The first time he saw the Schnabelperchten walking the streets in their black robes, with their gleaming shears and their enormous, bone-like beaks protruding from beneath their hoods, it did not surprise him that they passed him by. Their duties could not bring them to his doorstep, because of course he had none. No threshold, no door, no visitors, nowhere to mark the start of a new year, only the continued existence of life invisible, a creature unseen. Quiet, even when loud.

The Schnabelperchten were even quieter.

Tonight, he and his friend Bern were out together in search of food. Freddy had forgotten the date until he spotted the creatures. It was the fourth January fifth he had seen them, and each time they had ignored him. He presumed they appeared every year and that he had slept through their arrival in the years he had missed them.

He watched as they crept along the streets, leaving no trace of their passage through the lightly falling snow. They were delicate creatures, some with their brooms and others with shears, and no door was ever locked to them. Every home opened, no matter how tightly it had been shut up for the evening.

"Chi chi chi," they whispered in the hush of falling snow, and they went about their business.

Freddy climbed down from the side of the garbage bin, holding the bag of leftovers he had known he would find there. The kitchen staff always wrapped the food being discarded and placed it in a single bag along with the uneaten bread. The restaurant manager frowned upon this practice and had shouted at his employees for encouraging nightly visits from the homeless, but they were kind and waited until he was out of the kitchen before putting out the bag. This place was no Gablerbräu, but the staff there had never been so kind, and even if they had been, Freddy did not like roving around that part of the city late at night. It felt more empty, more open, as if anything could happen. Here, there were more homes, lived in by people who desired quiet evenings, away from the downtown.

A clang of metal echoed along the alley.

Bern had let the garbage bin's cover come crashing down. Freddy glanced anxiously around, afraid they would draw unwanted attention. If they created any nuisance, their lives would become more difficult. Sometimes he grew frustrated with Bern for his clumsiness, though never for his addiction. Alcoholism made Bern a fool, but it was the engine that drove him, as much a part of him as his left leg.

"Hush," Freddy said in German, more a plea than an admonition. "Don't be a fool."

Bern did not so much as look at him. Thin and gray, unshaven and unkempt, in an ill-fitting suit that did nothing to disguise the state of his dissolution, he staggered from beside the bin to stand next to Freddy.

"Don't you see them?" he whispered.

Freddy glanced from the alley into the street again. The Schnabelperchten were still passing by, spread out like a hunting party, perhaps twenty feet separating each from the next, some on one side of the street and some on the other. The most fascinating thing about them was the size of those beaks, at least eighteen inches in length, but wide enough that if one could draw back their hoods, the creatures would not have any face at all—or so it seemed. Only beak, the gray-white of bone. The first time he had seen them, nine years ago, Freddy had been reminded of old photos of plague doctors, but these were not masks, nor did they have anything like goggles to resemble eyes.

They glided along the road. Even as he looked, he saw one approach a door that led to a stairwell, rising to the apartment above the flower shop across the street. Silently, Freddy hoped the owners of that shop kept a tidy home.

"Freddy," Bern rasped, shaking him by the shoulder. "Don't you see them?"

"Hush. Of course I see them."

"Are they ghosts?" Bern whispered. "They don't look like ghosts—they seem solid enough. Are they demons?"

Freddy pondered that. "Honestly, I'm not really sure what they are, though they are certainly not people. They are Schnabelperchten."

The word caused Bern to screw up his face in a way that made him look like a toddler given an unfamiliar vegetable for the first time.

"I don't understand. You've just said they're not people, not human. Aren't you frightened?"

Acid burned in Freddy's gut. His laugh was bitter. "Of the Schnabelperchten? Certainly not. You and I have nothing to fear."

"But what *are* they?" Bern prodded.

Freddy gazed at him, trying not to let his friend see the flicker of distaste that passed through him. "I forget, sometimes, that you are not from Salzburg—"

"What has that got to do with anything?"

"If you were a child here, you would know the story," Freddy replied. He patted Bern's back. "Come with me."

His friend hesitated, but when Freddy began to walk along the alley, Bern followed. Most of the Schnabelperchten had already passed by, but there were a few stragglers who had gone into the homes along the street and only now emerged. Without eyes, it was difficult to know for certain whether the Schnabelperchten noticed them, but they showed no interest. They might as well have been dust motes in the air or dry leaves that skittered along the road.

"Do they not see us?" Bern asked.

"They are like most of the people in this city. We are invisible to them," he replied.

One of the Schnabelperchten passed by, and in the light of a streetlamp they could see blood on the blades of its shears, dripping onto the street. When Bern saw that blood, he looked as if he might be sick.

"Come," Freddy said. "Those two."

He pointed at a pair of the creatures further up the block. They approached the door of a two-story home. Bern followed anxiously as Freddy crept up behind the two beaked Inspectors.

One of them extended a skinny hand with long fingers like the legs of spiders and turned the doorknob. It ought to have been locked, and Freddy believed that if he or Bern had tried the knob it would not have turned. But for the Inspectors, no door was ever locked. They opened the door and stepped across the threshold. Freddy caught the door before the Schnabelperchten could close it. He heard Bern suck in a terrified breath behind him, but the Inspector who had tried to shut the door just left it and began to move through the house.

"I've followed them before," Freddy whispered, worried more about disturbing the family living in the home than drawing the attention of the creatures.

Inside, the Inspectors began to move about the place, spidery fingers gliding along tabletops in search of dust, beaks lowering to discover if the floors had been swept or vacuumed.

"Chi chi chi," they said quietly, without mouths.

One in the kitchen brought its head down close to the stove and seemed to study its surface for much too long, perhaps deliberating on its relative cleanliness.

Freddy leaned over to whisper into Bern's ear. His friend was trembling.

"It is the Epiphany," he said. "Christmas ends tonight. January first begins the calendar year, but tonight is truly the beginning of the New Year. The Schnabelperchten bring happiness and blessings for the coming year, but only to those who are properly prepared for this new beginning, who have set their houses in order."

"What happens if they enter a home that has not been tidied in anticipation of the new year?" Bern whispered.

Bern watched intently as one of the Inspectors went up the stairs, shears hung at its side. Freddy understood his fear, even found it somewhat delicious, but Bern was his friend and he knew there was cruelty in allowing him to continue in ignorance.

"Something horrible," Freddy said. He took his friend by the wrist and shook it, forcing Bern to look at him. "But we have no home. They are not here for us. Do you see?"

At last, Bern seemed to exhale.

Moments later, the Inspector who had gone to the second floor returned, its shears still clean. It joined its fellow Schnabelperchten and the creatures walked right past Freddy and Bern and out the door. This time it was Bern who led the pursuit of them.

Out on the street again, the breeze was chilly enough to remind them they were alive. Snow fell gently, a hush that felt like it made some sound just beyond the limit of their hearing, though it was only silence.

In morbid fascination, they followed the two creatures while other Schnabelperchten drifted along the street around them, wordless and intent. Moving amongst them, ignored as if invisible, long after midnight and in the quiet hush of gently falling snow, they might as well have been wandering the street inside some Christmas snow globe.

"What *are* they?" Bern wondered aloud.

"Spirits," Freddy replied. It was the only word that felt acceptable. He had so many questions but no real answers. The Schnabelperchten came out one night a year, which meant every other night they were somewhere else. If he could ask them anything, it would be about that.

Schnabelperchten glided silently from building to building. Up along the road, Freddy saw others crawling on the outside of several taller buildings, cloaks billowing in the breeze as they slid open windows that should have been locked. One perched at the edge of a rooftop, scuttled to a domed skylight, opened it and vanished within, its beak leading the way.

Somewhere, Freddy heard a baby crying. The infant's wail pierced the oh-so-silent night, and then abruptly ceased. He pressed his eyes tightly shut, forcing himself not to imagine the things his darker fears wanted him to imagine.

They reached the house where the two Schnabelperchten they were following had gone inside. Bern turned the knob and the door opened. It had unlocked for the Inspectors and remained unlocked, at least until the creatures departed. Bern did not hesitate now—he stepped over the threshold as if he had forgotten Freddy entirely, too curious. Too eager.

Suddenly this felt too intimate. They were intruding on this quiet moment, this breath taken and held until sunrise, when the new year would really begin in earnest. He had a spot behind an old, crumbling school building where heat vented from inside created a small bubble of warmth near the dumpster. The roof's overhang kept the elements off his head except on the worst nights, and he wanted to go back there now, to his spot.

"Bern," he rasped, trying to grab his friend by the back of his coat.

But Bern had passed through the home's little entryway, where coats hung haphazardly on metal hooks—too many coats, too few hooks—and three pair of winter boots were arranged along the wall. Not impeccably neat, but he thought they would pass inspection.

Then he followed Bern into the living room, and he froze.

Antlers hung from the wall above the fireplace. The room held an eclectic array of furniture, most of it threadbare and in mismatched floral patterns. A small black-and-white television stood on a tray table beside a fat armchair. Magazines were strewn across the coffee table and piled beside the armchair. An open box of biscuits sat amongst the magazines. A coffee cup and a plate of crumbs and grape stems had been abandoned there. The entire room needed to be straightened, vacuumed, dusted, but the worst of it was the stink of cat urine and the litter box in the far corner, in front of an overstuffed bookshelf that looked as if the books had been stacked and piled by an angry drunk.

Across the room, through an arched entryway that led into the hall, Freddy saw the two Schnabelperchten return from the kitchen and start up the stairs. Bern padded across the stained carpet to follow.

Freddy lunged to grab his arm. "Don't be a fool."

Bern turned to glare at him. "They can't see us."

"We should not intrude," Freddy said. When Bern ignored him, Freddy grabbed him again. "You don't want to see this."

Bern scowled, shook himself loose, and darted for the steps before Freddy could try to drag him from the house. Freddy cursed under his breath and followed. He reached for Bern's coat a third time, but the other man was younger, quicker, and reached the second floor before Freddy could catch up to him.

The top step might as well have been a brick wall. This was as far as Freddy was willing to go. On that last step, he watched as Bern slunk along the corridor and peered into one room, then moved on to the next. Before he reached that room, the noises began.

From the room at the end of the hall came a sound Freddy had heard once before in life, and far too often in nightmares. The sound of shears plunging into flesh—a wet, violent puncture—and then the hushed metal clack of the shears being used.

Bern reached the door from which the noises emanated.

Freddy had warned him, had as much as told him without telling him, but the fool had needed to see for himself. Grim fascination, perhaps, or pure sadism—Freddy didn't think it mattered which. In that bedroom doorway, Bern stood with his eyes widening and let out a scream of horror. Freddy knew he should run, but his feet moved him in the wrong direction, toward his friend instead of away.

He rushed up behind Bern and clamped a hand over his mouth. It muffled the scream, and a second later Bern went silent, perhaps realizing how foolish he'd been.

"Quickly," Freddy whispered in his ear. "Let's go."

Bern whimpered but did not move. Freddy nearly dragged him, but in glancing up at his friend, he had a view over Bern's shoulder and into the bedroom. One of the Schnabelperchten straddled the woman on the bed, using its shears to open her from groin to breastbone. The whole room was in disarray, clothes piled everywhere, plates and cups on the nightstands.

On the floor, the second Inspector knelt beside the corpse of the husband. His guts had been laid open by the shears of the Schnabelperchten and the creature had reached both hands into the dead man's torso and now slid intestines out from his steaming insides, hand over hand, arranging them around the body with a kind of artistry.

The Schnabelperchten disemboweling the man on the floor kept working, but the one on the bed had frozen in the midst of cutting, disrupted by Bern's scream. Shears in hand, it turned its eyeless, mouthless beak toward them and Freddy could feel the weight of its regard, knew that despite the lack of eyes, the creature studied them.

The dead woman's head lolled to one side. Perhaps she had not quite been dead, but now her sightless eyes seemed to gaze at the two men in her bedroom doorway as if accusing them. As if asking why they had not stopped this, why they did not step in, even now, to prevent the further evisceration and desecration that would unfold here.

Freddy held his breath, telling himself that none of this was his fault. These people had comforts that had been beyond his grasp for years. They had heat and running water and a roof over their heads. They had quiet nights in which they could pretend the rest of the world did not exist. They had food to eat, and they'd had each other. He told himself they must not be from Salzburg, or they were jaded young people who did not believe in the old stories. He told himself perhaps they had been unpleasant people whose neighbors and friends did not care for them enough to warn them, to teach them the importance of a tidy home.

"Freddy," Bern whispered, his voice cracking.

The hooded Schnabelperchten tilted its head, its focus more intent.

"Chi chi chi," it whispered, with no mouth.

Freddy backed away from the bedroom doorway, tugging Bern with him. The moment they began to retreat, the Schnabelperchten on the bed returned to gutting the woman, no longer interested in the witnesses.

Hauling Bern behind him by the wrist, Freddy bustled down the stairs and out the front door. It clacked shut behind them, the noise like a whipcrack in the night. The snow fell thicker and heavier now and the creatures on the street moved like ghosts, their soft *chi chi chi* carried on the wind.

Instinct sent Freddy down a side street. A Schnabelperchten emerged alone from a doorway, gore dripping thick and red from its shears. Its beak did not turn toward them, but it paused and stood in statuesque silence as they passed.

"Where are we going?" Bern whispered, voice cracking.

"My spot," Freddy said, as if it were the stupidest question in the world.

Bern twisted his wrist free and stopped, there in the quiet of Epiphany Night. "Too exposed. We need to hide."

For the first time, Freddy saw the tears in his eyes, the wetness of his cheeks, red from the cold. He wanted to tell Bern they had nothing to worry about, that they had no homes and therefore were in no danger, but he had not liked the way the creature inside that second house had noticed them. Looked at them, if it could be said to look at anything.

"Where, then?"

Bern wiped at his tears. He hesitated a moment as if making a decision, then waved for Freddy to follow. With Bern leading the way, they jogged along the street, then through a side alley, alongside an old stone wall, then behind an ugly, no-frills hotel. Through a gap in the fence behind the hotel, they emerged in the lot of a used car dealership and auto body shop. The pavement had cracks everywhere, weeds growing up between them.

Freddy looked back through the gap in the fence and felt a ripple of relief. There was no sign of the Schnabelperchten.

"I think we're okay," he said.

"This way," Bern replied.

He led Freddy to the other end of the car lot. There were junkers back here, probably only used for parts. Bern brought him to an ugly gray Auto Union station wagon from the late 1950s, tucked between the shells of cars in even worse condition. Rusted and dented, the windshield covered in snow, the wagon was otherwise intact. The tires sagged like an old man's belly.

Bern opened the driver's door, head low, and gestured for Freddy to get in on the passenger side. Aside from the wagon's rear hatch, those were the only two doors. Freddy glanced around, but he realized this wasn't the sort of place that would have a security guard. There were no brand new vehicles here.

Inside the car, he tried to close the door as quietly as possible, gritting his teeth at the rusty squeal of its hinges. Bern shut his door, and then they were out of the wind and the snow. From inside, Freddy could see the windshield was spider-webbed with cracks and covered in grime under the coating of falling snow. It was certainly cold in the car, but better than being outdoors tonight.

"The owner of the shop knows I sleep here," Bern said, his voice dull and hollow, as if all the life had been drained out of him. "We can hide until morning. They... those things will be gone by morning, right?"

Freddy nodded. It surprised him that Bern had brought him to this shelter. They had known each other for long enough that Freddy thought of Bern as his friend, but if the owner of the car lot really didn't mind Bern sleeping in this dead, rusty car, it was a secret he had taken a risk in sharing. If Freddy told others, soon there might be a dozen people trying to sleep in these cars, and surely that would lead to the owner having a change of heart.

"Thank you," Freddy said.

Bern understood. "I'm trusting you."

"I know."

That was it.

Freddy thought Bern would want to talk about what they had seen, but Bern only shivered and then climbed over the seat into the back of the wagon. There were blankets back there, dirty and musty, but warm. Freddy watched as his friend began to dig himself into a kind of nest of blankets and clothing. There were empty bottles and crushed cardboard boxes, and a squat wooden crate that seemed to be Bern's pantry, with a box of crackers, a jar of some sort of spread, and other things impossible to make out in the dark. In the front seat with Freddy were half a dozen dog-eared books and the debris of food cartons.

It wasn't much, but it was so much better than Freddy's spot. Safer, drier, warmer. He found his envy simmering and forced it away. If he played his cards right, and Bern really trusted him, maybe he could find a junker back here with intact windows and set up a similar berth without pissing off the car lot's owner. Wordlessly, he promised himself he would do nothing to jeopardize Bern's good luck.

"You have a spare blanket?" he asked.

Bern looked at him. With obvious reluctance, he peeled off one of his own blankets and pushed it over the seatback. Freddy knew words were not sufficient, so he tried to put the depth of his gratitude in his eyes and the nod of his head, and then he swaddled himself as best he could and lay down across the front seat.

He was sure adrenaline would keep him awake, that he would see the Schnabelperchten when he closed his eyes and be unable to sleep. But in the midst of such worries, he drifted off...

...And woke to someone screaming his name. A hand gripped his shoulder, shook him hard. Freddy twisted around in the seat and looked up to see wide eyes and a face etched with terror. Bern loomed over him from the back of the wagon, pointing, shouting.

Freddy finally got it, the words making sense.

"Start the car!" Bern screamed at him. "Start the fucking car!"

The words didn't make sense at all. The veil of sleep had finally been stripped away and Freddy knew where they were, in that stretch of junked cars at the back of the parking lot. How was he supposed to start this car?

"Get the keys, Freddy! Under the floormat!"

Bern started to drag himself over the seat.

Freddy grabbed his wrists and sat up, pushing him back. "Christ, Bern. Calm down. You've had a nightmare, that's all."

Bern tore his right hand free and punched him in the face. Screamed, spittle flying. "Get the fucking keys!"

Angry, Freddy nearly hit him back, but he still had Bern's blanket wrapped halfway round him and that reminded him that his friend had been hospitable enough to trust him with his secret spot, to get him warm and out of the snow.

Bern ripped his other hand free, but now he stared at Freddy from behind the front seat with pleading eyes. "Freddy, they're here."

He saw movement to his left. A dusting of snow clung to the passenger side window, but Freddy could see a figure just beyond the glass, and when he went still, trying to tell himself it was just some security guard, he heard a sound.

"Chi chi chi."

The bone-white beak, gray against the snow, leaned forward to peer eyelessly into the car. The creature tapped its bloody shears against the window, as if asking him to unlock the door.

This time, Bern whispered. "The keys are under the mat, Freddy. Start the car."

Freddy stared at the Schnabelperchten. It tilted its head, just as it had back in that house while it cut open the woman on the bed. He wondered if this might be the same one, but it didn't matter.

Another rapped at the glass of the hatch at the back of the station wagon. Freddy whipped his head around and could see the shadows of others beyond the snowy windows. They should not have been here. He had followed them in previous years and they had always treated him as invisible. Why would they follow him and Bern tonight? Why pay any attention to them at all?

"Freddy, please," Bern said, weeping in terror.

Then it struck him. The keys under the mat. He turned to stare at his terrified friend. "This is *your* car. You live in your car."

Bern smashed his hands against the back of the seat and screamed at him to get the keys. This time, Freddy acted. Shoved his hand under the mat, dug around, found the keys, chose the correct one for the ignition the first time out, jammed it home, twisted it... and the engine growled, trying to turn over. He wondered how often Bern started the car to keep the engine from becoming a block of useless metal and guessed the answer was not-often-enough, but still he tried. He let it rest, counted to three, turned the key again. The engine choked and snarled and tried its best, and Freddy let it rest again.

"You live in it," he said, mostly to himself. He glanced around at the debris of meals, of life—a dirty blanket, some dog-eared books, takeaway boxes stealthily donated by restaurant staff at the end of a night.

Bern lived in his car. It was his home. And it was an utter mess.

The rear hatch of the station wagon clicked and opened, letting in a gust of frigid air and a swirl of snow. It opened as if it had never been locked at all, just like the doors of each of the homes the Schnabelperchten had visited.

Freddy glanced in the rearview mirror as Bern screamed a different sort of scream. This one held as much sorrow as it did fear. One of the Schnabelperchten bent and thrust his arms and beak into the back of the wagon, grabbed Bern by the legs.

"Chi chi chi," it said.

Bern screamed and reached out, shrieked Freddy's name, cried for help, in the moment before the thing dragged him out into the snow. Perhaps Freddy could have caught his arms in time and given the Schnabelperchten a fight, but instead he turned the key in the ignition again.

Coughing. Growling. Not starting.

Freddy began to cry.

Out the window on his side of the car, another of the things leaned in close to peer at him through the snowy glass. On the passenger side, the first one he'd seen grew impatient and simply opened the door, the lock notwithstanding.

Freddy turned the key.

The engine roared to life.

The Schnabelperchten at the passenger door bent its head and reached across the seat toward him. "Chi chi chi."

Freddy ratcheted the gearshift into drive and hit the gas. The car hitched once and then surged from its place amongst the junkers. The creature inside the car snagged his jacket, but then the open passenger door struck the rusted shell of an old Volkswagen. The door slammed on the Schnabelperchten. Its cloak caught on the rusted, twisted bumper of that Volkswagen and the Schnabelperchten clawed at the front seat of Bern's car before it was dragged from the vehicle.

With the passenger door still hanging open, Freddy could hear Bern back amongst the junkers, screaming in the snow. He did not glance in the rearview mirror or try to look over his shoulder. The hatch at the back of the station wagon remained open and he might have seen what they were doing to his friend, might have seen those shears employed at their gory work.

Hands locked on the steering wheel, he drove through the snowy parking lot. The tires were so low they were nearly flat and he didn't know what that might mean, how far he could get in this weather on those tires. So he drove.

He clicked on the windshield wipers to scrape snow off the cracked windshield. They worked, but poorly, and not well enough to keep him from smashing into the front end of a used Mercedes proudly on display near the front of the used car lot. The Mercedes banged aside and Freddy kept going, shaken, headed for the front gate.

The impact shattered the windshield. Splinters showered around him as he raised one arm to shield his eyes. When he lowered that arm, face dotted with little specks of blood and glass, he was stunned to find the car still moving. His foot had come off the gas and now he floored it again, twisting the steering wheel, heading for the river. He needed to get away from Salzburg, away from the Schnabelperchten, but as he drove he saw them in the falling snow. They emerged from rowhouses and apartment buildings, some of them watching him go in silence, their heads swiveling to follow as he passed.

The car had been Bern's home. Did they consider it his, now? Bern was dead and the car was in his possession. What were the rules? Did they need to kill him because of what he had seen, or simply out of spite? Would they let him go?

The engine coughed. He wondered how far the car would get him, how much gas might be in the tank. If he could put the river between himself and this group, he thought he could escape the city before they caught him. How far would he have to go before he was beyond their reach?

One of the headlights had shattered when he hit the Mercedes. The other was weak. Snow and wind buffeted him through the broken windshield. But he saw three Schnabelperchten in the street as he approached one of the bridges across the river Salzach. Which bridge was this? The Lehener, maybe? In the snow it was hard to tell. And were there figures drifting across the bridge in the snow, dark robed creatures with bone-white beaks?

Freddy thought there were.

The engine coughed again.

The car isn't mine, he wanted to scream through the broken windshield. *I don't own it. Never sheltered in it.* His only home was the city itself. Not only the city, but all of Austria. His home was the sky and the ground below. His home was the whole of the world. The world might be anything but tidy, it might be insane and brutal and unforgiving, with all the mess and ruin the human race produced, but he could not be to blame for that. He refused. The people responsible for the mess of the world had never done anything but take from him.

Freddy turned toward the river. The old car jumped the curb. The impact would have blown those half-flattened tires, but the snow provided a cushion.

He popped open the driver's door. Its rusty hinges shrieked. He took his foot off the gas and let the car roll down the embankment.

Freddy hurled himself from the car, hit the snow and tumbled twenty feet. Heart thrumming, he struggled to rise to his feet, but once up he managed to remain standing. The old, rusted, dented Auto Union wagon plunged into the river, bobbed for a few seconds, and then the river poured through the broken windshield and the car began to drown. Bern's belongings, his blankets and clothes and the castoff debris of his life and home, floated up around the car and were quickly swept away by the river.

"Chi chi chi."

Freddy whipped around and saw them through the snow. Three of them, coming along the embankment toward him from where they had been standing in the road, near the foot of the bridge.

He faced them, cold and tired and bruised, not sure where he could run.

"Chi chi chi."

Too tired, in fact, to run. Angry, he walked toward them. Off to his left, the car vanished beneath the icy current of the river.

"It's not my mess," he said, staring at the one in the middle.

They kept walking, passing around him as if he weren't there at all.

He turned to watch them go. Back on the street, they split up, angling toward homes along the road, where they would leave coins for those whose homes were tidy in preparation for the new year, and where they would make a deadly ruin of those who could not be bothered to care about the state of their homes and lives.

From a distance, he heard the sound again, carried on the wind.

"Chi chi chi."

Freddy raised a trembling hand to cover his mouth, to muffle the sound of his sobbing.

Then he began the long, cold trudge back to his spot. He had to get the hell out of this city, as far away as possible. But not tonight.

Tonight he was tired and sad and broken, like the world. Tomorrow he would start over, and one day he would be glad and warm and joyful again. He wished he could have said the same for Bern, and for the world. It was too late for Bern. For the world, he could not be sure. After all, he was just one man without a home or a family. What did he know?

END

Salzburg, Austria is one of my favorite places on Earth. My wife, Connie, and I went there on our honeymoon many years ago and I managed to return shortly before the pandemic hit. It's as beautiful as ever, an intriguing, very self-contained city that nearly vibrates with the echoes of its history. It's also a place with all kinds of folklore, and it's the spot where I bought the Krampus ornament that hangs on our family Christmas tree every year. When I was poking around for something suitably unsettling for this story, it did not surprise me at all to find a bit of lore specific to the area around Salzburg. I loved the dichotomy of gentle household spirit or grotesque murder-monster, and that you get one or the other depending on how neat you keep your home. It's a much more visceral version of telling children to behave or the bogeyman will get them. It creeped me out to think about it, and I hope I've passed that feeling on.

THE ONES HE TAKES

Benjamin Percy

I T was nearly noon on December 25th, and Joel Leer still hadn't risen from bed. His wife Greta was awake beside him—he could tell from her breathing—but he did not roll over to nuzzle her cheek and wish her a Merry Christmas. He didn't say a word to her or even look her way when he peeled off the blanket and swung his legs to the floor. He was only forty-two but moved with the pained slowness of the arthritic when he pulled on his robe and stepped into his slippers and trudged down the stairs.

There was no tree choked with colored lights. There were no stockings hanging from the hearth or carols sounding from the stereo or gingerbread cookies baking in the oven. Not in this house.

In the kitchen he opened and closed a drawer, then a cupboard, finding nothing he wanted. It used to be their tradition on Christmas morning to eat stollen smeared with butter and drink coffee spiced with rum, but his appetite was gray.

The dog whined from her kennel in the mud room. She was a yellow, long-haired dachshund named Daisy. They had purchased her from a breeder six months ago. She was supposed to make them happy, and she did. But today happiness wouldn't be possible.

He opened the kennel's gate and she burst out of it. He leaned over and gave her some scratches and she licked his hands and wormed in and out of his legs, panting happily. "I'm sorry it's so late," he said, and she cocked her head, studying him intensely. "You probably want to go outside?"

With that word—"outside"—she jerked into motion, scrambling her short legs across the floor, claws clicking on the hard wood. At the front door she let out a high-pitched bark and turned in circles, waiting for him.

He pulled on a hat and tucked himself into a coat, but otherwise remained in his slippers. He didn't plan on stepping off the front porch. A cold blast of air greeted him. Vapor puffed from his mouth and he squinted in the light of the day.

Daisy raced to the porch steps and paused at the snow gathered there. Maybe five inches had fallen last night, with more to come later today. It always snowed on Christmas; that was practically a rule here in Minnesota. No one was out shoveling or scraping or salting their driveways. The plough hadn't even come through yet. The world was shrouded white, and he was alone. Or so he thought.

"Go on," he said, motioning toward the yard.

Daisy moved with hesitation, testing the snow with her paw and looking back at him.

"Go! Go potty!" He tried to muster some enthusiasm in his voice, but he felt like an actor forcing his lines. "That's a good girl!"

The dog started down the steps and moved across the yard.

Her legs vanished. Snow clung to her fur, forming a white skirt. She squatted to relieve herself.

Some clouds were piled up on the horizon, but the sky was otherwise a pale blue. Contrails were etched cleanly across it like the scrape of skates on a frozen pond. That's where he was looking—up—when Daisy began to bark.

He couldn't see her anymore—she had raced around the side of the house—but he could follow the messy trench she left behind. He called for her, "Daisy! Daisy, stop it! Daisy, come!" He tried clapping and whistling. But she would not come.

He thought about going back inside to fetch his boots, but there was something about the urgency of her barking that compelled him forward. The first few steps were a bracing chill. After that an ugly ache set in around his ankles that felt almost hot. He slipped and nearly fell at the corner, where the yard steepened slightly, and there he found Daisy.

Her long body was rigid, and her ears and tail were flattened. There was a metallic quality to her barking that made it feel like knives were being sharpened in his ears. A mound of snow, maybe blown by the wind or fallen from the roof, rested next to the house. This was the source of Daisy's fixation. Maybe a possum had burrowed into it. He kept saying, "Stop! Stop, Daisy!" but she wouldn't so much as look at him.

He wrenched her back by the collar, but even then she tried to keep barking, choking and hacking against the pressure.

He could see now what bothered her. From this angle the mound appeared like a sugary egg that was dissolving, and within it lay a body. A child's body. Curled on its side. Dusted with snow in some places, buried entirely in others.

Joel no longer noticed the slush soaking into his slippers. He kneeled and brushed away the snow on the child's face, revealing skin blued by the cold and eyelashes feathered with frost. A boy.

It couldn't be him. It couldn't be. But Joel said his name anyway, "Isaac?"

The boy's eyes snapped open.

They had last seen him on Christmas Eve, one year ago. Isaac had changed into flannel pajamas and the three of them had read *The Night Before Christmas*. They had laid out cookies and milk by the fireplace, and Isaac had asked if he could have one.

"Sure."

The plate was stacked high with krumkake, sugared rosettes, frosted cookies, and pinwheel dates. He selected a krumkake and the golden flakes crumbled down his chin when he bit into it with a crunch. "He's not going to be mad, is he?"

"I'm certain he'll get plenty of cookies tonight."

"I don't want to make him mad. I don't want to be on the naughty list." Isaac finished the cookie and took a sip of the milk as well and dragged his sleeve across his mouth to clean it.

"Time to brush teeth and get to bed, buddy."

Isaac asked if he could stay up for one more minute. Just one more. And they said yes.

He kneeled before the tree to rearrange some of the wrapped and ribboned packages, and stare at the ornaments in wonder. The colored lights made a candied reflection on his eyes.

One minute became five became ten. Joel wished they had

stayed there a thousand more. "Ready?" he said and held out his hand.

Isaac didn't take it. Instead he turned his head toward the hearth. It was cold and dark and bottomed with ashes. "Don't light a fire," he said. "If you light a fire, he won't be able to come. Okay, Dad?"

"Okay, sure."

"Is it open?"

"Is what open?"

"The thing you open? Inside the fireplace? To make sure the smoke gets out? If the smoke can get out, he can get in."

"The flue? Let's check." Joel knelt beside the fireplace, opened the glass doors, and swept aside the chainmail curtains. He craned his neck. "Good thing you asked."

"Can I do it?" Isaac asked and grabbed the metal bar and creaked it forward and back. A cold draft breathed down and made a sound like whispering.

Isaac stepped back from the fireplace with a fearful expression.

"Everything okay, buddy?"

"Yeah," the boy said, but he looked back at the hearth before mounting the stairs. "It was just darker and colder up there than I imagined."

He and Greta tucked Isaac into bed, kissed his forehead, and whispered, "Dream about sugar plums and fairies, and we'll see you in the morning."

But in the morning he was gone, the sheets thrown back, the dent of his head still shaping the pillow.

They called for him when they checked in closets and under

beds. They looked in the attic. They looked in the basement. They looked outside, walking the yard, where fresh snow had fallen that revealed no tracks. They returned inside, and again, and then again, they searched the house, shouting his name until their throats felt raw.

All the windows and the doors had been locked; they were certain of it. The only way in was the fireplace. When Joel felt the chill blowing down it—a whispery vacancy—he clanked shut the flue.

Joel hadn't lit a fire since. Not until today.

In the living room, on the couch, Greta clutched the boy in her lap and tucked the blanket around him. "He's so cold," she said. "Hurry."

"I'm hurrying," Joel said. The firewood bin was in the garage. He brought an armful of logs and kindling into the house. He found some matches in the kitchen drawer and snatched yesterday's newspaper out of the recycling. He twisted the sports pages into five wrinkly candlewicks. He flared a match and the paper caught flame. Onto it he fed sticks and then the split hardwood. Soon the room was full of dancing light and a popcorn crackle.

Joel joined Greta. He touched her but not the boy. Her cheeks were wet from crying. "It's him," she said. "It's our little boy. He came back to us."

Joel wanted—desperately—to believe. He was almost there. He gave her a stiff smile and did not mention the boy's eyes. Isaac's had been green. The boy staring back at them had eyes that gave off the strange blue light of glaciers.

His hair wasn't shaved so much as hacked away. The rough job of a barber working with shears or a knife.

They debated whether to take him to the hospital or call the police. But they had only just found him, and it felt wrong to let go so soon. He existed as long as he was in their arms. And the police had not been kind, questioning them repeatedly, pitting them against each other. "When a child goes missing, a family member is usually to blame," they had said.

The fire roared when the pressure shifted, and wind pulled at the chimney top. The orange light of the fire brought black shadows to the room. Color gradually returned to the boy's skin. The blanket and couch cushions soaked through. A dripping puddle formed on the floor.

After an hour he still would not speak, but he sat up on his own when Joel brought him a mug of hot cocoa. "I even put marshmallows in it."

The boy took the steaming mug with two hands and drank with tiny loud sips.

With the blanket off him, they had to acknowledge his clothes. He wore what appeared to be a leather onesie with shoulder straps. It was roughly stitched with what looked like yellowed ligaments. The gray mottled quality reminded Joel of a seal's hide. A rank, oily smell came off it. His arms and shoulders were bare, and the pale skin of his back was scarred purple and scabbed red as if he had been lashed. One of the wounds wept blood.

Greta reached for the tissue box on the end table. She dabbed at the blood. "What happened to you?" she said. She was referring to the cut, yes, but she was talking about something much bigger as well. What had been done to him? Where had he been? How did he get home?

The boy pointed up.

"The roof?" Joel said, and Greta said, "You were on the roof?" "You fell?"

"What do you mean, Isaac? What are you pointing at?"

The boy raised his hand even higher, as if to indicate he came from someplace even higher than they could imagine. He made a noise. It might have been a whimper or it might have been a word, "Sleigh."

Joel heard a low growl behind him. He had forgotten about Daisy. The dog was peering around the corner, showing her teeth.

In Minnesota, in the winter, the days were white, but the nights were blue. Joel had lost track of time. A gloom settled over the neighborhood as the sun set.

He went to the window. The clouds were thickening again. A few flakes fell. His wife snapped on a lamp and suddenly all three of their reflections hung on the glass, transparent as ghosts.

The boy was staring out the window as well. His eyes were wide. His breathing came in quick pants.

"What's wrong?" Greta asked him. "You can tell us anything, you know. We love you so, so very much."

Joel said, "You're safe here, buddy. I'll protect you."

The boy scrunched shut his eyes and shook his head. "No," he finally said with a voice like a rusty hinge. "You didn't before. You can't now."

"Isaac. Please talk to us," Greta said and knelt in front of him and put her hands on his shoulders. "Please tell us what's wrong. Please tell us how we can help?"

The boy stepped away from the window. The clouds appeared black now and the snow was falling more thickly, lashing at the glass.

His voice came as a shriek. "He's coming back for me."

"Who?" Greta said.

"Who's coming?"

There was a short stack of wood in the living room. The boy grabbed several more logs and dumped them roughly into the fireplace. Sparks sprayed onto the floor.

"Isaac, what are you doing?"

"I got away. I hid in a bag, and then, when he wasn't looking, I got away. He's going to be so mad that I got away."

"Who?" Joel said. "Who, goddamnit?"

"Him."

"Him who?"

"He needs us. He uses us." He holds out hands thick and glossy with calluses. "We build for him. Somebody has to do all that building."

Joel remembered what the police had said—about how a family member is usually to blame for a child's disappearance—and maybe they were right. He remembered the cookie he allowed Isaac to steal off the plate. He remembered the black gaze and the cold hiss of the chimney flue.

A sudden snow blinded the windows, as if a cloud had descended onto the house. The flakes swirled and eddied and fleeting shapes could be seen in them. There was a thump that shook the whole house. Several pictures fell from their hooks and glasses fell from cupboards and shattered on the floor. The dog began to bark, racing from a window to the door and finally to the fireplace. Then, above them, a creaking sounded as a great weight negotiated its way across the roof. With a whimper, the dog retreated to her kennel.

The three of them held each other and stared at the crackling hearth and waited for what was next. Christmas had finally returned to their home.

END

In the Andy Williams song, "The Most Wonderful Time of the Year," he sings not just about the joys of Christmas, but about the ghost stories, and that's how I always think of the holiday. It's Tiny Tim saying, "God bless us each and every one," but it's also the Ghost of Christmas Future pointing a bony finger toward a gravestone that reads Ebenezer. It's sugar plum fairies, but it's also the rat king creeping through a darkened living room. It's George Bailey shouting, "Merry Christmas, Bedford Falls," but it's also George Bailey perched on a bridge over a winter river. I can't believe in the good without the bad, light without shadow. And there's nobody who deals in joy and horror more than the big man—Santa—who's always watching, always judging, and punishes or rewards us like a terrible god. When I think of the dark throat of the chimney and something stirring inside it, I get the chills. Who's making all those toys? How do these so-called elves (the little people who... might just be children) come to find themselves indentured? That's the unsettling spirit of "The Ones He Takes."

HIS CASTLE

Alma Katsu

I T starts with banging at the door.

We expected as much. We'd been warned on our first night in this small Welsh village down at the Bloody Highwayman, the village pub. It's decorated for Christmas, garlands strung over the bar and festive red bows on each of the taps. The barkeep wore a red Santa Claus hat at a rakish angle. "There'll be revelers coming to your door one night," the barkeep had said as he drew a lager for my husband Trevor. "Nothing to fret about."

"Like carolers?" Trevor had asked.

The man behind the bar had laughed. "Not exactly. It's more of a local tradition. *Mari Lwyd*: the grey mare. You'll see... If they show up at your door, just give 'em a pint or a nip and they'll be on their way."

We hear as they approach, all drunken laughter and careless footfall echoing down the cobbled lane. We're outside of Llanbradach, not far from Caerphilly, which is just north of

Cardiff. If asked, we tell people we're here for the holidays, Christmas and Boxing Day and the New Year, that we needed to get out of London for a while and that we find Wales restorative. Uniquely restorative, you might say. We're both from here originally, though it was a long time ago.

We've no relatives left to visit.

Something besides familial obligation draws us back to the ancestral sod. Something not so easily explained.

We've rented a proper old cottage for our stay, just down the road from the local baronial estate, Phillips Hall. We could've stayed there, rented a room in the drafty wing they let out to guests, but found this place on Airbnb, a barely renovated farmer's shack. It's got low beams and tiny rooms, and the only heat source is the cast iron wood burner tucked in an inglenook. There's one bathroom and a single bedroom only slightly larger than the bed that sits in the center. According to the listing, it dates to the 1700s but to me it feels like home.

I'm interrupted in the middle of my thoughts by the knocking. *Bang, bang, bang.*

The revelers the barman warned us about. Why have they picked this house, I wonder. It's not festive looking, not compared to some of its neighbors, which glitter with strings of fairy lights and ornaments that wink from behind a window. The people who live there are likely to be celebrants and would welcome wassailers. Our rented cottage is cheerless. A blank slate.

There is no peep hole in the thick front door. Whoever has come to our cottage, they're on the threshold. We can hear them shuffling noisily about. The voices are male and thick with drink. Bells jingle as feet stomp on the slate walk. There's phlegmy throat-clearing, hocking, spitting. "Open the damn door," one of them finally growls. "We know you're in there. It's bloody cold out here."

Hairs rise on the back of my neck.

I can feel Trevor's presence close behind me. "Go ahead and open the door, Cate. I could use a good laugh," he says.

When I open the door, I'm confronted by a specter. A huge white horse's skull dances high overhead. It's smooth and pure alabaster, like a sculpture, with its gaping nasal cavity and narrow, elongated jaw. Shiny glass ornaments have been placed in the empty eye sockets and realistic leather ears have been fastened up top, making the skull look bizarrely alive.

It grins down at me. A voluminous white sheet has been fastened behind it, shrouding a reveler who hoists it up and down on a pole. Ribbons festooned with bells flutter from its crown. It is frightening and festive at the same time.

Even though I knew they were coming, I stagger back at the sight of that glowing white skull. This elicits a snigger from the two revelers flanking the ghoulish hobby horse. Custom dictates that they be dressed in costumes something like Morris dancers, but they've barely put in any effort. Only one of them has tied ribbons around his biceps and at the knees, though the two we can see have smeared paint all over their faces. God only knows about the one under the sheet.

"It's the Mari Lwyd, come to decide whether Good Fortune will smile on ye in the New Year," one of the revelers bellows like he's the town crier. He looks to be in his mid-thirties, with wiry ginger hair and an overgrown beard like a thorn bush. His eyes are on fire; he's already been celebrating, I think.

They try to push their way into the house but Trevor squeezes in front of me, blocking the narrow threshold. "What do you think you're doing?"

"Don't be a poor sport. You're supposed to fete us," the second man says. He's shorter than the ginger man and wears a knit cap over greasy brown hair.

Trevor crosses his arms over his chest. "From my understanding of the tradition, you're supposed to entertain the homeowners, and if you're good, they'll invite you in. You're being rather lazy about it, don't you think?"

"Then we'll give you a rhyme and you give us one in return," the ginger man says.

"I'm afraid I don't do rhymes." Trevor smirks. "Are you sure you know what you're doing here?"

The fire in the ginger's eye turns into a belligerent gleam. "You're Londoners, aren't you? I can tell from your accents—and that posh car parked out front."

That explains how they decided on this house.

The ginger man continues. "Mari Lwyd is a Welsh tradition. What would you know about it?"

Trevor's smile is confident. Fighting with the locals is great sport to him but I wish he would stop. We're here for a reason and these men are not part of it. Our quarrel lies elsewhere. "Oh, we've been to Wales a time or two. Besides, you're drunk."

"Aye, we've made a few stops already," the third man, the one under the sheet, says, his voice slightly muffled. He hiccups and stumbles back a step, the horse head bobbing. "We've been celebrating."

"I can see that," Trevor says. He's still blocking the door.

The ginger man is trying to look inside over Trevor's shoulder. It might be ungenerous of me, but I think it's to see what we've brought with us. Our luggage is within view—three Carl Friedrik cases, discreet but expensive—and Trevor's Burberry coat hangs from a nearby peg. My laptop, the latest Apple has to offer, is just visible on the table. Suddenly, I feel nervous.

The three men on our doorstep are not moving on, and Trevor isn't letting them inside. It's a stalemate, and it's starting to feel dangerous.

"You're here for the holidays," the ginger says like he's telling our fortunes.

We're here to fulfill a longstanding obligation but I'm not about to tell him that. "Yes," I say, hoping to make peace. "We're staying for a few days. We love Wales."

"It's a magical place, that's for sure," the man in the cap says by rote, as though it's expected.

"Then you won't object to participating in a local tradition. For the missus," the ginger adds. He's clearly trying to make Trevor feel like an ass for making his wife uncomfortable.

I place a hand on Trevor's shoulder. "Oh, do let them in. I brought the last of the Christmas cake down with us. We might as well finish it up."

Trevor holds his ground for one last second before he steps aside. Ginger and the man in the cap shuffle by us, the ginger giving my husband an ill-advised smirk. The man under the shroud goes to leave the hobby horse outside on the walk but Trevor lays a hand on his arm. "No, bring it in. You can't leave it out there. Someone might nick it." The man guffaws in disbelief—who would steal something so frightening?—but does as Trevor says.

The horse's skull is enormous, as big as a schoolchild. It could be a dragon's skull—fitting, for Wales is the land where dragons supposedly once lived. The skull fills the tiny entryway. The man sets it on a bench, swathed in its white sheet, the pole now blocking access to the front door.

They all troop by as I linger behind. It's the skull, calling to me. I touch the smooth bone, unable to help myself.

There was a white pony grazing in a field as we drove in, on a hillside just outside of Caerphilly. A beautiful sturdy Welsh, with thick mane and tail, snowy white against the last of the green grass. The green made the horse stand out, luminous as a dream. My throat tightened up at the sight of it. It reminded me of the horse I'd had when I was younger, a pale grey mare named Lucy. No plain chestnut or bay, Lucy was a beauty with dapples on her flanks and hindquarters. She made me feel a princess every time I rode her.

It has been so, so long since I'd last seen her.

These trips are meant to remind me of our childhood in this village and the things we did, Trevor and me, but *this* trip, for some reason, hits me harder than most. I felt it as soon as we crossed the border into Monmouthshire. I was only sixteen, Trevor a year older, when we decided we would leave Wales to make our way in the world together. By today's standards that's too young to be doing such a daft stunt, but in those days, there was barely such a thing as childhood. Out of swaddling, we were considered adults and our sins fell on our shoulders as adults.

It all seems an impossibly long time ago.

I look down again at the skull and shiver, before heading back into the kitchen.

⌒

Trevor stands by the refrigerator with the men. The kitchen is not meant to hold four people at one time, so they are forced to stand close together. Now I can see how seedy the revelers are. They are all in their early thirties with bad teeth and in want of haircuts.

Their eyes shift as they note their surroundings. "You're Londoners, aren't you?" the man in the cap asks.

"Is it that obvious?" Trevor says as he pulls bottles from the refrigerator. Our Range Rover squats in the gravel driveway like a tank. Typical Londoner's car.

"We get a lot of your kind, especially this time of year," says the man who had been carrying the horse's skull. "Wales for the holidays. It's that damned Dylan Thomas story. It's made us a cliché."

Ginger's face hardens by a degree. "Half the houses in town are holiday lets now. It's getting so a working man can't afford a place to live no more."

"It's a problem in London, too," I say gently.

"Take it up with your MP," Trevor says.

The man in the cap sniffs. "The man's a twat. Last of the Phillips—you know them?"

"I do," Trevor replies, back stiffening as he takes another sip. "But I wouldn't call them friends."

Ginger nods his head in the direction of Phillips Hall, down the road. "Then you know Clive Phillips, the second son, is the Baronet now, since his old man died a few years back."

"They say he died of a broken heart after his eldest son had that accident, ten years ago," the man in the cap says. "Broke his neck falling off Gower Rock, not far from here."

"Sad case, those Phillips. So many untimely deaths over the generations. Some say they're cursed," I murmur.

"Cursed for generations," the capped man says glumly.

"If being rich is a curse, I'd like to try it," the hobby horse man says.

"Clive lives in Harrogate now," Ginger continues. "Fat lot he cares about us trying to make a living out here. The estate's been turned into an Airbnb. That's the solution to all our problems, he says. Rent out your home to strangers. Easy for him: his family already own half the county. What if you can't afford a house to begin with? It's jobs we need, if they want us to stay put to tend their gardens and clean their holiday lets and make the place all charming and pretty for their guests," Ginger says with a snarl.

I'm sympathetic: it was jobs we needed, too, back in the day, but the peerage always told us we were responsible for our own problems. We didn't work hard enough. If we just wouldn't drink so much, we could afford a good pair of shoes.

Ginger may be nursing his grievances but the other two continue to peer and poke, and it all falls into place, sickeningly. Seeing them here in our kitchen, noses twitching like ferrets, it's plain: they're searching for things to steal. That's why they've painted their faces, so it will be harder for us to identify them to the police. Robbing outsiders who come down to stay in the accursed holiday lets is a pastime for the locals. They feel entitled to the fine things that are, otherwise, denied to them. It's more lucrative around Christmas, too, with houses full of presents.

Trevor pours a draught of porter for each of them while I slice the Christmas cake. The small kitchen fills with the scent of spices from the stale dessert. I leave a blurred thumbprint in the icing sugar as I cut it up.

They are shoveling cake into their mouths when Trevor decides to ask them a question. "So, tell us about your little tradition. Where did it come from?" He gestures in the direction of the entry where the horse's skull sits. "How does the horse head come in?"

Ginger grins, only too happy to school the Londoner. "It's for the feast of the ass, innit? Celebrating the humble ass what carried the Blessed Virgin."

Trevor furrows his brow. "No, it's not. You should at least get your story straight before you go round door to door, shouldn't you?"

Which makes Ginger go red in the face. "What would you know about it, Londoner? This here is a local tradition."

"A *Welsh* tradition," the man in the cap adds.

"Right. Welsh. Mari Lwyd means 'grey mare.'" Trevor drains the last of the porter from the bottle. "It may be Welsh, but it has nothing to do with Christmas. I daresay it's pre-Christian. Pagan."

"Are you calling us pagans?" It's the man who had been under the shroud. He's stocky, like a bulldog, but his voice is soft and high. He's impatient and strains for a fight, his dislike of city people palpable.

"You should be flattered," Trevor says, pointing the bottle at his chest to make a point. "The pagans were here first. Before the Christians. To be a pagan is to put you in very good company. Anyway, it has nothing to do with any virgin, blessed or otherwise. You can blame it on the lord of the manor, those Phillips you hold in such low regard. Aristocrats were crazy for hobby horses in the day. Fancy ones, all carved and painted and decorated with ribbons and whatnot. So, the poor folk decided to copy them and used what they had at hand—including the bones of the old family cob." He nods in the direction of the skull.

The man in the cap stares at Trevor as though he's mad. "I never heard such a thing. What are you—a historian?"

Trevor shakes his head. "No, but I've seen a thing or two in my time."

Ginger opens his mouth to snipe back but I can't stand to listen to their arguing any longer. I creep out to the front hall, to the horse's skull. I crouch low and, careful not to jostle the bells, touch the bone again. It's like touching a relic. I press my hand against its smooth surface and run my fingers down the length of it, stroking it. There is something very familiar about this skull—which is odd because I've never seen it before, obviously. But it's as though I know it from a previous life.

After another minute or two admiring its bleached whiteness and elegant lines, its noble yet melancholy expression, I rise and look out the tiny window over the stairs. There's no car nearby. If they intend to rob us, they may have parked out of sight so we wouldn't be able to identify it, but this trio strikes me as too lazy for that. No, they plan to steal our car to make their getaway. What will they do with us, I wonder? Tie us up and gag us, leave us to fend for ourselves? Or maybe there's a fire inside that needs an outlet... Maybe they will beat up Trevor once they've restrained him to salve their injured pride and rape me to assert their masculinity?

Some might say we deserve it. Trevor and I are no strangers to violence. We are part of the circle of violence, and we know it is never-ending.

I look down at the skull at my feet and feel a pang. That pang troubles me. I don't know what it means.

I creep back into the kitchen, where the conversation had continued during my absence. No one missed me, of course. They're too busy with their manly jousting. Faces have grown redder. The three men haven't noticed that Trevor has cleverly brought them to the precipice, readied them to do what they came here for.

I break into their bickering. "Where did you get the horse's skull?"

A silence falls over them. They look uneasily at each other. "From a farmer down the road," the hobby horse man finally says. "They save them when their horses die, knowing they're wanted for Mari Lwyd."

"No," I say. "You didn't get this from a farmer." I reach for the knife I used to cut the Christmas cake. It's still on the counter, dusted with crumbs, and point it at them. "The truth. Now."

Nervous looks are exchanged among the trio. Am I mad? What the hell is going on? Ginger turns pointedly to Trevor: *do something about your woman.* But Trevor grins. He's enjoying this.

It's the man in the cap who breaks first. I had him figured for it; he's the most nervous, that one. The least sure about what they're doing, the one with a smattering of conscience left. "It came from the peat bog over the hill. We pulled it from the bog."

The pang returns, stabbing at my heart.

Steady, I tell myself. *The skull could belong to any horse.*

An ancient bog lies not far from this village. We were warned about it as children. Plenty of animals have stumbled into these peat bogs and are unable to get out. Humans, too. The bog is deep and if you weren't looking where you were walking, you could easily find yourself sunk to the waist in cold, muddy water with no bottom under your feet.

And if you were riding across those wild, open fields... riding by moonlight, going fast and not paying attention because you were being chased... well, you could easily be well into the bog before you realized your mistake. Before you realized there was no getting out, that there was no one to hear your calls for help before the foul water closed over your head. Plenty of time to think about your wasted life and to beg God or the Devil for a deal because you are young, and you don't understand the ramifications of what you are asking for. *Why me and not that bully in the castle, eating his Christmas goose? The tyrant who raises rents every year until we can afford nothing and must resort to a life of crime. Crime they call it, when we call it survival. Where is the fairness in life?*

What no one tells you when you are young is that there is no fairness. None to be found in a peat bog. None to be found in a stranger's holiday let.

Trevor can see that it's time. No more fooling around. "Alright," he says, tossing his empty bottle into the bin. "You've had your cakes and ale, and I've tired of your company, so finish up. It's time you boys were on your way."

As the three men grumble, I flash Trevor a look. *You can't mean that. We're not going to let them go, are we,* and he flashes back a look that says *not on your life.*

But Trevor's barely gotten his words out when Ginger reaches across his chest, deep into his coat and then whirls around, pulling out... a gun. It's an old thing, heavy and clunky, and looks all wrong in his hand. "Not that we don't appreciate the hospitality, guv'nor, but you'll not be giving the orders anymore." By the ludicrous grin on his face, you can tell he's been dying to do this all evening. "There's one more thing about this village—not that you would know. It has been home to some famous highwaymen, once upon a time."

He's smug, so sure that he's now part of a glorious tradition. If he would only ask, we could tell him about the old days when there were serious consequences for burglary. The Phillips hung an iron gibbet over the road into town and you could be locked up for stealing a loaf of bread from the master's table. I watched my father's corpse decompose until it was just a skeleton dressed in tatters.

Trevor and I escaped the gibbet that night, but it didn't matter. We couldn't escape our fate.

I look over at Trevor. But he doesn't betray so much as a twitch. "And that's what you are? A highwayman?"

Ginger gives him a shit-eating grin. He nudges the gun in our direction, a cocky poke. "No sudden movements, neither of you. In case you can't tell, this is a robbery."

If he expected us to scream and wet ourselves in fright, he is to be disappointed. Trevor's laugh, hollow and merciless, has frightened better men than Ginger. "Is that all you've got? Is that *it*? You've done it all wrong, mate. For one thing, you should have *two* guns, not one. How are you going to cover the both of us with only one gun?"

His two pals glance at each other nervously—this is not going according to plan—but Ginger ignores them.

"Do either of your mates have a weapon? No? Maybe that's because you don't think you need to worry about Cate because, well, she's a woman, isn't she? Ooh, but you've made a bad mistake there. Cate—she's just as bad as me. Maybe worse. You should know your marks before you unsheathe your weapons."

There is about eight feet between Trevor and the would-be robbers. I have seen the expression on Trevor's face countless times. It's the way he looks when he gets to be himself, as he was born, the person he must hide every day. He grins wildly in anticipation of the violence he is about to commit, violence like an old friend met only too rarely these days.

He takes a step toward the revelers, unfurling his hands at his hips—the same gesture that Ginger tried to pull off when he whipped out his gun, but Trevor shows them how it's done. With all the force, all the flair like in the old days. *Stand and deliver, your money or your life.*

In Trevor's hands are two knives. Our three guests may be wondering where they came from. He certainly wasn't holding them a minute ago. Maybe he took them from the chopping block holding the kitchen set, but they don't look like kitchen knives. They look blunt and heavy and meant for something much more insidious, like gutting a stag or killing a bear.·

He takes another step toward them and another. The three would-be robbers scramble backwards like crabs, even Ginger. His eyes go big as he stares at the knives, their intent unmistakable. In that split second, however, he seems to remember that he's got something better than a knife in his hand. He's holding a gun. He raises it, shakily, and takes aim mere feet from Trevor's chest.

To which Trevor laughs. "Go on—take your shot. Better men than you have tried, God knows."

They have forgotten all about me. Forgotten what I was holding the entire time.

Before he can pull the trigger, however, there's a zing and a flash, a streak of silver come seemingly out of nowhere and now there is a kitchen knife sticking out of Ginger's hand. It's the eight-inch chef's knife I used to cut the Christmas cake, crumbs and all.

It makes him drop the gun, which spins under the range cooker. The knife tip sticks out of the far side of Ginger's hand and he is howling like a stuck pig. His two chums have recoiled in fright, unable to take their eyes off Ginger's copiously bleeding appendage. And then, when they realize who threw that knife, they gawp at me as they slowly come to realize that they have stepped into a nightmare. Nothing is as they thought. We are not the clueless victims from London and they are not the dashing highwaymen going to save the village.

Trevor laughs as he advances on Ginger and his two cowering pals and there is no denying that there's a distinctly menacing air about him. You can almost smell the sulfurous reek and heavy, peaty undercurrent swirling around him.

It brings that last day back to me. I remember our last moments fleeing through the bog like it was yesterday when, in truth, it was hundreds of years ago.

Centuries, and yet so little has changed.

We were doomed to a life of sin and crime, just like you, I want to tell these boys. *We don't blame you. There's no escaping. So, chin up and face your destiny like men.*

But they don't, of course. They try to run but Trevor and I stand between them and the cottage door. There's no time to try to break the window and crawl to safety, and the nearest window is too small anyway.

They can only scrabble for purchase on the oak floor, now slippery with Ginger's blood, but they're trapped by the counters and narrow confines of the kitchen. We advance on them slowly, Trevor brandishing the knives in his hands with maniacal glee. "You should know better than to try to rob a man in his own home," he says to the trio. It will be the last thing they will ever hear. "It may be a holiday let but, still, a man's abode is his castle, don't you know? Even for a Welshman."

The slaughter takes nearly no time at all. Trevor is very good with those knives, which were originally used for cutting up game. He disembowels Ginger because, let's be honest, he was begging for a comeuppance with his obnoxious behavior. It brings a smile to Trevor's face to spill those intestines to the floor. I draw another knife from the chopping block and slit hobby horse man's throat before he can call for help, and then it's a quick, mad scramble into the hallway before tackling the man in the cap and dispatching him with a bread knife to the back.

It's over too soon, really, for something that only comes around every ten years.

We are wrapping the bodies in a tarpaulin when we make the decision to put them in the bog. Normally, when we return to have our revenge on the gentry, we leave our victim in the woods to be found by the police. We'd never chance that they might be resurrected, as we were. They don't deserve to be.

But these boys? Rude as they were, well, we know in our hearts that they should have a second chance. They are no more guilty than we were when we held up carriages on the high road, fighting and clawing our way out of the desperate straits we'd been born into.

The village is silent and unseeing as we load the bodies into the car. We pass dark houses, not so much as a lone light in an upstairs window to guide our way. Our vehicle is whisper-quiet as we drive past farms and forest to the peat bog. We drag the bodies the last few yards after driving as close as we dare to the crumbling ground. We use the tarpaulin to roll them one by one into the loose, muddy water.

Better luck in the next life, boys.

Dawn is breaking as we pull up in front of the farmer's cottage. Our time back home is winding to an end; I can feel it in my bones. We pack our fancy bags and carry them out to the SUV, ready to dissipate like the morning mist. There's one good thing to come out of all of this, which is that I've been reunited with my Lucy. I wrap her skull tenderly in a blanket and nestle it in the boot, ready for the trip back to London.

END

Lately, social justice themes seem to creep into all my writing. "His Castle" started out as a collection of things I enjoy or am drawn to—horses, village life, highwaymen (oh, to write a novel featuring highwaymen!)—but along the way it became a statement on the problem of homelessness. Thanks to Airbnb making it easy for people to turn property into hotels, all over the world real estate investors are buying up property, particularly entry-level, making it impossible for the working class to live in the towns where they work. However, as the story explains, this is not really a new phenomenon: the wealthy have long claimed land as their right and privilege, and the poor have suffered for it.

THE MAWKIN FIELD

Terry Dowling

I N Australia it's always high summer then – those final weeks of the year – and, what with the heat and the glare, things feel like they're being completed, rounded off somehow. Maybe that was it. Even more so out in regional New South Wales, with the harvesting all but done and the long views through the car windows. So seeing the refrigerator in the middle of the field seemed like something to mark the time.

It was a battered old white thing, standing upright about twenty metres in from the road, and apparently functioning, because a series of power leads, one connected to the other daisy-chain fashion, stretched over the newly turned earth through a hedge to a house sheltered by pines in the distance.

Not so much who would do a thing as why? A long walk back to the house barely covered it. These were rural folk hereabouts; the nearest town was, what, eighteen kilometres away. These people were used to distances.

Though little went on in Briarley, to be fair. The bigger towns drew the tourists, the dollars, had the regional events like the Southern Stars Festival, the Wings, Wheels and Wine Airshow, the Ute Muster, and the Down Home Elvis Revival. So keeping a fridge stocked with beer and soft drinks in the middle of a field was what someone did once, kept doing it till it became a thing, their thing, this thing.

I slowed the car to consider it, fix it all in place, then noticed the metal box on the ground beside the fridge. A coin box, I bet. Those in the know stopped by for a cold one, just pulled over, made their selection and left their money.

I had to come back and see.

And, sure enough, on day three, late in the afternoon, there were four director's chairs set up by the fridge, all turned *away* from the road, facing out across the ploughed fields to a broken line of trees in the distance, with more fields beyond. Not two chairs for a private thing, but four, for company if company turned up.

A sunset watch, I was sure of it. Or some neighbourly pre-Christmas thing around the longest day of the year. Sit back and enjoy the magic hour at the end of a long day. Had to be. And it was quite a view: wide land under a vast sky, enough trees to provide perspective, one or two other houses far off. The immense quiet, just birds sounding now and then, crows and currawongs, the sudden rush of a passing car before the silence settled again and ruled it all.

The traveller's truism came to mind: try it and see. That seemed the intention, the invitation. Take one of the chairs, put some money in the box, have a beer.

I stepped out of the silver CSIRO rental car, climbed between the strands of fence wire, and crossed to the fridge.

The day was winding down, already soft at the edges, so having the fridge light come on when I opened the door was oddly comforting, a bit like stepping into someone's parlour where you're expected and welcome. Sure enough, there were a dozen cold beers, several brands, as many cans of soft drink. I grabbed a twist-top bottle of Hahn Light, added what I judged a fair price to the assorted change, then took one of the chairs.

I sat looking out across the fields with my back to the road, relaxed for the most part, feeling I'd read the set-up correctly, yet still just a touch concerned in case I had it wrong.

Now and then a car passed behind me on its way to Briarley, Yento, or points beyond, and I'd listen till all sound of it vanished. Then it was birds settling, insects and distances again, the ticking of the car engine cooling, the stir of a soft breeze, the smell of turned earth. It truly was the magic hour.

A good fifteen minutes passed before someone came ambling over from the house where the power lead ended.

"Evenin'," a man's voice called, still a way off.

"Evening," I replied. "Hope I got this right."

"You have. Thought I'd give you some time alone. I'm Geoff. Geoff Spicer."

"Colin, Geoff. Colin Traynor. I'm with the CSIRO team doing the natural gas survey."

Geoff looked to be in his late forties, early fifties, a heavy-set man in work shirt and dusty overalls. He grabbed a beer from the fridge and took the next chair but one. "Locals won't have it, you know."

"We know. But the funding's been allocated. We have to be seen to be trying."

"You're staying in Briarley then?"

"Rest of the week." I left a pause. "What's with this?"

Geoff chuckled. "Someone dumped a fridge. Seemed too much trouble to move it."

I chuckled in turn, but Geoff's tone shifted. "Actually my Dad's out there somewhere. The fridge was his idea. He was sitting out here one day, just like this, and saw something jigging about over by the treeline. Went to have a look and didn't come back."

"You're kidding me."

"Ask about it in town. They'll tell you about Dad. Gus Spicer. Missing person report MI-213214GS."

"When was this?" I naturally expected one more tale of financial worries or marital strife leading a guy to walk out on wife and kids years back.

"A year ago, right about now."

"You spoke to him before it happened?"

"I was in town doing some last-minute Christmas shopping, just going to head back. He called on his mobile, said something was jumping about and wanted to check it out."

"And no trace since?"

"Nothing. I've been going to shut this down, keep meaning to. But it's a link, you know? I just come and sit as if maybe he'll see the fridge light, see us out here, and wander back any moment. Keep going over his words. That Buller had himself a mawkin and it was jigging or jiggering about, something like that."

"Excuse me?"

"What he said. Buller's our neighbour back there. Dad said something like: 'Buller's got himself a mawkin'. That's a scarecrow."

"Right. Never heard the expression."

"There's a whole string of 'em. Dad's family was from Sussex originally and they're mawkins there. In other counties they have other names. Gus – that's Dad – grew up with mawkins."

Maybe Geoff was winding me up. Maybe he did this every time someone stopped by. A topic for the magic hour. Weird story time.

I let it play like that. "But this one leaped up, you say? Jiggered about?"

"You can get 'em like that. Like those blow-up figures you see outside car yards to get the motorists' attention. You know, long things that lunge back and forth waving their arms. You can get 'em battery-powered too, work on a timer. They spring up with a shriek or whistle through this thing they have, even glow in the dark. Anything to keep the birds and possums away."

"But you've seen nothing."

Geoff shook his head. "Nothing. Buller says he's never had such a thing, just three shifters over the other side, closer to the house."

"Shifters?"

"Pinwheel arms. Cantilever things that turn and wave all of a sudden. Have strips of tin on their arms to flash and raise a clatter."

"No jigging, no jiggering?"

"Nothing over by the treeline. There's a creek there. Bit of a gully."

Another figure was heading towards us, ambling across the turned sods.

"This is Bamby, my kid sister. Bamby with a y. Dad's pet name. Bit slow on it."

That was clear when Bamby reached us and took a soft drink from the fridge. The light showed a stocky mid-thirties form in scruffy overalls, with a slightly slackened face, sweet looking in a way, and with tousled curly hair above a really good smile.

"Bamby, this is Colin Traynor."

"Colin Traynor." Still lit by the open refrigerator, she tested the words, must have found them to her liking. "Colin Traynor."

"Telling Colin 'bout Dad. What he saw out there."

"A mawkin," Bamby said, sitting in the chair beyond Geoff. "It was a mawkin."

"Right," I said, nodding and smiling, keeping it easy.

"It's a mawkin field," Bamby said.

"Told 'im, Bam."

"It's a mawkin field, Colin Traynor."

"A maw-kin field. Right." I made sure she saw me nod. It was clearly important.

Bamby had a serious look on her face. "Something jigging – jigg—"

"Jiggering about," Geoff Spicer added, used to helping out. "What it sounded like."

His sister was nodding. "Jigging, Colin Traynor. Jiggering. A mawkin."

"Over there," I said, helping out too, keeping it easy, not hurrying to finish my beer. Not yet.

The highway, the car, the director's chairs and coin box, the daisy-chain leading back to the house were here, the fields and trees way over there, parts of a story, just that right then.

"Feel like walkin' out a ways?" Geoff Spicer said, changing it in an instant. "Show you where it happened."

Everyone has had moments like this. People who usually refuse to sit in the back seat of a two-door sedan suddenly finding themselves trapped in precisely that situation to make a flight deadline. Agreeing to blind date someone to a friend's wedding or to help transport something precious. Being asked to keep a secret. Moments where you find yourself a hostage to fortune in some way or other you know never to allow.

"Kind of like the view here." It was all I could think to say right then.

"Halfway then," he suggested. "I don't like going too near the trees either." As if that had been it. "Have to admit, Colin, the whole thing gets to me. This'd help. Buy you another beer."

"Right."

Halfway seemed okay, mostly because it was so open and there was still enough light. I started up out of my chair, letting him see I was willing.

We were maybe twenty paces on our way when Bamby began her litany.

"Mawkin!" she called out. "Sussex!"

Geoff laughed and called out "Sussex!" in reply, which pleased his sister enormously and clearly encouraged her.

"Hodmedod!" she called after a half dozen paces. "Berkshire!"

"Berkshire!" her brother chorused, giving me a sidelong grin that may have included a good-natured wink; I couldn't be sure.

"Berkshire!" I echoed.

That really pleased Bamby, I could tell. She giggled with delight.

We were another dozen paces across the turned earth when the next one came.

"Murmet!" Bamby called, and giggled in the growing dark. "Devon!"

"Devon, it is!" Geoff said.

"Devon!" I affirmed.

It wasn't far now to what I considered the halfway point, preparing my *Shouldn't leave the car – didn't lock it* excuse.

"Gallybagger!" Bamby called with glee, making it sound like a favourite. "Isle of Wight!"

"Isle of Wight!" I echoed, this time with Geoff trailing me with his own "Isle of Wight!"

"Tatty bogal!" What it sounded like. "Isle of Skye!"

"Isle of Skye!" Geoff and I chorused in unison.

And I stopped, as if heeding a special cue, and Geoff and Bamby did as well, with the line of trees before us, Buller's fields beyond and the lifeline of the highway at our backs.

"That was fun," I told Geoff, making it sound like the truth.

"She knows them all," he said, as if there were a list I was meant to know about. Then he pointed. "It would have been there. Near that gully at the property divide. Not much of one. You can see the fence. Figured that's probably where it was."

We stood in silence for a while as if we truly were looking for some kind of clue. Then Geoff turned and started heading back to the fridge, the fence line, and the road.

Bamby called out as before, names and places we chorused

in reply until we were back at the chairs and I had the beer he'd promised.

"Need to pee," Bamby said.

"Go do," Geoff answered, and I half expected his kid sister to move off a way, drop her overalls and do it right there, but she headed back to the house.

We sat in silence until she had disappeared inside.

"Thanks, Col," Geoff said then. "Ploughing during the day is one thing. You're up in the cab. Walking the fields 'round when it happened is somethin' else."

"She really loves it, doesn't she?"

"She wasn't always this slow. It came on. Blame myself a bit, stayin' out here. She would've done better in town. Now she wouldn't have it."

More silence. More watching the skyline softening, old gold blurring into slow rose-purple now.

I came back to it obliquely. "You married, Geoff?"

"Not now. It can be a hard life. You?"

"Not yet." Though not now would have covered it. I'd come close before career choices meant different priorities, different cities, different countries. Which naturally made me think of Sheridan in New York, in the northern winter, the northern festive season, at the *northern* solstice. So different from here.

The comfortable silence held, so I went back to it. "Did your Dad ever talk about selling up? Relocating?"

"He was starting to. Didn't tell Bam though, far as I know. She wouldn't have taken to it. Why, what are you thinkin'?"

"Not my place to say, Geoff."

"Go on."

"It must get wearying. Everything at the end of distances. Opened out like this."

"It does get that way."

Silence again. More falling away of the light as the minutes passed.

Then it struck me.

"You don't have a scarecrow yourself."

"Do now," Geoff said. "That'd be you, Col."

And I really did think of the movies and the solstice and harvest yarns that had *those* endings. And I really did feel a quick grab of fear.

"How you figure that?"

Geoff smiled. "Look see."

And there was Bamby walking back from the house, carrying what looked like a garden stake and a hammer, but heading not towards the chairs but out to where we had been a short time before, the point we'd reached on our walk, seeming to know exactly where we had stopped before turning back.

And, framed against burnt umber heading towards indigo, she was calling out all the way, names and locations, her usual litany.

Geoff gave his soft throaty chuckle. "She's a good girl. We agreed that the next one to stop by would help pick the spot, and now, right around the solstice when Dad went missing. You did that for us just now. Means the world to Bamby. A lot of people don't stop. Don't read it like you did. Don't care to. You're something the world served up."

"Geoff—"

"Let her have it, Col. It means everything."

"But—"

"Col, it's as Bamby says: don't disturb the cupboards."

"Excuse me?"

"People coming last minute. You tidy up quick. Tuck it all away fast. The place looks great. But, whatever you do, you—"

"Don't disturb the cupboards!" I barely hesitated. "Tuck much away, Geoff?"

"Didn't have to. Like I say, you were meant to be here."

So we sat finishing our beers. The birds had pretty much settled for the night, and the only sound now was Bamby hammering in her stake.

"Better be off, Geoff," I finally said, figuring enough was enough and, for some reason, wanting to be gone before Bamby returned. Then I stood and placed my empty bottle in the plastic tub left for the purpose.

"Drop by anytime," Geoff said.

"I'll do that." Then I called out across the dark field. "Good night, Bamby!"

A tiny voice called back. "Night, Colin Traynor!"

Night.

And that was that.

Though it wasn't. I kept thinking about what had happened to Geoff and Bamby's dad, most of all what had been started, what the new scarecrow post might have become while I was away.

My scarecrow. My sighting at least.

I had to see if it had been added to and how.

The movie endings and tall tales were there on cue, of course – *keep away, keep away!* – but it was a clear moonlit night, and that part of the field was certainly open enough.

And Geoff had said it. *Drop by anytime.*

So I left the motel and Briarley behind, and drove with the windows down out through the night-fields, smelling the land, enjoying one moment the fragrances of dusty wheat ready for late harvesting, the next, the spicy crispness of lucerne or the richness of freshly turned earth.

I made out the white shape of the fridge even before I identified the Spicer place behind its hedge and two sheltering pines. I pulled up opposite the familiar white shape, switched off the engine and sat waiting. It was just after ten, still early, but the house was already dark, everyone in bed, which had to be the way of it for all the early risers hereabouts.

The chairs were still there, folded and stacked now, though the coin box had been taken inside.

When no house lights came on, I finally got out, climbed between the fence wires and crossed to the fridge. Working on an excuse if needed, I set up one of the chairs and took out a light beer, letting myself be clearly seen in the glare of the interior light. No coin box at this hour, but I knew I could settle up later.

Still no lights from the house, so I just sat regarding the night-locked distances.

What was out there, I wondered. What had been added?

I needed to go see, but made myself wait, enjoying this warm summer night just before Christmas, smelling the earth, tracking the oldest rhythms any of us can know.

You're something the world served up, Geoff had said.

I was part of it, which made me easier about my handy excuse, how I couldn't wait to see how the 'Colin Traynor' scarecrow was turning out, about being restless, unable to sleep, needing somewhere to go, somewhere obvious and known. At the end of a night drive, somewhere that could *be* an end, a turning back point. Somewhere that courted strangers. Welcomed them.

Which tipped it back *that* way again, though the night soon eased those thoughts away with its rhythms, harvest smells and insect sounds. The distances were still out there, yes, blunted by darkness but sweeping away regardless, never caring who came or went.

Still no lights.

I laid my empty bottle in the plastic tub. Then, leaving the chair set up, showing my intention to return (and smiling at the additional cinematic flourish in that), I headed out to where I decided the post would be.

I must have missed it, misjudged badly, for I was soon much closer to the treeline bordering the gully than I'd intended. I could see the low post-and-rail boundary fence, could make out other fields beyond, other distant clumps of trees, Buller's land.

Way too close.

How did that happen?

I immediately turned and located the dim silver shape of my Toyota by the highway, then saw the welcoming light of the open fridge door, a white rectangle, clean and clear.

Someone was getting a drink.

But that couldn't be right! The fridge was facing the road, facing *away* from me. Seeing the full patch of light was impossible!

The fridge had been turned!

Had turned itself!

I blinked, looked round, glanced back.

Nothing now. Just the car, the dark outline of the Spicer place and, yes, the white shape of the fridge, but showing no light, no impossible light now. The door had been closed. Had closed itself.

Crickets sounded along the gully. A night bird, too, as it settled again. Otherwise there was just the silence of the fields.

I started back, needing to be away from this little fold in the land, and felt immense relief to see the lights of a passing car on its way to Briarley, confirming the highway, the world, the other world.

"Found you, Colin Traynor!"

I yelped in fright, heard Bamby giggle. She'd been crouching down, waiting, a dark lump on the earth.

"Came to see the post." It was all I could think to say. My heart was pounding.

"More tomorrow," she said, which I welcomed, having the prospect of tomorrow when I needed it most.

And Geoff's words from our first meeting were right there.

She knows them all!

Of course she does, whatever that meant right then. Knows them all. Knows all.

And Geoff's more recent caution was there too.

Don't disturb the cupboards!

Which I was probably doing even now, though Bamby seemed not to mind.

As we continued walking, she began calling her stations of the way, not tuned down to darkness and the hour, but as full-voiced as ever.

"Mommets! Somerset!"

And I dutifully added the refrain – "Somerset!" – not daring to make it hushed and furtive.

"Bodach-rocais! Scotland!"

"Scotland!" I cried into the night, tracking the unfamiliar words as best I could.

And so it went, through shoy-hoy, shewel, craw-deil, scarehead, tatterdemalion and jack-of-straw until we were back at the chairs.

Thankfully, the house lights stayed off, with no sign of Geoff, no need to justify the intrusion. But I made a big thing of setting up another chair, getting us soft drinks from the fridge and showing my intention to sit a while, no rushing off.

It seemed to be a companionable silence.

"I'll fix you up for this tomorrow," I said.

"Fix me up?"

"Pay for the drinks." I was instantly wary, so careful, and resolved to keep it easy between us before heading back to town.

Time helped, with the drinking, the calm breathing, watching the night together. She hadn't seemed to mean any kind of innuendo, thank goodness.

Which made me try for more. "What happened to your Dad, Bamby?"

"That's the thing, Colin. That's the thing. And at this time of year. What could it be?"

This first-ever omission of my surname made everything different, laden, intense, so much more personal. Did I imagine it, or was she more focused too, more alert? There really was the distinct thread of something other.

TERRY DOWLING

"Mawkin comes from malkin," she said. "A naughty name for a woman."

Skewing it even more, provoking again.

"Is that so?"

"Yep. A bad name. And Papa wouldn't ever have it that the jigging or jiggering was woman's business."

"Oh?"

Two strikes. I dared not say more, but Bamby made up for that, took it further herself.

"A jigger is an odd-looking person too. Another old word. He *saw* a jigger."

You make a bit of a jigger yourself, I immediately thought, but no, no, that wasn't true now. That wasn't fair.

"But that could have been a mawkin, right? A jigger jigging?"

I couldn't believe what I was saying, how the words came out.

And Bamby might have been marvelling at the wordplay. The moonlight gave so little, but her face was angled towards it and there seemed to be fascination in her eyes rather than confusion.

"Can't be that now," she said. "There's just me, see."

I couldn't track her meaning, though what was there to lose?

"Where were you when it happened, Bamby?"

"I have good days, Colin." Again, no surname. "Like now. Now is a good day. Right now. That's the thing. And I was inside making us coffee on a good day. I can use the jug on a good day, do all the good day things. And he was gone when I got back out. Papa was gone. Geoff was home soon after."

I nodded, allowing that she could probably see me do that and that it was answer enough.

And allowing more, something sensed about her, not at all clear.

Not slow. Distracted. Calibrated to something else, the workings of something other that took the mind, so much attention. Bamby was concentrating, turned elsewhere. Fiercely so. This was just what was left, all she could manage while doing something else.

Which led to the question. What did setting up this new scarecrow mean to her? And more. At what point was setting up a scarecrow simply making something functional to keep unwanted birds and animals at bay? At what point was it about so much more: obstructing, working, protecting, something totemic, talismanic and placatory? We all had rituals, some set about families and harvests and years ending, some around hopes and expectations. We found purpose however we could.

Don't surprise her. Don't distract her.

"So this is good, Bamby?"

"Of course."

"Did you add to it?"

And she shot back, alarmingly fast: "Did you find it?"

"No. No, I didn't. I went too far."

"Not quite."

And I longed to have a 'Colin Traynor' added right then to scale it back, make it less.

Which in turn made seeing what my scarecrow had become more important than ever.

"*Did* you add to it?" I asked her.

"Of course. If you count thinking about it."

So quick, so sharp now.

"Can *I* add something?"

"It would have to be right."

"How can I tell?"

"You're bright. You'll know. Now I'd best be getting back. We're up early."

I immediately rose, began folding and stacking the chairs. "I'll pay for these tomorrow."

"Fix me up."

"Of course. Good night, Bamby."

"More tomorrow, hey?"

"More tomorrow," I said, and headed for the fence.

Heading back to Briarley, the fields seemed to go on forever.

There was a late-notice meeting for the regional reps that Thursday afternoon, followed by pre-Christmas drinks and dinner at the RSL in Briarley, after which I had to drop two colleagues off in neighbouring Yento. I didn't get back for the sunset watch until the special hour was nearly done. The fields were already a spread of darkness against the lustrous blues, with just a run of treeline filigree and the tiniest edge of spoiled gold and verdigris to show where the sun had been.

I found Geoff sitting alone with a beer in one of the director's chairs.

"She's out there," he said, after I'd been to the fridge, grabbed a beer and settled. "Won't come in now, Col. It's her job."

I couldn't make out any sign of Bamby or the post. "Can I go say hello?"

"She won't thank you for it. Not now. Not yet. It's your mawkin though."

"My mawkin. She said I could add to it."

"She did? Well, it would have to be something good."

"She said."

"It's her thing, Col."

Geoff, what's going on here? I almost asked. *Why the scarecrow now? Why now? Tell me about the others. There must have been others. What happened to them?*

But I didn't ask any of it, rather found my own answers, my own deflections and reassurances.

Old year ending. New year ready to start. Everything coming back. The oldest clocks reset.

Which troubled me even more, what I kept bringing to it, finding, forcing on all this. It warned me off, brought the bitter ironies, the movie outcomes, the inevitable, too-obvious twist before a high-pan ending showing a solitary mawkin in a field.

All that was there.

More to the point, was I imagining it, or did Geoff seem short with me, more distracted and abrupt, just as Bamby had seemed sharper, smarter the night before, with a different light in her eyes? Geoff seemed duller now, closed down a bit. Or, again, was it all me?

Either way, it was enough to stop me asking if there were any news about his dad, any of the usual things that recent conversation and neighbourly courtesy allowed. Had it been otherwise I might have even asked him if he'd ever been out there and seen the full light of the fridge turned towards him, visual tricks like that, but not now, not tonight.

Don't disturb the cupboards!

I made a lot of standing and stretching, putting my coins in the cash box and laying my empty bottle in the tub, being seen against the low wash of light from the highway, but nothing came of it. No word from Bamby, no link with what was happening out in the dark field.

She had to know I was here – that is, if I could trust her brother that she was out there at all. Though I sensed that she was. It felt right, seemed right. And it was what *I* needed somehow.

I bid Geoff goodnight and drove back to the motel, feeling disconnected all of a sudden, cut adrift, all the magic trimmed back, just me projecting, bringing things to it, like we all do, and most of all when it comes to relationships and connection.

I woke the next morning determined to distract myself, to put in a good day's work and only then go see if the new post had been added to.

But I made preparations as well, went online and scouted out whatever I could find to earn me a place in the scarecrow game, things to surprise and, hopefully, delight Bamby.

"It would have to be right," she had said. "You're bright. You'll know."

I had a list of special 'tokens' soon enough, obvious ones really but hopefully sufficiently unexpected to blindside her, just as my called-out responses with Geoff had at that first visit.

I printed off my list at the motel's front desk and kept looking it over as I went about my official duties that day, visiting the nearby properties, getting responses to the mailed-out questionnaires, the polite refusals and precious few compliance agreements, carefully timing it so I'd be swinging by the Spicer place at the special hour on this, the actual day of the summer solstice.

"Come see the mawkin, Colin Traynor!" Bamby called as soon as she saw me getting out of the car, the old behaviours in place. She was sitting in one of the chairs as if awaiting my arrival. There was no sign of Geoff.

"Please," I answered. "But today I have to take the lead. Have to, okay?"

Which first confused her, then brought wonderment and a happy glow.

"Okay."

Then, when we were a few steps along, before she could start a recitation of her own, I called out.

"*Épouvantail!* France!" And looked back at her, flashing my best smile.

Bamby stopped in her tracks with a look of absolute joy on her face, as if the heavens had opened and some amazing miracle had been displayed. Then, still disbelieving, still processing what had just happened, she cried, "France!"

I continued walking, counted nine paces, carefully shaping the next word on the list in my mind, wanting to get it in before she could intervene with one of her own. She knew them all. I was giving her things she didn't know.

"Spaventapasseri!" I yelled when I had it. "Italy!"

And she chorused, "Italy!" with a run of giggles for the unfamiliar nonsense word.

"Espanta pajaros!" I continued. "Spain!"

More happy giggling from behind, more delight at the wondrously funny words. "Spain! Spain! Spain!"

And more funny words it was. I first pictured each one as it sat on my own list, getting it right before calling out.

"Fågelskrämma! Sweden!"

"Sweden!"

And after straska, kakashi and pugalo, we were at the post in the field, so strikingly lit in the last of the light.

It was still unadorned, not even a crosspiece added.

I wanted to ask *when does the rest happen,* wanting more, just as anyone does, whether in a spooky scarecrow tale, a movie or a life. But the old tropes and folktales, the cupboards, were right there, and I went to steer clear.

Then remembered the other words she'd said, and what they could truly mean.

Fix me up.

Those words as a cry from the heart.

And I called it out with all the joy I could find amid the doubts.

"Colin Traynor! Briarley!"

And Bamby echoed it in the last flickers of gold across the fields. "Briarley!"

There were things left unanswered, but that's life, isn't it, at all times of the year, in all years? Why Papa Spicer went missing like he did. And Buller too, we soon found out, but no surprise there. Life, time and chance come to us even behind locked doors. But no real surprises. Not even why the fridge still seems to work on days when the power is off. Why my girl is looking better and better, sharper every day, and Geoff slower and slower, completing whatever handover it is. Why it matters that the mawkin post stays unadorned as far as I can tell, nothing else needed.

I take the beer Bamby hands me and sit, watching the twilight working itself around everything.

"Colin Traynor!" Bamby calls. "Briarley!"

And I never fail to answer, even as the light fades and magic hour fills the world.

E N D

I've long had a fascination with scarecrows, but approached 'The Mawkin Field' knowing that any story featuring one had to keep well clear of the clichés, focusing rather on moments of recognition and deep knowing we all experience in our lives. Aware that it would involve the solstice around Christmas in the southern rather than the northern hemisphere, there then came three elements occurring at just the right time: learning of the origins and meaning of the word 'mawkin', having the sighting of an actual working fridge in a country field, and a picture-book garden scene by Valerie Littlewood showing rain veils against a far horizon at sunset. Put together, the story became what it needed to be.

THE BLESSING OF
THE WATERS

Nick Mamatas

G REEK coffee at midnight was Gus's last bad habit, except for his vain belief that he only had one bad habit. That was a sin. He also tended to snap at his wife, which wasn't good, and rolled his eyes at the members of the Ladies Philoptochos Society when they'd phrase their confessions in such a way as to complain about one another, and then there were the members of the church board—every one of them was some kind of jerk. They'd mutter "Gamo tin panagia sou" right in front of him, steal pens from his desk, and call him Gus instead of Father. And yet, here Gus was, at midnight a few days into the New Year, making his own coffee, counting up his own sins, and feeling proud of it except for the coffee habit. So much for resolutions. What was everyone else doing? Sleeping? Watching TV? Screwing?

A pebble hit the window over the kitchen sink. Gus wiped away the condensation and squinted. *Nasos.* His brother-in-law was outside, in a half-shredded and bloodstained orange prison jumpsuit, snow up to his shins, breath steaming from his mouth like his belly was a coal-fired furnace. The moon was high and set the snow drifts glowing. Gus gulped his coffee, burning his throat, rushed to open the door, and waved Nasos in. A freezing wind pushed past Gus and filled the kitchen; Nasos took his sweet time coming in, and didn't even kick the snow from his feet.

"Sweet Lord, you must be freezing! You're going to lose your toes!" Gus hissed. Another self-interested prayer: *Please Lord, don't let Nasos call out for his sister.* "Let me get you towels, a foot tub full of warm water. There's some coffee left in the briki."

"No," said Nasos in his normal voice, as if he did want to wake up Elpitha, the parish presbytera, Gus's wife, a lady who would definitely do the right thing and call the police immediately and scream at Gus until they showed up. "I'm fine. It'll be okay. And I don't want you running off and calling 911... Father."

"I won't," Gus said. "Sit, but I'm getting a towel first. I'm not explaining bloodstains on the kitchen chairs to Elpitha tomorrow morning."

"You know I don't drink coffee. Do you have any—"

"No." Gus had plenty of what Nasos was going to ask for. Retsina. Ouzo. Beer. Wine. Even rubbing alcohol. A couple cans of Sterno, for that matter.

"I'm cold," said Nasos. He followed Gus to the linen closet in the hallway and took three fluffy towels that weren't going to be white for much longer. He wrapped two around his thin body as he stepped back into the kitchen and carefully arranged the third over a chair before sitting in it.

"How about eggs and toast. No wait, just eggs," Gus said. Nasos raised an eyebrow. Gus tilted his head toward the bedroom, where Elpitha was, he hoped, still sleeping. "The toaster makes a noise when it's done," he explained.

Nasos was wiry as ever. He could have been an Olympian in swimming, in track and field, had everything not gone wrong for him. The flunking, the fighting, the drinking, the alienation from Elpitha and his brothers and cousins, the wrong crowd, the accident, the two parishioners Gus had to bury. Gus crossed himself.

"I'm not a vampire, Gus. You don't need to make the sign of the cross," Nasos said.

"So, it's Gus again, is it?"

"May I still have those eggs, Father?"

"Yeah," said Gus. He focused very hard on extracting a frying pan from the cabinet without making too much noise, and even harder on not asking the question at the top of his list—*how did you escape?* Nasos had obviously performed an amazing high jump or pole vault from the prison yard to the top of the fence, got tangled up in the razor wire, but managed somehow to tear himself free and run for it. Don't prisons have guard towers full of snipers, helicopters fueled up and ready to go, bloodhounds trained to find escapees? There was nothing to be gained from knowing, so Gus asked the second question on his list as he poured a bit of olive oil into the pan.

"Why did you come here to ruin your sister's night? Why not Johnny's house—"

"He'd turn me in as soon as look at me," Nasos said. "Hell, he'd shoot me and try to collect the bounty."

"Is there a price on your head, Athanasios?" Gus asked.

"So, it's Athanasios, is it?" Nasos asked.

"Scrambled or over easy?"

"Anything's fine. And no, there isn't a price on my head, not that I know of. But you know Johnny."

"I do." Johnny was Gus's age. "How about Peter?"

"He has cats, and I'm allergic," Nasos said. "The man has six cats. What kind of man has six cats?"

"How about Billy?"

"Too far," said Nasos. "I'd've been snagged before I made it halfway to his place in Mastic Beach. I'm not here to talk to my sister, Father, I'm here to talk to you. You know my godfather, Harry Pappas."

"I baptized you, didn't I?" asked Gus. "Harry? More like *the Godfather*. Scrambled's fastest. Let me get you a plate and a fork."

"He still tithes from prison," Nasos said.

"Tell me something I don't know," Gus said as he set the small plate of eggs before his brother-in-law. "You can't buy your way into heaven, but Harry Pappas is giving it the old college try." He crossed himself again. Nasos was the baby of the family. Elpitha was twenty years older than her youngest brother. Gus had baptized baby Athanasios, took Harry's big fat tip for it, taught the kid folk dancing in the church's basketball court. And now look at him. Gus didn't know whose neck he wanted to wring first—the kid's, Harry's, or his own.

"You canceled the blessing of the waters," Nasos said. "I saw it in the church newsletter you send Harry. It's practically the only thing they let us read in jail. They don't even let you read *The Amazing Spider-Man.* He has a problem with authority, that Spidey."

"So do you, Nasos. I told you to tell me something I *don't* know. I know they don't let you read your Spider-Man. Your sister told me all about it. I get the Weekly Prison Report from her after every visit. I know I canceled the blessing of the waters. Plain and simple, the parish is graying. There aren't any young guys left who want to dive into the Long Island Sound in January to swim after a cross, even when there isn't a bomb cyclone forecasted for Epiphany, and the bomb cyclone was coming. Lord, Nasos, you were out in it."

Nasos ate the eggs with both hands, shoveling it all into his mouth like there was some secret written upon them he had to hide. At least Gus wouldn't have to wash the fork. *It's funny what people think,* Gus thought.

"I know, I was outside in the weather," Nasos said. "Now you're telling me what I already know. More eggs please." He tapped the plate, licked a filthy finger, and wiped his hands on the bloody towel hanging over his shoulders. "Here's something you don't know—this is all your fault, Father Konstantinos. That's why I'm here."

Gus sighed and took a seat, his wife's seat, at the tiny kitchen table. A wave of exhaustion overcame him. He hadn't even had a sip of his coffee, which was now cold in its little cup on the countertop. Gus was definitely not going to make any more eggs for Nasos. The kid could eat them raw in the shell if he wanted. *Little pissant.* "I'm listening," Gus said.

"When I was ten and I swam for the cross," Nasos said. "The first time. And I got it."

"You were a strong swimmer. You beat the Spanakos brothers, and they were both in high school, and varsity."

"It was so cold that morning. I'd never been so cold. I've never been so cold since." Nasos's gaze drifted toward the window. "That's why the cold doesn't bother me. The blessed water is in my bones. It froze the marrow, forever. Some blessing, eh?"

"Maybe you can say that having every boy in the parish dive into the water after a cross the priest throws to bless the waters makes more sense in Greece than in New York, Nasos," Gus said, "but I don't control the temperature. The weather isn't my fault. It's not even God's fault these days."

"I was so cold. My mother was hugging me, my father too, and kissing me. It was like when Marika used to visit me in the joint and we kiss through the glass. I didn't feel a thing. And Elpitha too; her arms were so cold. Are these the same towels from back on that day years ago?"

"I'd say that they're the same make of towel," Gus said. "We're not going to have to worry about waking her up if you keep at it like this, kid. The sun's gonna come up and her alarm will go off and we'll *both* be eating our next plate of eggs in prison."

"Remember what you did, because I was so cold?"

"Uhm..." Gus was frozen for a moment. The years melded together like slush on the Sound. And Nasos had retrieved the cross four or five times before deciding to dedicate his life to other things, like whatever Harry Pappas needed doing. "Oh yeah, I gave you a little brandy from my flask."

"A little brandy," Nasos repeated. "I liked it. You know what you say about Holy Communion, like it's God's blood and body, and connects us with Jesus and with one another?"

"Yeah, I know what priests say, Nasos." Now Gus briefly prayed that Elpitha *would* wake up.

"That's what the brandy tasted like to me. That sweet, that holy. Why do you think I kept swimming every January 6th, every Theophany, Epiphany, whatever you want to call it?"

"There are easier ways for a kid to get a snootful," Gus said. "Had you stuck with being an altar boy, you could have stolen the wine between liturgies." Nasos's face, calm and too white till now, flashed red as his bloody clothing and twisted into a rictus. *Maybe he is a vampire, Athanasios means immortal!* Gus found himself thinking for a moment, before calming himself, and the situation. "I'm sorry. I'm sorry I said that, and I'm sorry I introduced you to alcohol. I didn't know it would be a problem, and it was just what we did in those days. Like a Saint Bernard with a little barrel around its neck in the Alps, you know? It was just a sip."

"Just a sip," Nasos said.

"The blessing is canceled this year," Gus said. "Probably next year too. I don't even know how long the Archdiocese will let us keep Saint Katherine's open. If not for the Pappas tithes, we wouldn't have survived the pandemic. So it won't happen again. I'm sorry, Athanasios. I'm a sinner. Please forgive my sins and pray for me, and I'll pray for you. I'll write a letter to the warden, I'll try to help."

"You can't cancel it, Father. It'll be your fault, what happens next, if you do."

Gus didn't know what to say. Not even a few words of prayer sprang to mind.

"I kept coming back for three reasons."

"Your father was so proud—"

"I don't give a shit about him!" Nasos slammed his fist on the Formica. Gus could hear Elpitha groan in her sleep just a few yards and three thin walls away.

"Endaxi, eh!" Gus said, holding up his hand and spinning it. "Fine, fine, what are the three reasons? Brandy is number one."

"Brandy is one," Nasos said. "I liked it. A lot. Two, the cold. I didn't feel it after the first time, like I said. Made it real easy. I could have been at the beach near Yiayia's house in Paros, in August, for all I felt the weather. I'm going to walk back to county after this. I don't want no trouble."

Gus struggled to control his eyebrows. "Okay. The third reason?"

"You know how you said that, when we ask God to bless the water, it becomes holy. That you make holy water by pouring a drop of holy water into regular water, so when we bless the Long Island Sound, it becomes holy. The Connecticut River becomes holy, the Atlantic Ocean becomes holy. All the water in the world becomes holy?"

"Yeah, I know what a pries—"

"It's true. I used to see something down there, every year, Gus. Something like a man, big though. Maybe twelve feet long."

"A long... man?"

"Long, not tall. Because he was on his back, resting. Not sleeping, like half-sleeping. Little bubbles coming out of the holes in his face. I wouldn't call them nostrils. And he was surrounded by other figures, little creatures with claws for hands, and big, I don't know, fins on their heads, and then I saw other things down there too. Bones of things that wouldn't, uhm, *work*, if it was a body with flesh and skin. Things that glowed *black*. Does that make sense? Not glow-in-the-dark, a dark that glowed black. And I'd find the cross every year before, you know, the kelp or the tentacles or the eel-headed arms, or whatever—name an appendage, they were all down there, like I said, the main guy was a guy—could grab it and I'd see them all start to dissolve."

"Dissolve?" said Gus. "Like an Alka-Seltzer?"

"Like an Alka-Seltzer," Nasos said. "Fizz fizz."

"You and I have fished off that pier a hundred times when you were a boy, Nasos. There's nothing down there like that," Gus said. "It's not rational."

"It is," Nasos said. "It takes them all year to regain their strength, to regenerate. People flush their toilets and run their jetskis and take their leaks off the sides of their boats and spill their oil in the ocean and the waters turn foul again, turn profane. They regain their strength slowly but surely. Like those goblins, what do you call them, kokoretsi."

"Your Greek is terrible, Nas. Kokoretsi is lamb guts shoved into lamb guts. You mean kalikantzaroi," Gus said. "Those are the Christmas goblins. Who are also not real."

"Whatever. I had a bad day. Anyway, Gussie, if you don't bless the water..." Nasos shrugged expansively, the way Greek boys learn to do from their fathers.

"Nasos, Nasos, I'm sorry. Let's pray. I'm sorry you've been made to see those things when you were a kid. It was probably just..." What were you supposed to do in a situation like this? Just say *a lack of oxygen* or *your overactive imagination*? Or *you are just a crazy person*. There had been all of two days of pastoral training on dealing with believers who hallucinated demons and devils, and not even a footnote about dealing with mobbed-up prison-escapees who had the same sloe eyes and royal nose of your wife who was definitely going to wake up and start shouting *Gamo tin panagia sou!* in the next two minutes.

"Look, if those things were down there and the only reason they don't come up and start eating people like on the late late movie is because we bless the waters every Epiphany, why were they asleep for thousands of years beforehand? Why didn't they pop out of the Sound and eat all the Montauks? Or the Puritans, when they came, or those Lutherans your papou and Harry Pappas bought the church building from back in '73?"

"Maybe the Indians had their own blessings. Maybe it's pollution, global warming, those earthquakes that came when they started fracking. I'm just telling you, Father. Gus," said Nasos.

"Why didn't the Spanakos brothers see it?"

"Maybe I'm special," said Nasos. "Maybe I'm mama's special boy. Maybe they didn't dive deep enough. Listen, you gotta do the blessing. Get someone to swim. Just borrow a kid from a parish in the city, or Jersey. You need to—" Nasos's eyes twitched and he looked past and behind Gus. "Oh, hi."

Gus slowly turned around. There was Elpitha, in her housedress. She had her old pistol—Harry Pappas's idea of a wedding present ten years ago—in one hand, and her ancient flip phone in the other. Elpitha's face was inscrutable to Gus, unnerving after two decades of marriage. Her eyes were wide and ready, but wet like it was time to cry. Was that a tremble along her lips, like she wanted to smile for Nasos?

Elpitha pointed the gun at her brother. The phone she tossed to Gus. "Call 911."

"Yes," said Gus. "Elpitha, please, put the gun down. I was hoping you'd wake up and we could all handle this together, as a family."

"Me too, Gussie," said Elpitha. "That's me. Hope."

Gus opened the phone and looked down at it. The screen was dead. Then something huge and hot and sudden filled the tiny kitchen and the phone hit the floor.

"I hate driving at night," said Elpitha as she put her weight into turning the steering wheel. "And I hate driving in the snow. How's he doing back there?" She glanced at the rear-view mirror.

"Alive, still. Go fast," said Nasos. "He's the holiest thing we have to offer the... them. I don't know if it'll work if he's..."

"I'm sorry, Gussie," said Elpitha, mostly to herself. "I don't know if this will work period, no matter what we do," she told Nasos. It was a short ride downtown and to the pier. January was tourist off-season, the snow was ridiculous, and it was two o'clock in the morning. The town hadn't taken down Christmas lights from around the lampposts and trees yet. The waters of the Sound churned black despite the red and green twinkling and the bright white moon. Gus was a little man, and Nasos so strong, but as long as Gus was still breathing, they had to work fast, and be at least a little careful. Elpitha grabbed his ankles, and Nasos wrapped Gus's neck and arms in a full nelson. Together, they manhandled Gus to the end of the dock and together they counted ena, dio, tria, and they tossed him in.

There were no roiling bubbles or glowing black aurorae, no grasping claws and slimy appendages, just a man who floated for a few moments and made a human noise, then sank. It was early morning, January fourth. Nasos and his sister had two days to clean up and get down to Pennsylvania where they had some cousins who had a cabin in the woods. Elpitha's phone wouldn't work down there, so maybe they couldn't be tracked. In the cabin they could pick up the Long Island news on the AM radio and, God willing, hear headlines no more shocking than the mysterious story of an escaped convict and a missing priest. And then they could start planning what to do next week, where to go next month, how to survive what they had done. But the big unspoken question was this: what the hell were they going to do for next Epiphany?

END

I am from a small Greek and Greek-American enclave on Long Island, where the local congregation practices the blessing of the waters to celebrate Theophany and the end of Christmas season. The Sound is nearby and easy to access. It's just freezing. Once, before I was born, my cousin Peter dove for the cross and won it; my grandmother would frequently tell of swaddling him in towels and feeding him brandy afterward to ward off serious frost damage. I often pictured my cousin, who with his beard and long hair as an adult, looked a little bit like Jesus, flattened and limbs splayed out, being carried up Main Street, a bottle of brandy at his lips.

Years later, in high school, I went on a school trip to the local county jail. It wasn't a Scared Straight program or anything, but the prisoners and guards did their best to terrorize us all. One story a guard shared was of a local Olympic hopeful who had turned to drugs and ended up in the jail. He nearly managed to escape by high-jumping into the razor wire topping the fence, she said, but just managed to tear himself apart.

Two young men, all arms and legs, either covered in towels or wrapped in barbed wire. That was image enough to spark "The Blessing of the Waters." After that, it was just the coin flip of "supernatural horror" or "noir betrayal." The quarter (in my mind) landed on its edge. A Christmas miracle!

DRY AND READY

Glen Hirshberg

"HELP Grandma out of her seatbelt," Aliyah says as she shuts off the motor. Through the mist and the beads of drizzle on the windshield, the wooden gate at the entrance to the park looks like it's dissolving, or overrun with raindrop-colored beetles. Either way, her father would have approved.

In the backseat, Aza neither acknowledges nor lowers the headphones that may or may not be blasting beats into her brain. Aliyah watches and waits.

With a sigh, Aza turns to her grandmother, and Aliyah risks—allows herself—a smile. Little victories. The only actual or sustainable kind with teenaged daughters.

Or anyone, she thinks, right as Shoshana snaps, "I don't need help," then scowls and sits still while Aza unhooks her.

Moments later, they're standing together in the lane of black walnuts and larches outside the park she will always think of as her father's garden, while droplets float around them like ash. The ghost of ash from the fires that blazed across these hills a few months back, and very nearly relieved her family of this obligation for good.

So close.

Aliyah doesn't actually wish that, or want it. Not really.

"Know what some families do for Hanukkah traditions?" Aza mutters as they start forward.

This time, Aliyah doesn't just allow herself the smile; she turns it on her daughter. "Go ahead. Let's hear the list."

"Well, let's see." Aza is wearing mittens, which doesn't stop her ticking off rituals she'd prefer on her fingers. "Joan's whole family blasts that 2 Live Jews album—"

"It's Hanukkah here," Aliyah chants, and Aza actually gurgles.

"Hanukkah? That song has nothing to do with Hanukkah, assuming you were trying to sing just now. You not only have zero memory, you have zero rhythm. Anyway, they blast that all day, and at night they light candles while vats of oil are heating on the stove, and then they don't even eat dinner, they just fry up sufganiyot all night, all of them, together, and eat them blazing hot until they pretty much throw up."

"Why didn't we think of that?" Aliyah says, and Aza swats her.

"Wait," says Shoshana.

Aliyah slows—Aza, too, automatically, because she's a good kid—and each of them takes one of her mother's arms. Spindle-arms. They start forward again. Their feet make shushing sounds in the ground cover. Overhead, drizzle taps the last leaves off the branches of the walnuts. Gifting the trees back their winter forms, her father would have said. He'd cribbed his definition of sculpting from Michelangelo: the act not of giving material shape, but of digging out shapes already cocooned in the material.

Aza's not done, of course. "Then there's Brian's family."

"Who's Brian?" Aliyah asks.

"Nice try, Mom. No one you're going to know or know about. They open all their presents on the first night, so they can get that Christmas present-orgy feeling—his dad's Christian—and then they ball up all the wrapping paper and have snowball fights with it for the rest of the holiday. Also, I think they use the balls to bowl down each other's dreidels."

"So, more of a marking-the-military-victory flavor to their Hanukkah."

"More of a playing games emphasis. With present orgies."

"Know what we did on the first night of Hanukkah when I was a kid?" Aliyah asks as they reach the gate. The wood, she notes, has warped more in the past year because of the perpetual northwestern Washington wetness; it also has new black streaks down it. Dozens of little punctures, too, as though something with talons swept by and tried to pick it up. Aliyah taps Shoshana's arm. "Remember, Mom?"

"Hi, Avvy," her mother says. To the fence. To *in there.*

Aliyah squeezes her elbow, but Aza rolls her eyes. Then she glances across her grandmother's head at Aliyah.

Stop it, Aliyah mouths. But what she says is, "We went to synagogue. Maybe you'd prefer that."

"You mean, seeing friends and singing with everybody and then having a communal latke feast? You're right. Sounds awful. Think we can make it if we turn around right now?"

Letting go of her mother, Aliyah tugs the frayed rope that releases the latch, pulls open the gate, steps through, then swivels suddenly to her right. She stares down the slope into the mist and tree shadows.

"What?" Aza asks.

Someone's here, she almost says.

But why shouldn't there be? People do come—it's an official city attraction, and has to stay one; that was one of the conditions for granting her father the land, and now this place has become a treasured little county secret. The reclaimed sewage and landfill dump turned art park plus heron and black deer sanctuary.

Her father's garden. Lab. Zoo. Studio. Whatever he thought it was.

The smell slips into her lungs with her breath. So faint, Aliyah always wonders if she's imagining it. Remembering it, because unlike Aza, Aliyah was here when her father first got the grant. Used to come here as a kid to... play? Wander? Watch her father dig and shovel out space in repurposed waste-earth, and sing to it.

Again, she swivels, gazing this time between the firs, past the Garry oak toward the pond, where her father lies buried. Where their ritual will end for another year, half an hour or so from now. She always thinks of her father's garden as still, which is weird, because it never is. Even on Hanukkah eve, when she and Aza and Shoshana are always the only people here.

Hello, deer, she thinks, wondering for the thousandth time how they even get in. She hopes they'll let themselves be seen this year.

Hello, Dad, she doesn't quite say, and beckons her mother and daughter onto the path beside her. From the pockets of her rain shell, she pulls out the little pads of paper and pencil stubs.

"Right. It's cold. Quick round, today, okay? Let's go feed Grandpa's animals."

"Hi, Avvy," says her mother again, all breathy, like a little girl.

"Fuck's sake," murmurs Aza, not quite quietly enough. Before Aliyah can tell her off, she grabs paper and pencil and starts to her right toward the clam. Land-clam, as Aza calls it. The trees above her shudder, settle. There are always birds up there, no matter the season. Herons, sometimes, even in winter. Owls, though mostly Aliyah only hears those. Occasionally, she sees their humped, black shadows—half-sculpted, her father would have said—way up in the bare branches. Seemingly emerging from the bark. She used to see squirrels, too, but hasn't for a long time. Possibly, the owls have eaten them.

"Meet at the pond in fifteen minutes. We'll light the candles," Aliyah calls.

"Right," Aza calls back. "Maybe this time we can *trigger* the fire."

"You know, daughter, this is in fact a Hanukkah tradition. Our family's tradition."

"A made-up and really weird one."

"A fulfilling of obligation. A mitzvah. To your family. What else do you think tradition involves?"

"Being home with Dad making sufganiyot. Present orgies. Pleasure vomiting."

Shoshana has shuffled off to the left, toward the sculptures she always goes to first. Her favorites, and Aliyah's least: the bulbous raccoons that always have to be swept clear of leaves, the squirrel on the black walnut trunk that always looks a little too much like it's pinned there, half-squashed into the bark. Then the little eaglets. Eaglet-smears, Aza calls them, and as usual, she's not wrong.

Cruel, sometimes. Rarely wrong.

Aliyah knows she should follow her mother. Should, in fact, be right next to her, supporting arms at the ready. Instead, she stands and watches the old woman bend over the raccoons, slowly write her first message of the day on her pad. The peculiar peace of this place wafts across her without quite settling her. Her father's sort of peace. The stillness inside motion, he'd called it, once. The death inside life, always waiting to be given its shape.

Weirdly cheerful guy, her father. Cheerful-inside-doomy. Or maybe the other way around?

"Hi, Dad," she whispers quietly. Watches the words mist from her mouth.

When she next looks, Shoshana is talking to the squirrel blob affixed to the walnut trunk. Eventually, she slides the note she has just written into the little slot that passes for squirrel mouth, like a supplicant at the Wailing Wall. When she starts gingerly downslope toward the eaglet grove, Aliyah follows fast. Her mother's steps are so unsteady on the ground, now. She has shrunk in the eleven years since her husband's death, but also widened, as though she's being squashed from above.

Aza is nowhere to be seen. If she has a favorite sculpture—other than the land clam, she loves the land clam—she has never said. For her, this ritual has all the resonance of a treadmill jog.

Aliyah would still rather be with her, though. Arguing. Teasing. Doing anything but acknowledging how *she* has come to feel about this particular mitzvah, laid on them for life by her mad dad.

Her remote, mad, sometimes marvelous dad. Who'd spent most of Aliyah's childhood behind this fence, on this hillside, under these trees. Making animal-blobs. And singing to them.

The fastest way to the other side of the worst is through. Aliyah's life has taught her this. Everyone's life teaches them this. Therefore, the fastest way to the rest of Hanukkah—to latkes and sufganiyot and laughing with her husband and 2 Live Jews—is to finish the rounds.

Her mother has made it safely into the eaglet grove. So Aliyah veers off along the steeper switchback path toward the grove her father called The Paddock. "Stay there, Mom," she calls. "Feeding the horse. Be right with you."

Shoshana doesn't answer. Very possibly doesn't hear. Her mother mostly doesn't hear, these days, and also doesn't seem to notice.

Around and above Aliyah, the drizzle sharpens, or else the trees are dripping. Wetness taps the sleeves of her jacket, trickles down her cheeks like brook water over stone. Nothing about this wetness reminds her of crying. She has never cried here, in all these years. Not once.

Does her mother, she wonders? Has she ever?

Right as she slips into The Paddock—just an asymmetrical quadrilateral of hedge, Aliyah isn't even sure her father did anything to it except cut a secret-garden arch for an opening— something sails up from the dirt and darts across her vision.

Circles back, then hovers in front of her. A little black winged line. A shape sketched from mist, vibrating at eye level. When it vanishes, she can't tell if it has zipped off or melted.

Dragonfly? In December?

Why not? Always, there is so much life here. Under the lily pads and its skin of algae, the pond at the bottom of the garden has long housed living tadpoles that dart and dive among the blob-approximations her father molded and anchored there. Plus frogs, possibly fish, though Aliyah never put any there and doesn't think her father did. But she thinks she has seen them. Aza claims she definitely has.

Her shudder is automatic. Familiar. Weirdly redolent—if shudders can be that—of her dad when he came home from sculpting. The faint but unmistakable odor of this specific Earth, ruthlessly treated, bleached and sanitized, hovering around him like an aura. The clay and marble smells clinging to his hands. Becoming his hands.

She is as close as she can remember to tearing up as she approaches the horse. "Hello, Bob," she says.

There it stands where it always stands, on its two good hooves. The two finished ones her father allowed it. It's a pony, really, barely four feet high, maybe seven feet long, its black sides pebbled and grooved, as though it were once riverbed before her father tilted it upright and planted it here. Its mane tight and twisted, like dreadlocks. Hence her name for this piece, which she'd thought might make her father angry. But it had made him laugh.

Bob, as in Marley.

Abruptly, she pulls her hand back, stares right into the horse's eye. It isn't quite rounded, but perpetually pooled with water along the bulbous bottom of its socket. As though it is either only now congealing into eye-ness, or else liquifying.

As always, Aliyah feels her gaze drawn down Bob's body toward those hooves. They dig at different angles into the mud. Mid-gallop, her father claimed when he first invited them into The Paddock to see it, when she was maybe twelve.

Her mother had snorted. Suggested scrabbling. Or rearing.

Aliyah is practically singing now as she grabs pencil from pocket, scrawls on her notepad. Her lips shape the lyrics, or catch at them. Cling to the shape they give her mouth.

Please stay up, Bob.

Ripping off the top sheet, not thinking—she prefers not to think about what she writes when she's here—she folds the paper and slips it into the horse's just-open mouth, through the space where the top lip pinches upward as though dragged by a bit that isn't there. Or the memory of a bit. Promise of one. As usual, Aliyah expects to shiver as her fingers slide between the jaws. As usual, she doesn't.

Because there's absolutely nothing in there. Like all her father's sculptures, the horse is hollow. More than hollow, somehow; empty.

And so, actually, less than hollow? What's less than hollow?

She lets go of the paper, listens for its falling. But wherever it lands, it does so silently. From across the park, she hears shuffling in the ground cover and dead leaves. Too fast and stompy for deer. Aza, most likely, cycling through her assigned stations as quickly as she can. But doing her duty. Leaving wishes or curses or hopes or hellos. Saying the blessing at each stop. It really is like a sort of Hanukkah Tashlich, this ceremony her father invented.

Except instead of casting off sins, as in the Yom Kippur ritual, they're just making contact. Saying hello.

With a sigh, Aliyah lays the back of her hand on the pony's forehead, the way she used to in order to check Aza's temperature. The way Shoshana did for her.

"For comfort, see?" her father had told her the first time. The day he'd showed her how. Before even he had realized this would become his legacy. Commandment. Dying wish. Gift. "Gently. Like you're helping him sleep. You're giving them the Word!"

"Baruch atah a-d-o-n-o-i," Aliyah murmurs. The prayer mixes weirdly with the Bob Marley lyrics still flitting around her brain. Her voice rings more than it should in this dripping, empty space, as though sounding the hollow of the horse. By the time she gets to She'kacha Lo Be'Olamo, she's just mouthing again, *thank you, God, for wondrous things,* leaning forward to whisper, so that the explosion of knocking almost rocks her off her feet, has her ducking sideways even before she hears Shoshana gasp.

"Mom?" she calls.

More knocks, rapid fire, straight up from where Aliyah stands. Pushing away from the horse, Aliyah shoots a glance up the trees, thinks she maybe sees a red crest way up the trunk of the nearest fir. A Williamson's Sapsucker. Beautiful bird.

In her chest, her heart thumps. Sounds her. She blows out breath.

"She'kacha Lo Be'Olamo," she murmurs again. For Bob, and maybe the bird. Her thumping heart. She gives the horse a final stroke across his withers, which are wet, as always. Colder than the air. "Don't get caught." She doesn't have any idea what she means.

"'Liyah?" her mother calls. Then coughs.

Across the park, Aza laughs. Hopefully not at her grandmother. *Please don't let that be the girl I've raised*, Aliyah thinks. Except, how could one blame her? Her grandmother is not the person she was when Aza was born. Shares only a name and shrunken, sagging outline with the woman Aliyah thinks of as her mother. Is mostly a skinful of stabbing, whole-body pain, half-accurate memories, barely contained bitterness, and exhaustion.

"I need help," Shoshana calls, and Aliyah hurries out of The Paddock toward the eaglet grove.

When she spots her mother sitting in the dirt, legs straight out in front of her and half-buried in leaves, Aliyah has a horrified urge to laugh, herself. The tableau is ridiculous: Shoshana in little-girl pose, right underneath that sculpted, silvery nest in its sculpted bush, with her face tilted up, mouth pursed in what could be surprise or even hunger. She almost looks like an eaglet herself, fallen from the nest.

A really old one.

And not one of her father's. The eaglets are only partially formed, mostly blobs. Blobs with wide open mouths, plopped into a nest that is mostly bigger blob, and which clings like a giant raindrop to a bush that resembles a bubble ballooning from the Earth.

"Mom," Aliyah says, hurrying forward. "You okay?"

"What?" says her mother, not even looking at her. Or anywhere, exactly.

"Did you fall?"

"What do you mean?" The question is a challenge. But she lets her daughter help her up.

Aliyah is about to lead her out of the grove, but turns first to check the eaglets. To make sure her mother fed them, if she's honest.

There they sit. Their tiny, dripping, half-formed beaks. Barely-there bodies seemingly spreading across the interior of the nest, which looks molten. Cold, and molten.

There are no crumples of paper she can see. Not in any of those mouths. "Mom," she says. Casually. "Did you feed the... Did you leave the chicks a note?"

"Who?" says Shoshana. And then, right as Aliyah sighs, starts to reach for her own pad, "Oh. Yes. I left his fucking note."

For one moment more, Aliyah, stares at the eaglets, holding her mother tight around the shoulders.

His fucking note.

Sometimes, especially lately, she really does see her father's sculptures through Shoshana's eyes. The cruelty in them. This pitiful huddle of abandoned chicks with the rain pelting them. Cloud shadows taunting them as they pass overhead. Hint of warmth, shadow of wing. Memory of mother, but not one.

Other times, she sees them as she's sure he intended. As new life, forming.

Almost sure.

Tucking a hand under Shoshana's arm, she pulls her mother gently up and away. "What did you write in your note?"

"Just that they should eat." Her voice surprisingly like her old voice for a moment. Like Aliyah's mother's voice. "They look scrawny."

Hint of warmth. Shadow of wing.

Aliyah leads her down the leaf-riddled path toward the pond. On the far side of that, she spots Aza emerging from the woolly mammoth enclosure, moving fast toward the jackrabbit warren. Then the ship. Almost done already. Except that, even as Aliyah watches, her daughter darts sideways, doubles back uphill toward the entrance. As though she has forgotten something. Or wanted to write a message of her own to Bob and the eaglets and squirrel.

It is amazing, Aliyah thinks. The accruing weight of rituals that stick. The way obligation becomes the foundation of meaning. Or just meaning.

Sometimes.

Goddamn you, Dad.

But she's not sure what she's damning him for, or even if she is. She mostly loved him, and has mostly loved this obligation. The all-generation, once-yearly return to the world her father dreamed.

Way down at the bottom of the garden, in the tall hedges that line the fencing, branches shudder. Twigs snap. Deer, almost certainly. They, too, are usually here at this time of year, foraging for any foliage still alive enough to eat. Unless they're always here. Maybe they are. Maybe this really is a refuge Aliyah's dad made. Somewhere safe from coyotes and speeding cars, home to prayers and wild things. Some of them living.

She scans the hedges, now, hoping for a glimpse. Those amazing black pelts she has only seen on these deer. Their black-splotch tails. Gestural tails. Something her father would have carved and stuck on them. Some years, the deer come right out in the open, wander up the hill. Venture surprisingly near as she and Aza and Shoshana tend the sculptures. Stand still, watching. Not like they're afraid. Almost saying hello.

The next stop is the tortoise, which looks even more like a mushroom than it always has. Its shell mottling orange, its tucked-under head less hidden than halfway dissolved. On its way to being reabsorbed. In the firs above it, an owl hoots. Across the garden, another answers.

Her mother makes no motion to write anything, so Aliyah takes out her pad. Without thinking, she scribbles a single word. She doesn't know where it comes from, doesn't want to interrogate the impulse. But she does stare at it for a second. Almost shows it to her mother, but that's not the ritual. You can tell afterward, if you want. But the words are meant to be yours alone. Yours, and the sculptures to which you feed them.

Stay.

Tearing off the page, Aliyah folds it, gives it a kiss, and tucks it into the space between head and shell, ignoring another impulse to yank back her hand. She lays her fingers against the turtle's grooved brow, which feels wet. Her father's sculptures always feel wet, even on the rare days they've come when it isn't drizzling. The materials he used retain water, somehow. Or produce it. Less clay or metal than sponge skin.

Or skin, period.

"Almost done," she sighs when she finishes the blessing. "What's left?"

"Just the snot," says Aza, appearing suddenly behind them, half out of breath. As though she has been running. Certainly, she has been grinning. She's barely controlling that, now.

"And the bat," says Shoshana.

But Aliyah watches Aza, whose mouth keeps twitching. Whose eyes dart sideways, away from her mother's.

"What?" she finally asks.

Aza just laughs. "Oh, right. Bat, then snot."

"They're not snot."

"Bat, snot, light the candle, wave to Grandpa, *home* for latkes. Dreidel. You and Dad giving me presents. I've done all the rest. Fed them their words, gave them their blessing, the works. Come on, Grandma." To Aliyah's surprise, she grabs Shoshana's elbow and leads her carefully away.

Down the hill they head toward the Garry oak. Around them, the air stirs, rippling the branches overhead and the leaves at their feet, draping droplets on the bushes and tree trunks and the sleeves of their jackets like seeds. Everything here is constantly in the midst of either getting soaked or drying. Taking shape (like Aza) or losing it (like her mother).

Aza glances around, doesn't so much flash that grin of hers as suck it back in. Again. Aliyah narrows her eyes. Her daughter looks away.

Under the Garry oak—beside it, really, the branches forming no discernible pattern but shooting off in every possible direction like flung paint across a canvas—they stop. Not for the first time, Aliyah wonders if this tree isn't the whole reason her father's garden exists, or at least exists here. The only native Washington oak, he told her once. Impossibly rare on the U.S. mainland, now. A tree with deep roots but no distinctive shape, its bark so grooved it looks furrowed, or would if the grooves ran straight. The whole edifice on its way to formed, nearly-tree (or recently-was). Just the way her father liked it. A protected tree, to some degree, growing here amid the waste, which is part of what had prompted—or forced—the state to do something with this land other than build over it.

She pokes a careful finger into one of the tree's grooves, feels the scrape of its bark, the softness down in the hollow. The mosses that only grow in these furrows, on this specific tree. The little creatures only this moss houses, crawling over and slowly suffocating the only world that sustains them.

"*You*," Shoshana snarls abruptly—*to the tree?*—and Aza startles and lets go of her elbow. Starts a response, but the look on her grandmother's face stops her.

Aliyah knows that look all too well. It's the one Shoshana always flashes in this precise spot, for whatever reason. Also the one that seemed to have frozen on her face during the whole year her husband withered away in the medical bed they'd set up in their living room.

It's not hatred. Not quite. It wasn't, then.

Because he was actually there and with her, for the first time in their marriage? Or because she'd suddenly remembered why she hadn't always minded that he wasn't? And also what she'd loved about him, once?

Maybe, of course, that look is something else entirely, something between her mother and father that she will never understand.

Ssh, Aliyah mouths at her daughter, but makes no sound. She lets her mother hate, or commune, or whatever it is she has always done in this spot.

Much sooner than usual, Shoshana looks up. "Your grandfather," she says to Aza, with a quivery half-wave at the branches. "In his glory."

"The bat?" says Aza, and looks up, also.

There it hangs. Bat-shaped blob, bark-colored, dangling from its reinforced branch maybe eight feet up. Dripping.

"Upside down. Half asleep. Oblivious. Except when he's flapping around in the air chasing invisible things so he can eat them. How much more your grandfather could it be?" Disdain doesn't just lace Aliyah's mother's voice, these days. It *is* her mother's voice. The last component of her vocal cords that still makes sound.

Except for that hint of admiration. Or maybe affection.

The ghost of love?

Aliyah can never decide if she's imagining that on the rare occasions she hears it, now. Can't even decide if she'd *always* imagined it.

With a silent sigh, she slides an arm around her mother's shoulders. If she squeezes hard enough, she can still feel Shoshana in there. The bones of the woman who raised her. Got her to school and put her to bed. Helped her survive trig/pre-calc. Taught her trig/pre-calc, truth be told, which was such a surprise, and shouldn't have been. Stayed married to a crazy man who'd dedicated the last thirty years of his life to shaping a garden out of what was once landfill, then populating it with creatures he couldn't bear or just didn't want to bring fully into being, except for their mouths. Their gaping, desperate mouths. By the end—really, by the time Aliyah had become a teenager—her father had all but vanished into these clearings, sunk into this earth. Become a thing only glimpsed about its own business. As remote and magical as the black deer in the hedges, and at least as hard to know.

Shoshana has taken out her writing pad, is scribbling. She finishes fast, tears off the page and folds it. Takes a step forward, and for an amazed moment, Aliyah thinks she's going to step into the notch in the Garry oak's trunk and climb up to feed the bat herself.

Instead, she holds out the paper and waits, as though expecting the tree to take it. Aliyah starts forward, but Aza is faster, grabs the page from her grandmother's hand and jams a sneakered foot into the notch.

"Thank you," Aliyah calls to her daughter.

"Oh, don't thank me," Aza calls. Glances back, and lets the grin flash.

"O... kay...?" Aliyah murmurs. She squeezes Shoshana's shoulders again as Aza climbs, reaches out her arm. The bat does not lean or twitch. Stays asleep. Continues to drip, and dream.

Almost, Aliyah doesn't see it happen. Then, for one blissful second, she thinks her mother hasn't seen.

Then Shoshana snaps, "Put it back."

Above them, her face right next to the bat's—*too close*, Aliyah thinks, without any idea why; the feeling has nothing to do with the bat or even its mouth, but its weird, wet skin. *Don't touch its skin*—Aza grins down. She looks like a bird. Williamson's Sapsucker, mid-peck. A creature of the oak.

"What do you mean?" she says.

What are you doing? Aliyah mouths. But she stirs fast, starts to tug Shoshana around and away. "Come on, Mom. Last stop."

For a moment, her mother looks confused. More than confused; like she's forgotten not just what they're doing but where she is.

Or who she is? Was?

Shuddering, furious at herself or maybe Aza, Aliyah keeps tugging, and her mother doesn't so much resist as go solid. Like clay hardening. Aliyah tugs harder, and her mother swings back to the tree.

"Say the blessing."

Aza has climbed down. "Already said it on my way up. Didn't you hear me?" She steps to the other side of her grandmother but doesn't take her elbow again.

"We'll say the last one together," Aliyah says. "Over the candle." She very much wants them to do that together, suddenly.

Because, really, how many more times will there be?

"Come on, Grandma," Aza says, moving just far enough ahead that Aliyah can't see her face. "Snotward!"

It takes longer than usual, but after a few steps, as they move down the hill toward the pond, her mother finally says, "It's not snot."

Right on cue, Aza chimes in, her words and teasing tone as predictable and familiar as Torah trope. Turning this whole exercise—rain, complaints, scribbled words, the sculptures' open mouths, the half-seen deer and ghost-echoes of her father— back into a recitation. Commemorative ritual. So much more satisfying than visiting a grave. Her family's version of the Mourner's Kaddish. Of *We miss you, Dad. Whoever you were.*

"It's a smear," Aza chants.

"It's tadpoles."

"Of what? Giant melting snot-frogs?"

"There's something wrong with your daughter."

"She's your granddaughter."

"She's..." But Shoshana stops. Not as if she's forgotten, but as if the conversation disintegrated in her mouth.

With a jolt, Aliyah realizes she herself doesn't remember what they usually say next, either. There was something else. And now there isn't.

GLEN HIRSHBERG

Yet another piece of life with her father—of her father's life—draining away. Her mother is still picking her way toward the pond and her husband's final resting place, each step just a little more careful and anxious than the last. Someday soon, Aliyah knows, she and Aza will be coming here alone. To leave notes for both her parents.

Would that be right, though? Would either of them really want that?

Aza has reached the pond and is facing the water down there. "Aww," she says. "Hi guys."

"Deer?" Aliyah calls, instinctively speeding up. Then she turns around. Does not say, *Come on, Mom.* The scowl on her mother's face is stunning, almost a sneer.

Or else just concentration. The expression of a frail and failing person checking footholds she knows won't support her much longer.

"Mom?"

"I'm fine," Shoshana snarls. Sounding nowhere near frail. "Let's get this over with."

To keep from reproaching, Aliyah moves ahead. She reaches the lip of the pond just in time to see raccoons appear on the other side. Three of them, a mother and two kits emerging from the hedge. Like a mirror image of her own family. Except in raccoon.

Is that what you were thinking, Dad? What all this is?

The raccoons have seen Aza and Aliyah, too, but seem neither concerned nor interested. One of the kits scratches at leaves, dips a paw in the lily-smeared surface of the water as though stirring it. The mother stops, holds still. They all do. Then they wander off into the hedge.

116

Ritual completed. Duty performed.

Fuck you, Dad, Aliyah thinks abruptly, balling her fists and very nearly tearing up. The ferocity of the feeling gets more intense every year. Because it's her mother's, she has long suspected. Runoff from her mother, unchecked now by weekend afternoons alone up here with her father.

Meaning, not exactly with. Afternoons in the space he happened to be in, also. Her presence as significant to him as it was to those raccoons or the black deer as he dug up sterilized earth and trucked in clay and marble and squeezed and buffed and chiseled and shaped. And sang. Always that same, so-old song. "My golem ode," he used to tell her. "Remember, 'you and I, too, were nipped from clay...'"

"Happy Hanukkah, snot," Aza says to the water, patting around in her jacket pocket for her pad of paper, and accidentally spilling three other little folded sheets she has stored in there. Immediately, she grabs for those, tries to stuff them back in. But she's too slow.

It's too late.

"You little bitch," Shoshana hisses from behind Aliyah. "You put those *back*."

"Mom!" Aliyah snaps, then blinks in surprise. Sways where she stands. Right up until the word left her mouth, she had thought she was going to reprimand Aza.

Shoshana has gone stiff, straight-backed. "You put them back. Right this minute."

Having collected the sheets, Aza balls them in her fist and shakes them in front of her face. "Have you seen what she writes, Mom?"

"No. And you shouldn't either."

"It's horrible. She's horrible."

"Pisher," Shoshana spits. "Snake."

Aza glances at Aliyah. "Pisher?"

Which gives Aliyah the de-escalation opportunity she needs. The chance to remind her family that they're family. "Means bed-wetter. It's barely even an insult. She could have gone for much worse."

"She has," says Aza. Once more, she brandishes the papers.

"She has to return those," Shoshana mutters. But she has softened, or weakened. Either way, she's quieter.

"She will," says Aliyah, coaxing her mother toward the water. "Why don't you leave the message for the tadpoles?"

"Snot," Aza mutters.

Aliyah ignores her. "We'll light the candle and say the blessing. Then home for latkes and dreidel and sufganiyot." She holds her breath. Waits to see what her fading, furious mother and her righteous, furious daughter will do.

They turn to the water. Aliyah exhales, forgets momentarily even to glare at Aza. Instead, she strokes her daughter's hair, then helps her mother kneel at the water's edge. At first, she thinks Shoshana's trembling is from the effort of hunkering down. The strain of all this movement.

Only as she hunches over her notepad does Aliyah realize she's crying.

Which reminds her to glare at her daughter. But when she does, Aza holds out the papers from her pocket. The notes her mother left her father's sculptures, and which her daughter has stolen out of their mouths.

Momzer, reads one.

Ruen zol er nisht afile en keyver, says the next, and Aliyah's mouth starts to open, but she clamps it shut. Why does she even know this curse, or remember what it means?

Because my mother taught it to me, when I was young. Because she thought it was funny. Same reason I taught it to my daughter, on a car trip somewhere. All of us laughing. So funny, the things Jews used to say to hurt each other. So vicious and clever. Rueful and sad:

May he lie in the ground and bake bagels.

For as many years as he's walked on his feet, he should walk on his hands.

May he find no rest even in his grave.

For a second, Aliyah considers ripping up the papers. Or balling them and hurling them into the pond. But that feels like a desecration, somehow though God knows of what. And maybe worse. A curse on things that must not be cursed.

Her mother is still writing, Trembling, and writing. Aliyah steps back, beckoning Aza to her side. "You have to put these where she left them. Okay? On our way out?"

"Why?"

"Because that's the ritual. That's what Grandpa wanted us to do. He said we had to feed them our words. He didn't say we should police each other's."

"She's so mean."

"She's lonely, Azzy. She's so lonely."

Always has been, Aliyah realizes. No—remembers. Part of the bargain and curse of that sort of marriage. When your partner's passion or craziness or brilliance or mania so eclipses you that even your children half-forget you're there.

"It's not fair to Grandpa," Aza says.

"Grandpa doesn't care."

And wouldn't have then. Aliyah hates that she thinks that. Wonders if it's true.

At the water's edge, Shoshana leans forward, her hand twitching in the air, magical in that moment, dewed and flecked with misting light. A dying dragonfly. Together, Aliyah and Aza watch that hand, with its folded paper, dip toward the water's surface, her father's black metal splats seemingly suspended there, just offshore amid the drab, flabby lilies. Slicked among them.

"It really does look like snot," Aliyah murmurs.

Abruptly, Aza darts forward and kneels next to her grandmother. "Here," she says, lifting the paper from Shoshana's fingers. For a second, Shoshana clenches. Then releases the message into Aza's hand.

"Don't steal it," she says.

Without answering, and also without reading what Shoshana has written, Aza slides the paper into the slot—the stingray-style slit-mouth—on the top of the tadpole sculpture. Snot-slick. Stays kneeling next to Shoshana.

Eventually, both of them shuttle sideways toward the foot-high, rusted metal candle holder that sprouts like a decapitated reed from the scatter of actual reeds at the edge of the pond. Aliyah joins them, carefully clearing space around the holder so their flame doesn't catch on anything. So they can say the yearly blessing her father has demanded of them. The one thing he specifically asked in his own memory.

Moving fast—wanting to get through this moment while the peace holds—Aliyah fishes candle and matchbook from her pocket.

She digs dirt and debris out of the holder, presses the candle into it. Aza stands. Aliyah considers asking her to kneel back down, decides not to push her luck. But then Aza does it anyway, settling between her mother and grandmother, so that they form a semi-circle.

Without another word, just a brush of her sleeve against her daughter's that she hopes Aza realizes is intentional, Aliyah strikes the match. Snaps it in half, swears, and strikes another. This time, she gets the candle lit.

Automatically, as though triggered by the flame, all three of them cup their hands near their faces, and light catches in their fingers. The glow suffuses their skin. Nothing that can be held. But something to sing to.

We are all golems, Aliyah thinks. Mud and clay momentarily illuminated by wind and light. Animated by the promise we found in our mouths at the moment we were born.

"Baruch atah adonai," she sings. Her mother and daughter sing, too. The words in their mouths and the light in their hands. "She'hechianoo. V'klmanoo..."

Thank you, God, for letting us reach this day.

We miss you, Dad.

They are halfway back up the hill before any of them speak again. The drizzle has intensified. But in the aftermath of their little ceremony—or the anticipation of being home, of menorah lighting and latke feasting in their gently glowing house—a peace seems to have taken hold. And so Aliyah forgets for a second, right up until Shoshana jerks to a stop.

"Put them back," she says.

Aza is several steps ahead, and continues as though she hasn't heard.

"She has to *put them back*," Shoshana hisses.

"Okay, Mom, it's okay, she'll—"

Lurching forward, Shoshana almost sprawls face-first as she grabs for Aza's jacket. She catches hold on the second try and yanks her around.

"Ow, *get off*," Aza snaps, right in her grandmother's face.

Shoshana teeters, and Aliyah jabs out her arms to steady her. Her croak, this time, is an old, old woman's. "Put them back."

"What is *wrong* with you?" says Aza, trying to shake off her grandmother's grip. But for once, Aliyah's glare freezes her.

"What," Aliyah says, holding her daughter's gaze, propping up her mother with her hip. "Is wrong. With *you*?"

The screech yanks all of them around just in time to see the heron lift from the Garry oak—seemingly spring from its bark—and sail off dripping and squawking. The top of the tree shudders, and the whole garden hums like a wire being struck.

Shoshana is shivering against Aliyah's side. Is wet through, and freezing.

"I'm taking your grandmother to the car," she says, low and hard. "Meet us there when you're done."

She knows Aza will do what she's asked. *Almost* knows, despite the defiance on her daughter's face.

"Let go, Mom." Aliyah taps the hand still clutching Aza's jacket. Eventually, Shoshana lets go, allows Aliyah to ease her toward the exit.

"Mom," Aza says, holding up the scraps of paper. "Why are you okay with this? How is this any kind of version of Tashlich? Why is this okay?"

"I didn't say it was okay," Aliyah answers. Against her side, Shoshana shivers without seeming to hear what's being said, or to notice that she's shivering. "It's just not worth... Just do it, okay? Hurry up."

But Aza stays standing in the dripping wet with her grandmother's curses curled in her fist. Hood down, head exposed, which is another act of defiance.

Finally, Aliyah hears her move off back into the garden.

Tightening her arm around Shoshana's shoulders, Aliyah hustles her toward the gate. "Come on. Let's get you warm."

For answer, her mother hums. Makes a humming sound.

"She doesn't understand," Aliyah continues. Her words a hum of her own. She's not really thinking about what she's saying. Is thinking instead about her daughter's fury. And her mother's. The years-long, unrelenting heat of that.

The last heat in her?

They're through the gate, now, back in the parking lot, and Aliyah has tears in her eyes. The car chirps as her fingers push the key in her pocket. Her mother is still shivering.

"He wasn't worth it," Aliyah says, not even sure who she's talking to, now. Speaking the words she has found in her mouth. But these are for her mother. The tears are for her father, and the magic he made. For the way he'd really seemed to need Aliyah— to see her, really— for the first time in his life, right at the end, as he lay there in that awful bed in that darkened living room, rasping, *"Ali. Ali."* Rising half out of the blankets, straining so hard he looked like he might burst. Would have, if there'd been anything left in him but dust.

The moment he'd made her promise. Saddled them with

this task, forever. Gifted it to them. The lighting of the candle. Saying of the blessing. Feeding of the words. "So they know they're remembered."

Not *so* I *know*, Aliyah thinks, now—her thoughts whirling, wild—as she lowers her mother into the backseat, with more force than she usually applies.

What did you think you were making here, Dad? And laying on us? A mitzvah, or a threat?

The feeding of the words. Any words. So his monsters don't come looking for the company they missed?

Shoshana isn't resisting, but she's not helping. She's still shivering, too. Her sopping coat presses against Aliyah's face as she tries to click home the belt, which makes her want to scream.

"Come on," she says instead. Not to anyone. Just making sound.

Wind through metal. Breath through people.

With a grunt, she gets the belt locked, straightens so fast she goes dizzy and has to grab the roof of the car, sucking in lungsful of air. This air. The smell of this place. Clean sewage. Sprayed, cleansed, refurbished Earth. All of it rendered safely dead, then granted to her father. So he could resurrect it.

"Shut the door," Shoshana says, and Aliyah all but slams it on her.

She starts around the car, but takes her time, watching the tops of the walnuts and larches rattling in the rain on the other side of the gate. The branches grabbing at the falling drops like children chasing bubbles.

Shaking her head clear, which proves easier than expected, she glances toward the gate, wondering what's taking Aza so long. Wanting her to hurry.

Then Aza's there. Hurrying. Waving, even. And Aliyah is smiling as she pulls open the door and drops into the car. By the time she's settled, Aza is in, too, seatbelt locked.

"Monsters milked," her daughter chirps. "Stables swept. Herculean labors completed. Sufganiyot, please."

"Sufganiyot, ho," Aliyah says, and starts the car. Feels the tires grip, and they're rolling toward paved street with the heater on for the first time all year and that dusty, dead-heater smell filling the car as the mechanism coughs and resuscitates. Into her head—into her mouth—pops the dreidel song. She has already started singing, hit the first "I made it out of clay," when Aza and Shoshana both cry out.

"Grandma, *fuck!*" is Aza's.

"I knew it," is her mother's, as she holds up the crumpled paper she has just reached around and fished from Aza's pocket. "Go back. Go *back*."

She's straining at her seatbelt, practically throwing herself against it as though she keeps forgetting it's there. Which makes her look way too much like her husband in that bed. His last bed.

"*Go BACK!*" Shoshana roars. Then she coughs—the sound like glass grinding—and sags into her seat. Whimpering, "Go back."

Aliyah stops at the parking lot exit, but she doesn't turn the car off or around. Yet. She pins Aza's gaze once more with her own.

"You really didn't return her notes? You lied to me?"

"I did, too. Okay? I forgot that one. Missed it, I guess." Sullenly, Aza turns her jacket pockets inside out.

Abruptly, Aliyah is so sick of all this. Of the ritual, and the day, and the person her mother has become. Of trying to explain that to her daughter. Remind them both of who Shoshana was before.

"You hear that, Mom? She returned your notes. Of course she did. This is your good granddaughter." She starts to reach out a hand, stroke Aza's hair free of her face.

But in the back, Shoshana shakes her head. She's clutching the seatbelt as though gripping a railing at the edge of a chasm.

Right then—with a lurch of her stomach—Aliyah sees her daughter through her mother's eyes. Sees what Shoshana sees. The very real resentment there. Disgust, even. All of it aimed at the pathetic, crumpling wreck in the backseat.

"Azzy," Aliyah says. "You put the notes back? You really did?"

Tears spill from Aza's eyes. Which does nothing to soften the look on her face. She shrugs. "I put them back in the *garden*. In the trashcan by the gate where they belong."

On the roof, rain drums. Except it's not just out there, it's in Aliyah's head, in her blood, which beats in her throat and wrists, triggers a spasm in her arms that she realizes only afterward is an urge to slap her daughter straight across her face.

And then turn around and do the same to her mother.

Somehow, she keeps her hands in her lap and her voice low. "Go back," she says. Her voice is neither hiss nor whimper. *Is just me talking to my girl. Teaching and shaping her. The way mothers are meant to.*

Aza sits there crying, mouth half open. Not defying, exactly. Not throwing a teen-Aza fit.

But she's also not moving. Isn't going to.

And shouldn't? Why should she, really? Why should she be deliverywoman for her grandmother's poison? And why should I be a chauffeur for it?

"I can't believe you," she half-whispers. The words taste wrong. But they're the only ones that come. "I can't believe you're the child I raised."

Because you are way too determined to do what's right. Because you are way too sure, at too young an age, of what that is. Because you are too much like me.

With a sigh, Aliyah returns her hands back to the wheel and her eyes to the windshield. "Mom, I'll take you back tomorrow. Just you and me. We'll go early, and we can..."

For one second, she lets the silence fool her. Thinks Shoshana has let the argument go, or forgotten. Then, right as her foot lifts to the accelerator, Aliyah glances into the mirror. Just in time to see the shadows pouring over the fence out of the garden.

Shadows? Shadow? One thing, or many? Wing, horse-leg, furred snout, mouth.

Mouths.

Almost, she wheels around, guns the car out of the lot. She would have, she decides afterward. If she hadn't glanced down first, and seen her mother melting.

"Aza," Aliyah barks, tangling herself as she tries to unlock her seatbelt. Then she's free, half-climbing over the seat, but her mother's expression freezes her.

Or. No. Not her expression. Her *face.* The way it's sliding off itself. Into itself. The Michelangelo effect in reverse. Sculpture sinking back into the clay that birthed it.

Shadows boil over them like floodwater.

Just shadow, Aliyah thinks desperately,

But bubbling. Surging up onto the trunk and into the back seat. Into her mother, who closes her eyes.

"Oh," Shoshana says suddenly. From somewhere so deep inside her throat that Aliyah gasps, reaches out fast to grab her mother's hands. Which are cold. And wet. But not rain-cold or rain-wet.

"Mom!" she says.

"Ali. He's pulling."

Absurdly, Aliyah pulls back. Yanks hard at the hands, and her mother's body flops forward, the head tilting on its neck, face frozen except where it seems to be *running,* spilling into the seat fabric. Mouth open but not moving, words falling out of those motionless, colorless lips like echo.

"I feel myself going down."

Then she's gone.

"Mom," Aza whimpers.

Aliyah lets go of her mother's hands, which are no longer her mother's hands. Are hand-shaped things that were her mother's. She grabs her daughter's hands, which are rain-wet. Rain-cold. Her instinct is to turn Aza away, or bend her head down against her chest. Keep her from having to see, so that she won't remember.

But Aliyah doesn't do that. Partly, she knows, because she herself needs the company. Needs the seeing, breathing girl beside her, so they can withstand the sight of the body in the back.

Eyes rolled up. Skin stretched, as though pulled wide, pressed flat. Mouth open. Like Bob's. Like the eaglets', and the bat's, and the tortoise's.

Helplessly, Aliyah lifts her gaze to the back window. To her father's garden. The shadows flitting atop and along the fence, where they always do. Tree-and-leaf patterned.

Receding?

The words that rise to *her* lips, that spill involuntarily from her mouth with her breath, are, "Thank you."

If Aza hears, she doesn't acknowledge. She is teetering on the edge of sobbing, Aliyah knows. From fear. Guilt. Maybe residual sadness, who knows, because for a brief while—when Aza was very young—Shoshana had been a good grandmother. Taught her to make rugelach. Took her on glass-bottom boat trips to see whales. Giant, magical shadows in water.

It's just as well she hasn't heard what Aliyah said. Because neither Aliyah's *thank you* nor the sob in her throat are for her daughter.

They're for her father, and whatever he'd loosed here. Which had noted today's transgression. The debt unpaid.

And chosen who should pay it.

E N D

As with most diaspora cultures, I suspect, many of the most meaningful and lasting rituals for American Jews have developed within homes rather than places of worship, and signify ties to individual family trees at least as much as they do to shared religion in the traditional sense. Hanukkah seems especially permeable, given its relatively minor significance except for its proximity to winter breaks from school and ubiquitous Christmas celebrations. *"Dry and Ready" came partly out of that, and partly from my second kid's deep and lasting fascination with Yiddish culture, and partly from a particularly memorable, misty twilight wander amid the sculptures at Big Rock Garden in Bellingham, Washington.*

LAST DRINKS AT BONDI BEACH

Garth Nix

I T is dark in the garage carved from the rock, cellars being hard to come by in Sydney. There is the smell of raw earth, the concrete floor clawed up to make way for the necessary dirt, transported at great expense and no small difficulty from the other side of the world. The Mother has dug herself into it. She needs only the earth, and the yearly slaking of her modest thirst with the blood of her close kin. The Mother does not drink mortal blood, those diluted, distant descendants of her kind. *Homo Sapiens* are fodder for her spawn, but not for her.

Mother. Wake.
Yes, daughter.

You're sure this is the last of them, Mother? You see no others?

Yes. She is the last of my sisters, come to this far side of the world.

She's clever.

I should have thought long ago. Where their little, lesser folk go, they too can go.

But not easily.

No. She must still have her earth. Have you found it?

Yes. A tree was brought here, long ago, in a huge tub. A tub of her earth.

A tree? How could she lie between the roots? She must have grown smaller, far smaller than I. Weaker.

I know not, Mother. But that is how the soil came here. The earth is no longer in the tub, but in a place such as this, beneath a house higher on the hill.

Which one is she?

I do not know, Mother. You said—

But she is one of my twelve sisters? A mother? Not some errant daughter?

Yes. You told me so—

Did I? I forget.

You told me. You told me only one of your sisters remains. Ricagomor, you said, Ricagomor—

Ricagomor? She was only tenth. I was first... but at last, I will drain her and there will be only one of the thirteen. Only me. Oh, how long it has been... how long... how long?

Uh, are you really asking—

I have forgotten. I sleep too much. I forget.

Sixteen thousand times around the sun and one hundred and fifty-one more. Will you... will you be strong enough, Mother? You will drink Ricagomor to the final death?

I will. Ricagomor is the last of my enemies. The last feast—

(...)

What was that?

Naught. Dust upon my tongue.

What of those who were here before even our first waking? The original powers of this land?

They have gone deep, their people slain, scattered. I do not think they will interfere.

We should not be here. But we must be. If Ricagomor is here. You're sure she is here?

I told you so.

You have seen her?

No, I dare not approach her earth! I do not wish to slake her thirst. Yet she is here. I am your daughter. I know.

My daughters, my lovely daughters...

Concentrate, Mother! She is here. She hides in her place of strength. But she cannot hide tomorrow.

The one day. Festival...

She will come out. She must drink, but who can she drink from? Only her lesser offspring, the mortals of her line. That is all she has.

Ricagomor was the one who started it. She suborned our sisters. They broke the compact, they drank from the lesser breeds, they bred with them. And look what has come of it. They brought their fate upon themselves! I had, I have, good reason to drink my sisters' blood, they were... they were...

Rebels?

GARTH NIX

Fools. But Ricagomor is the last. Tell me again what you will do. I forget. My thirst grows close, I cannot think.

Ricagomor will leave her earth a moment after the sun sinks in the west, take mortal shape, and go to the sea strand. Like the festivals of old. She will not be able to resist. So many mortals, so much blood for the taking.

What do they call her people now? Here?

They are mostly found among the British and the Irish. There are a great many of them, under this southern sun. Thousands will come to the sea tomorrow, tens of thousands.

To celebrate Mithras, the birth of their god?

No. No, you really are wandering, Mother. It is the Christ-child they celebrate, remember?

Ah, ah. Yes. What is that?

What?

That!

The curtain across the door wasn't properly fastened, that's all. There, that's better. It was only a little light. The sun has almost set.

A little light! A little light!

Calm down, Mother. You were in no danger. Concentrate on what lies ahead.

You woke me too soon. Full dark! That is the time for waking.

Yes, Mother. I'm sorry.

You forget, you who can bear the sun. You forget your duty to me!

Yes, Mother.

So, she will take some mortal form and hunt upon the sands. You must let Ricagomor drink, but not too much. Enough to slow her, that is all, so you will prevail. Then you must bring her here. Into the dark. Bring her to me.

I know. I know.

How will you know her? How will you know Ricagomor?

I will know her by her shadow. I will know her by her stench. I will know her by the blood she drinks.

Yes, yes, that's right. But how will you bind her?

I will bind her with iron.

How will you compel her?

I will compel her with mirror-glass.

And bring her to me, to my earth, for my drinking in the darkness, for my feasting.

I will bring her.

Yes, yes. And I will drink the pure, pure blood of my last sister.

And what then? When Ricagomor is gone, what of the next Yuletide—

I must rest. You must prepare the chains, the shard of mirror glass, so bright and terrible.

Yes, but what—

Tell me. I have forgotten. My daughters. How many of my daughters live?

Only I remain.

You are Heldvar, the eldest?

No, you must remember. She was the first, the first you... when we could find none of your sisters to slake your thirst. You—

Yes. I remember. Yet I must drink. Which are you?

I am Sinnevan, the youngest. The strongest. Remember? Sun-sister, the others called me—

That is not strength. True strength is found in the dark. It is found in the earth.

As you say, Mother. But the sun is stronger here. Much stronger. Stay in your earth.

Yes, yes. Bring me Ricagomor. Into the dark. I will drink deep, and need no more for many turns about the sun. You understand?

Yes, Mother! Sleep now. Rest. Prepare yourself.

Oh God! Oh God! Why are you... where is this... what do you—

Ah. Ricagomor.

What? What? Who's there? Help! Help!

Save your shouting. Your pretence. We know what you are.

Help! Help! Oh God, somebody please... what, what is that... no, don't touch me, don't touch me!

You saw her shadow?

She has no shadow.

What the fuck are you... please, please, just let me go. Help!

And the stench? I smell nothing now. Nothing.

You have lost that sense, Mother. You cannot smell even the stench of your own kin.

Yes, yes. I fear it is so.

Help! Heeellp!

She feels a frail vessel, too frail, even in this mortal shape. Has she not fed?

Don't touch me! Don't, whatever it is, I don't, I don't, don't—

She has fed. I saw her drink from a young mortal. Red-haired, like so many of her people, in the long ago. She wrapped herself in glamour, no other mortals saw the deed.

I will drink now, Ricagomor. You are the last. The last sister.

I have drunk them all.

What the fuck are you going to – ah, ah, no, don't! Don't! Don—

This is not Ricagomor! This is mortal blood, nothing more, nothing more! Why have you brought me this, this poison! Where is Ricagomor?

Ricagomor walks the sands and drinks from the mortals she and her sisters made long ago, so they need not feast upon each other, so there need not be the bitter enmity among us. So a great, bloated beast like you would not kill us all! Ricagomor told me mortal blood would weaken you!

Ricagomor told you wrong. I am a little weakened, yes. But not so much I cannot take you, smash your limbs, drink your blood here in the dark, here in my earth. What are you doing?

I like it here, Mother. I like this beach. I even like Ricagomor. We drank together not an hour ago; we have sealed our alliance. And I know you will not be ended by mortal blood alone. Oh, don't scrabble so stupidly! I chained you as you slept, with the iron meant for your sister.

What are you doing?

It isn't after sunset, Mother. It's closer to noon, on a bright, bright, beautiful Christmas Day.

What are you doing!

What are you do—

I'm letting in the sun, Mother.

(*screaming*)

I'm letting in the sun.

E N D

I lived in an apartment on the headland at the northern end of Bondi Beach for several years and got to see firsthand the tens of thousands of people who congregate on the beach and the park behind to celebrate Christmas Day, many of them British and Irish tourists. It occurred to me that if there was some entity who preyed particularly on people of this background then Bondi Beach on Christmas Day would be like a penned shoal of fish to a shark. Add in the fierce sunshine of an Australian summer Christmas, it seemed obvious to me that any such predator would either fear and shun the sun, or love it. Or maybe there would be two, related, predators...

RETURN TO BEAR
CREEK LODGE

Tananarive Due

December 26, 1974

I N Johnny's dream, he is running in white, snowy woods.
He hears music—distant, tinny-sounding trumpet fanfare
from the Duke Ellington Orchestra—before he sees the light.
The vague glow is brighter with every step, until darkness parts
to reveal the wooden rail fence of his grandmother's lodge. One
rotting rail has fallen out of place, leaving a breach he can easily
run through.

But he doesn't. He stops short, staring at the lodge. And the
back porch.

And the woman sitting there.

In his dreams, Grandmother doesn't look the way she did the
last time he actually saw her, when she was already emaciated and
sharp-jawed from illness. This is Mazelle Washington the way

she has immortalized herself in her photos framed all over her house: hair hanging long and loose (*straightened*, of course), in radiant makeup, shoulders nestled in the fur collar of her shiny silk bathrobe, the kind of garment only movie royalty would wear. She shines so brightly that the light seems to glow from her.

Something rustles just beneath her on the porch steps, snow flung aside by a long neck and then a head with a snout the size of a long weasel, white fur almost camouflaged by the snow. It rises between Grandmother's knees... as if she is giving birth.

Grandmother's face snaps into focus: but her eyes are the color of blue ice. She opens her mouth, and her jaw hinges beyond any human length, revealing rows of long, sharp teeth.

He screams as—

"Wake up, hon. We're here."

Johnny's mother's voice coaxed him to open his eyes, and his dream had come to life. Snow. The wooden fence rails. Grandmother's lodge. The back porch. He tried to rub it out of his eyes, but the nightmare was real this time. Mom had parked the rental car they'd picked up in Denver in Grandmother's snow-dusted driveway after driving up the mountain. He'd fallen asleep to static-filled AM radio, which was all the car offered. *Shit. We're actually here.*

Grandmother's lodge would seem like an ordinary two-story wood frame house if it weren't so secluded in the Rocky Mountains woods. Its isolation alone made it seem luxurious to have electricity lighting the windows, or a fence claiming five or six acres. Thirty yards from the main house, three small cabins stood in a perfect triangle as relics of a time when Bear Creek Lodge had provided dignity to Black celebrities lucky enough to get an invitation. In those days, fine hotels nationwide did not accept them, no matter who they were. Once, he'd been told, Grandmother had her own ski lift for her guests.

But all of that had been a long time ago.

"My stomach hurts," Johnny said. He had learned that his mother wrapped herself in silence like warm clothing, but he vowed he would never be like her. "This place already gives me nightmares, Mom. I want to leave."

"I know, baby. And I understand."

"But you don't care."

"Of course I do. If I could've left you somewhere else, I would have. I didn't want you here either. I don't want to be here my own self."

"Then why?" Johnny's voice hitched, but he would *not* cry.

"Because she owes us." *There. She finally said it.* "She owes *you*. She's got a college fund set aside for you. If I just... say goodbye this weekend. Two days. Her last Christmas. I haven't seen her at Christmastime since I wasn't much older than you."

Mom was thirty-one, although her face was still round and girlish. With a scarf wrapped around her Afro—probably hiding it from Grandmother—Mama reminded him of Aretha Franklin. Johnny had always assumed she ran away from home at seventeen because she was pregnant with him. Uncle Ricky's blue VW bug was already parked beside them in the lodge's driveway, a reminder that his uncle kept coming back—although he had good reason never to speak to his mother again either, much less stay with her in the woods.

Based on his own short visit last year, Johnny could hardly imagine the horror of growing up in a house raised by

Grandmother. His mother and uncle had lived in a mansion in Los Angeles, but Johnny would choose his two-bedroom apartment in Miami with Mom any time, even with the flying cockroaches that kept coming back no matter how much she sprayed.

"I don't care about her money," Johnny said. "She can keep it."

Mom blinked as if he'd struck her. If she'd convinced herself they were making this trip for his sake, he had just stolen that lie away. Good. Johnny wondered what other ways Mom had been lying to herself, or to him. He could never trust her again, not the way he had before. That idea, worse than his nightmare, cramped his stomach again.

"You'll be in one of the cabins, like I said," Mom said. "You won't even have to see her. She stays in bed in her room. Rick's been here looking after her, and a nurse comes in the mornings. This is our burden, not yours—okay?"

None of it was okay, and never would be. At fourteen, Johnny was already certain of this. His birthright was soiled to the core; not just Grandmother, but Mom and Uncle Ricky too.

But he nodded, a lie. Mom looked relieved, choosing to believe him. Or to pretend she did.

"All money ain't good money," Mom said, "but bad money can be put to good use."

When she got out of the car, she headed straight for the back porch that haunted him. And the small mounds of snow beside the three back steps.

"Can we go in through the front, please?" Johnny hated being afraid that a dream might come to life, but if he stared at the snow long enough, he thought he might see it move from something buried underneath. His mother cast him a confused look over her shoulder, but she changed course to walk around to the front double doors.

Inside, the smell of Grandmother's dying was everywhere. The smell froze him in the open doorway. Mom, behind him, patted his shoulder.

"You don't have to go in her room," Mom reminded him. Her whisper smelled like the peppermint candy she'd used to mask her cigarette smoke; she was still apparently afraid of what Grandmother might say if she caught her smoking. She cupped his chin in the way she used to when he was younger. "I'm still so mad at your Uncle Rick for not watching you like I told him to. And you heard me cuss Mama's ass out on the phone last year, didn't you? What she did to you is *not* okay, cancer or no cancer."

No one had said the word *cancer* before now. But Johnny swore he knew from the smell.

It was all in place: the white grand piano, the oversized fireplace with gleaming stones, grinning celebrity photos framed on the wood-plank walls, even the film projector where she'd caught him playing her old reels from the 1930s movies that filled her with shame. "You shouldn't have gone in Mother's things," Uncle Ricky had told him during the drive to the airport to go home last year, nudging blame back toward him after a night of consolation.

Nothing in the living room had changed in the year since Grandmother had burned leering teeth into his arm from her steel hot comb, scarring him with dark marks that would never go away.

Uncle Ricky had gained at least ten pounds in the past year, his hair cut Marine short. He had trouble meeting Johnny's eyes— maybe because Uncle Ricky's eyes were so red from smoking grass every chance he got. The smell of grass baked from his uncle's clothes as he hugged him. Johnny saw his mother's lips tighten as she glared at Uncle Ricky. For an uneasy instant, Grandmother's rage was reborn in his mother's eyes.

"Good to see you, lil' man," Uncle Ricky said, speaking as quietly as he would in a hospital. "Front cabin's all yours. Star treatment all the way. Nothing but the best for—"

"Oh, hush," Mom said. "Nobody wants to hear all that."

Uncle Ricky was still in trouble with Mom, so after saying hello, Johnny escaped to his cabin.

The cabin was decades past any elegance, but it was a good size, with a bunk bed, sofa, and a table near the front picture window. A too-large crack beneath the door couldn't keep out a bold breeze and traces of snow that melted in a pale ring on the floor. The air near the door felt ten degrees cooler, too. At least. The space heater's coils stank of roasting dust when he turned it on and they glowed bright orange.

Johnny pulled aside the fading curtains to stare out at the snow-covered woods beyond Grandmother's wood rail fence. He'd been excited to see flurries for the first time last year, but now snow was the backdrop to his nightmares. *You saw something in the snow,* his mind whispered, a reminder. *Or did you?*

All he knew for sure was that he kept having the same dream, when *something* popped up from the snow, its head appearing between Grandmother's knees. A pointy nose, so pink it was almost red. Long, active whiskers near its mouth. And white fur so tight across its frame that it seemed bony instead of soft. Not quite a reptile, not quite a mammal. In the year since, he had decided that maybe his waking mind had conjured a creature that mirrored Grandmother's true self—a vision for the casual monstrosity she hid from everyone except her own family.

The door to the back porch opened abruptly. He expected to see Grandmother glide outside in her fur-lined robe, staring straight at him. The thought raked the back of his neck with icy pinpricks. But Mom and Uncle Ricky came out instead, neither of them wearing a coat, and Mom was hugging herself tightly as she leaned close to her brother. They were trying to keep their voices down, their argument spilling outside from the kitchen.

Johnny knew they were talking about him.

"...All I asked you to do was watch him in the goddamned cabin," Mom was saying to Uncle Ricky in the cold. "*Never* let him be alone with her. I haven't asked either of you for shit his whole life, and that's all I asked. *That's all*, Rick."

"Sadie, she said—"

"Damn what she said! You were supposed to stand up to her for once. You're a grown man! How's a sick old woman gonna' make you do shit? You want the Baldwin Hills house that bad? Is that what's got you so cowed that you couldn't do one simple thing? You *knew* better."

Uncle Ricky didn't have an answer for that, hanging his head. He listened in that childlike pose for some time, a big man made small. Mom's words knit his face until he finally said, "You acting like I'm the one who burned him! You know who you really need to be mad at. I wish I'd done more, but I ain't the one who did it."

At last, Mom had nothing else to say. She went back inside, slamming the door.

"What's all that noise?" he heard another voice call, perhaps through a cracked open window. Reed-thin, but he heard it. The dying woman was awake.

Johnny stepped away from his window. Even if the cabin was cold and only a short walk from the back door, at least he wasn't in the same house with her.

"Coming, Mother!" he heard his mom call as if she were a child again too. Johnny braved another peek through his window.

Uncle Ricky didn't go inside behind Mom. Instead, he sighed a cloud of breath and walked carefully down the stairs, nursing the knee his mother had hurt when he was young. He glanced up at Johnny's cabin as he passed on his way to his own and waved. But he didn't smile. Johnny did the same, running his fingertip across the raised bump of the dark keloid scar on his upper arm. His mother told him it would never go away unless he got plastic surgery—which meant they might as well find a doctor on Mars. A scar for life. More like a brand.

"How could she do that?" he'd asked his mother, tearful, when he came home with the fresh scar and its story.

Mom had met his tears with her own and said, "I don't know, baby. My grandmother told me she changed after she started working in pictures. Playing Lazy Mazy turned her into somebody else. I swear I used to think she sold her soul."

Mom insisted that he come inside to eat at the long dining table with her and Uncle Ricky, and that part wasn't bad. She served heated up leftover ham, macaroni and cheese and greens from Christmas she'd carried in Tupperware on the plane from Miami. Then she lit a candle, explaining that she hadn't had room to bring the kinara from home, but she reminded him that the first principle of Kwanzaa was Umoja, which meant *Unity*. She squeezed his hand on one side and Uncle Ricky's on the other.

"So I'm glad we're all together," she said. She wanted to say more, but shook her head in a way that told Johnny she was trying not to cry.

Uncle Ricky said he had a surprise for Johnny and put the Jackson Five's "Dancing Machine" on Grandmother's console— oh so softly, if music could whisper—a peace offering like sage, since Grandmother had confiscated his cassettes and tape player last year. After venting at Uncle Ricky on the back porch, the anger had left Mom's eyes and she was already smiling and twisting to the music in her seat, especially after her second glass of wine. She and Uncle Ricky toasted "getting rid of that asshole Nixon," both of them tossing their heads back to drink. Mom's empty wine glass slipped from her grip, shattering on the wooden floor, and they both froze and waited to hear their mother call out, as they no doubt did as children, terrified of making her mad. When she didn't make a sound, Mom and Uncle Ricky smothered giggles. Johnny didn't like it when his mother drank, but it was good to hear her laugh.

Johnny was taking his empty plate to the kitchen, in the hallway just behind the kitchen doorway, when he saw, in a slant of shadow, Grandmother's partly open door at the far end of the hall. His heart batted his throat at the sight of the space beyond her open door, a dim light shining out. Was she awake? Johnny ducked into the kitchen at the thought that she might be about to walk out of her room. He closed the swinging kitchen door behind him, breathing fast. He threw his plate into the sink so hard that dishwater splashed on the floor.

Why don't you go see if she's awake, chickenshit? Pussy. Mama's boy. Sissy. Lil' bitch.

Johnny thought of every name he'd been called at school, shouted across the P.E. field or whispered through his bathroom stall door. And didn't all those names fit? Wasn't he scared of a sick old woman, trapped under the same hex as Mom and Uncle Ricky?

Johnny's breath tickled the roof of his mouth as he walked closer to the sickroom, touching his feet down lightly until he was standing just beyond her doorway. Through the slit he saw a bed table and the side of her bed frame—not the fairy-tale princess bed with a canopy she'd slept in before, but a curving metal rail like a hospital bed.

A low *hisssss* floated from the room, the sound of a giant snake close enough to touch him. Johnny jumped back, startled. A mechanized click made him realize that the sound was coming from an oxygen machine somewhere near the bed. This time, he used the rhythmic *hisssss* to hide the sound of his movement as he cracked the door open wider to peek in. The sole tea lamp on the bed table offered the room's only light, patterns of green in panels of stained glass. Most of her furniture had been pushed aside, but he recognized the fur collar of her fancy bathrobe hanging on a hook beside the door.

Grandmother's bare brown arm lay straight at her side, the flesh at her elbow a mass of jellied wrinkles. She had lost weight, and her frame had been slight and bony in her clothes a year ago. Her face was hidden from him by the lamp. Her sheet rose up and down with her breathing; maybe she wasn't quite awake, not quite asleep.

"*I hate you,*" he whispered loudly enough to be heard over the hissing, but not loudly enough to escape the hallway. "I hope you die."

The words exploded inside of him, a shock to his own ears. His knees felt unsteady, so he leaned against the door frame with a small pant. Was she awake? Had she heard?

He waited three seconds, four, five, to hear any response except measured hissing. With each thin breath, his fear gave way to triumph. A celebration rose in him that he wished he could share with Mom and Uncle Ricky. *You'll never believe what I just said to that old—*

A chair across the room tipped so wildly that it almost fell over, rocking back and forth. A scrabbling shook the window above the chair, and for the first time he noticed it was open nearly six inches. (Had it always been open?) Something had bumped the chair and was crawling—snaking?—back outside through the narrow gap.

The creature from his nightmares with a long snout looked back at him, white whiskers sweeping back and forth across the pane like a dog's wagging tail. Two ice-blue eyes glittered at him. The creature's odd chittering filled the room.

It's real, he thought. *It's real and it's here.*

Johnny had not imagined how a demon might look until he saw the thing at the window. Maybe it had possessed Grandmother. Maybe that was what had brought out the meanness in her.

But these thoughts didn't come to Johnny in the doorway: they would only come later. In that instant, all thought had vanished. His body was stone except for his savagely blinking eyes.

The thing at the window rattled the frame, and a mouth yawned open, revealing a row of top fangs so long and sharp that they gleamed in the moonlight. A white fox-worm from Hell.

"Johnny? That you?" *WAS IT TALKING TO HIM?*

The demon smacked against the window... and then it was gone. Outside, its slithering scattered the snow as it raced away in an erratic pattern, here and there almost simultaneously, moving *fast*. Impossibly fast.

"Johnny?" Grandmother's voice was louder, recognizable despite its deep hoarseness. Not the demon's voice, then. He was torn about which frightened him more—the demon in the window or Grandmother calling for him. She might have heard the terrible thing he'd said, the words he was certain had conjured that thing. What if she got up and staggered toward him...?

"I'm sorry," Johnny whispered, just as he had as she burned him that night, senseless with surprise and pain. He closed her door and ran back to the kitchen, where he helped his mother and uncle dry the dishes, trying to hide his shaking hands.

He didn't tell them about the cracked open window. Or the demon. He didn't say a word.

That night, Johnny didn't sleep as he sat sentry fogging up his cabin's window, watching the back door and snowy patch of yard, reciting the Lord's Prayer like a record needle caught in a groove. He held a snow shovel in his hands, the only weapon he'd found in his cabin. Even with only the moonlight to guide his vision, he recognized the path the creature had left in its wake, a sinuous pattern of burrowed snow from Grandmother's window, between the cabins, toward the gate and the woods beyond. He might not have seen it if he didn't know it was there. All night he jumped at falling clumps of snow from the treetops, or rustling in the dried brush, believing the creature had come back for him. His fingers shivered, but not from the cold.

He only realized he'd fallen asleep by the window, slumped over the cabin's rude wooden table, when a knock at the door scared him so much that he fell to the floor.

"Hey, J!" Uncle Ricky's voice called. "You up? Said I'd take you rabbit hunting, right? Gotta get 'em early if we're gonna get 'em."

Johnny's head felt blurry. Then he remembered Grandmother's room, the thing at the window, and he leaped to his feet to unlock the flimsy pin and open his cabin door. He'd tried keeping the secret, but silence was burning a hole in him. He would have to confess, that was all. He would have to tell Uncle Ricky what he'd summoned from the snow. But how could he make Uncle Ricky believe him?

"You're already dressed, huh?" Uncle Ricky said. Johnny stared down and realized he was still wearing his jeans and aqua blue Miami Dolphins sweatshirt from dinner. He felt a strong certainty that he must be dreaming, that maybe he wasn't at Grandmother's property at Bear Creek at all. "Grab your coat and gloves. Cold as a witch's tits out here today."

Outside. He'd tell him while they were outside. He'd show Uncle Ricky the—

"Uh oh," Uncle Ricky said from the cabin doorway as he surveyed the snow, tipping back his suede black cowboy hat. He walked a few paces and squatted, staring down. Johnny ran outside, still pulling on his coat. Of course! As a hunter, Uncle Ricky had seen the creature's tracks right away. And Uncle Ricky had a gun! Now they could—

"Lookie here!" Uncle Ricky said, grinning up at him. He was squatting in the middle of the fox-thing's swishes in the snow, but he was pointing to much smaller tracks in an unthreatening, predictable pattern just beyond them. "The rabbits are out, see? Told you. You can always tell rabbit tracks cuz they land with their hind legs first, up front. They're bigger. And that's the front legs behind them, kinda off center... see?"

Johnny didn't see, or want to see. He only saw the evidence the fox-thing had left behind, a trail like a broom pushed by a madman. He was agape that Uncle Ricky was missing what was right in front of him.

"They don't like to come out in the open, so I'm surprised to see tracks here," Uncle Ricky said. He leaned on his rifle stock to straighten to his full height and shook out his bad knee as if to wake it up, or quiet it down. "Let's go out in the woods where there's some brush. They like bushes, pine stands. Places they can hide."

Johnny swallowed back his disappointment that Uncle Ricky didn't know, that he must explain it all. And time was wasting. Who knew how far the thing had traveled overnight?

"This way," Johnny said, pointing toward the fence and the old growth forest of pine and spruce trees beyond it.

Following the fox-thing's trail.

They waded through snow so deep that Johnny wished he had cowboy boots like Uncle Ricky instead of the new Converse sneakers Mom had given him for Christmas. Fighting through a dreamlike feeling after so little sleep, he realized that he and Uncle Ricky hadn't talked about rabbit hunting at all on this trip; the proposed hunting lesson last year had been one more thing cut short by the burning.

Johnny never let his eyes veer from the wild flourishes of the fox-thing's path in the snow. Uncle Ricky seemed content to let Johnny lead, but he was studiously ignoring the creature's trail. Instead, Uncle Ricky pointed out places where he'd found rabbits.

Then... the trail was gone, as if the thing had burrowed more deeply underground and never resurfaced. Or vanished outright. Johnny stopped walking, panicked that the hidden beast might yank him by his feet and drag him away. He didn't know what he'd expected on the outing, but the lost possibility, once within reach, crushed him. They were beneath a towering old cottonwood tree with a dark gap, like a doorway. A mound of snow in front of the tree looked undisturbed, but who knew what it was hiding?

And were those blue eyes glowing from the folds of the dark? Instead of moving toward the shadowed hole, Johnny stepped away. He hadn't wanted to trade familiar terror for a worse one, sharpening the claws of his nightmares. With Uncle Ricky beside him, he hadn't felt scared until he lost the trail.

The morning woods were not quiet. Bear Creek was east of them, the babbling water of its stony bed suddenly loud although most of the creek must be frozen. To the west, a coyote's far-off yipping startled him. He looked toward every noise... then back at the old tree.

"What's wrong, youngblood?" It might be the first time Uncle Ricky had looked him dead in the face since he knocked on his door. Uncle Ricky's eyes were an invitation to tell. And his eyes weren't red from grass, for a change. He had come to hunt with a clear head.

"I did something," Johnny whispered.

Uncle Ricky and his sober eyes waited.

"I... said something to your mom last night. Outside her door. But I didn't go in." He added the last part in case a respectful distance somehow made it better. He tried to bring the words he'd said to his mouth, but they seemed worse in daylight. "I said something bad."

"What'd you say?" Uncle Ricky's voice was only curious. No judgment.

Still, Johnny shook his head. He couldn't tell him. He would never tell anyone.

Uncle Ricky chuckled. "Listen—I'm sure you didn't say nothin' me and your mom didn't think up first. And she probably didn't even hear you. That what's got you all freaked out?"

"When I said it..." He wanted to say *A demon came.* That explained it best, but it would sound the worst. "...something climbed out of her window. It was in her room."

Now silence draped the woods. Uncle Ricky's eyes moved away, scanning the landscape. Beyond the cottonwood, they were at the base of a steep incline knotted with fir trees. Finally, Uncle Ricky stared toward the old cottonwood and its large gap before turning back to Johnny.

"Did you see it?"

Johnny nodded. "Kind of. It moved fast. But... I saw the teeth."

Uncle Ricky grabbed Johnny's shoulder, his fingers tight through his thick coat. "Did it hurt you?" For the first time, he sounded worried.

"No. It ran. It doesn't go straight, it goes like..."

Johnny scraped his shoe in the snow in a zigzag to show him. His toes were so cold inside of his sneakers that they burned. "...here... and then there. It doesn't go in a straight line. The tracks are right outside her house. They come out here... and then they stop."

Johnny pointed at the spot in the snow where the tracks ended a few yards in front of the cottonwood tree and the mass of snow that might be a perfect hiding place.

Johnny wanted Uncle Ricky to jack a cartridge into his rifle's chamber and say *Let's go see where it went.* Instead, a stormy uncertainty grew on Uncle Ricky's face. He tipped up his hat to run his hand across his forehead, fretting.

"What kinda animal did it look like?" Uncle Ricky finally asked.

"Didn't look like *any* animal! It looked like a demon that crawled out of the ground."

There. He'd finally said it. He expected Uncle Ricky to laugh at him... but he didn't.

"Then you shouldn't try to go chasin' after things you don't understand." Uncle Ricky's voice was sharp with scolding. "Should you?"

The change in Uncle Ricky was troubling in an entirely different way. Johnny's ears rang as if his uncle had shouted at him.

"You already know about it. Don't you?"

"Don't ask me that." Uncle Ricky stared at the ground like when Mom told him off.

"Because it's a secret?"

Uncle Ricky's jaw flexed so tightly that he was afraid his uncle would slap him. "Hard headed, ain't you? What'd I just say? You listen to me good: we ain't gonna talk about it. You're not gonna say nothin' to your mama, neither. What you saw is just between me and you."

"But you believe me," Johnny said, testing him. His heart was pounding in his chest so hard that his lungs barely found room to breathe.

Uncle Ricky half-shrugged and half-nodded, the way he would if they were talking about when it might snow next. Or if Grandmother's private nurse might be late on the icy road.

"Say it," Johnny said. "Say you believe me."

Uncle Ricky nodded. Close enough. The pressure in Johnny's chest eased, but he was shivering despite his coat and gloves.

"I told you!" Johnny said. "I told you I saw something last year!"

"Yep, sorry." He didn't *sound* apologetic. "And you don't yell when you're hunting."

Despite his anger and a dizzy feeling from doubting everything he thought he knew about the world, Johnny obediently lowered his voice. "Well, why—"

"Come on," Uncle Ricky said, and walked toward less steep ground, away from the cottonwood tree and its yawning maw. "Let's get us a hare."

WHAT. THE. HELL. Johnny came as close as he ever had to cussing out an adult. He breathed in angry puffs, struggling to keep pace in the deep snow. The creek burbled ahead.

"You know what a nervous breakdown is?" Uncle Ricky said. "I'm not crazy," Johnny said, still quiet. "I know what I saw."

"Not you—my mom. Remember I told you how she had to step away from Hollywood and spend some time by herself? They were forgetting her, or worse: calling her a coon. Oh, she hated that word. That grinnin' and foolishness she did to make all that money off white folks in those old movies came back on her after times changed. When I tried to visit to see after her, she just fussed and hollered and sent me away. Hell, she threatened to shoot me once. For five whole years, it was just her out here in these woods."

Johnny sensed that his uncle was winding to the point—*the creature?!*—so he tried to slow his breathing so he could hear past the pounding of his blood in his ears. Uncle Ricky held up his hand: *Stop.* Johnny stopped abruptly, nearly stumbling into him.

"Snow hares are brown in summer, but in winter their fur turns white," Uncle Ricky said. He nodded toward an arrangement of stones a few yards from them. Something moved, barely visible against the gray rocks—but it was small, not the creature from Grandmother's window. As Johnny stared, a form took shape: a white-haired rabbit was standing against the rocks, rubbing its face with its paws. Johnny couldn't help thinking of the hare from *Alice's Adventures in Wonderland,* as if it might pull out a pocket watch next. That wouldn't be any stranger than what he'd already seen.

To Johnny's surprise, Uncle Ricky slipped his hunting rifle into Johnny's hands, guiding him to raise it high with the stock beneath his chin. The gun didn't weigh as much as Johnny had expected, given its deadly power. Still, his arms trembled beneath its weight.

"So…" Uncle Ricky said, his voice low in Johnny's ear. "…one time I came out here, just like you, and I saw it's not just rabbits and ermines out here with white fur." He gently moved Johnny's arms to reposition the rifle slightly. "You see 'im?"

Johnny looked all around for the fox-demon, but Uncle Ricky was only pointing toward the hare. "Get 'im in your sight. You ain't even lookin'." Uncle Ricky pointed out the nub of the rifle's front sight and used his palm to push gently on the back of Johnny's head so he would lower it to a proper hunting stance.

The rabbit changed position only slightly, unaware that they were so close, favoring the other side of his face for cleaning.

"Where did you see it?" Johnny whispered.

Uncle Ricky chuckled. "I was sittin' outside in my old truck tryin' to figure how to talk sense into her… and that thing came runnin' out the back door."

"It opened the door?" Johnny remembered Grandmother's cracked open window.

"*She* opened it," Uncle Ricky said. "Let it out like it was her pet pooch. And then… boom. It was gone in a flash, just like you said. She saw me, too. That was the night she threatened to shoot me. She said to get the hell away from her and never come back."

A sound from closer to the creek made the hare stick its head up high, alert.

"Hurry," Uncle Ricky whispered. "Don't miss the shot."

But Johnny could barely remember who and where he was, imagining Grandmother feeding the fox-demon. It *hadn't* been a dream. He had seen with his own eyes and then in his dreams. His mind whirled with the dizzy feeling again.

By the time his wooziness passed, the hare was gone, only a pile of stones left behind.

"Dammit," Uncle Ricky said.

"What is it? I thought I made a demon come. Like... saying something so bad was praying to it."

Uncle Ricky didn't seem to hear him, staring with longing at the spot where the hare had been. "I got no goddamn idea, but it's no demon," he finally said. "All I know is, it's been out here with her, the two of them hiding from the world, I guess. She's been feeding it, and it's been here a long time. It was smaller when I saw it. Maybe it thinks she's its mama."

"So... what will happen when...?"

For the first time, Johnny noticed that his uncle's eyes were red after all. And moist. "When the time comes... I suppose I'll have to come out here and take care of it. So it won't hurt nobody. Whatever it is... it ain't natural. Is it?"

Johnny shook his head. The cold hadn't been as bad when they were walking, but now that they were still the frigid breeze was slicing into his bare cheeks and ears.

"Don't feel bad about whatever you said to Mother..." Uncle Ricky said. "She brought it on herself. Besides, there's worse. Way worse. If I tell you something, will you keep it a secret? Never let your mama know I told you?"

Something screamed inside of Johnny that he should say *no*, that his mother would never want him to make that promise. It was bad enough he couldn't say anything to her about the odd creature—not that she would probably believe him. Maybe secrets, and silence, were a part of the key to becoming an adult, but they also took something away.

"Okay," Johnny said despite himself.

"It's hard, watching somebody dying," Uncle Ricky said. For a while, Johnny thought that was the end of the secret. "You know what bedsores are?"

Johnny shook his head.

"Believe me, you don't *want* to know. A body laying in bed a long time gets… holes in it. Big ones. *Sore* ain't even the right word. I could fit an orange in one. The nurse comes in and cleans her up, but… it hurts a lot. So anyway, last night your mama and I stayed up late talking about whether we should mash up some pills and… let her rest. Put a stop to her pain."

The world's axis tilted again, but this time Johnny fought the dizziness, staring into Uncle Ricky's eyes to make sure he understood. *They had talked about killing her.* A tear escaped the side of Uncle Ricky's eye, and he didn't wipe it away. "Only thing that stopped us? We couldn't be sure if we wanted to do it out of love. Your mama's mad as hell about that burn, and killing out of hate's a sin. Neither of us wants that demon on our backs. But it could be a worse sin to let her suffer. If she was a dog, we would've put her down a long time ago."

Uncle Ricky's confession sat heavy in the morning air, how he and Mom had weighed whether or not they loved their mother enough to kill her. Or if they hated her so much that they must let her live. Johnny wished he could unhear all of it. The confession felt like a curse that would follow him. One day his mother would get old too, and she might get bedsores big enough to put his fist into.

"I'm cold," Johnny whispered.

Uncle Ricky nodded and took back the rifle Johnny had forgotten he was still holding. "Yeah. We better head back and

Return to Bear Creek Lodge

make sure the nurse made it on that road. Always take your shot, Johnny. Now I gotta drive to town or we're gonna eat leftover ham for dinner. Again."

While Uncle Ricky walked ahead, Johnny noticed how his limp was worse in the cold; Grandmother's lasting gift to him in her moment of rage with a tire iron that had ruined his chance to play football when he was in high school, or anywhere. A year ago, Johnny thought it was the worst story he had ever heard. But not anymore.

Johnny landed his feet inside his uncle's deep footprints, hopping from one to the next, trying to keep the snow from burying his new shoes.

The nurse, a white woman, jounced up the driveway in an old blue station wagon with snow chains, but Johnny never saw her except through his cabin window. He slept leaning in his cabin's hardback chair much of the day undisturbed, except when Mom brought him a ham sandwich for lunch. Her smile was so sweet that it made his stomach ache again. His secrets stewed inside of him while he mumbled his *thank you*, trying to pretend he didn't know what he knew. This trip had ruined more than Christmas and Kwanzaa; he couldn't even reclaim joy from his mother's smile. Instead, his groggy mind kept flashing him the creature's sharp teeth.

He was nodding off at the table again when he heard the scream.

Johnny's hands tightened around the waiting snow shovel as he jumped up to stare out of his window. He saw the back door ripped away, the windows shattered, a bloody heap quivering in the driveway from a sudden attack—but all of that was his imagination, vanishing when he blinked. Uncle Ricky's VW bug was gone, leaving only the nurse's station wagon and Mom's rental car parked near the back door, but there were no new tracks. No blood. A bright light from Grandmother's bedroom shined through her window, which was now firmly closed. Last night's swishes from the retreating creature were unchanged because no new snow had fallen yet.

Another scream clawed through the stillness. He was sure it must be from Grandmother's room. Was Mom alone with her? Had the nurse gone on an errand with Uncle Ricky? A well of panic swallowed Johnny as he imagined his mother as a knife-wielding killer like in *Black Christmas*, which he had snuck into a theater to see while Mom was at work a week ago.

"Shhhh... it's all right..." Mom's muffled voice soothed, a plea nearly as sad as the screaming. "Emma's almost done... Please hold still. It's all right, Mother."

Mom wasn't alone! *The bedsores*, he remembered. That was why his grandmother was yelling: the nurse was doing her difficult work. Maybe Uncle Ricky hadn't left just to find something else for dinner; the suffering might have driven him away.

Another scream. Even muffled, the sound made him drop the shovel and mash his palms against his ears so hard that it hurt. He had never heard a person in so much pain. Sick people in movies and on TV didn't wail like wounded animals. Was *this* how people died? And last night he had heaped his horrible words on top of her suffering. Johnny could barely catch his breath.

Why had Mom brought him here for this morbid ritual?

Why had Uncle Ricky told him a secret he would be forced to remember with every scream?

As he stared outside, Johnny glimpsed Uncle Ricky's hunting rifle leaning unattended against his cabin door on the other side of the yard. *Always take your shot, Johnny,* he had said.

As soon as Johnny saw the rifle, he rushed to put on his coat and sneakers, which he had dried in front of his space heater. Several facts fell into place: He had a gun. The creature's tracks were visible. He still had the chance to conquer his nightmares. He had missed his chance to fire at the hare, but he would not hesitate to pull the trigger again.

The tracks had ended right near that big old cottonwood tree, and the hollow in the trunk looked just like a doorway, didn't it? That thing in the woods was dangerous, or else Uncle Ricky's eyes wouldn't have widened so much when Johnny told him he'd seen its teeth.

Somebody needed to do what needed to be done, even if nothing could be done for Grandmother. Anything was better than waiting. Johnny grabbed the rifle, ducking under his grandmother's wood rail fence to run into the graying woods.

Farther behind him with every step, Grandmother was still screaming.

His feet, it seemed, remembered every dip and crevice as he followed the slashing, senseless trail between the firs and pines. This time, the creature's passage was accompanied by Uncle Ricky's boot tracks and Johnny's smaller ones beside his, sometimes intersecting, sometimes roughly parallel. Johnny panted with his mouth open as he ran, his breath charging in bursts from his lips. He held the rifle like a bayonet, ready to strike.

Fear made his legs heavy, but he pushed through until he was sweating despite the cold, until he could see the large tree ahead, dwarfing the surrounding conifers with a massive canopy of feathery branches made ominous without their leaves.

Yes, this was the place. He had no doubt. The tracks stopped abruptly, but the end of the creature's trail was a small heap, a sign of burrowing for sure. When he nudged the snow heap with his foot—jumping quickly away, of course—lumpy snow fell away into a hole as wide as a basketball. And the cottonwood stood only yards away from the creature's tunnel.

Upon his second visit, the mound of snow in front of the tree seemed like a wall, and the gap itself looked bigger; an archway of inky blackness against the snowdrift.

"Come out! *I'm not afraid of you!*"

In that moment, it didn't feel like a lie because his terror only felt like rage. He was enraged with his mother for bringing him on such a horrible trip. Enraged with Uncle Ricky for the secrets he kept, and the one he had shared. Enraged with himself for cursing Grandmother to die and then pitying her and for feeling anything for her after everything she had done. His rage poured out of him as tears, and his throat grew clotted, but he yelled again, "*Come on out!*"

He had never wanted to kill a thing, but he did now with a ferocity that felt primal. If he could turn back time, he would shoot that hare until his rifle clicked, empty. Maybe this creature had no more to do with poisoning his family than the hare, but he hoped that killing it would help him sleep without nightmares.

The silence infuriated him. Johnny picked up a stone and threw it at the dead cottonwood tree, missing the cavity by two inches. The second stone he threw flew inside and vanished in the blackness with a *THUNK*.

The chittering he had heard in Grandmother's room floated from the gap, but much louder than before. Agitated. Rising in pitch. A slithering sound echoed from inside the tree trunk, something moving fast, perhaps racing in a circle. Would it come outside?

Always take your shot, Johnny.

The rifle snapped into place beneath his chin, the perfect shooting stance. Johnny's sight was aimed directly into the dark crater, barely wavering despite his heaving breaths. Nothing else in the woods existed except the inky maw and his breathing.

Two ice-blue eyes emerged from the darkness. Moving toward daylight. Toward him.

Johnny's breathing stopped. The world stopped. For a moment, neither of them moved. The urge to kill, so consuming before, withered. *Might think she's its mama*, Uncle Ricky said.

"Don't come back!" Johnny said, although phlegm tried to strangle his voice. "You hear me? She's dying, so stay away!"

More chittering, but it seemed softer this time. Plaintive, even. Could it understand?

A large twig cracking from the creature's motion in the darkness sounded like a gunshot, snapping Johnny awake from his fugue state. Without realizing it, he dropped Uncle Ricky's gun when he turned and stumbled to run away.

His own scream was bottled in his throat, ringing between his ears.

～

When Johnny made it back to the lodge, the nurse's car was gone.

Mom was bundled up in her coat and scarf on the back porch bent over with her head wrapped between her arms; the same spot where Grandmother was always sitting in his dream. He had never seen his mother look so weary and sad.

He thought Grandmother might be dead until he heard a soft moan through her window.

Mom sobbed so loudly that Johnny thought about sneaking back into his cabin unseen. But he decided to go to her instead.

Mom heard his feet crunching toward her and looked up with a smile she tried to paste in place to greet him. When she saw his face, her smile died unborn. Wildness was playing in his mother's eyes, and he suspected she saw the same wildness in his.

"This is no kind of Christmas for you, Johnny," she said. "I'm sorry."

"You neither. I'm sorry too."

He sat beside her, so she scooted to make room on the narrow stair. The part of him that wanted to tell her everything quieted, obsolete, when she hugged him close. And he hugged her, comforting, not merely comforted—different than when he'd been younger—something new.

Johnny knew then that he would never tell his mother about Grandmother's strange creature in the woods, perhaps the only one of her children she had not scarred for life.

Three weeks after their trip to Bear Creek, Grandmother died at a Denver hospital. Neither Mom nor Uncle Ricky gave her the pills to end her misery, although Johnny could never forget that only their fear of hating her had stopped them. Her lodge sat empty for a year, but then Uncle Ricky moved in. He and Mom split the proceeds from the sale of their childhood home, and Mom bought a three-bedroom house in North Miami with a yard full of mango and avocado trees. It was the best place Johnny had ever lived, but that didn't stop the bad dreams.

Five years after Grandmother died, Uncle Ricky vanished on a hunting trip near the lodge. His mother, of course, was devastated. By then, Johnny was in college in lily-white Iowa on a full academic scholarship, never needing a cent from Grandmother's estate— and the story of his uncle's disappearance didn't sit right. Uncle Ricky had been a seasoned hunter, and he knew those woods well.

Johnny called the local sheriff's office to find out more, since a Black man missing in the woods surely wasn't their top priority. But the deputy who picked up the phone told him he drank beer with Uncle Ricky on Friday nights and had been a part of the search party. He didn't need to pull up a report to tell him the facts: a set of footprints they thought held promise had simply stopped cold in a clearing. The dogs sniffed Uncle Ricky to that spot and no farther.

"In front of an old tree?" Johnny said. Beyond his doorway, music blared from an impromptu dance party erupting in his dorm to celebrate the weekend. Metal rock. Johnny and his classmates were in two different worlds, yet again.

Come to think of it, a deputy said, there *had* been an old husk of a tree near where the tracks disappeared. The dogs had whined and circled, and one of them had started digging.

But all they found was snow.

E N D

Often when I write a short story, the character's journey has finished—but when I wrote a story called "Incident at Bear Creek Lodge" for the Other Terrors *anthology, co-edited by Rena Mason and Vince A. Liaguno, I believed I had room to expand that incident in a story that could both complement the original and exist as a standalone story. (I actually think I might be working my way up to a novel where both of these stories are the backstory to a creature story in the present day.) This story expands my premise of intergenerational trauma.*

THE GHOST OF CHRISTMASES PAST

Richard Kadrey

I T wasn't the holiday season until, a week before Christmas, the scar on Laura's left arm began to ache.

It always started with an itch that grew into a pulsing, burning sensation. Without fail, she'd stare at the crescent-shaped bite mark—the teeth marks still perfectly visible—half expecting the heat to radiate through her skin and turn the scar a bright crimson. But it never happened. If anything, in the twenty years since she'd received the bite, the mark had faded to bone white. Still, she insisted on wearing long sleeves, even in the heat of summer.

Every year Laura and her husband, Jordan, would put up the same small artificial tree in the living room and top it with the felt and yarn angel her mother had made when Laura was just a girl. The holiday ordeal didn't end there. They would also go to a Christmas tree lot and select a large wreath for the front door, Jordan holding her anxious hand the whole time. With these grotesque holiday signifiers in place, Laura could relax a little knowing that the house fit in with the neighborhood so that no one would ask why she spent every holiday locked in seclusion.

If they only knew, she thought each Christmas Eve. *If only they knew about the shotgun.*

"Are we still going to do the other stuff?" said Jordan wearily from the sofa.

"It's a holiday tradition," Laura replied.

"Not a good one."

"Please. I don't want to have this argument again. I was doing this year's before we met and if I have to do it by myself I will."

Jordan got up and said, "Relax. I'm sorry I brought it up. I'll get the nail gun."

With that, Laura and Jordan began the final touches securing the house.

They nailed the windows and the basement door shut and made sure the chimney flue was securely closed. A few years earlier Laura had become nervous that her neighbors might begin to ask questions about all the hammering that went on at her place, so she bought an electric nail gun at Home Depot. Jordan loved using it and the job, thankfully, went quickly and quietly. It was one of the reasons she'd been drawn to him after so many years of being alone. He knew how to use tools. He was steady where she was not. He listened and didn't judge. Until recently.

Things were changing between them. Things *had* changed, and the holidays made it worse.

When they were done securing the house, Laura and Jordan went to the kitchen for a snack. After a decade of prepping, she knew to lay in a fridge full of their favorite food to get them through their Christmas lockdown. Since they'd finished work in the afternoon, she set out a pot of Earl Grey tea and large slices of fruit cake on the kitchen table. The cake was Laura's one pleasurable concession to the holiday season. Still, she had to choke down the first few bites before she could relax enough to enjoy the snack. Gryla, she remembered, had smelled sweet, like the candied fruit on her cake. It's why she'd let the old witch get close enough to bite her arm that Christmas Eve—the old woman's sweet, reassuring scent. Ten-year-old Laura had made that mistake, but thirty-year-old Laura would never allow it to happen again. The nailed-up house and shotgun would see to that.

As she was finishing the tea her cell phone buzzed. Laura picked it up to check the caller ID and almost set the phone down unanswered. Taking a breath, she thumbed the button to answer knowing that if she didn't Aunt Theodora would keep calling back all day.

Better to rip the bandage off the scab now and get it over with, she thought.

"Hi Aunt Theo, how are you?" she said as casually as she could.

"I'm fine, dear. Just worried about you. I'll never understand why you and Jordan won't ever join the family for Christmas dinner."

Laura sighed. It was the same conversation every year. The same deflections and lies. "You know how I feel about Christmas," she said. "It's not my time of year."

"I know," said Theo sympathetically. "It seems so unfair."

"You're so good at Christmas. You'll just have to celebrate for all three of us."

Theo laughed lightly at that. "Okay. I know when I've lost the argument. Again. Did you get the card I sent?"

"Yes. It's lovely. Thank you. Jordan put it next to the tree."

"How nice. I assume that you're not going to Mass?"

Laura rubbed her brow wanting to end the call. "I'm afraid not. But I have my rosary fired up and ready to pay penance after the holidays," she lied.

"I'll light candles for the two of you, dear. And, of course, one for Reiner. Even though you're not going to church you can still light a candle for him too, you know."

Laura drew in a breath. It was the same damn thing every year, so she told another lie. "Of course, I have a candle for him. I'll light it tonight."

"Good girl. Please don't forget."

"I won't."

There was a long pause, which surprised Laura because this was usually where Aunt Theo would give up and end the call. But this time the call didn't end. It hung there in silence until Theo said, "After all these years you have to forgive yourself. There was nothing you could have done."

Laura made a face as she felt a stabbing pain in her scar. "I know. We've been over this," she said quietly.

"Reiner's kidnapping, well, you were both children. I thank

the Lord every year that you got away with just..."

"A scar." Laura fought to keep her voice from getting hard. "I know, Aunt Theo. And I appreciate it."

"You have to forgive yourself," Theo cut in.

"I'm working on it. I promise. And please don't tell me to go to church and ask God for help. I prayed and prayed after Reiner was gone and all I got was radio silence."

"Please don't talk that way, dear. God has a plan for us all."

Another twinge of pain in her arm. "That doesn't mean we have to like it. I sure as hell don't. And I know Reiner didn't. I'm the one who saw him being dragged away, not any of you."

When Theo spoke again, Laura could tell she was crying and felt a small pang of guilt. "Oh my dear," said her aunt.

"Hey, Aunt Theo. I'm sorry. I didn't mean it like that. Please forgive me."

Laura heard sniffling on the line and Theo said, "I'll pray for you. Pray for you both," then hung up.

She set the phone down and for a moment considered calling her aunt back, only what would she say? Would she finally tell Theo the truth, that she'd seen an old witch eat her little brother alive on Christmas Eve? No, that was never going to happen. So, she let the phone lie there and sipped her tea, but it had gone cold during the call so she set the cup and pot in the sink.

"Theo never gives up, does she?" said Jordan.

"And she never will."

"What if, and don't get mad at me, she's right? What would be so bad about one Christmas dinner with your family? Don't you get lonely this time of year? I do."

"That's not the point," said Laura tensely. "The doors, the windows, it's just for a few days. I'm not good enough company for a few days?"

"I didn't mean it that way at all." Jordan got up from his chair, but before he could go to her Laura's phone rang again.

Without looking at the caller ID, she thumbed it on and said, "Aunt Theo? I'm so sorry I was mean just now. Christmas is so hard..." No one answered. The call crackled with static, long seconds of white noise interspersed with crackles and pops. "Aunt Theo?" said Laura. The static stopped for a few seconds, then came back loud enough that she had to move the phone from her ear. Underneath all the white noise was a sound Laura couldn't quite identify. It was a screeching, almost laughing sound, like someone happily torturing an animal.

"Hello? Who is this?" she said, and the laugh-screech came back louder than ever. Laura thumbed the phone off and dropped it on the table.

"What was that all about?" said Jordan.

Laura didn't answer but went to the living room and held the shotgun on her lap until she was calm again. Jordan followed, stopping at the kitchen door just looking at her.

"I'm not going to end up like Reiner," she said.

No, I'm not. You monsters. You've all tried. Over and over for twenty years and I beat you every time. I'll do it again this year too.

Memories of all the child eaters that had come for her through the years flooded Laura's mind. Old Gryla. Krampus. A Namahage yokai. Jolakatturinn, the winter cat. Frau Perchta, a shapeshifter, almost got Laura one year by appearing as one of her friends. There was even the Swiss bastard, Kindlifresserbrunnen. She didn't know why they wanted her and it didn't matter. She'd beaten them all, staying alive for twenty Christmases while keeping her secret. This year would be no exception.

From across the room Jordan said, "You want to put the gun down, babe? You're scaring me."

Laura glanced at her watch. It was early enough that the sun was still out. None of the eaters ever came until after dark, so she propped the shotgun on the floor next to the sofa.

"Thank you," said Jordan. He went to sit with her and spoke quietly. "You know, when I saw my therapist last week I mentioned your... condition."

There was another shot of pain in Laura's scar and she turned to glare at him. "You're talking about me to your psychiatrist?"

"Of course. You're a big part of my life. We talk about our relationship all the time."

"No. I mean about me and Christmas."

Jordan nodded. "He thinks that these unresolved feelings about Reiner's disappearance..."

"Death," Laura said. "He's dead. I know it."

"You see, it's assumptions like that that worry him and me. He gave me the name of a couple of other psychiatrists—both women—that he thought you might want to talk to."

Jordan held out a slip of paper that he pulled from his shirt pocket.

Laura didn't reach for it. She said, "You've been waiting to spring this on me all day, haven't you? Why else would you have the names so handy?"

"I suppose so. I get so worried. Each Christmas seems worse than the last. I don't know how much more of this you can take."

"You mean you don't know how much more *you* can take."

Jordan set the slip of paper on the coffee table and nodded. "I can't stand seeing you like this."

Laura stood up and said, "If you're planning on leaving me, do it now while it's still light out. I'm not opening any doors after dark."

Jordan got up, went to her and hugged her tight. "I'm sorry. It gets to me every year. Nailing the place up. The gun. When are you going to make a mistake and shoot me in the middle of the night?"

"I haven't pulled the trigger once the whole time we've been together," said Laura. "Isn't that enough?"

Jordan let go of her and stepped away. "No. It's not. One mistake and it will be something you can never get away from."

Laura looked away for a moment. When she turned back, she gave Jordan a small smile. "Would you like to know a secret? Something no one else knows?"

He gave her a puzzled look and said, "I guess."

She walked to him and said, "I know Reiner is dead because I saw him die. She killed him. Gryla. She ate him in front me. Swallowed him right down. But she wanted me. It's why I have her bite mark. Only Reiner hit her, so she took him instead. And she's going to come back. Her or someone like her. The Christmas child eaters. They want me and they'll never stop. So now, you tell me how irrational it is for me to be afraid when I saw my little brother ripped apart and devoured before my eyes?"

Jordan stared at Laura for a minute, then sat down on the sofa. "Oh," he said finally.

Laura went and stood over him. "Is that all you have to say? I tell you the greatest secret of my life and all you can do is grunt '*Oh*'?"

Lifting his hand, Jordan let it drop back down onto his lap. "I don't know what to say. If you were in my position what would you say when you hear your partner tell you that a monster ate her kid brother?"

"I'd say I'm sorry. I'd say I support you."

Jordan took the slip of paper from the coffee table and pressed it into Laura's hand. "After the holidays, please call someone. You need help."

Laura stepped back. "That sounds like an ultimatum," she said. "Go to a shrink or I'm leaving you."

"I promise you that's not what I meant. But something's got to change. I mean, answer me this: in all the years we've been together why haven't I ever seen anything strange? Any of these eaters?"

Laura gave him a weary look. "Because there's nothing to see. Because I keep them out."

"Right. How very convenient. No one ever sees the monster because you keep the monsters away."

"I'm telling you the truth. And I'm not keeping the eaters away. I just don't let them get in."

"Laura. I want to believe you, only it's all so—I'm sorry—insane."

She stood at the far end of the sofa and shook her head. After a moment she said, "I need a drink. Do you want a drink? Of course you do. A toast and a cheery sendoff for your new bachelor life after Christmas."

Jordan put his hands to his forehead. "Please don't do this."

Laura went into the bathroom and then to the kitchen where she poured them both shots of good bourbon, careful to make sure that Jordan got the proper glass. Laura raised hers in a toast.

Again, Jordan said, "Please don't do this."

"If you ever loved me, then drink with me now," she replied.

Slowly, he raised his glass, clinked it against hers and downed his drink in one gulp. Laura drank hers and sat down behind him on the sofa. "Should we watch a movie?" she said lightly.

Jordan stared at her. "Seriously? We're having the most important discussion of our lives and you want to watch a movie?"

"I thought we could both use a break."

He leaned back against the sofa and said, "Sure. Fine. Whatever. But you need to call one of the numbers my psychiatrist gave me."

"Of course, dear. *A Christmas Carol* is on. The one with Alastair Sim. Shall we watch?"

Jordan waved a hand at the screen. "It's your party."

Laura turned on the movie. It was already at the Ghost of Christmas Past sequence where Scrooge saw the happiest and most miserable moments of his life. Laura watched intently and poured them more drinks during a commercial break. By the time Scrooge awoke on Christmas Day, Jordan was blinking and shaking his head.

"I don't feel so good," he said.

"Don't worry. It'll pass," said Laura.

"What do you mean?"

"Remember the Oxycodone the doctor gave me after my hip surgery? I had some left over, so I put one in your drink."

Jordan lurched unsteadily to his feet. "You did what?" he said. "I have to leave."

Laura shook her head. "You can't in your condition. You'll crack your head on the ice outside before you make it to the garage. And you certainly can't drive. Plus, by the time you sober up it will be night and too late. I'm not opening the door, so you'll have to stay."

Jordan took another step away from her and almost fell over. "Why would you do that?"

"So you'll stay. I'm going to let the eater in this year so you can see. Then you'll know I'm not crazy."

"But you *are* crazy," said Jordan dropping down into an easy chair across the room. "I know it now."

Laura picked up the shotgun and put it on the sofa where he'd been sitting. Getting up, she took a blanket from under the coffee table and draped it over Jordan in the easy chair. "You rest up now. It's going to be a long night." Afterward, she went back to the sofa and channel surfed as Jordan half-floated, half-napped the afternoon away.

Around ten that night, Laura grew tired of the Christmas nonsense on TV and muted it. Jordan still lay like a heap on the easy chair.

What a lightweight, she thought. She called to him, "How are you feeling?"

"Still fucked up."

"You never could hold your drugs. Remember that time we tried Molly and you cried all night?"

Jordan struggled to get up. "Please, let me go."

"No. I left one way in. You have to see."

"See what? There's nothing out there!" he shouted.

Laura put a finger to her lips. "Quiet. Did you hear something?"

"Only your bullshit."

She sat very quietly. After a moment, came the faint sound of scratching. First on the windows. Then the front door. Laura picked up the shotgun and looked through the peephole. There was nothing outside but a snowy sidewalk. The scratching resumed, this time behind her. She ran to the nailed-shut basement door and listened. Nails or talons raked down the door and crept around the bottom, trying to claw through. The house quieted for a moment and she let out a long breath. Then a loud crash came from the basement door, so intense that she almost dropped the shotgun. Something threw its body against the door, over and over again, so that the sound shook the house. The wood around the hinges and nail heads splintered a little, but they held and the door didn't buckle under the blows. Finally, the sound stopped and Laura thought that she could hear footsteps going back down the basement steps.

When the house was quiet again, she ran to the living room and shook Jordan's shoulder. "Did you hear that racket? Now tell me I'm crazy."

He looked at her blearily. "I didn't hear anything."

"Fuck you. Yes you did."

A sound came from above her. The rhythmic thumping of someone running across the roof.

"Now tell me you didn't hear anything," she shouted.

Jordan tried to stand. "Just you screaming. Let me go. I'm feeling better."

She pushed him back down onto the chair. "You're not going anywhere until this is finished."

Laura knew that there was only one logical place large enough for someone to get inside from the roof and that was through the chimney. However, the flue was shut and she knew that the eaters didn't operate through logic. They operated through hunger. Still, she waited until the gun grew heavy in her hands.

From the kitchen came a sharp metallic *pop.* Then another. She ran from the fireplace and turned on the kitchen light in time to see the aluminum vent above the oven distort and expand, like a silver throat trying to choke something down.

This was it. This was finally it. The place she'd left open—the trap she'd set. Which eater would it be? It would have to be a small one to fit through the oven vent.

An idea came to her. Laura set the shotgun down on the kitchen table and, as the vent over the oven distended and throbbed, she turned on all the burners. Then she ran back and grabbed the gun.

Something alive in the vent shrieked. Great screams and the sound of metallic kicks filled the house.

A voice came to her. It screamed, "Help me, Laura!"

She ran back to the living room for Jordan and found him half-sitting in the chair trying to pull himself up.

"Do you hear it now?" screamed Laura.

He nodded. "I do. What is it?"

Laura grabbed his arm and pulled him into the kitchen, shoving him against the wall so he wouldn't fall. "Look," she said. "Look and then call me crazy."

Something like a black bubble hung from the oven vent. It slowly pulsed inward and outward like it was breathing. The smell of singed fabric and flesh filled the room. Then, with one more kick and a muffled howl, the thing oozed out and onto the oven in one glistening, ichorous mass. And began to scream, even as the liquid flesh flowed slowly onto the linoleum floor. The ragged clothes it wore burned and smoldered. It was roughly the shape of a man, but its slug-like body was pooled at strange angles. Slowly, however, the burned figure began to pull himself back into human shape.

Laura didn't hesitate. She pulled the trigger of the shotgun, and missed, blasting a jagged hole in the kitchen floor. The gun's kick knocked her backwards and by the time she was steady again the slug man was gone.

She ran into the hall beyond the kitchen, but it was empty. Swinging the barrel back the way she'd come, all she saw was Jordan in a corner of the kitchen with his hand out before him. "Please don't shoot me," he shouted. Laura ignored him and crept into the living room.

When the slug man ran off, he seemed much bigger than Laura had expected. When she went into the living room, she did it looking for a tall man. It didn't occur to her that he'd expect that and sat crouched by the door. The moment she set a foot in the room, he sprang and swung a fist into the side of her head. Stunned, she dropped the shotgun and it went off, shattering the TV. Before she could react, the slug man grabbed her by the hair, threw her to the ground and kicked her once in the stomach. "Stay down there until I say you can get up," he said.

The pain in Laura's scar burned her like never before. Even after being punched and kicked, it was the one sensation she truly felt. Still on the floor, she turned her head and watched the slug man pick up the shotgun and point it at her.

"Okay. Get up," he said. "I didn't kick you that hard."

Trembling, Laura braced herself on the sofa and pulled herself to her feet. When she was upright, she finally got a look at the man. His hair was wild. Greasy and matted. He was filthy and his clothes and skin were scorched almost black, though the worst thing about him was his face and the shredded holes where his eyes should be.

After a minute he said, "Hello, Laura."

Something awful turned over in her mind, a long-ago memory. She said, "Reiner?"

He smiled bleakly. "I wasn't sure you'd remember." He ratcheted the shotgun several times, ejecting the shells and when it was empty, he set it down.

"You're my eater?" said Laura. "Did Gryla do this to you?"

Reiner leaned back against the wall, leaving a dirty smudge where he touched it. "Gryla," he said. "I'm glad you still remember her. I mean, I knew you had to. I would have beaten you bloody if you'd denied it."

Confused and scared, Laura leaned heavily against the sofa. "She ate you. I saw it. How are you here?"

"That's all you remember? Nothing else?"

"What else is there? It was horrible."

The brows over his hollow eye sockets raised a fraction of an inch. "Oh, it was horrible. More horrible to feel than to watch, I assure you. You really don't remember the rest of it, do you?"

"What? What else is there to remember?"

Reiner shot forward from the wall, grabbed Laura by the shoulders and shook her. "How you held me for her," he said between clenched teeth. "You held me in front of you the whole time, so she'd eat me instead."

Laura shook herself from his grasp. "No. She bit me and you hit her. That's why she attacked you."

"Bit you?" said Reiner. He laughed. "Those are *my* teeth marks in your arm. I bit you trying to get away when she was swallowing my guts."

"No, no, no," said Laura. The scar on her arm burned and when she touched it, her mind was swept back to a dark room twenty years earlier. A sweet smell in the air. A hungry old woman with Reiner between them. He never cried out once. The old witch kept a tight hand across his mouth. Laura crouched behind Reiner trying to stay out of the hag's eyeline. Grinding her teeth to keep from screaming as Reiner bit her arm to get away.

"No. It wasn't like that," she said.

"It was exactly like that. But you know what the worst part was? It was the last thing I saw before she finished me off. She pulled out my eyes and gave them to you. 'Eat these, my child,' she said. 'Eat these and be like me or join the little squire in my belly.'"

"No. It's a lie."

"And you ate them."

"No!"

"I could still see, you know. That was part of her magic. I watched you take my eyes from her hands and swallow them down in one gulp."

Laura's head swam and she fell to her knees. Her brow was cool and sweaty when she put a hand there. And there was something else wrong with her face. Her cheeks and jaw felt strange.

"You lie to yourself each Christmas," Reiner said. "Leave yourself a secret exit through the nailed doors so that when Jordan is asleep you can go out and eat."

Tears formed in Laura's eyes. "No. It's a lie."

Reiner reached down and pulled her from the floor. "Every year you nail yourself up and tell yourself it's from the monsters, but you're the monster—and what's been trying to get inside all this time is me."

"Why?"

Reiner shrugged. "I can't move on. You have my eyes. I need them to see my way to the next place."

As he said it, the memory of the night came back stronger than ever. All that he said was true. Holding him. Hiding behind him. Swallowing his eyes.

"Oh God," she said, then looked at him. "I'm sorry. I can't give you your eyes back. I ate them."

He put a hand out toward her face. "Then let me have yours."

"I can't. I need them..."

"To hunt?" said Reiner.

Laura's head felt tight and she could hear her pounding heartbeat. When she put a hand to her face, something was very wrong. Turning her head to a mirror on the wall it took her a moment to understand that the face she was looking at was hers. She looked so much like Gryla, though not quite. It was as if they'd spawned a child together. A subtle mixture of them both. Laura opened her mouth and admired her rows of razor teeth.

"Every year?" she said.

"Every year," Reiner replied.

Laura laughed a little. "The lies children tell themselves."

Her brother approached her again. "I want your eyes," he said more insistently.

"You can't have them," she said and shoved him away. "But I have others."

Reiner frowned. "Others?"

There was a sound from the kitchen and Jordan lurched into the living room swinging a frying pan at Reiner's head. He dodged it easily and Laura slapped Jordan to the floor.

Her husband looked up at her, his eyes still a little unfocused. "Laura?"

She looked from Jordan to her brother and said, "I don't have your eyes anymore, but I do have a spare set around."

"Please let me have them. Any eyes will do," he said pleadingly.

Laura knelt beside her husband. He blinked at her a few times. "What's wrong with your face? Did he hurt you?" Jordan said.

"He didn't," she said. "I understand now and no one will hurt me again. Or call me crazy."

Laura grabbed Jordan and twisted his head until there was a loud *crack*. As he lay limply on the floor, she knelt beside him and used her talon-like nails to pluck out each of his eyes. When she was done, she stood and gave them to Reiner. Her brother eagerly pushed the orbs into the empty sockets in his face and laughed.

"Oh man. It's been so long," he said and looked at Jordan. "These eyes were his? Who is he?"

Laura prodded her husband's body with the toe of her shoe. "Just some man. I thought I knew him. Sadly, it turns out I didn't. I should have never let him in."

Reiner stepped forward and gave his sister a brief hug. "Thank you. I'm going now. You won't see me again."

Laura took his hand and squeezed it. "Safe travels," she said and wrenched the front door open with strength that surprised her.

Reiner stood in the open door for a moment and said, "What will you do now that you don't have me to be afraid of anymore?"

"I'm not really sure. I only know one thing."

"What's that?"

"I'm very hungry."

"Goodbye, Laura."

"Goodbye, Reiner."

She locked the door after her brother left and went back to Jordan's body, which she ate quickly and ravenously. But she wasn't sated. Not at all. She needed more.

At midnight, she crept quietly across the roof tops of the nearby homes knowing that, if any children heard her coming, they'd think her light footfalls were Santa's reindeer come to bring them Christmas cheer.

END

Winter isn't just a time of celebration. It's a time of cosmic retribution. During Christmas, bad children can forget about Santa and instead brace themselves for a visit from Krampus when they'll get a beating, or worse, be whisked away forever to who knows where?

I thought that was as bad as things could get for kids, but as I read more about the darker aspects of the holiday season, I discovered that Krampus was a softy. Around the world were entities ready to attack and even eat hapless kiddies while they sat around waiting for reindeer on the roof. People have tried to explain these beliefs as ancient responses to the death of children before the advent of modern medicine. And, of course, there's the gruesome specter of religion. If kids were too young to understand ending up in the eternal flames of Hell, they'd certainly understand vengeful monsters sent to cleanse the world of tiny troublemakers. So, put your socks away, kids. Be sure to make your beds and hang up your clothes or who knows whose bones your neighbors will find when the snow melts in spring?

OUR RECENT UNPLEASANTNESS

Stephen Graham Jones

1.

"WHAT if you don't decompress enough this time?" Sheila asked Jenner, pooching her cheeks out with air and letting her arms rise around her sides as if she were inflating, inflating, about to explode.

"Yeah, two seconds less'll do it," Jenner said, leaning in to jab a kiss onto her puffed-out cheek, which made her lips turn into the spout of an untied balloon, sputtering warm breath and more than a bit of spit down the collar of his jacket.

He pushed her away in play, of course being so, so careful—pregnant women shouldn't take spills in the foyer, even if this was only the second trimester.

The joke while Jenner had been getting Winty, their Labradoodle, into her harness and leash was—this being the official shortest day of the year—Jenner's usual before-dinner dog walk was going to be shortened by maybe *a whole two seconds?* And the daily walk was where he always left barely a survivor of the office, then came back a husband, a soon-to-be-father, his outlook dialed back from grim to... at least less unoptimistic?

"I'm putting the bread in at five 'til!" Sheila announced, swishing the door open and presenting the neighborhood to Jenner and Winty, and heating her eyes up at Jenner about how he wasn't to be late again. Yes, walking along the creek is nice, yes, the Christmas lights two streets over are Santa's wet dream, but lasagne night's lasagne night, and garlic toast is best fresh out of the oven.

"Scout's honor," Jenner said, falling into his usual routine of trying to make the peace sign or wolf ears or whatever Boy Scouts actually did, but playacting that his fingers were traitors, were Vulcan, were Alice Cooper, were Three-Stooging him in the eyes.

Sheila shut the door on this repeat performance.

Jenner waited for the deadbolt to turn, patted the belt loop he kept his dog-walking key on, nodded, and they were off, out into the evening.

It was cool but not quite cold yet—thank you, changing climate.

Winty, a creature of habit, pulled to the left at the end of their block, looking over her shoulder at Jenner for the confirmation she always needed, that she was being a good girl.

"Go, go," Jenner told her, and they went.

Instead of ducking down Maple into the winter wonderland measured in light bulbs and wattage, they hooked right at the last instant, Jenner's mood already lifted enough for him to—like the boy he wasn't, at thirty-two—jump with both feet into Winty's shadow. She took no note of this small violence, so Jenner stayed there, pretended to be standing on the tightrope the leash's shadow now was under the streetlight, but, after two of three steps of plunging into his own shadow on the sidewalk, he gave the stupid game up. Because... he was here again, wasn't he? The circle. If he followed it all the way around, it would continue onto his own street, meaning, really, this was a completely rational and normal route to take to get back for lasagne, wasn't it?

It was.

Still, to make it make even more sense, in his head Jenner was explaining to Sheila that what he was doing here was dutifully ignoring the extravaganza Maple was, because of how it would overload Winty's senses, get her too hyped for the night.

Which was two or three bullshit excuses piled on top of his turning right instead of going straight *more* than that decision really called for, he had to admit. Especially when the real reason was right there: their first week after moving in, on one of his and Winty's inaugural post-work, pre-dinner walks, which he guessed was some six months after what they'd then been calling their "recent unpleasantness," which involved Sheila's personal trainer Dan and how from here on out she was only going to work with fitness experts who were *women*—Jenner had been scuffling down the sidewalk, checking out all the house fronts he passed, just because they were homes he hadn't yet had a chance to catalog. Before this, he and Sheila had walked Maple hand in hand, and it had been idyllic enough that the only thing missing were pairs of ice skates slung over their shoulders. Walking it without her now would have felt like a betrayal, though, like "getting even with her for her dalliance," as the marriage counselor had phrased it, so Jenner had turned right instead, stepped into that puddle of darkness that was his own crisp shadow under the unwavering streetlight, and set out to explore this circle.

And he wasn't being lecherous, he wasn't a peeping tom, didn't need *that* reputation in the neighborhood, they were planning to make a life here, thanks. Still, passing by 1872, he'd—not even remotely on purpose—dragged his eyes across the house but caught on the wide, tall, clear front window.

It was framing a grand staircase that curved up to the second floor, and, just starting to walk down that staircase was a woman about his and Sheila's age in a black slip and a black bra with scalloped edging or whatever at the top, her head hidden by the arched top of the window, and for a bad instant Jenner's heart clutched in his chest, because he thought he recognized the way her hand was opening up to accept the bannister... but it couldn't be Sheila.

Jenner turned away before the woman's head could dip into view—before she could catch him lurking—and it was a dramatic enough backpedal that he stepped off the curb a bit, tweaking his ankle, Winty looking back to him about this, and... that was that. End of the moment.

Except it wasn't.

For months afterward—until now, really—Jenner, when he let his mind go slack, would be on that sidewalk again, looking in. Was this woman going downstairs for a blouse in the utility room? Was she on her way to the hot tub in the backyard, and stripping down as she went? Did she, like Sheila used to, years ago, just prefer this state of undress for being alone in the house at night?

Though Jenner and Winty practically wore a rut in the sidewalks of the neighborhood with their daily walks, he only turned right onto black bra circle in his weaker moments.

That house's lights had never been on again so far. It was as if the woman coming down the stairs had been staged just for Jenner, that one time. Walking up to 1872 now, its lights were off again. *Thank you*, Jenner said inside. He hated coming home feeling guilty. He owed Sheila better.

Thing was, though, seeing that one woman coming down the stairs that one time? It had conditioned Jenner to the possibility that this might happen again. Meaning, every house he passed, he'd sneak a fast look up, just on the chance.

He wasn't a peeper, though. He was just checking things out. Neighborhood watch, dogwalker style.

At the top of the circle, Winty finally stepped out onto this lawn in the gentle, timid way that meant she was about to "make like a plane," as Sheila said: her pee-stance, where her legs looked like the wings of a Concord, taking off.

Jenner looked all around to see if anyone was there to witness this. On his street, everyone was at war with the rabbits—their thousands of pees were withering lawn after lawn. And, every few houses on the circle, there'd been signs of cartoon dogs straining to use the grass, with that red circle-and-slash over them.

But it was just dog pee, c'mon. What about when the deer came through? What about trash day, when the raccoons take over? What about birds, and squirrels?

This was just nature. This was the outdoors.

Still, Jenner kept Winty's leash tight while she peed, in case he needed to make like he was scolding her.

Because it's impolite to watch, though, he scanned the house this lawn belonged to.

The only light on was on the second floor, above the garage.

A woman was sitting at a vanity, the window framing her perfectly from the back. She was just adjusting her hair, doing or undoing her make-up, it didn't matter—*don't look, you didn't see anything,* Jenner told himself.

She was wearing a pajama top, green and soft it looked like, and, most importantly, she was looking into the mirror, not to the crime happening down on her lawn.

"C'mon, girl," Jenner said, giving the leash an obligatory tug.

But his eyes were climbing the house.

The woman's hair was mounded on top of her head in a fashion he thought wasn't in fashion anymore. Not quite "beehive," but not *not*-beehive. And she had both her hands at the back of her head, like patting the hair in place or something, which made her breasts under those pajamas thrust—

No no no, Jenner told himself.

Winty, back on the sidewalk, pulled ahead, and, in farewell of sorts, for what could have been, Jenner cast one last look up, guiltily hoping for a snapshot to take with him, one he'd have to hide in his head behind the taxes and baseball stats, but... *what?*

The woman's hands were still up like they'd been, her back ramrod straight like she *was* from the fifties, or maybe a music video—if there were still music videos—but one of her hands had worked around to her chin, now.

The same way you'd twist the lid off a sports drink, she pushed her chin to the side, the back of her head the other way, and, easy as anything, lifted her head off her neck.

Jenner stopped on the sidewalk, felt Winty looking her question back to him.

"I—uh—" was all Jenner could manage.

Moving very deliberately, her arm movements exaggerated, maybe because of the whole "my eyes are somewhere else"-thing, the woman set her own head down on the vanity while her hands did something below the mirror, and, and—

She'd set her head down backwards to her.

Meaning her eyes were looking down right at Jenner.

"No, no," he said, and stepped back into the empty space past the curb, his tender ankle collapsing again, the leash slipping from his hand, and had the asphalt been slurry, a tar pit to drink him in, that wouldn't have been surprising at all.

Instead, the woman's headless body rose and crossed the room, her face still watching Jenner from the vanity, and somehow those blind hands found the light switch, plunged the house in complete darkness.

Jenner rose, scrambled past this lawn, this... this whatever-it-was, and by the time he got back to his own front door, Winty was there waiting for him.

He stood for a moment, watching the street behind him, sure a headless body was going to be lurching after him, but there was just a few dry flakes of snow, sifting down.

By morning, the neighborhood was white.

It would make the squirrel on the walk out to Jenner's car more distinct.

Squirrel *body*, to be specific.

There was no head.

Sitting behind the wheel, waiting for the defroster to heat up, Jenner breathed in deep-deep, made himself hold it, and shook his head no, no, this wasn't happening. And it hadn't happened last night either.

And, until late late spring, summer really, when he sneaked away from changing diapers to scoop the rain gutters out and found the squirrel's desiccated head in the gutter over the garage, he was able to keep on believing that.

It was good it happened, though.

He never walked the circle anymore.

Really, he hardly decompressed at all.

2.

Jenner carried the fame of summer well into fall: *he* was the one who, in July, had finally gotten the police out to deal with the project cars spreading out from 1216, four houses down from his own.

The guy who lived there had inherited the house from his mother, as far as anyone knew—the old-timers had known the mother, vaguely recalled she'd had a son—and apparently some money as well, as his pastime was buying cars-with-potential and parking them all along the curbs up and down the street. Not always facing the way they should be facing. Not always even close to the curb. It was like their driver had just stopped driving, left the car there when it puttered down.

Other neighbors had been able to get the ones out of registration ticketed, but, it turned out, those tickets tucked under the windshield wipers were basically useless. What you needed was a police offer to call the tow truck in, bring those project cars to where they'd always been heading anyway: the impound yard on the other side of town.

How Jenner, of everyone else who'd tried, finally got a black and white to come to their neighborhood, was by calling in to report a prowler.

"Like, a real *ne'er-do-well?*" Sheila had asked while he was dialing, doing the Dickens-ey accent while bouncing Taylor-girl in her arms.

A few minutes later they were all at the front window, peeking through the curtains, waiting to see if this officer would show or not.

"Who wouldn't want to creep around, catch a glimpse of you?" Jenner asked, hip-checking her softly and taking Taylor. They danced around the living room, her giggling, Jenner lost in her baby eyes, until Sheila waved them down, made "cop eyes" at him, which he didn't even know she had.

Jenner explained the "prowler" to the officer in high detail, telling himself the whole while that, pretend or not, the police being aware of this neighborhood in a new way had to be good, didn't it?

"Show up on your doorbell thing there?" the officer asked, ready to note it on his flipped-open pad.

Jenner looked back to his front door, hadn't considered that.

The story he'd just told the officer was that the prowler had been peeping in the front window, so, yeah, he *should* have been recorded, shouldn't he have?

"Didn't even consider that..." Jenner said, and hiked Taylor to his other hip so he could open the app on his phone.

There was no prowler there, of course. He showed it to the officer.

"While you're here," Jenner said then, and walked the officer to the late-seventies Camaro, the little hot-rodded Datsun, and the Monte Carlo that he actually kind of liked. Then he pointed to the other three cars up and down the street, making sure to mention which ones had bad tags, which ones' doors were unlocked, could be a hazard to curious kids, and... by dark, one tow truck had been back to the street enough times to clean things up.

Jenner was a champion, a hero.

And all it took was making up one peeping tom.

Who definitely wasn't him.

Still, at all the backyard barbecues and front yard beer-while-the-kids-playathons, he often found himself studying the women's necklines, throat, collarbone areas.

For... for what? Suture lines? A joint? The shadow of a seam?

He hadn't seen what he'd seen, though. He couldn't have. For one, there'd been zero blood. For two, the head had been distinctly alive and aware after being removed. For three—like two wasn't enough already?—bodies don't walk around without their heads.

He couldn't explain what he'd seen, but he did take the lesson: keep your eyes straight ahead, don't concern yourself with what goes on in other people's homes. That's their business.

His business was Sheila, and Taylor, and, okay, Winty too, but not on the same level as wives and daughters, of course. Well, wives and daughter *singular.*

And the squirrel didn't even factor in. He'd seen bright white pigeons in parking lots, their heads cleanly severed, probably by cats, and he'd seen gophers or marmots or something on the trail, similarly torn up. Nature's tooth and claw, bub. That's just the way of things. Like it or lump it.

So summer shaded into fall, and fall became winter. The grills were covered, the Christmas lights went up, Maple glowed like a Christmas concert, and suddenly it was the 21st again.

"How am I supposed to get this ready if the stupid solstice is stealing two seconds from me?" Sheila said from the kitchen island.

Jenner swirled Taylor around by the arms like she liked and didn't answer, knew this was a rhetorical joke, if that was a thing. He'd just heard it, though. That meant it had to be a thing.

"Oh, hey," he said to her, miming buttoning his own shirt: Sheila'd missed one.

One full cup of her black bra with the scalloped top had partially exposed, when she was leaned forward for the spice rack.

"Just what I need..." Sheila muttered, and, when her fingers were too suspect to attend to a white shirt, she walked over to Jenner to help.

He buttoned it, maybe letting the backs of his hands wander a bit. Sheila play-bopped him on the shoulder, swished back to the cutting board.

After being wined and dined all through the last few months for his heroics, they were paying the neighborhood back with their "Solstice Celebration"—*not* "Christmas Party," because that assumed things it wasn't safe to assume.

"So we're Druids now?" Jenner had asked.

"If so, we're Druids short of cocktail napkins," Sheila had informed him back, sending him down to the store one more time.

But tonight was the night, at last.

And, since everyone would just walk over, the wine could flow.

Every time the doorbell rang, Jenner waded there with Taylor, did the welcome thing until the living room was packed, the kitchen was standing room only, and the back porch was pretty thick with neighbors as well, all of them huddled around the heater.

The highlight, repeated over and over, was Jenner holding both of Taylor's hands over her head while she took a few tentative, not-completely-her-own steps, her feet really just pedaling, only about a quarter of her weight on them. The women with kids already in high school pressed their lips together and batted their eyes, and Jenner was happy for them, and for himself, and for Taylor. For everything.

Until he saw *her*, standing on the other side of the kitchen island, her hair piled on top of her head just like last time, a wine glass to her mouth, her eyes locked directly on his.

He went cold inside.

Instinctively, he moved Taylor around to his other side, as if this woman with the detachable head were going to raise a pistol crossbow, fire a bolt through the crowd at him.

"Time?" Sheila asked, suddenly right there.

"Um," Jenner said, not completely able to form words yet.

"Nighty-night?"

"Yeah, yes, nighty-night," Jenner said.

They'd coordinated this well in advance: Jenner, being better at getting Taylor to sleep, would disappear for long enough to do that, and Sheila would double her hostess efforts to make up for his absence.

Up in the nursery, Jenner changed Taylor then paced with her, rocking her gently, singing the song he was pretty sure she liked. Sheila said it was just her father's voice that soothed her, but Jenner was pretty sure that Taylor, being his child, maybe had a certain affinity for Bon Jovi as well.

On one of the flipturns—the room was only five steps wide— he thought to close the wooden blinds. Because, he would hardly admit, he didn't want to have to think about the woman from downstairs standing on the roof out there, looking in. Or, no, standing in the driveway and lobbing her *head* up to second-floor height, to look in.

It was ridiculous.

Someday Jenner would tell a temp in the break room at work about it and they'd explain back an unexplainable terror they had just the same—a giant evil caterpillar humping past their window at night, a closet door that always creaked open, that darkness thick with whispering—and in this way the specter of this supposedly headless woman would recede, and then keep receding, and one day Jenner, probably with a different dog by then, might even walk back along the circle, to prove to himself that he could.

But not tonight.

Tonight he was holding Taylor close, even though she was already asleep, and, when he finally crept out of her room, he fingered three pennies up from the jar in the hall, and did that old dorm trick of jamming the pennies in between the door and its frame or jamb or whatever it's called, so that it was effectively locked, unless you knew to shoulder it hard and turn the knob at the same time.

"Druids can't be too careful..." Jenner smirked to himself on the way back down the stairs, to, hopefully, engage this surely nice and normal woman in conversation.

She was already deep into something with Sheila, though. They were sitting on the hearth together, their empty wine glasses precariously tilting from their hands.

Jenner swept in, collected Sheila's glass and opened his hand, asking this stranger *with a head that was connected to her body* if she needed a refill?

When she looked up, Jenner couldn't help it: his eyes skated down, down. He wasn't trying to sneak a peek into her blouse, he promised. He was just looking for anything... *wrong* about her neckline.

The joint was perfect, though, wasn't a joint at all. No seam, no line.

Because he hadn't seen what he'd seen.

She grinned and held her glass up, said, "Pinot?"

Jenner took her glass and leaned back to suddenly study the painting above the fireplace, which was really making a show of how much he *wasn't* looking down her blouse, but when he came back from that probably excessive display, Sheila was already holding his eyes.

She one-hundred-percent knew what was going on. Not the headlessness, or *non*-headlessness, but the fact that his standing vantage point had afforded him certain, um, views.

That was later's problem, though.

"Pinot Noir it is," Jenner said back.

The woman's name, it turned out, was Desi, which was old-fashioned like her hair, and she'd been here for thirteen years now, and this was the first solstice party she'd ever been to, she was pretty sure. And, since Jenner could think of no natural way to ask if her head ever detached as part of her nightly ablutions, he toasted her and Sheila and folded himself back into the party—his and Sheila's strategy, which they'd gone over and over, was to never be in the same talking circle, but to circulate, attend, *host*.

Thirty minutes later, which was fifteen after this celebration was supposed to have wrapped, Sheila and this Desi were still leaned into each other to—and this had to just be how it looked from across the room—*conspire*.

But surely it was actually just confiding, or commiserating, or consoling each other about the hecticness of the holiday.

Jenner toasted them in his head, glad Sheila was making a connection, and circulated, hosted, sliding stray coasters under various wine glasses, until he found himself in the driveway pointing Cassiopeia out to the Wilbanks' oldest son. Looking along the ramp his extended arm was supposed to be, launching the Wilbanks' son up into the stars, and maybe his heart too, Jenner sensed... what?

He turned, saw immediately: Desi walking through the light crust of snow on the lawn, back to her circle. She raised her fingers to him in toodle-oo, which also seemed old-fashioned to him somehow, and... so she came alone, then?

"It looks like a W," Grant Wilbanks said, about the constellation.

"It's an M from the Southern Hemisphere, I think," Jenner said back, and kept from smiling until Grant had thoroughly interrogated him with his eyes, not sure if this was a joke or not.

And so the party wound down, petered out, was a success, as these things are measured. Jenner and Sheila shared a celebratory glass of wine in the kitchen, Jenner wearing his robe with the big hood, that hood pulled over his head so he could be a real Druid, and... six days later was when the police showed back up. It was the day after Christmas.

Not one officer this time, but five or six cars.

It was about the house with the guy or son or whatever who'd had all his cars towed.

Evidently the grocery store that delivered to him every week hadn't gotten a response, and, since they were responsible for perishables until the actual person-to-person handoff, they'd called and called, and finally requested a wellness check.

It turned out—and nobody knew this until well into the new year—the guy, this son, this wannabe mechanic or hot rodder or just general car enthusiast, had been found in an upstairs room overlooking the driveway, with his severed head set neatly on an end table by his rocking chair.

Word of mouth had it that his shirt wasn't even bloody.

All Jenner could see was Desi, swishing away through the cold, back to the circle. After she made one fast stop?

All *he* could remember about that night after the party was he and Sheila on their hands and knees in the living room scrubbing up wine splashes, and then walking hand-in-hand down to their bedroom, trying so hard not to wake Taylor because this was adult time, only his bare right foot had stepped onto a peculiar coolness in the carpet.

A penny. One of three fallen there.

Jenner had let Sheila go on, had shouldered fast into his daughter's room, and for a moment she'd been standing at the jail bars of her crib, which her head usually just crested.

It was just her hands, though.

As if her neck was now a clean stump.

Jenner fell back onto his ass, something moving in waves up from his core to his awareness, and—

And Taylor was just hanging on the safety rail like the little monkey she was.

Of course.

Of course.

3.

At his desk at work the following December—no party this year, the whole block still reeling and grieving, whispering and changing the bulbs on their security lights—Jenner found himself lightly exploring the stability of his own head. Just one hand at the chin, the other at the base of his skull.

"It's just a meeting, J-man, no need to get dramatic," Kyle said from the doorway, because the crew in A/R was so hilarious.

Ha ha.

Jenner quit messing with his head, rose from his desk for the meeting he guessed he now had a chaperone for.

"Should we leave breadcrumbs so HR can find us if this goes forever?" Kyle said, ripping the bagel from his mouth carelessly enough to rain crumbs down onto the carpet.

"Them or the rats," Jenner mumbled.

"There's a difference?" Kyle asked, and Jenner did have to smile at that.

All fall, after the leaves were finished with their fanciness, Jenner had been compulsively checking the gutters. He wasn't sure for what. Or maybe he just liked being up on the ladder. It gave him a different, better-feeling angle on the street.

The car guy's house was still for sale, no surprise. The house beside it had a sign in the yard now as well. The neighborhood wasn't going downhill by any means, but last year was still close enough in the rearview that Halloween had been a desultory affair, the yard decorations more compulsory than fun. And no blood or skeletons or corpses or headstones. And every little ghost or ninja or pirate had a parent stationed on each side of them for the whole trick-or-treating journey, their digital flashbulbs flashing.

Taylor was a cute bumblebee, buzzing up this sidewalk, those stepping stones—which was cute enough, sure, but all the same, Jenner didn't think anyone would be getting nostalgic about these snapshots anytime soon. There was a pall over everything, it felt like.

Jenner had been a hero for keeping the junkyard from metastasizing, but, in retrospect, had that been the first domino? Was the last when that wellness check went south?

It had to be. What bigger, more ominous domino could there possibly be?

Well, okay: if it turned out to be one of them who'd killed the guy, if someone from the neighborhood had done it, *that* would be worse, Jenner knew.

The bad thing was, of everybody up and down the block, in all the cul-de-sacs, tucked back on the circle, even over on Maple, he was the only one who knew the tableau that had been recreated in that second story bedroom.

Well, Desi too. *Maybe.*

But now that he knew her better—Sheila and her had become tight—there was no way he had... seen what he'd seen. That wasn't even the way to say it. Better: it had been a trick of the light, the angle, the night. Maybe the moon on solstice nights cast misleading shadows—*some*thing.

It hadn't escaped him that it had been two consecutive solstices, though.

Or that the third was around the corner, was barreling in, was—

Today.

"I want my two seconds back, please," Jenner said, harnessing Winty up, which, with her squirming and barking, was no small chore.

"Be careful?" Sheila said, holding her lips lightly together in that caring way she had. It was how you hold your lips when you're watching a baby duck in a video try to get up a staircase.

"Book club tonight, right?" Jenner asked her back.

He switched his huge flashlight on and off in the foyer, and it was like a sun had sparked up between them.

"Desi's down with that thing," Sheila said, shrugging it true.

Book club was supposed to be at Desi's, her first time to host, everyone else having done it twice, Jenner was pretty sure, but this flu was taking no prisoners, didn't care about the vaccine at all, it seemed.

"Always careful," Jenner said in late reply, and leaned forward to peck Sheila on the lips like always.

Now on dog walks, everyone out with their own dogs would raise their hands to each other well before they would have before, to signal their good intentions, and show that this area was safe. No decapitators behind these bushes. No neck cutters crouched up under that eve.

Jenner had planned this to be his and Sheila's forever house, but forever was turning out to be sort of a grind. Maybe it would be better to test the market, see about getting out? If you don't see awareness of the unpleasantness at 1216 in the eyes of everyone you talk to at the mailboxes, then it's got to be easier to stop thinking about it, doesn't it?

And of course, the kids on the block had their own version of things. Their own stories. According to Ted and Cyn next door, the going creepypasta making the rounds on the playground was that the headless car guy was stalking the streets now, looking for his lost head. Or that he'd finally gotten one of his old cars running, and if you heard those pipes rounding the corner behind you, it was best not to look, because you might not see a face over the steering wheel. Or, worse, you might stick your thumb out, catch a ride with him into wherever he lived now—if you could call it "living."

Did Jenner really want Taylor growing up with that story? And what about when she finds out it started just four houses down?

Jenner hissed air through his teeth, ditched the beast of a flashlight in the package slot under their mailbox like always, to prove how unconcerned he was with the darkness, then leaned into the walk, half-wishing he'd brought sunglasses for the drain-on-the-grid Maple was again, but what can you say? Please don't care about Christmas so much, Maple? Anyway, Taylor had liked it when Sheila and he had pulled her in her little red wagon up and down it. So it was good it was there.

Say a thing enough, it's sort of true, isn't it?

What Jenner couldn't seem to *stop* saying in his head, though, was that Sheila had stayed up nearly all night last night reading the book she'd been expecting to be talking about over wine.

The flu's the flu, though. And Desi wouldn't make something like that up—she wouldn't duck her turn to host.

She wouldn't have to duck, Jenner hissed to himself. If she wanted to hide behind something, she'd just pop her head off, right?

Sheila hadn't even enjoyed the book, though, that was the thing. It had been a chore of a read. "Dr. Turgid," she called it, a play on the title more clever than anything in that mass of pages, the way she talked about it.

Now she was pacing the kitchen, Jenner knew. Pacing and staring into her phone, to track his location, his and Winty's walk.

Had she made the solstice connection? Jenner didn't think so. As far as anybody else knew, yes, 1216 probably *had* been… done in the night of their party, but one doesn't make a pattern. Really, two doesn't either. You can plot a *line* from two points, though, Jenner guessed.

Where that line pointed was here, tonight. The third solstice—fourth since they moved here, Jenner guessed. And… really? Could he have seen the woman in the black bra on the first solstice?

Surely not.

That would make each of these December 21sts dominos falling, wouldn't it?

"Don't be paranoid," Jenner told himself out loud, to stop this line of thinking, and followed Winty up the flatter of the two sidewalks towards the incandescence of Maple, the lights there bright enough for Winty to have multiple dog shadows blasting out from her, both of them in step with her.

Both of them *with* heads, too.

Jenner hated the way he was always checking for that, now. Was this going to be his life from here on out? It was like he'd allowed one little splinter of "maybe" through, and it lodged deep enough in him that it was coloring everything.

It didn't have to, though.

Was Desi faking her flu, for some obscure solstice reason?

That was the first reason to take the right, onto the circle.

The other reason was to prove to himself that he could. That he wasn't scared. Not in his own neighborhood.

Giving himself no time to reconsider, Jenner turned right at the last moment, his shadow deep enough black in front of him that he teetered for a moment before stepping into it, like doubting it would take his weight. Winty sensed the hesitation, looked back to him, but he just nodded her on, girl, let's go.

The first ordeal, like Jenner guessed he expected, was 1872, the house he'd seen the woman coming down the stairs in, once upon a more innocent time.

So you saw someone in their bra? Who cares? If she didn't want people to see her like that, then... maybe put a shirt on? Close the drapes? He was just walking his dog, hadn't been looking for trouble, didn't ask for his whole life to nudge over this direction instead of that direction.

The lights were on in that house for once, but the fast glance Jenner allowed himself didn't show him anyone behind the windows. Just a lifeless living room.

Good.

Mission almost accomplished.

Winty whined with anticipation and Jenner cast about for a cat, the usual source of her excitement.

Nothing. Just the rattle of leaves in a dry bush—raccoon, probably. Surely.

Soon enough Desi's house was rolling in around the bend.

Jenner drew his phone like a shield, buried his attention in it, then fake-fumbled it a few steps later. In reaching ahead to catch it, he managed to look over to Desi's.

It was dark like the real and actual flu. Even that top bedroom. Where he hadn't seen anything. Where he shouldn't have even been looking.

Desi was normal, Desi was good, she'd been over so many times the last year. Granted, Jenner had noticed Sheila sort of conceiving of the world differently, now that she had a close girlfriend to tell her what was what, like Desi did, but... that had to be normal. People go through stages. They change with every person they let into their lives. Nothing to worry about.

Satisfied, Jenner made the motion of sliding his phone back into his front pocket, except he was satisfied enough, apparently, that he wasn't paying attention to things—he missed his pocket, instinctually tried to kick his phone back up to keep the screen from shattering on the sidewalk.

Predictably, it clattered ahead, plunked right into a storm drain. Perfect.

Just great.

Holding Winty's leash with one hand, Jenner bellied down to reach in, fully expecting to be thrusting his whole arm into stalagmites of the worst gunk.

It was just open air.

Until something with fur brushed his forearm.

Jenner jerked his hand out desperately, hard enough to knock the tender inside of his elbow on the concrete lip and scrape the top of his hand on the underside of the sidewalk. Rationally, he knew storm drains were raccoon highways. But it's hard to be rational with your arm in the sewer at night.

Winty whimpered again, pulled, and Jenner jerked her hard, not in the mood.

At which point he saw a pair of legs beside him. Woman's legs. Yoga pants.

He looked up and up them to the hips, the torso, and he was one hundred percent in pre–wince mode about there not being a head when...

"Jen?" Desi said.

She was holding a tissue over her mouth, and had one of those wispy scarves tied over the rollers in her hair.

People still *used* those?

"Just, you know," Jenner said, cranking himself up to a standing position, "making my annual sacrifice to the gods of technology."

Desi pressed her lips together in a sort of chuckle, and when Jenner took a step toward her, she backed up, shaking her head no.

"We can't let Tay-Tay get this," she said, about her flu.

Jenner nodded, was definitely in favor of that.

"She's like me," Jenner said, knocking his knuckles twice against his sternum. "Naturally resistant."

"She is?" Desi asked oh-so-innocently, holding his eyes about that long enough that Jenner tumbled back through a montage of her and Sheila with their heads together over a thousand cups of coffee over the last year, and, when it felt like he was falling towards some inevitability he knew he couldn't face, he faked a cough to try to reset his thinking.

What was Desi trying to say, though?

Jenner fake-coughed again, turning away now and holding his hand out for Desi to give him a moment, then breathed in for the mother of all coughs, the cough that would stop this fit, but, instead of letting it out, he brought his eyes back around to Desi to see if she was buying this. Because he was supposed to be turned away to cough, she wasn't ready, was looking down the circle Jenner had just watched, and—no no no, please no—a dark slit had opened up about where her larynx should be. Maybe a quarter inch at its widest, spanning from jugular to jugular, and black and empty inside instead of red and spilling, but definitely a little horizontal slash, a distinct little fracture in reality, a narrow chasm that made Jenner *really* want to cough.

Right when that slit closed, with Desi coming back to face him, was when his phone rang. In the darkness under the sidewalk.

"Sheila," he identified, for Desi, being so sure to showcase how much his eyes were only looking down to the storm drain.

"Here," Desi said, and called Sheila herself, started to hand the phone across but then shook her head no about that, took a step farther away, her other hand clutching her shirt to her throat as if she'd felt that sudden little influx of dry December air invading her neck, her phone out like a shield, just, one on speaker.

Jenner leaned in, squinting to hear better, but—

"Can you—?" he asked, doing his right hand for more volume, please.

Desi punched it up so Jenner could hear better, but... was that even Sheila? He was pretty sure those were words, just, they were the kind of words someone makes from underwater, that pop on the surface, mean nothing.

"*Sheel?*" Jenner said, closing his eyes all the way now, to really tune his ears in.

Still the same burble, but now mixing with hisses and static and distance, as if Sheila were on the landline, had maybe walked out into the yard for an eyeline on him and Desi?

"Bad connection," Jenner told Desi, and she flipped the phone around to face him, held it to her ear, then studied him like "Are we hearing the same call?"

How could they not be?

"I'll send him home," Desi said in goodbye to Sheila, and held her phone over her stomach the way women will sometimes, like muting it.

She was waiting. It was Jenner's move in this impromptu chess game.

"Thanks," he said, his hand lifting in farewell almost like a salute—what was he *doing*? Desi toodle-oo'd him then turned to get her sick self back inside.

After she was gone, Jenner came back to the storm drain and reached in again, damn the raccoons, let whoever wants to see him being this undignified just *see* him, and from that position, his face against the curb, he saw the porch light way down at 1872 glow on.

It's those extra two seconds, the Sheila in his head joked, loving it.

Those seconds the solstice always stole each year, she meant.

Anything could happen in this slice of extra time, couldn't it?

"I do need to decompress," Jenner told himself oh-so-humorously, and clambered up as best he could, still no phone, and, telling himself anyone watching probably wouldn't be invested in which direction he'd been heading, he strolled back down the way he came, only, two houses down from the house in question, a patrol car eased onto the block, moving the kind of slow that said it was responding to a call from a concerned citizen.

Jenner sucked air in, held it, and looked down the leash to his excuse for being out here, officer: Winty. Just walking the dog, sir, anything wrong?

Except the leash was just hanging there. No Winty.

Jenner let his breath out.

The patrol car was splashing its dummy light back and forth across the street, looking for the prowler who was at it again, apparently, never mind that he was supposed to have been just a one-time-use, officer.

Shit.

Jenner took a knee to attend to his laces, which needed no tending to, and, low enough to maybe be out of sight, now, he scurried left, forced himself into a wall of bushes, his hands a cage over his face to keep his eyes from getting poked out.

The patrol car stopped in the street right beside him, its light heating up the rattly bushes he was standing in, some of that light even warming a spot on his neck, Jenner praying to every god he thought might listen.

Of course, what came next was a door creaking open, the springs of the patrol sighing up about two hundred pounds.

Now the yellow beam was tighter, twitchier: the officer's flashlight.

I'm supposed to be home already, I'm supposed to be home already, Jenner chanted in his head. Because of the garlic bread, right? Sheila had told him.

Jenner had walked back into the missing two seconds, it felt like. Back to before police officers ever included this neighborhood on their patrol. Back to before the party, earlier, earlier, to—

No, not that far, please.

Back to when Taylor was born, and so, so happily had his hair color.

You need to be here, now, he told himself. Because this was where Winty was. And coming home without the dog was going to be hell to explain.

He'd miss her too, Winty. Of course he would. That should have been first, not second.

When the patrol car finally eased away, Jenner stepped out, brushed off the yellow windbreaker Sheila insisted he wear after dark, in these dangerous times. He'd joked that it was so his corpse would be easier to find, but that wasn't so funny, now.

Winty was home already. She had to be.

Jenner should be too.

He thrust his hands in his pockets because that posture was more obviously innocent and started back the way he'd been going in the first place. It would mean passing Desi's again, and she was evidently parked at that second story window watching passersby, but screw it. This could be a funny story someday, so long as there was a "someday." As long as her head was, you know, *attached*.

Jenner hissed a laugh out, grinned a secret grin—he was being idiotic—and, instead of looking side to side like a prowler, he faced forward, only forward.

Where a tiny form was stumbling toward him.

In a flash like terror can do, he pictured Sheila still on the porch, leaning out into the street to try to see him coming, or to wave and shrug to Desi, while, while...

While Taylor toddled out, hugged the house, fell into the darkness between their place and next door, such that Sheila went back inside without her, assumed she was in the other room with her multi-colored blocks.

Really, though, she was coming to find Daddy herself on her pudgy little legs, having to run on her toes because walking was still sort of a controlled fall, at least in bare feet on a cold night, in the darkness, unfamiliar houses and lawns all around her.

But she was reaching for the one stable thing in her field of vision: Jenner.

"Tay, Tay!" Jenner called, skipping forward, ready to take a knee, but, but—

When Taylor lunged out under a flickering yellow streetlight, instead of her cute little face, what he saw was... her neck was a stump, looked like an in-process mannequin in a department store: no blood, no windpipe or spine, just more skin, sort of?

No cute little head at all.

Of course she couldn't get her balance.

Jenner fell back, looked past her when a couple of houses almost around the last of the circle flashed blue and red—the patrol car, burbling its light bar, the siren chirping almost politely.

Below Jenner's feet, then, Winty barked once, harshly, like when she was guarding the front door from delivery people—her *real* bark, the one she saved for delivery people, stranger dogs, and unusual sounds like sirens.

So she was in the storm drain too.

Wonderful.

Jenner pressed the heels of his hands hard into his eyes, starbursts popping darkly behind his lids, and when he looked ahead on the sidewalk again, at first it was just blur, but when that smeariness gained lines, the sidewalk was... just the sidewalk.

No Taylor.

Jenner's eyes were full of tears now, he realized. One of them took the emotional plunge, trailed down.

He wiped it away with the back of his hand, looked behind in case Taylor had taken to the lawns, gotten past him—kids are sneaky like that—and...

No, please.

No more.

It was the woman in the silky black slip and matching black bra.

She'd walked into the back edge of the yolky glow from the next streetlight, such that she was only visible from the chest down.

He could tell *she* had a face, though. A head.

But, whose?

Jenner's skin went cold. His arms, his back, all of it.

What if—?

No.

But: *could* it have been? Could that really have been *Sheila* he was seeing, descending that grand staircase in a pretty fetching state of dishabille? Was this why she always insisted on his nightly walks? Had she been taking walks of her *own* again? Would that explain why the Taylor he'd just not-really-seen didn't have a face? Was this his own mind whispering to him that there was no resemblance between him and her? Was that what Desi had been asking him, about Taylor being like him with the flu?

Jenner coughed for real, couldn't stop, had to cock his hands on his knees and lean over.

Finally he coughed from deep enough that he threw something up: wine. Specifically, pinot noir. Which they hadn't had in the house since having to have the carpet cleaners in after the party, because pinot's the hardest of all the wines to get out.

And of course he hadn't drank any today. He would remember that, he was pretty sure. It was—it was like the last three solstices were bleeding across to each other? The last *four*?

No.

It was that he'd stepped into his own shadow to get here, wasn't it? It was a spell, a magic formula, an accident that could only happen on the shortest day of the year? An accident that made the circle not the same circle it was the rest of the time, but something much more personal. When you step into your own darkness on a night where the borders are already weak, you can step through, and fall into yourself.

In *this* circle—this version of the circle—Jenner was the prowler, Taylor was headless, it *had* been Sheila wearing that black bra, and Desi's head wanted to Pez dispenser back.

Down with Winty, Jenner's phone rang again and Winty, alarmed, barked once at it.

"It's okay, girl," Jenner said.

It's just Mommy, calling to see when I'm coming home.

If, Jenner realized he should say.

If he was even speaking at all.

Which he wasn't.

Because he didn't want to be where he was anymore, he looked up and up, to Cassiopeia hanging on the horizon like a letter of the alphabet, one he was planning to teach to Taylor next year if not this one—you can't start too early—but then he had to bring his eyes sharply down again, to the patrol car's reverse lights.

It was making a J-turn, was coming back.

And this time it would find him, he knew.

He was the one who'd had a beef with the guy who turned up dead, wasn't he? He *had* voyeured the nice woman down the block, right? And was that *his* kid unattended out in the night, alone?

Yes, officer.

To say nothing of animal abuse.

Still, Jenner shook his head no, that he could explain this, only, his peripheral vision pulled the rest of his eyes around. To that second story window of Desi's house—where all this had started.

Her body was standing there like the first time, her head watching him from the vanity.

Her right hand came up slowly, deliberately, still holding her phone, which it positioned in front of her face so the fingers could follow the eye's orders, touch the person's face she wanted to touch.

Under the sidewalk, Jenner's phone rang, and its light filled that darkness.

Up on Desi's vanity, her mouth was saying something into his voicemail, some catastrophic tidbit Sheila had told her in confidence, so Jenner had no choice but to fall back onto someone's grass, rise from it, and run as best he could back the way he'd come, towards the insistent lights of Maple, because nothing bad could happen in a winter wonderland.

Just, one house on his left, its garage door was already open? Just a wall of yawning darkness, inkier than the rest of the night.

Headlights stabbed out from it and Jenner flinched away, fell down but scrambled up, kept going.

He couldn't ignore the exhaust leaks when that engine rumbled to life, though.

He didn't have to look back to know 1216's primered Camaro was easing out into the road behind him. Its underinflated rear tires crunched the loose gravel on the asphalt, then the car guy behind the wheel gunned it like he liked to do, the headlights throwing Jenner's shadow out so far in front of him, so there was nowhere *left* to step but into his own darkness.

It made him run faster at first, but in a house or two he slowed, just stood there, his shoulders slumped, his hands working each other in front of his gut.

Twist, pull, twist harder.

His back straightened when his left hand snapped off.

Behind it, the stump under his knuckle was dry, and there wasn't an actual hiss, like air escaping, but there was some sort of decompression, Jenner was pretty sure. And that was the least surprising of all of it.

He turned around, held his left hand up in his right to flag his ride down, and jogged out into the street when the Camaro rattled to a stop.

The long passenger door swung open for him, and Jenner stepped inside its arc, took one last look at the neighborhood he used to think he knew, and then he settled into the cupped, sprung seat, slammed the sagging door shut, and the headless driver behind the wheel gunned it again, surged them out of the circle, the twinkling lights of Maple smearing past faster and faster, and Jenner fitted his left hand back into place and held it there in his lap, just watching it, the fingers moving numbly at first, but then with feeling. When this driver put his foot all the way into it at last, the Christmas lights streaked away and the dull halogen headlights of the Camaro sucked back in, along with any remaining hope Jenner had.

Two seconds, he said in his head.

Probably less.

It was how much shorter today had been.

But, he was just realizing, didn't that also mean that this was the *longest* night of the year?

Long enough to live in, yes.

Jenner had the dim notion of applying pressure to his chin with the heel of his hand, like to pop his neck, but there would be time for that, he knew. There would be forever for that.

Instead, he slipped the wedding band off his ring finger, being careful not to tug the whole finger off, and held it out the window, let it fall like a breadcrumb.

The car's exhaust was too loud to hear the *tink* of the ring, but Jenner felt it all the same, and closed his eyes, the acceleration pinning him to the seat, Cassiopeia a monstrous letter M through the windshield, and, like that, he moved to a new neighborhood. One that went forever.

E N D

There's this one house I walk by with my dog nearly every day, and I always am thinking about it, What if somebody in that place can take their head off? *Not sure why. The house is no different from any of the other houses up and down the block. But, this one particular place, it concerns me. I always try to be on my best behavior, slipping by it on the sidewalk again. Pretty sure my dog walks a little better there, too—sort of like she's faking it, like she also feels we're being not just watched, but sort of dissected with each step.*

ALL THE PRETTY PEOPLE

Nadia Bulkin

B Y the time she'd gotten more ice into the cooler and
restocked the cans and adjusted the music per request,
Candice had almost managed to forget about Sam.

But then "Here I Go Again" came on the party playlist and she
thought of karaoke—of sharing Sam's flask and the mic and the
melody, and most of all her energy. This was the buzzy feeling
Sam used to give her, back when Sam still talked to her—the
warmth of a held hand, a shared joke. Safe like a child would
want to be. Candice sniffled over the Festivus pole; these last few
months without that lifeline had been hard.

Still, she had others, she told herself; they were in fact gathered
around her on this very night for her sixth annual Festivus
party. Eddie brought a pole he'd found on a street corner, and
helped Candice wrestle it into a planter filled with rocks. Marnie
brought the engagement ring Eddie gave her when they met up
in Madrid. Nina and Lawrence brought a bottle of their new

gin recipe, which was very floral-forward. Sheldon brought his attitude.

Alan brought his date, a huge-eyed coworker named Monica who was way too pretty for him. He left her with Candice while he went to get them drinks.

"It's nice you guys do this Festivus thing," said Monica.

Candice's voice automatically calibrated to a higher, hostess pitch. "I think so! We started it in grad school, so we could get together before everyone went home for Christmas. It's crazy how hard it gets to find time to actually see each other outside a group chat."

The very fact they'd all shown up was itself a Festivus miracle. By then, everyone in the group was at the rotten end of their twenties, when bills had started coming due and muscles had started seizing up and a creeping dread had begun to follow them to work, to happy hour, to the gym: the sense that they didn't have a lot of time left, so they'd better get going to wherever they were going. Nina and Lawrence, for example, were going to rent a warehouse in Ivy City and open their own distillery. Marnie and Eddie were going to get married as soon as her contract with Wildlife International ended and she could come back from Tanzania for good, instead of just for Christmas. Sheldon was going to Kathmandu. Alan was going to get a promotion, and hopefully a girlfriend.

Candice wasn't surprised to hear that Monica was new to the company and hadn't known Alan long. He was nice, she said, albeit too eager for her taste. "He did call me Sam a couple times," Monica said, forcing an awkward laugh. "Not like, you know... just randomly. At lunch, or whatever. I wasn't sure if she was an ex-girlfriend, or..."

Sometimes Sam seemed like Candice's own ex. An ex-friend, perhaps, who would largely ignore her messages but very occasionally send an inappropriate one-word text *(lol)* or a slew of drunken nonsense *(what else is there except this life?)*. The ex-friend who still sometimes showed as "active" on Messenger but never actually seemed to read her messages. These random bursts of life, tantalizing hints of the friendship they'd once had, were almost worse than silence. Sometimes it was easier to pretend Sam was dead.

"Oh, no. No. We just all went to grad school together. I don't think they ever…"

There was, of course, Alan's habit of standing a little too close to Sam at happy hours, of occasionally accidentally rolling his hand down her back and onto her butt. The way he used to hover over her when she talked to other guys, until he showed up uninvited to what was supposed to be girls' night at the Lame Duck Cantina and Sam had to tell him to back off.

"Sam actually dated our friend Sheldon during grad school." This was not entirely relevant—they were several years out of grad school, and Sam had no lingering feelings toward Sheldon— but it was an easy way to divert the conversation, since Candice could point to Sheldon pouting by the mantle. To be honest, she was surprised he'd shown up. He hated them for what he saw as their basic, bourgeois interests—even when trying to be nice for Sam's sake, he couldn't hide his derision when Marnie talked about conservation and Nina talked about books.

Speaking of Nina, she caught Candice's eye across the room and made a cycle motion with her finger, signaling that it was time for the Airing of Grievances.

When Candice started hosting Festivus parties, her socially conscious guests would dutifully use the Airing of Grievances to rail against toxic elements of society: Big Pharma, Big Oil, Big Tech, Big Government, Big Gun, Big Media, Big Food. Big Death, as Sheldon once summed it up. Although these screeds could be funny, they always cast an uncomfortable pall over the room, a sentiment somewhere between guilt and despair—made worse when some guests inevitably got jobs at these institutions, because everybody needed to make rent. So this year, Candice put a moratorium on Big Grievance. *Grievances should be directed toward a person you know*, she wrote in the invitation. *Remember, this is supposed to be fun ;)*

"Guys!" Candice called. "Let's air grievances!"

Before anyone inside Candice's apartment could react, there was a knock at the door. Marnie yelped, then started laughing as Eddie put his arms around her, calling her a scaredy-cat. "But seriously," Marnie said, "who else is coming?"

The answer should have been no one; they had lost several friends to the transient nature of their city and the call of the distant Virginia suburbs. And anyway, the buzzer hadn't gone off, which meant it was probably a neighbor. Surely they weren't making too much noise, Candice thought, wiping her hands on a dishtowel before moving toward the door.

Standing in the hallway with her back to the apartment was Sam. Wearing a golden puff-sleeved dress that looked totally gauche, totally extra, totally and wonderfully Sam. Candice felt her pulse tremble like a snake inside her chest and Sam spun around with a big empty smile, as if she could hear the call of Candice's wayward heart.

When Sam first ghosted her back in August, Candice had been too embarrassed to admit it to anyone. She thought Sam had finally had enough of her pathetic neediness, her always-a-beat-too-late humor, her striking lack of stories that did not revolve around her job. Maybe Sam had simply decided her time was better spent with people who could run alongside her free spirit instead of stumbling awkwardly at the back of the pack. It was only at Nina's birthday party the following month that she realized Sam had ghosted *everyone*. "Must be in one of her moods," everyone said, because Sam practiced Irish goodbyes and wandered off on nights out. It was as if she had simply been lured away by smoke from a distant hookah lounge, and would resurface when she was satiated, when she was ready to grow up.

Most of the party greeted Sam as if she, like Marnie, had merely returned from a temporary overseas gig. Candice would have expected Eddie to keep his distance out of respect for Marnie, but no—he embraced Sam as usual, wincing only a little as she dug her nails into his back. Sheldon, meanwhile, practically leapt onto her, asking her where the hell she'd been.

Candice, though—Candice froze. When Alan came back with a pair of Old Fashioneds, the sight of Sam took all the light from his eyes, too. Out of everyone in the group, Alan had been the only one whose agony over Sam's disappearance seemed to rival Candice's—probably because he had no one to fawn over anymore, but Candice still appreciated the camaraderie. And while they'd exchanged maybe three dozen texts overanalyzing their last interactions with Sam, Alan had told her recently that they would eventually have to accept that Sam had simply chosen to stop being their friend. He was sure she hadn't meant to hurt them, he said.

"Is that really her?" he whispered to Candice.

"I guess so," she whispered back, unsure of who else it would be. The invitation had gone out to everyone on the group chat, though of course Sam had not responded. Apparently she had seen it after all. "Does she seem weird to you?"

"No, she seems... fine." Sam had glided through the living room without acknowledging either of them—well, maybe she had smiled at Alan?—and now she was in the kitchen, playing with the refrigerator magnets as Sheldon kept trying to talk to her, his head dipping toward her in increasing urgency. The word "fine" plucked a raw string of hurt that Candice hadn't quite been aware of—anger, perhaps, that their estrangement didn't seem to have affected Sam at all.

Nina and Lawrence, the group's PTA parents, tried to get the party back on track by airing their harmless, vanilla grievances. Lawrence complained about Nina taking too much time in the bathroom in the mornings; Nina complained about Candice flooding the group chat with stupid videos, a grievance that drew more laughs than Candice would have liked. Eddie suggested Candice needed a boyfriend to torture, a joke that seemed to be a dig at Marnie's corny sense of humor but in truth came at Candice's expense. That was another thing she'd lost since losing Sam: another "spinster" to laugh about gender doomerism with. Being "sad and alone" hit harder when one really was sad, and alone.

Candice finished her drink and raised her voice: "Thanks, Nina. I guess I'm up, right? Good. Then this one's for Sam."

Sam had finally pulled away from Sheldon and was now staring at Eddie, not with longing but with thirst, like a hunter might gaze upon a deer. When she heard her name she rolled her eyes at Candice, so hard that Candice only saw her bone-white sclera: bulbous, strained, empty.

"Why the hell did you stop responding to my messages?" It was embarrassing, being ghosted by a friend—friends were supposed to be the easy people to keep around, the connections even kindergarteners could make—but she hoped Sam would be more embarrassed to have inflicted this kind of pain. "I sent you like, a thousand. It feels like shit, you know? I missed you."

"I'm sorry," Sam said. She stuck out her chin and her bottom lip, in a mockery of regret. From Candice's vantage point her neck looked twisted, broken. "I tried calling."

Then, and only then, Candice remembered: before Sam stopped talking to her, there had been a phone call. No, two. Two midnight phone calls at the end of a long week in August that Candice had been too tired to answer and too lazy to follow up on the next day. Deep down, Candice knew the reason she'd sent Sam "a thousand" messages since—the reason she spent September asking everyone if they'd heard from Sam—was because she'd left Sam hanging first.

Candice closed her mouth, shame churning beneath her skin. She jolted again when someone clammy grabbed her arm—it was Sheldon, trembling and covered in goosebumps like he had the DTs. "Open the door," he hissed, squeezing so hard she felt the pain all the way down in her fingers. "I need to leave."

"Okay..." Sam used to call Candice's front door a lobster trap, because it always took her at least two tries to let herself out of the apartment, regardless of her sobriety. She'd keep twisting and trying and twisting and trying... "Just turn the lock. It can be a bit fiddly..."

"I *did*. It's *stuck*."

Candice had always been mindful of Sheldon's demands, given the shortness of his fuse. But the pathetic absurdity of Sheldon's current need, so counter to the man who'd defiantly cursed out their economics professor for calling poor people a drain on society, was making it very easy for Candice to ignore him. Especially when Sam was sauntering into the center of the room, looking very clearly like she wanted to say something— dropping her mouth open, licking her lips.

"Candice, come on!"

"Okay, okay. Just wait a second."

Under the glow of the LED lamp, Sam cleared her throat. "I have a grievance too," she said.

Sam stuck out her index finger and looked around Candice's living room with an exaggerated sneakiness, like a cartoon witch looking for the party's naughtiest child. Eventually she locked onto her target, and grinned.

"Eddie..." Her voice would have been playful if it didn't sound like it had been run through a garbage disposal. "It was super rude of you to leave me alone that night at Quorum. You know I was in no shape to find my own way home."

After Marnie left for Tanzania, her geographical distance

from the group had allowed everyone a certain mythmaking when it came to Eddie's bad habits. A few forgot Marnie existed, at least on Friday nights. Several believed he and Marnie had an "understanding," a perception backed up by Marnie's avoidance of any inquiry into Eddie's activities while she was away. At this year's Festivus, however, Marnie's gaze looked hot. Heated. Maybe it was the ring on her finger.

Eddie's mouth dropped open an inch, a space he immediately filled with the rim of an IPA. "I don't remember this happening," he said after swallowing.

"You don't? Really?" Sam stepped into the center of the room, the shine of her golden dress somehow so oppressive that Lawrence and Nina were flinching, shielding their eyes. Still rapt, though. "Let me remind you. It was in the middle of August..."

Sweat pooled in Candice's palm, nearly making her drop her phone as she checked and then re-checked her call log: Sam had called her at 12:08 a.m. on August 14th. And then again, two minutes later. She bit a growing welt on the inside of her cheek.

"You begged me to come out with you, Eddie. Begged me to come."

"Just shut the fuck up, Sam."

"You got me Molly. Said you liked me nice and loose." The "ess" of loose floated like a fragrance through the room. Like Sam's favorite fragrance, thick with musk and sandalwood. "I thought you were going to take me home. But then you just disappeared on me."

As Marnie burst into tears, fiery panic licked at Candice's skin as she imagined Sam collapsed on the club floor, strung out on the sidewalk, walking crooked down that lonely strip of downtown that always emptied after midnight, and encountering... what?

"You promised!" Marnie warbled, punching Eddie's shoulder. "You promised you would stop!"

"I did! I haven't even seen her in months!"

"Oh yeah, so it's fine you tried to fuck her right before you proposed?"

"I wasn't gonna—look, maybe I wouldn't have to hang out with other people if you just came home when you were, supposed to, you know, I'm not the one who extended my contract..."

"Don't you dare throw this shit at me! Oh, and you! You!" Marnie whirled around, pointing at Nina and Lawrence. "Here's a real grievance for you. Why the fuck didn't you tell me?"

Lawrence's hands were stuffed deep in his pockets; when he shrugged, he looked like he was in a straitjacket. He had always claimed Eddie would change once bound by marriage, and children. Beside him, Nina was silent, her jaw locked up and her fingers flicking at the hem of her sweater. Nina had an aversion to Eddie that some uncharitable people in their graduate program had assumed to be jealousy, the type of disdain that disguises desire—but seeing the way she moved now, like a nervous mouse, Candice knew that wasn't the case.

"You know how he gets when he wants something," Nina muttered, and Lawrence quickly added, "You know how Sam is when she's high."

Wild child Sam. Hot mess Sam. Whoever knows with Sam.

Once again, Nina caught Candice's eyes across the room and motioned a cut across the throat: time to shut things down, before any more damage was done. But a strange thing had happened over the last fifteen minutes: Candice no longer cared about the damage done to any of them. And anyway, she was no longer in control of this party. Sam was.

Sam dropped her jaw as if to laugh, or swallow a mouse. "Well, I am so sorry to hear that," she said, "But thanks to Alan here, you'll never have to worry about me again. Will they, Alan?"

Sam sharply swiveled her head to beam at Alan, her gaze like the spotlight of a cop car. Alan retched under its gaze, then ran into the kitchen and vomited into the sink.

Candice knew as soon as he threw up that Alan was the one to blame. To blame for what, she still wasn't exactly sure—for the phone calls Sam made that night in August, for the silence that followed, for her sudden appearance tonight? Truly, Candice had been more than ready to direct her rage at Eddie; she fully believed he deserved it. But then Alan mumbled through vomit that he hadn't known Sam was on Molly, and certainty like cement settled in her gut.

"Sam called me from Quorum," Alan said after reluctantly slinking back into the living room. "She needed a ride home. I thought she was drunk, so I gave her a bottle of water, you know, and I thought everything was fine. She was so thirsty, she wanted another one. I swear I didn't know she was on Molly or I wouldn't have given her any water, I swear to God. That's why I got so confused when she started getting sick. Like, really sick, frothing at the mouth and everything. It was awful. I thought she was gonna choke. So I shook her, you know. Hard. I just... I was just trying to help her."

Candice had to turn away to keep the anger from exploding

out of her mouth, her hands. This stream of babble was all bullshit, and if their so-called friends had known Sam half as well as they should have after six years of parties and brunches and late-night cab rides home from bars, they'd have known Sam would have called her deadbeat dad before she called Alan. Gnawing her thumbnail, Candice thought back to that one night at the Lame Duck Cantina, when Sam put her finger in Alan's face and told him to *back off.*

Meanwhile, the boys kept arguing. Alan was blaming Eddie for leaving Sam while she was too high to explain what she was on. Eddie was insisting Sam was fine when he last saw her. "No, when *you* walked away!" Alan yelled. "I saw the state you left her in. Sitting there on the curb all limp. Maybe if you didn't treat everybody like a single-use tissue, none of this would have happened!"

"Shut up!" Candice snapped, whirling around. "I wanna hear from Sam." The golden girl was still standing in the middle of the room, listening to the boys' volleys whiz over her head, but she hadn't spoken since Alan puked. "Can you please tell us what happened?"

Alan covered his eyes before doubling over. "That's not Sam," he howled. "I told you, she drank a ton of water. It must have made her brain swell up. I even... I even smacked her in the face before I realized she was dead."

And in that moment—for just a moment—she was not Sam. Not the Sam they all remembered, anyway. Her flesh had receded into her bones, her golden dress hanging off her shoulders as it would have on the rack. Where she'd once had big brown eyes there were now hollow pits. Where she'd once had lips like a stretched pink heart, she was now all teeth.

The lights dimmed. In the few dozen seconds of darkness, someone—Marnie?—began to sob, saying she wanted to go home, and Candice's eyes adjusted just in time to see the silhouette of the body that had been Sam's fall like a sheet ghost without a wire.

When the electricity steadied, Sam was gone.

Candice felt faint. She batted her hands back, hoping for a wall, a pillar, a person—and found the Festivus pole instead. It was cold, slightly slick. A blunt and moderately heavy object.

The only way to end a Festivus party, according to tradition, was for the host to challenge and be bested by a guest in a feat of strength. Candice was not particularly strong, so ending parties was easy for her if she could remember not to panic. Ever since Emma Ridge's girl-gang ambushed her in fourth grade she'd had a fight reflex that had her drawing blood when she felt threatened, which was why she never challenged men. Last year she'd picked out Sam, who'd playfully bear-hugged her onto the couch, her bleach-blonde hair getting in Candice's mouth.

This year Sam was gone, and Candice had no intention of submitting. She didn't want to end the party; she wanted to destroy it. She pulled the Festivus pole out of the planter and charged Alan.

"Candice," he was saying, putting up his hands. "It was an accident."

It curdled what little pity Candice had for him. She told herself afterward that when she raised the pole in her right hand, she only meant to scare Alan—give him a taste of true mortal fear— but maybe this was delusion. Maybe her heart was uglier. Their friends screamed and ducked, but all she saw was Alan moving as if to escape and all she felt was a need to hold him down. She drove the pole toward him and pinned him against a wall before he could weasel away. *Let him go*, her friends were saying, but what had he done to Sam? Had he let her go?

Candice was not used to a position of dominance, and this one did not last long. Alan soon pushed the pole out from under his chin and shoved her with it, hard. Her feet slipped from underneath her and in her futile attempt to stay upright, her command of the pole slipped too—and then he was the tower, and she was the floor.

It was fear in his eyes, she knew it. But fear transformed people in different ways, and the trembling stones that his eyes had become were the head and tail of a battering ram.

She couldn't move. She couldn't breathe. If anyone was yelling, she couldn't hear it. Black spots like cigarette burns filled her vision as Lawrence's blurry shape struggled to pry Alan's weight off her. For all the time Lawrence spent at the gym, it took so long to free her that Candice did wonder if Alan was that much stronger than he looked or if Lawrence perhaps wasn't trying very hard.

In the full light of day, Candice could tell herself it was the former, console herself with the thought that at least now she understood the hateful determination that Sam's body had endured, even if her mind had already gone. But in the half-light, when the sky turned amber and the night-cold came rushing in, she saw another truth.

Unlike Sam, Candice would move again. She would breathe.

It wasn't until she momentarily slipped into unconsciousness that the door opened, at which point the pole came off her trachea and Alan's body came off her own and Alan ran out of the apartment. When the door latch clicked open and he walked out of the apartment, tears sprang to Candice's eyes—not because her last Festivus party had ended, not because she'd almost been choked to death, but because Sam's hold on the world was well and truly gone.

Alan did go to the police, eventually. He pled guilty to concealing a body and paid a fine of two thousand five hundred dollars, then moved away to the other Washington. On winter nights to come, Candice would sometimes look him up—always while the wind was rattling the windows, always while drinking wine—and scroll through what felt like hundreds of photos of Alan with a smiling little woman and a growing little boy. Every so often she'd hit "like," just to remind him she was there. That someone remembered.

Because everyone else committed to forgetting. They averted their eyes, wiping snot from their noses, because they no longer wanted to hear Sam's name at all. They were ready to move her into the column of things they simply did not talk about for the sake of the social peace, along with Eddie's infidelity and Lawrence's questionable stance on certain political issues. But those people hadn't laughed themselves into a state of aching delirium with Sam.

After Lawrence and Nina opened their distillery—not in Ivy City, but all the way in California—they started telling people that the woman in the gold dress who came to the Festivus party wasn't really Sam, but a lookalike playing a malicious prank. By the time Candice heard this story from a mutual grad school acquaintance, it was Sam's twin sister who'd shown up at Candice's apartment, trying to get to the bottom of Sam's disappearance by shocking her friends into admitting something. Never mind that Sam had no sister, let alone a twin.

Nina, Lawrence, Marnie, Eddie. They all left without a word. Eddie and Marnie also left without touching, though as far as Candice knew they were still together and living in Wisconsin near Marnie's parents. They didn't really keep in touch, though. It became too hard.

Sheldon spoke before leaving. "You fucking people make me sick," he said. As it so happened, he would die in a Kathmandu hostel of a virus that might not have killed him, had someone known to check on him. Maybe this was what Sam had whispered to him as he cornered her by the refrigerator: that soon he too would take that long, lonely road into the dark.

The only one who didn't trip over someone else hurrying down Candice's three flights of stairs was Monica, who helped Candice pick up plates and glasses and shovel leftovers into little plastic boxes. The whole time, Candice was imagining herself packing up Sam's room—recycling her national park posters, giving away her dresses, dragging her refinished blue desk out to the sidewalk for another passerby to pick up on the way to another house party. She imagined herself sweeping away the last traces of Sam so another lonely transplant could sit on Sam's windowsill, dragged down by the strange heaviness of a city with too much open sky.

She took a deep breath and turned to Monica. "You never got a chance to share your grievance," she said, trying to find the hostess pitch once again. "Happy to listen, if you want."

Monica sighed. "My last boss—my boss at my last company—was a piece of shit. Always saying gross stuff to me, asking me weird sex questions. I reported him to HR. They said they'd look into it. Weeks and weeks go by. Nothing happens. Come to find out they asked my coworkers to corroborate my story and none of them backed me up. They all saw what he was doing. Some of them even told me to go to HR. And then they just..." She shrugged, her voice trailing off. "I still don't know why."

Candice knew why. Because it was easier. Just like it was easier not to pick up Sam's calls that night in August, and easier not to call her back the next day—because she decided she simply didn't have the energy for whatever emotional upheaval Sam was undoubtedly experiencing, and she figured if it was really important, then Sam would reach out. It took her five days to notice she hadn't heard from Sam since a conversation about bagels the previous Friday.

"That's fucked up," was all she said to Monica, because Monica would not understand. Monica didn't know her well enough to know that these easy decisions ate at her stomach lining every time she opened her messages and saw her failed attempts to make contact with a ghost.

"Yeah. I know it is," Monica replied. And then she, too, picked up her coat and disappeared.

In the ensuing silence, Candice deep-cleaned her apartment. Not just the typical post-party wipe-up of bile and spit and half-processed vodka but a full reset, the kind of scrubbing that she would come to learn came only from profound terror. She bleached every contour of her toilet, scoured every pot and burner, bled from both hands as she did. While she was taking out her refrigerator shelves, her gaze caught on the magnet words that Sam had strung together into a burst of meaning when she floated into the apartment earlier that evening: *I lie like blood in the water / could cry but love is beating me.*

END

I chose a Festivus party because I wanted to write about the type of winter holiday gatherings I went to in my twenties in Washington, DC—secular, ironic, caught between wanting to mock tradition and wanting to recreate it. These are dress-up parties, in a lot of ways, and for me as an insecure young person they came with a lot of pressure, a lot of sadness. But at least they do tend to teach you who your real friends are.

LÖYLY SOW-NA

Josh Malerman

F OR a man who had never thought much of love, who had devoted his life instead to pursuits of personal triumph, it was quite a revelation to find himself fully across the globe, entirely unclothed, in a tight, enclosed space with the father of the woman he had finally fallen for.

There was no music opportunity here in Finland, or rather, he had not come specifically for that reason, and could not recall a time he'd been motivated by anything else. He was still a young man in his field; thirty years old being yet nascent on the piano. He'd witnessed colleagues losing their drive once they'd "settled down." In this way, he'd watched the field narrow. Not without some glee.

"Russell *Gold*?" the father asked. "Is that Jewish? My best friend is Jewish. People tell us Finnish and Jewish is a unique combination. Our respective neuroses fit well together. His guilt comes from what he has *not* done."

The older man stood naked before a large plastic barrel full of water from the lake. The sauna was made up of two rooms: the changing room, where Russell's clothes hung on wood hooks and here, the steam room itself, where the stove burned, and rocks surrounded the stovepipe. The barrel was big enough to fit inside, and Mikko reached far down to fill the bucket he held.

"Jewish, yeah," Russell said. He looked to the three benches. "Born that way anyway. I don't go much for religion. I find that in music. Where do I sit?"

Mikko set the bucket on the second bench. He spread two towels on the third.

"Up there," Mikko said. "That's where it's hottest."

Russell eyed the thermostat. Seventy-six degrees Celsius. He didn't know what that was in Fahrenheit, but he knew it was hot. Would it get much hotter?

"Music and religion serve very different purposes," Mikko said.

"Yeah," Russell said, climbing up to the third bench. He didn't feel much like talking music with someone who likely didn't know anything about it. But he was here for Hannele.

Or was he?

"The bucket of cool water is for your feet," Mikko said. "So long as your feet and your ears are cool, you can withstand most heat."

Heat. Indeed. Russell hadn't ever quite experienced it before. It smelled of cedar. A hint of menthol. He put his feet in the bucket but retracted quickly.

"Whoa, cold!"

This was the Polar Night, the Kaamos, as Hannele's mother Marjatta had dubbed it over the phone. Back when Russell and

Hannele were only toying with the idea of spending the darkest day of the year in Finland. Marjatta insisted. And how could they resist? Having passed the six-month mark, they were no longer feeling each other out: they were dating. Hadn't he considered the day would come when he'd be required to meet her parents?

Beautiful musician though she was, Hannele could only help Russell's image so much before he had to make a concession. And couldn't he find inspiration in Finland? Couldn't this *benefit* him?

Marjatta was ecstatic when they called to tell her they were coming. Russell thought then Hannele must've got her free spirit from her mother. It wasn't until he was standing naked in the lakeside sauna with Mikko that he understood two parents can contribute to a singular trait in a child.

He recalled what Hannele had said on the long flight over.

Oh, just wait 'til Dad gets you alone in the sauna. Oh, just you wait.

"You and Hannele share a bond with music," Mikko said. "I think so long as people are hearing the same song, that bond is a strong one." He was a large man with a large voice, and Russell wasn't quite sure what to make of him. Their home just up the hill was a comfortable one. But the woods, and the free-standing sauna, all spoke of people who lived more off the land than they did not. Hannele was certainly earthy, and as naturally beautiful as a snowfall, but Russell was a city man. He'd met Hannele in Detroit at an art show in a decidedly unartistic space. He'd followed the curious, quirky violin music to the woman who played it. Hannele's blonde hair hung to the black sleeves of her long dress. She played what Russell considered "experimental" music, standing alone by a large painting of what looked like a nose. She was smiling as she played, her green eyes bright, and he was taken by that smile. Had he himself ever looked so happy playing piano? Was there a secret here, in this woman? A thing to be coveted?

Something that could benefit *him?*

"Hannele's the first Finnish person I've ever met," he said, looking for a way to bond. But Mikko had other ideas, as he handed Russell a can of Olvi beer and opened one for himself. He dunked the second bucket into the cold water.

"Lot of Finns in the Upper Peninsula," he said. He set the bucket further down the second bench.

"You know about the U.P.?" Russell asked.

Mikko laughed. "Of course. Hannele's lived in Michigan since she was eighteen. We've been up there. Have you not?"

It wasn't the first sense Russell got he was being evaluated, possibly even interviewed, since their arrival. He'd readied himself for just such a thing.

"Of course," he said. "But Marquette is some four hundred miles from Detroit. So, I haven't been since I was a teenager."

"You ought to play music up there," Mikko said. "Finns make an honest audience."

Russell laughed. "But who wants that?" he joked.

But was he joking? And did Mikko perhaps catch he was not?

He checked the thermostat. Seventy-nine Celsius now. It felt hotter. Some sweat at his brow and on his body. He'd watched Mikko in the adjoining room when the older man carried in pieces of wood for the stove. Hannele had told Russell how much her father loved chopping that wood. By the light of a string of holiday lights, Russell had seen the cottage Mikko and Marjatta called home, the sauna nearly flush to the large, cold lake, and the wood pile, too, where it looked as if the wood got older, darker, the further the pile stretched toward the water.

Now, eyeing the smooth stones arranged around the stovepipe, Russell knew that very wood was heating this room.

"Getting hotter in here," Russell said.

"I should've started it hours before you landed," Mikko said. "But I thought you'd like to see how it's done."

There was a trace of Hannele's voice in her father's Finnish accent. Russell thought of quick trills north of the middle C.

This was a nice thought. Felt like he was getting something out of Finland already. Something for *him*.

"I gotta admit," Russell said. "I know nothing about saunas."

"You didn't need to tell me that," Mikko said. "I can tell by the way you stood covering your privates."

The older man laughed. Russell did, too. But was he so obvious? What else could Mikko determine about Russell without him knowing?

"The sauna is a special place," Mikko said. "People get married in here. People give birth in here. People die and part of their funeral ceremony takes place in here." He eyed his spot on the third bench, then said, "I'm going to add a little wood first."

He exited through the strong wood door. Russell was alone with the rising heat. He could hear the man out on the sauna porch, then no more footsteps. He must be over by the firewood then. Russell's mind wandered to where it most often went. He imagined himself interviewed, his hair perfect, his clothes styled by someone smarter than him. He thought how worldly it would sound to mention Finland in an interview. If he could come up with a little melody now, he could always cite this trip as his inspiration. Maybe he'd write a piece about December in Finland. The darkest day of the year.

He liked these thoughts. He relished them. And, lost in them, it took him a second to recognize Mikko's face in the small window beside the sauna door. The older man was back.

"This'll get us where we want to go," Mikko said, re-entering the hot room. The wood he held was black.

Russell, understanding more heat was coming, eyed the thermostat. Eighty-two Celsius. Real hot now.

"Keep your feet in that bucket," Mikko said as he added the dark wood to the stove. "Soon you may want to pour it over your head."

He climbed to the third bench at last and took his seat on the second towel.

"Are you ready?" he asked.

"For what?"

"Now we throw steam. Breathing in through the nose and out through the mouth helps."

He dunked a small pan into the bucket at his feet. He tossed the water onto the smooth rocks.

The hiss surprised Russell. And a distant smell, too.

"Gamey," he said. But Mikko didn't seem to hear him.

"You see the steam? Curling up at the ceiling? Coming toward us?"

The wave was hot. Real hot. Russell thought it might be too much for him.

Mikko dunked the pan again. Tossed more water on the stones.

Russell didn't think he'd be able to handle a second wave. The first hadn't faded yet. He steeled himself. Felt it first in his shoulders, then everywhere at once. Tiny, thin needles of heat. He considered getting up, leaving the sauna.

He glanced over at Mikko and saw the older man hunched, elbows on his knees, staring ahead. Or was he? Russell couldn't be sure. The steam, like a blanket, a sheet between them...

Then the heat gave a little. Russell could breathe free again.

"Holy shit," he said. "That was the real deal, huh?"

Mikko looked to the thermostat.

"Not quite that yet," Mikko said. "You'll see."

How long did Hannele hope he'd stay in here with her father?

"Hannele says you hunt," Russell said. What else to say? Russell didn't hunt. Had never held a gun. He thought then of writing a piece called "The Hunter." Imagined interviewing for it.

"Aye," Mikko said. "Reindeer."

"What?"

Mikko smiled.

"Yes. But demons, too."

Russell laughed. Hannele's father was interesting, that was for sure. First night meeting his daughter's boyfriend and here he was naked, drinking beer, talking about hunting—

"Wood demons," Mikko said. He tossed another pan full of water on the stones before Russell had a chance to speak.

Russell braced himself, gripped the bench. Mikko tossed another. And another. And—

"I don't know if I can handle—"

"In through the nose, out through the mouth," Mikko said. "Here."

Russell took the pan handed him just as the needles of heat reached him. He scooped up the cold water and dumped it over his head.

"One more steam and then we'll do it," Mikko said.

"Do what?" Russell said. But it was hard to get the two words out. Mikko took the pan back and tossed another load on the stones. Then another.

Russell thought he might suffocate.

"Ready?" Mikko said.

Russell couldn't speak to answer. But the older man was up and leaving the room and Russell followed him out through the changing room, onto the sauna porch. Was that it then? Was Russell free to head to the cottage?

Mikko took the wooden steps down to the dock.

"Come on, *hurry*," Mikko said. He yelled it. "Before you lose the sauna!"

Russell couldn't believe what was being suggested. While it wasn't freezing outside, the thought of that water on the darkest day of the year sounded mad.

Mikko dove off the end of the dock, vanished into the dark lake. Russell looked to the cottage. Hard to see up the hill. Was Hannele in the window? Marjatta? Was Russell really supposed to—

"*Come on!*" Mikko yelled.

Russell took the steps down, ran the length of the dock, imagined his entire body seizing up if he were to leap into the water. Imagined dying out here without having done a single interview about his experience. Then...

He leapt.

And the relief he felt, in every pore, shocked him more than any temperature could have.

He exploded up out of the water, thoughts of a world-famous piece about Finland on his mind. He could taste the champagne, sharing glasses with the Detroit Symphony Orchestra back home.

"This is *amazing!*" he said. But Mikko was already near shore again, climbing up and out, heading for the dark woodpile by the side of the free-standing sauna.

Russell went under again. It had to be the coldest water he'd ever swam in. And it felt fantastic. Felt like the water was doing something for him. Revitalizing. Rejuvenating.

Inspiring.

But... not for long. As the true cold of it started to seep in, as the heat from the sauna began to fade, he headed toward shore. Up on the porch, Mikko was carrying more black wood into the sauna for the stove.

"Wait," Russell said. "We go back in now?"

"Of course," Mikko said. Naked up there. Black wood in hand. "That's the way it's done. Back and forth, back and forth. Didn't Hannele teach you this?"

Russell looked to the cottage again. He couldn't see anybody in a window. Did Hannele expect him to do this all night? Was it all a test? The father of the girlfriend, testing Russell's endurance? He hadn't agreed to *that.*

"Come," Mikko said. "We've only begun."

Russell bounded up the steps and followed Mikko through the changing room. But when he entered the steam, he had to step back.

It was a wall of heat. And the smell. Stronger now.

Gamey.

"Hurry so I can close the door," Mikko said. "We don't want to lose any heat."

Russell stepped inside.

"It's all about the internal," Mikko said. "All about what's inside."

Russell breathed in through his nose, out through his mouth. Could he take another round?

He climbed to the towel on the third bench. Mikko was already there.

"A wood demon," Mikko said.

"What?"

But the older man scooped up some water in the small pan and tossed it on the stones. Russell thought he'd be more used to it this time.

He wasn't.

The smell had become something closer to a stench. He imagined a gutted reindeer seated at the piano. Imagined hooves upon the black and white keys.

"Do you smell that?" he asked. Because he had to. But Mikko didn't answer. He scooped more water and tossed it on the rocks.

Did Mikko speak then? Did he say *wood demon* again?

Russell went quiet. Hannele had mentioned how her parents were into Finnish folklore. The pride with which they told stories. She mentioned myths, in the days leading up to the flight and on the flight itself, but Russell had been thinking of the piano then. He'd been making a list of the pieces he might put together for an album. He was so close to playing with the Detroit Symphony

Orchestra. And if he could just keep his priorities in order
between now and then—

The wave of steam struck him, and he moved a bench lower
before he decided to. It didn't just sting like needles. It felt like
steel spider legs, crawling up his arms and legs, up his back, up
the back of his head and into his hair.

Russell smacked at the back of his head. But the steam was
more bearable on the lower bench, and he turned to face Mikko.
The older man's face was obscured by dark steam, only his white
hair still visible.

"Come back up here," Mikko said. His voice emerged from
the steam like a distended sound, prerecorded, like it could have
been spoken with nobody there. "Come back up and we'll jump
in the lake together again."

Russell stood up. His head and shoulders entered that hot
upper level of steam, and he ducked as he retook his seat on the
third bench.

"What are your motivations?" Mikko asked.

Russell, still trying to get his bearings, still worried about that
smell, turned to the old man and saw only his green eyes in the
dark mist.

"My what?"

"What are your motivations?"

The older man dunked the pan into the foot bucket and tossed
fresh water on the stones. Russell wanted to tell him not to do it.
He couldn't handle another round. But Mikko's question: Russell
felt nailed to the bench. For, who could answer such a question by
fleeing? Escaping even one bench away?

"I want to make great music," Russell said. He nearly yelled the last word as the dark steam curled under the sauna ceiling, engulfed the green eyes facing him, reached Russell in full. If it was spiders before, it was scorpions now. Russell thought of the endless darkness he and Hannele had driven through from the airport.

What are your motivations?

And why did it feel like he'd lied with the answer he'd given?

He thought of that woodpile, illuminated under the holiday lights, and how it grew darker the closer it got to the lake.

"Why?" Mikko asked.

His voice was distended, again. Russell looked to the small window that showed the changing room, but the steam obscured it in full.

"Because..." Russell started. But it was getting harder to talk. Thoughts. New thoughts. Thoughts he hadn't quite had before. Why indeed did he want to make music?

"The wood demons are so truly evil," Mikko said suddenly. "They're hard to hunt. They stand still just long enough to tease. You line up your shot, sure of yourself. Then, as you pull the trigger, they move. They're gone. And you find them again, easily enough. And you believe you have another clean shot. But you don't. You only get so many of those in your lifetime."

Russell was too hot to make sense of these words. He wanted to play along. Wanted to say something witty. But he was stuck on the question.

What are your motivations...

And so, what were they? In the layers of dark steam he saw himself seated at a piano, a breathless, sold out theater. He saw, too, a second man at a piano at home, playing the same song.

Yes. The exact same song! The steam like a stage, the backdrop of that stage, and curtains parting, too.

Then... it faded.

"Did you see that?" Russell asked.

Because it really did seem as if the vision was real.

Mikko tossed another panful on the stones. Then another.

"Hey, wait," Russell said.

"The opposite of evil is not good," Mikko said. "It is *honesty*."

The older man's profile showed, a moment's reveal, before the rising steam swallowed him again.

"A few seconds longer and we'll do it," Mikko said.

Russell could barely stand it. The heat. The smell. And these thoughts...

The vision in the steam returned. Russell signing autographs, taking pictures with fans. The other man worked at his upright at home, loose papers beside him on the bench.

"Truth serum," Mikko said. "The bones of a wood demon..."

Russell jumped at sudden movement to his right. A quick shadow in the dark. Then the sauna door opened, and he saw it was Mikko, exiting again.

Russell followed him out.

Mikko hurried down the steps and ran the length of the dock. He dove into the lake. Russell went too and thought he heard a voice from the sauna behind him as he leapt. He sank into the cold, wonderful water.

First thing he did when he came up was look to the sauna porch.

Had he heard something?

Mikko was submerged to his nose. His eyes on Russell.

Then Mikko went under. And it felt to Russell like he was alone with the lake, the sauna, the lodge, Polar Night, the stars, Finland.

What are your motivations?

He didn't like this question. Didn't like it at all.

Above the sauna chimney, ghostly movement, a misty film rippling in the cold. It was the smoke from the stove, Russell understood. And it, too, was dark.

He heard Mikko by the woodpile. The old, naked man, taking two more blocks.

When had Mikko got out of the water?

Russell stepped fast, splitting the water with outstretched hands.

"Come on," Mikko called from the porch. "Round three."

Russell got out of the water and looked back. When did Mikko leave the water?

"Coming," Russell said.

But what he thought was: *honesty.*

Truth.

What are your motivations?

Out of the water, up the steps, back onto the porch. Through the open door, he saw Mikko placing the fresh blocks of wood into the stove. Did the older man talk to them as he did? And was his tone one of anger? Hannele had used Finnish around the apartment before. She'd tried to teach him some. Was this that? Was her father scolding the blackened wood?

Mikko looked over his shoulder.

"Don't just stand there," the older man said. "You can't let the hot get too cold or the cold get too much colder. Round three."

Russell looked up to the cottage. Nobody there that he could see.

He stepped through the changing room and past Mikko to the benches.

"Refill the buckets," Mikko said, taking his place on the third bench. "Now we've got started."

The thermostat was in the red.

Russell took the first bucket, hot to the touch, and dunked it in the cold barrel. He set it before Mikko. Then he did the same with his own and sat on the hot towel.

"Pay attention," Mikko said. He drank from his beer. In his other hand was what looked like a bundle of old lettuce. Russell was already sweating hard. He feared what was to come. "The sauna is a place of honesty. Do you know how to find the truth about yourself?"

Russell thought. What was there to say? What kind of question was this?

"This is the vihta," Mikko said. He held up the bundle of lettuce. It wasn't lettuce. "You whip your muscles in the sauna. To relax them."

Russell eyed the bundle.

"Birch twigs," Mikko said. "Usually."

They didn't look like twigs. Looked more like bones. Thin bones with polished knobs on their ends.

Mikko dipped the pan into the foot bucket.

"Hang on," Russell said. "I don't know if I can handle another round of that steam. I'm sorry, Mikko. I'm new to this, is all."

"I don't want to steam you out," Mikko said.

"Thanks. Yeah. I think it's good how it is. For me. I'm sweating up a storm. Are Hannele and Marjatta coming down?"

"One more round," Mikko said. "But try it my way. Here."

He tossed the water on the stones. Black steam rose to the sauna ceiling.

"Hey," Russell said.

But Mikko was already scooping cold water, pouring it over Russell's head.

"In through the nose, out through the mouth."

He took Russell by the ear.

"Hot," Mikko said. He dumped more cool water over Russell's head. But the steam had arrived. Spiders, scorpions, fingertips...

Russell turned quick. Had Mikko touched his back? Yes. But no. He'd whipped his back with the vihta.

"Hey," Russell said. But it was hard to keep his eyes open. Hard to talk. The black steam. He could only see parts of Mikko. Someone threw water on the rocks.

"Hey," Russell said. "Who's there? Hannele?"

Because Mikko was using both hands. Both on the vihta. Yes. Russell could see that.

"Who's there?"

He made to get up, but Mikko whipped his back again.

"What do you want with my daughter?" the older man asked.

"What? Hey, I need to get out of here. I'm sorry, I—"

"What do you want with my daughter?"

It wasn't that the whip hurt. Hannele had told him about the vihta. She'd laughed about it. Russell getting whipped in a sauna in Finland. The idea was preposterous. But it's what they did here. It's how her parents lived. It's how Hannele herself was raised. No, it wasn't the pain of it.

The steam enveloped Mikko whole.

Russell got up. He stepped down a bench, another, almost fell, found balance on the lowest one. It was cooler down here but no easier to see. And the smell. Of meat. Of fur. Burning.

"I'm gonna step outside," Russell said. "I gotta get out of here."

He stepped down, carefully, expecting to feel the concrete floor of the sauna. He found another bench instead.

Russell stepped carefully again. But there was only more wood.

Then again. Another bench.

Another.

How many benches were in here? Three, right?

"What are your motivations?" Mikko asked.

Russell turned, looked up. How deep was he? How far down into the sauna?

Water tossed onto the stones again. A hissing eruption.

"No, no," Russell said. "Honestly, I'm overheating. My mind is playing tricks. I feel fucked up."

He stepped down onto another bench. Another.

Another.

More water on the rocks.

What are your motivations?

That gamey smell. Russell saw visions of two piano players swirling in the thick steam. Saw the woodpile. Black wood.

Wood demons...

Hard to hunt...

"Come on, come on."

He stepped again, missed the next bench, fell forward, and—

"Got you," Mikko said.

Mikko held Russell's arm with one hand, the door open with the other.

"Let's do it," Mikko said.

Russell, wide-eyed now, watched the older man step through the changing room and onto the sauna porch. Russell followed. At the top of the steps, he looked back. To the window where, beyond, black steam swirled and orange rocks glowed in the sauna.

"*Come on!*" Mikko called.

Russell heard the splash. He walked to the end of the porch for a better look at the cottage. A light on upstairs? Maybe. He heard giggling. He turned fast.

Hannele was on the porch, a foot from his nose.

"Boo," she said.

"Jesus!" Russell said. "You just freaked the hell out of me!"

"How goes it?" she asked. "I brought you some water in case Dad was only giving you beer."

She held out the glass for him.

"Hannele!" Mikko called from the lake. "He's gotta jump in before he gets too cold!"

"Okay," Hannele said. "Go on! Jump in the water. Have you done it yet?"

"Yeah," Russell said. He was out of breath. The smell was gone. *What do you want with my daughter?* "It's crazy in there," he said.

Hannele's smile was tempered. "It can be," she said. "Hurry up, though. You don't wanna lose the sauna."

Russell took the steps, walked to the end of the dock. He didn't see Mikko out there anywhere. Was he under? He looked back to the porch. Hannele smiled, waved.

Russell jumped in.

What are your motivations?

The water felt just as good as it had the first time. Exhilarating. Cleansing. His head cleared up within seconds. By the time he came out, he wondered if he'd been overreacting.

Still… those questions remained.

What *did* he want with Mikko's daughter? What *was* he doing here, across the globe, with this woman who stood on the sauna porch? Hannele was happy to see him hanging out with her Finnish father. But what made Russell happy?

"Round four," Mikko said.

"Oh wow," Hannele said. "You guys are already on round four?"

The man was by the wood pile. Still naked. Reaching for the black wood.

"No, no," Russell laughed. "I'm done. But thank you. I really did like it. One day I'll look back and—"

"Oh, come on!" Hannele said. "You gotta go the full four rounds with Dad. You gotta!"

Russell stood to his waist in the cold water. The darkest day of the year. Finland. Deep December. Holidays upon them.

He'd never felt so far from home.

But it wasn't quite that. And an unsettling thought came fast: *You've never felt so exposed.*

Naked? Yes, but more. Something about the smell. The questions.

He did not want to go back into the sauna.

Mikko carried the wood into the changing room, then vanished beyond the strong, wood door, into the steam.

"One more round," Hannele said. She winked and Russell felt colder. He'd been out here too long. He knew now: you got hot inside the sauna, you jumped in the water, back and forth. There was a rhythm to it. Just like playing the piano. You had to find the right hand/left hand. The right hand was the water: melody, trills, moonlight reflecting off a dark Finnish lake. But the left hand *supported* those melodies. The left was the rich quilt upon which the music slept. The right hand was what you told other people, how you presented yourself. The left was the subconscious. Who you really were. Who—

"Round four," Mikko said.

He was standing on the porch again.

"Alright," Russell said. But why? Why return to that room? "Are you going to join us?" He asked Hannele.

"No way. I don't need to sit with my gross naked dad."

Mikko eyed Russell from behind her. As if he and Russell had a secret, were in the middle of a journey, and hadn't quite finished what they started.

At the porch, Russell took the glass of water. He drank quick.

"There," Hannele said. "I'll see you up at the cottage. After the grand finale."

The sauna as stage. The sauna as theater. Russell recalled the swirling steam, the two piano players within. One, obsessed with fame. The other with expression.

Hannele held up a hand for him to slap her five. He did.

"Good luck..."

Did she say that?

"Come on," Mikko said. He handed Russell a fresh can of beer from a cooler in the changing room.

Russell followed him back into the sauna.

The heat now, without any steam, was greater than when Mikko had thrown steam the first time around. Russell breathed in through his nose, out through his mouth. He could stand one more round. Yes. Okay. Fine. One more, then the lake. Four rounds with Mikko. He could do this.

Mikko set fresh buckets of cold water on the second bench. Only three benches in here. If Russell felt too crazy, he'd just get up and leave. Nothing to it. This was a vacation. Or something like it. He shouldn't feel trapped. Shouldn't feel—

"Exposed," Mikko said.

"What?"

"Did you not hear me? I was talking of the wood demons. Detectives would do well by caging a few. Truth serum. Greater than any lie-detector. You put a man in the same room as a wood demon and the man cannot lie."

Russell looked to the barrel of cold water. To the stovepipe rising from the smooth stones.

Mikko laughed.

"You think I would let a living wood demon free in my sauna? Come, sit."

Russell climbed the benches. He sat on the towel. The fabric was near scalding now. But he was doing it. And he could leave. If he had to.

The thermostat was as high as it could go.

"*This* is a sauna," Mikko said.

He tossed water on the stones.

Russell tried to remain upright. And the word *upright* reminded him of the player at the upright, not the grand; the player who worked tirelessly in his apartment, for the love of the music.

"It's in their blood," Mikko said. "In their bones. And their bones burn. And you can sauna to their bones..."

He tossed more water on the stones.

The steam was black, obscuring the door, the window, Mikko, the benches, Russell's own legs and feet. Still, he was able to put his feet into the bucket. These were not spider legs or scorpion legs or even fingertips or bones upon his shoulders and neck now. These were teeth. Teeth of the heat. Biting him, all of him, at once.

"Tell me, Russell," Mikko said. "Who are you?"

Russell breathed in through his nose, out through his mouth. It sounded like Mikko. Maybe. It smelled like something from the woods. Something that didn't exist in Michigan. Something that, if Russell smelled it on the street near home, he'd turn the other way. And if he'd smelled it in the woods, he'd have considered himself dead.

Who are you?

These questions. They were too much. Or should have been too much. But Russell thought he understood now. The steam like a key into the lock, behind which he kept the truth of the matter, all matters. The black steam and the gamey stench like giant green eyes, the moon and the sun both in Finnish sky.

"I saw your daughter playing violin at an art show. She was so beautiful. A musician. I thought she'd look good on my arm. I thought she'd help my career."

Through the steam, Russell saw a shape squatting upon the stones. It pissed upon them, and the steam rose black, curled up and along the ceiling, came toward him. In it, an image of himself, all smile and sparkle, a faceless beauty by his side.

"I think only of myself," he said. "My career. What Hannele can do for *me*."

He was saying it. Just *saying* it to her father.

More piss on the stones. Breathing from the stovepipe. Russell wanted to cover his nose, his mouth, avoid the smell, but he couldn't. He had to breathe in, breathe out, even as the teeth of the heat sank into his body.

"I don't care about the piano at all," he said. The steam, so dense now. "I never have."

He stood up and his head did not touch the wood ceiling. He felt no bench beneath him.

"It's just something I'm good at. I memorize it. I play. People cheer. The piano, for me, is attention. The piano can be fame."

What are your motivations?

Russell knew them well. They'd propelled his every decision for as long as he could remember.

"I have no interest in love. Family. Even friends."

Tears then. Rendered boiling by the black steam.

"What's the wood made of?" he asked Mikko.

But was Mikko still here? Had the older man walked naked into the darkness, leaving Russell alone with whatever squatted upon the stones?

"Bones," Mikko said. "Of the beast. I cannot lie in here any more than you can."

Russell saw nothing in the blackness. No musicians, no Mikko. He felt for the bench, to sit again, but felt none there.

The sound then of steam rising, without any water to command it.

"I'm empty inside," Russell said. "Hollow. I have no good intentions. No hopes to help anyone but myself. I'm a leech. I leech off the people who listen to me and I leech off your daughter. I only wanted a beautiful musician by my side so I could tell people I had a beautiful musician by my side."

Breathing then, close to Russell's ear. And the swish of a whip through the air.

Whatever struck him, it was not the vihta. It was not for the relaxing of his muscles.

Russell cried out and fell to one knee. But upon what? Not wood.

A forest floor, perhaps. Russell out in the woods now, perhaps. And behind him—

A second slash, as fresh steam rose.

"I'm selfish," Russell said. "Everything I do is for *me*. Not even the music is for anyone but *me*."

Another slash. Was he bleeding? He felt blood upon his back. Breathing by his ear.

"I don't know how to change," he cried.

"You want to change?"

Mikko's voice?

"Yes. *Yes*. I want to be something real for Hannele. For the world."

"By the bones of the wood demon, burning bright, you want to change..."

"I do. I do..."

Steam so thick it gripped him, like fingers upon his neck, his chin, forcing open his mouth, then *into* his mouth, over his teeth, down his throat.

Russell was going to die in here. Round four. *Just wait 'til Dad gets you alone in the sauna.* He tried to pry away the fingers. It was all steam, only steam, and he couldn't hold it, couldn't touch it, couldn't—

"What are your motivations?"

He couldn't talk. He'd failed. He'd flown to Finland with Hannele, hopes of bringing home some melody that might make him famous. Never a thought of her, *Hannele* with her family, *Hannele* coming home, the happiness *Hannele* might feel.

"What are your motivations?"

Not Mikko's voice now. Couldn't be. Far too deep. No Finnish accent. No fatherly accent. No man at all. Russell choked. The steam, the stench, the piss, the bones—all filling him up, his body, his mind.

How can I change...

He died then. He believed it. A man cannot change if a man cannot breathe. He fell backward, toward the forest floor, arms crossed upon his chest, eyes closed, he fell, back, back, into the steam, into the darkness, into the—

Water.

The sound of the splash woke him before the cold lake did. He was under quick, water up his nose, water in his open eyes.

He scrambled and broke the surface, gulping for air.

Mikko was just stepping onto shore, Marjatta handing him a towel, the sky a steamy ceiling.

"You did it!" Hannele called from the porch. The moon sparkled in her green eyes. A vitality he wanted to see there always.

"I did it," Russell said. The reality of the water, the moment, upon him.

He went under again, came up. He threaded the lake back to shore. Hannele had a towel for him, too.

"You've successfully been naked with my dad," she said. Russell watched her mouth laugh, her eyes laugh. He took her in his arms for a hug.

"You're cold!" she said.

"And now we know each other," Mikko called. "And now we begin a real relationship. Now we begin to share this life."

"Your dad," Russell said, "he must think I'm a monster. I *am* a—"

Hannele put a finger to his lips.

"He told me he likes you a lot," she said. "He said you have hyvä in you. *Good* in you, Russell."

Russell watched her parents pass the woodpile. He eyed the closest, darkest logs.

"Bones," he said.

"Come on," Hannele said. "Let's go play cards."

"Bones..."

Hannele told me you're a hunter?

You think I would let a living wood demon free in my sauna?

"Yes," Russell said. "Cards..."

They started toward the cottage.

"And now we celebrate the holiday!" Mikko called from ahead. "Now that we are clean!"

"Did you come up with any good melodies in the sauna?" Hannele asked.

"Me? No. I can't... No. I don't care about that right now."

"I get some of my best ones in there," she said. "When we met? I was playing one I'd been calling 'Wood Imp.' That's why it went all over the place. That's why it sounded experimental. Because a loose wood imp is like a loose ferret. A loose hyena. It goes in every direction at once and you have no choice but to let it be what it is. And people say you have to be what *you* are when you're near one."

"Wood imp..."

"Dad calls them demons. But what kind of demon gives you truth? What kind of demon does *that?*"

Russell eyed the wood as they passed the pile.

Bones. From here. No question. Whether reindeer or something else...

"Thank you for bringing me here, Hannele."

"Oh, I knew you'd love it. How could you not? It's the kind of place that teaches you what's important. And it lets you know you still have time to learn that. You always have time to learn."

END

I hadn't ever hung out regularly with a Finnish person until I met Allison Laakko, my fiancée. We've been together almost eleven years now and, as you can imagine, I'm close as can be with her family. Her parents are nearly one hundred percent Finnish and they one hundred percent live that way. They own a lodge they call The Huvila, deep in Michigan's Upper Peninsula. The Huvila features a freestanding sauna right up against the lake. The first time I ran from the sauna to the lake I thought it had to be madness. Had to be too cold to handle, right? But no. It's glory. And it's something I look forward to, deeply, every year now, spending time with Allison's family in the closest thing America has to Finland, i.e. the deep U.P.

COLD

Cassandra Khaw

THE cold no longer troubled her after her eighth year in this distant point of Quebec. There were days when she thought about leaving, packing her scant belongings and beginning a pilgrimage to somewhere warmer. Anywhere warmer. She was tired – *exhausted,* really, because how could she be anything else under these conditions – of being cold. Of how the ice jewelled every eyelash, how her breath stung with every inhale, and how the cold blazed in her lungs like a flame that wouldn't light. Half her endless fatigue was because she was human and humans loved their comforts, and half was because she'd somehow become old enough to remember being warm. Remember how easy it was to dream about the summer and its lazy, late-evening light. She remembered wine. And parks. And lying on the grass as fireworks burst over Hell Gate Bridge. (And telling people why such a bucolic construction had such an utterly metal

271

name. She recalled those exchanges in particular with heart-shattering clarity.)

The problem with leaving was there wasn't anywhere to go. The problem was the world was gone.

Oh, the radio chatter insisted there were still enclaves out there, encysting the continent. Montreal barely took note of the apocalypse; most of its survivors simply migrated to its underground city, repurposing twenty miles of shopping and subway stations for dormitories and hydroponic farms. Oklahoma City was increasing in popularity even though the trek there was a slow death, played out over weeks of agonising travel: disease riddled the roads there. Butte, Havre, the Greenbrier Bunker in West Virginia, even Albany's Empire State Plaza were alive too, although they were all ferociously guarded and lethal to refugees; prions mattered a lot less at the end of everything. (Starvation made disease someone else's problem.)

But what was the point? Their rations would run out. The power would go. Already, there was apocrypha of how Washington guttered to a cannibalistic orgy, how every living thing in the reclaimed cities of Cappadocia bit their tongues and swallowed them at the same time so they'd die and not have to worry about stranding their beloveds on the wrong side of existence. She'd seen one world, the one that had avocado toast and cable TV, cats in frilly skirts and bodegas, daydreams and the certainty there'd always be another summer, another year to waste, end already. It had died slowly, by degrees, choking wetly on denial of its circumstances. She knew how it really went: not with a bang, but with a bitten-down, drawn-out howl. This earth was as dead as dead could be. What they were experiencing now was an extended death gurgle.

Even if it wasn't, she had a responsibility here to keep.

She was a girl when the saint collapsed at her door, which is how all such stories begin. At that time, she'd been fourteen and the saint four thousand, but no passer-by would have been able to tell there was any gap between them wider than a few weeks. Her mother might have, but the woman was gone, eaten by cancer.

"Help me," said the girl at her threshold, a white hand raised up like a votive.

And she had said *yes* then, because her mother taught her kindness but not fear, *yes* because it was dark and it was too cold to worry about the risks strangers meant, *yes* because she could see where the girl's skin had blued, because she had a sister once, because her sister had said help and no one had listened.

"How?" she said, already gathering the saint inside. Cote-de-Neiges glowed with the blizzard, blinding even in the dark.

"Let me sleep," said the saint. "Let me rest. Let me close my eyes in a place you know to be safe. Let me dream through the Imbolc to the first breath of spring. Let me rest. My girl, let me rest. The world is so much to carry. Please, will you let me sleep?"

And of course, she said *yes*.

She drained the last of her coffee, savouring the bitterness, even the grounds. When the cup had been emptied, she ran a finger along the white plastic base, dabbing her tongue with what drops remained: there would be no more in the morning, or any morning after. But she didn't mind. There was a last time for everything. Even coffee, even love. She was old enough now to know this, older than she thought she had courage for.

Candlelight twitched and glowed at the windows, the glass webbed with spokes of frost. It made her think of Christmas and how supermarkets once carried a veritable parade of winter ornaments, sparkly and kitsch, a dollar or less for each if you were frugal or had children (furless or otherwise) and were happy with cheap plastic. The celebration hadn't excited her then, having grown up far – she was just old enough to remember her parents' country, if only as watercolour blots – from where they were anything but a novelty. Now, however, she found herself nostalgic for the pageantry.

Especially today, with the cabin feeling so peculiarly small. A frisson of worry – would her guest take offence at the lean offerings? – travelled through her as she went from her sofa (old, scavenged, more thread than stuffing, still redolent of someone else's dog) to the sparse kitchen (a camping stove mounted on old boxes, a butcher's block that doubled as a prep area) towards the back. On the burner sat an ancient, meticulously seasoned cast iron pan, and in it simmered a stew of venison, wild enoki, the last of her home-grown garlic. Hardly the feast she once welcomed her annual guest with, but circumstances were so very different now. She found, in the one cabinet she possessed, a dusty bottle of wine, the label rotted away. *It'd be a nice touch*, she thought. A good send-off for them both. If the alcohol was still good, at any rate – which it was, much to her relief. The bottle was then half-emptied into two mugs (ceramic survived better than glass) before both, together with the last artifact she needed, were ferried to the squat table beside a bed of dried rushes and mummified lilacs.

The apocalypse had been a clarifying influence, whetting her understanding of herself. Particularly, it taught her she was enough of a misanthrope to be pleased at how her voice had rusted, and how it rasped from disuse the rare times she needed to speak. So, she smiled as she croaked the first invocation: "Brede, Brede, come to my house tonight. I shall open the door for Brede and let Brede come in."

The saint wasn't, as the girl quickly learned, who she had advertised herself to be. Wasn't human; wasn't even mammalian, really, under the milk-rime of skin. But she was close enough in appearance to be made into an effigy and as the saint explained it, once too young to know what being a symbol entailed.

By then, though, the girl was in love.

As everyone knew, there was no magic that could cure *that*.

Imbolc. That was the name for it, for when winter begins to feel the weight of its age and spring kindles like a cancer in its belly. In another life, it was a promise, a warning, an invitation to dream of when the evening sky would wear the sun like a crown. These days, such a celebration was extraneous, important only in the archaeological sense. No one had felt warm in years. Nonetheless, she would conduct the ritual – if only for one last time.

"Brede, Brede, come to my house tonight," she said again. "I shall open the door for Brede and let Brede come in."

The wind groaned a reply, and the candle glow grew dim.

"Brede, Brede," she said, voice husked. "Come to my house tonight."

She drew a sharp whistle of breath when nothing followed, closed her eyes, a palm rested on the pitted flat of the cleaver she had laid on one narrow thigh. The world quieted.

"Please."

In answer then: a soft crackling, like wood in the fireplace or lake ice waking to the weight of an ill-placed foot. The noise grew louder, becoming a frenzy of something tapping, scratching, testing the glass of her windows, as though a thousand hands were seeking egress into the cabin. She kept her gaze trained on the front door, afraid that if she looked, she would find her imaginings weren't fictitious hyperbole and there were hands there, waiting to be let in. Lately, her dreams were suffused with small gods, little things that presided over the hyperspecific. All of them offering her everything if she'd choose them over Brede, but she was monogamous – in everything, not that it mattered, here and now at the end – in her worship.

Just as the din became intolerable, there came three knocks on her door. Silence followed, sudden as a broken neck. She looked up, tensed, swallowing her apprehension; in the next breath, she was up and limping to the threshold. Had it always ached like this to move? Had her joints always felt so stiff? She was sure it was yesterday when she could do cartwheels without restriction, tumbling through green grass, unafraid of whether that would bring about consequences in the morning. Where *had* she misplaced that effortlessly limber version of her?

Groaning, she sank first to one knee and then another, wincing each time she was assailed with a tinder-flash of pain. Getting up wouldn't be pleasant. But this obeisance was a necessary part of the observance, so she gritted her teeth and bowed her head, heart going a thousand miles a minute.

"She's welcome," she said to the dark.

The door opened.

What came in was her saint but not. It moved in stutters, a stop-motion horror made on a shoestring budget: its limbs too long, its joints too loose. What wasn't mouldering fabric was charred skin and scorched bone, the latter striated with cracks through which she could see marrow, most of which had been cooked by whatever fire had enveloped the creature. The face was the same as it had always been: pale, constellated with brown freckles, with a rosy cupid's bow of a mouth and strawberry blonde lashes, the right cheek dimpled and the left not, a look of peace giving her the appearance of statuary. It stared at her with peacock eyes – the colours shifted as she watched, as did the number of pupils and the structure of the irises – and the iridescent gaze was so mesmeric, so compelling in its familiarity, she could almost ignore how the saint's face sat in a sopping frame of red cartilage.

"Let me rest," it said in her love's voice, each syllable underpinned by cicada sounds, by moulting noises, cuticle sliding apart, tearing, coming agonisingly undone. "Let me sleep through the Imbolc to the first breath of spring."

"I can't," she said, her voice breaking. "There's no spring anymore."

The thing swung its head, lowing like an injured stag.

"Let me sleep—"

"Yes, that I can help with. But there's no more waking after this. Your work is done. One last long sleep for both of us, and for this broken world."

"Sleep," it said, resting its head atop her knee, all of its eyes shuttering, even the nebulae of smaller ones deep in the snarl of its hair. "Let me sleep."

"Yes," she said, leaning down to kiss its cold cheek. The skin on her hands and her face were blistered by the wind raking through the open door, but she knew from experience if she just waited, the flesh would go hypothermic and deaden. Pain did not last; only grief. She stroked its throat, skin flaking to ash under her fingers. "I can do that."

It was not good, what it did to the people who let her sister die, nor was it quick. The saint took its time out of love for the girl and for love of the kisses she laid on its brow each time it returned with another wet strip of meat. When there was nothing left, neither skin nor tendon, muscle or sinew, the girl bade the thing that was almost a saint to burn the clotted remains, which it did. And they stood there together until there was no more smoke, until the air smelled again of winter and not fat broiled by an impossible fire.

After that, the saint permitted the girl to lead her to its sleep.

When it came again the next year, filthy with the detritus of the forest, she guided it to the door of a man who had beaten an elderly woman so badly, her skull was stoved in. Though plumes of brain rose from the ruin, he did not stop, only kept hitting her, until she was almost paste and broken bird bones.

The year after that, a woman who'd pushed a young girl onto the subway tracks. And after that, two boys who did worse to a single mother, who kept her alive long enough for her to beg her death to come. The saint ate them all. None of it was enough, of course. No amount of gore would return the dead to their families, nor make right their loss – but it was something, which was more than the girl ever dreamt of having.

The saint had wings now, she realised. Eight in total, its feathers oilslick black, gleaming like lacquer. Under the down, there were eyes, as many of them as there were stars, small and golden and slit-pupiled, regarding her with unconditional tenderness. Sometimes, she forgot it loved her too.

It pushed its face into the cup of her palm.

"Not yet," she said, rousing herself to shut the door. The saint took up the entirety of the cabin, filled it with shadow and staccato movements: its head twitched like a clock hand as it tracked her. But for all its size, it was no obstacle, flowing away whenever she approached, rearranging itself so it could monitor her without interruption. With the door shut, she shooed it towards what passed for a living room in her cabin, the saint settling atop its pallet bed, ready for its repast.

"We eat first," she said. "Then there is sleep."

The saint nodded. As it did, antlers speared through the mask of its face, a velvet tine growing from the socket of its right eye.

Membrane clung to the prongs, but the saint seemed unperturbed by its own mutilation, its expression still beatific. The velvet ran crimson and the air smelled sweetly of cooked fat.

She gave it her wine and sat down opposite the saint, staring. The knife sat between them, gleaming atop the table, its edge honed to particulate thinness. To her, it almost seemed to glow. The saint lapped at its wine like a cat, its gaze never leaving her. Cow-eyed, her father would have called it and laughed.

"You have to die," she blurted before she could stop herself.

The saint said nothing.

"If you keep this going..." Her teeth chattered. She couldn't tell if it was the cold or the adrenaline, her grief at seeing the end. It no longer frightened her, the thought. Death had made a home of this world, and everyone was just renting rooms. But it saddened her nonetheless, this knowledge, this idea there'd no longer be spring mornings or birdsong, no exulting in the discovery of a cache of oyster mushrooms, the ruby flash of a robin passing through the foliage, no more deer and their white-tailed fawns, no more anything ever. "This will never end. It's time to let go."

In answer, it only held out its hands, this wet puzzle of bone and carbonised muscle, staring at her with animal trust. It did not move even when she rose to take the knife, did not stop her as she rested the edge to its throat, though its eyes shuttered halfway then.

"One last sleep for both of us," she said. "For all of us."

She tightened her grip, ready to cut. A single slash across the saint's throat; a matching one across her own once she was sure it had bled out, would not rouse from its bed of rushes and dried lilacs. But for all that she'd practised in her mind, her hand still trembled. If she was right, the saint's death would mark the proper end of everything. The trees would not wake, the grass would continue their torpor. What little could be wrung from the world would dry up.

If she was wrong, well, it wouldn't be too much of a loss.

So, why was she hesitating?

"Rest," crooned the saint, her monster, the last thing she'd ever love. It traced her jaw with the edge of a talon. Its million eyes opened wide. And in her voice, it said, "It's time to let go."

But she couldn't. Not really. The apocalypse hadn't done what every sociologist had insisted would happen. People hadn't bettered themselves. Warlords made pyres of anyone who resisted them. Men remained insatiable, corruptible. Humans remained cruel. The relentless horrors that the panopticon of the internet once broadcasted to anyone who would pay attention was still happening, still bitterly present. People still hurt each other.

If she was right and the death of Imbolc (and her saint, trusting, ravenous) would mean the death of days, all of those bastards would have their rest too.

It didn't seem fair.

"I'm sorry," she said, reversing her grip. The light in the saint's eyes grew to a furnace. It grappled through the air for her, but it was too slow and she was entirely too desperate. The blade did not hurt at all. The wound she made was effortlessly, ruinously deep.

"It's as they say," she whispered, as the blood welled and drooled from the gash she'd made. "No rest for the wicked. Make them hurt for me."

END

What inspired this story? Exhaustion, really. Sometimes, I get tired. Sometimes, I look at the world and all the malice in it, all the hatred running unchecked, all the pain that exists and the joy some people take in causing hurt, and I wonder if we deserve seeing another sunrise, another spring. Sometimes, I wonder if it's easier to stop fighting and keep my head down, to focus instead on surviving.

But then I think about how happy it'd make those bastards for me to lay down and die, and I get up again, ready to upset them with my existence.

GRAVÉ OF SMALL BIRDS

Kaaron Warren

If you want to make a gravé of small birds, put the birds to cook in a pot all covered with crisped bacon, and add wine and water and pepper and ginger, and keep well covered that steam doesn't escape that all will be cooked.

© 2005 Daniel Myers (trans.)

T HE island of Brennan. Most don't know it exists. But like a magical shop in an Enid Blyton book, it appears when you need it.

Each person there needed it for a different reason. Each person had a reason to stay, as if the island shifted and moved in the desire to keep people there.

There were those who came for the Twelve Feast Days of Christmas, spending those days enjoying the rare food and wine.

Some came for the winter solstice, in the hope of being blessed by the light, or named as the year's Beauty, chosen to shepherd the island towards a better future.

And those who came for Wren Day, when rights were wronged and justice was done, symbolically at least.

For Jackie, it was the chance to cook for the famous Twelve Feast Days at the Light House Inn. She'd been invited by Nigel, the Head Chef, who'd seen her on *The History Cook Off* and by some miracle wanted to work with her. It was her medieval knowledge, and her famous *Gravé of Small Birds*, from an old French recipe, that overtook her reputation as a cunt. "You were robbed. You should have won," he'd told her when he sent the invitation.

Nigel stayed on Brennan because his wife had died and was buried there. He was also an artist, so he was there for the light. Many people came for the light. "There's an almost religious belief in it," he said. "I see it from an artistic point of view, but some of them go way beyond that. They'll start flocking in, you watch. As we near the winter solstice, they'll all show up to see the light on the tomb." It was hard to imagine. The tomb was nondescript, more like a burrow but with old stone protuberances and concealed window slats.

Adam, who looked after the livestock, the food supplies, the wine, and pretty much everything else, was there for love, forever love, unlike Maria, the pastry chef, who was there for love that lasted an hour or two.

The restaurant was booked out for Halloween, although it was the least of the coming events on the island. Jackie had only arrived the week before but already felt part of the whirlwind. She loved the restaurant itself, which had been built by an architect who wanted to win awards for design, but no one would let him. It really was a beautiful building. It had a glass roof, hundreds of clear tiles layered upon one another like a snake's scales that let the sun in all throughout the day. It was a triumph of engineering, and once Jackie had worked there a few days she forgot to be anxious about it. The staff were all even-tempered and very funny. Jackie loved a kitchen where humour was key rather than bad temper. Having worked in both, one filled her with dread, the other with a sense of wellbeing.

Apart from the glass roof, the inn boasted a complex series of rooms, deceptively large, where visitors to the island could sleep comfortably. Staff stayed in the purpose-built prefab huts a five-minute bike ride from the restaurant. These huts sprouted like mushrooms around an oak tree, all of them placed higgledy-piggledy rather than in neat rows, something deliberate but also random, as each house was placed to catch the best light.

You couldn't get away from the light.

Jackie shared her hut with Maria. They'd already clashed over "privacy," with Jackie (quite reasonably) refusing to vacate the hut when Maria had someone over. "There are rooms everywhere," Jackie said, although this wasn't true. The island was filling up with tourists (one of the reasons Maria was so busy with her love life) and there were very few rooms left. "Why don't you use the architect's house? There must be hundreds of rooms there."

"Yeah, all filled with rats and spiders and ghosts. No thanks."

It hadn't been lived in for decades, not since the architect's wife, a celebrated beauty, had left to become a movie star and he had died of self-neglect. It was still quite beautiful, the remaining glass reflecting the winter sky.

It was a deceptively simple building, designed to catch all the light there was, solid to the core, and Jackie was seriously tempted to move in. Nigel told her absolutely not. It was too dangerous.

The architect's house was one of four points of interest on the island, along with The Light House Inn, the old village, and the tomb. On her second day, Jackie had been walking along the beach that abutted the restaurant, gazing out to sea, wondering at the lack of seagulls, when she found a small hut sheltering a series of bicycles. A worn, easy-to-follow path led her first to the architect's house in the north of the island. It stood on a dangerously steep cliff. Jackie peered through a broken window. Even in this state it looked beautiful, with pale wooden walls and slate floors. A lot had been stripped but the design was still clear.

The old village to the east, there long before the architect built his house, had been abandoned for many years but was in remarkable condition, although crumbling in places.

To the south lay the tomb. There was nothing exciting about this mound of grass; only once a year, at winter solstice, did the light play magic on the place. Still, it was quiet, and gave her a kind of meditative calm to be near it.

In the centre of the island lay a series of small houses which once accommodated the staff near the architect's house, a five-minute bike ride away, and were now used for visitors and restaurant workers. This was where Jackie lived.

~

Jackie showered in their tiny bathroom, kept clean by mutual agreement, and dressed for the day's work.

She pulled her bike into the small shed at the side of the restaurant and felt great delight in leaving it unlocked. It seemed there was a genuine spirituality about the customers who ate and stayed at the Light House, true believers, and there had never been a problem with theft, or violence, or even people complaining about the service. Not that there was any reason to do so. The Light House was five stars all the way. She rode to the old village, collected some dill and sage, and rode back to the restaurant.

Nigel, who was also the maître d', laid the tables, decorating them with the special lanterns that looked like the tomb and glowed from within. He put the finishing touches to an astonishing sculpture made out of butter, a perfectly carved naked woman, covering herself modestly.

Jackie thought it had her face. She nodded approval, then headed into the kitchen where the team waited for direction.

They prepped dozens of small cakes decorated to look like vampires, zombies, and other monsters. The canapes were creepily body-like: snacks made to look like severed fingers, eyeballs, ears. Jackie surveyed them all and gave an exaggerated shiver. They were perfect. It was all fiddly and annoying, but part of the job. They would begin planning and prep for the solstice in another couple of weeks. Meanwhile, she had time to settle in and explore.

"The good thing for me about this is it's all pre-prep, no meals for tonight," Maria said. She was already in costume, a pink, skin-tight body suit that covered her neck to knee. "I'm a white girl about to be autopsied," she said.

Adam laughed and said, "Best dead body I've ever seen. Also only dead body." Maria had told Jackie he wanted to be exclusive. He was in love. Jackie was pretty sure Maria wouldn't do better.

The restaurant filled with people dressed as witches, ghouls, ghosts, and monsters. They wore rubber masks or ones made out of papier-mâché, many provided by the Light House. They'd be hung carefully in the storage room, to be used for the winter solstice.

"Love your mask!" Maria said to Jackie, who wasn't wearing a mask. She had dressed for the occasion, though, wearing a tight-fitting shirt, thin and transparent, with a red bra underneath. She looked good. Jackie had no intention of covering her face. She'd always been proud of her looks and totally aware of how many doors were opened because she was pretty. It wasn't that she used it, exactly, but she didn't *not* use it, a distinction her father found infuriating. More than once he'd wished aloud that she'd have a disfiguring accident, to bring her down a peg or two.

She hadn't seen him in three years and had no desire to do so.

"I know it's because you're jealous," Jackie said to Maria. "And that's okay."

"You're the jealous one!"

"I'm not jealous! Nothing really upsets me, except when someone gets what should be mine and it isn't fair." It was like a curse. Everyone knew she'd thrown burning hot oil at the person who'd beaten her in *The History Cook Off*; she was hoping Maria wouldn't mention it. If she didn't, Jackie might let her have the hut tonight for her fucking or whatever she wanted to do in there.

While Jackie specialised in authentic medieval food, she also loved the basics. Tonight, it was char grill, done on the restaurant floor, and already the patrons were gathering. She cleared off one of the tables for mise en place and had the fireplace set higher. The yule log from last year had something left to burn and that seemed right. The fire blazed high, bringing a warm colour to her she thought looked good. Admiring glances told her she wasn't kidding herself.

"Is your name really Jackie Baker?" one of the men asked. He'd come with a group of four, the others perhaps his father and some uncles. He was sweet and shy and she liked him.

"It is! Hilarious, huh?" She used to tell people she was a descendent of Lady Baker, whose portrait hung in the Wellington Museum with the quote "The Exceeding Joy of Burning." She loved that. She told the man about it, explaining why she loved char grill. "It's in the genes," she said. He was too shy to play with that, but she could see him desperately wanting to.

Nigel pulled a chair up close to the fire, a sketch pad on his lap. "Your colour is amazing, Jackie. Your cheekbones. Beautiful skin." He sketched. She stretched her neck as she cooked, tilting her head sideways, showing her best angles. "You are easily the most beautiful woman on the island. You will win Beauty for sure."

Maria pressed up against Adam. She had her eye on him for the night. "She *is* lovely, isn't she? For sure you'll be chosen, Jackie."

Others wanted details of the competition. Nigel told them it happened on winter solstice, after the light shone in the tomb, while the whole island was gathered. That it was a pretty special thing to be chosen, and he named four or five previous winners, actresses and famous models.

"As if I'll be chosen," Jackie said. She served the beef, with a chimichurri sauce on the side, and chargrilled zucchini done to perfection. Her mouth watered just looking at it.

"Would we lie to you?" Maria said, leaning harder into Adam.

Jackie drank too many Bloody Marys and ended up stumbling to her bed before the party ended. She needed to take herself out of Nigel's path. His pants were soft, up against her leg. He told her they were made out of the skin of mice he caught in the cellar.

She didn't need that complication – not yet, anyway.

They didn't expect big crowds again until winter solstice. Nigel said the time was best spent looking after the few patrons who remained, and practising all the dishes. "With plenty of time off to explore the island," he said. Most of the staff took the chance to hit the mainland for a few weeks, finding work if they wanted but mostly surviving off savings.

Jackie stayed put. She loved not being recognised on busy streets, enjoyed the patchy internet which meant she wasn't constantly bombarded with footage of herself. She worked on her dishes and enjoyed the beach, as well as walks along the northern cliff.

Solstice. December 22.

The next few weeks were spent in prep, practising and perfecting the dishes. The dish of the day would be the *Gravé* of Small Birds, advertised and promoted widely and already giving Jackie stress. She found Adam tending their chickens, coaxing them to lay in his gentle voice.

"Birdman!" she said. "You're the one who can help me. I need a supply of small birds for solstice. Quails, usually, but I can work with anything. Have you got a small aviary hiding somewhere? I don't think I've seen a single bird since I've been here. Not even seagulls."

"Yeah, birds hate this island. I reckon it's because of all the glass, they think they'll be surrounded by enemy birds. Who knows. You'll have a shitload of wrens when we open the tomb on solstice. They nest in there and once a few of them appear, the island is overrun."

"Weird," Jackie said. "I can work with wrens."

"A heap of them die each year slamming into the windows," Adam said. He shook his head. "It'll be good not to just chuck them back around the tomb."

They always hired extra staff in preparation for the Twelve Feast Days of Christmas. It was the house speciality and people came from all over the world, some attending all twelve days, at a cost Jackie found almost obscene. The business would feed thousands during the midwinter.

They'd also package meals to be enjoyed on the mainland – charging an arm and a leg – but no one ever felt ripped off. In a good year, the restaurant would sell hundreds of these meals, making enough to see them through the quieter times when the only patrons were locals.

The day before solstice, Nigel – freshly showered and dressed all in black, a small easel under his arm and a strap bag full of paints over his shoulder – stood near the doorway and called, "All those wanting to come painting today need to join me now. I'm heading for the old village. It's mostly intact, but there are some ruins there. Perfect for the artist's brush! There are mushrooms, Jackie, of all kinds. And birds' eggs if you're lucky. Maybe even a wild pig or two."

He snorted, and Jackie laughed. She knew there were no pigs, but asked him to bring her back a basket of mushrooms.

There were always artists there to paint or sketch, especially the old village. One said, "I like the village more than the tomb. With the village it is all there on top to be seen. The tomb, you have to envisage what's underneath."

Jackie thought, *a good artist could do just that,* but she didn't say anything. They all set off to the old village, a forty-five-minute walk away. Jackie and the rest of the staff took a short break, then she got them on prep for the evening meal while she baked bread and pickled beetroot for the next day.

Solstice dawned, the weak sun pale, lacking warmth. Still, there was a sense of excitement, of change, that made Jackie's heart race. She spent longer getting ready, drying her hair smooth and shiny, drawing lines of makeup, shades of colour. She'd lost weight with all the exercise and it suited her.

She would be chosen, she was sure of it.

A tour group had arrived overnight on the ferry, too late for dinner, so now they were desperate for breakfast. Jackie and her team were energised, pumping out plate after plate of city-quality food. Her own porridge, beetroot pancakes, honey toast on her own bread, date slice. In a pause, as the barista made a round of second coffees, Jackie watched the tourists through the kitchen hatch.

"Hey gorgeous," Nigel said.

"Don't look at me! I'm a mess!" Too little sleep, food smears all over, hair tied up in a messy bun. She knew she still looked good.

"Even at your worst you are stunning." He was too young to be a widower.

There were about thirty tourists in the dining room. A lively group, there was one woman who stood out. She was in her mid-twenties, curly black hair falling to her shoulders, an angelic face. When she laughed her whole body shook, and laughter rose around her. She seemed to glow in the morning light, and she picked at her food like a fairy princess.

"Wow, she is magnificent. Truly, classically beautiful. She must be here for the contest," Maria said.

"I didn't know it was a contest. I thought someone was just chosen."

"Not a formal contest. But… sorry, Jackie, you might have some competition."

Until that moment, Jackie hadn't really cared, or at least she hadn't thought she did. But she enjoyed being the most attractive woman on the island. She'd been the best-looking one on *The History Cook Off,* by far, and she'd enjoyed the online comments about that. Regardless of her behaviour, people said, "But she's so cute."

There would be no lunch beyond sandwiches and chocolate chip cookies, small cheese pastries and tiny sugar birds the diners took in neatly folded white cardboard lunch boxes to eat near the tomb, but dinner would be a BBQ feast, with the beef smoking since the evening before, the pork on a slow roast in the wood-fired oven, the chicken marinating before a flash burn. The fish would arrive last minute, straight off the coastline. "Still panting if we're lucky," Jackie said, only halfway joking.

The *Gravé* of Small Birds would be the treat for the next day.

They spent the morning preparing the salads and other accompaniments. There were some historical elements to the food, with Jackie relying on her expertise, but for the most part this would be a modern meal. She hoped they would appreciate the food.

Nigel finished his next butter sculpture, definitely Jackie this time, her head tilted demurely like Princess Diana, her knees apart. He'd placed a bunch of herbs, collected in the village, between the sculpture's thighs.

⁓

The tour leader called out, "Let's start making our way to the tomb. Light will fall at noon precisely and there will be massive crowds to get through."

"Do we get to go inside?" an older man asked. "I want the light to fall on me."

"John, you know this." The tour leader was clearly exasperated. "There's only room for one in there, and the light falls for a few minutes only. *One* person gets the glory each year. Long since decided, and it isn't you."

"Must be a local?" Jackie said to Adam.

"None of us give a shit about the feckin' winter solstice light!" he said. "Big feckin' deal! We leave that to the idiots who'll pay out good money for it."

Jackie abandoned her bike with the passage tomb still a few hundred metres away. She laid it carefully on the grass, avoiding the puddles of thick mud, the soft piles of cow manure. She hadn't actually seen a cow and for a moment she was distracted, curious, poking at the poo with a stick as if she could learn something.

Wiping her hands on her trousers, she kept on towards the tomb. From this angle, this distance, it seemed to tilt as if about to fall over. She had been here a number of times by now, but never with this many people. It looked different.

The tomb had been cleared of debris on top but left covered with grass. The opening was small, rectangular. There were many dozens of people milling around, keeping their distance from the tomb. Around the base, bones piled up, and people added to them.

"All our beloved pets rest here," Nigel said. "They've saved up the bones all year to bring them."

Any animal that died on the island, from bird to dog, was buried, then disinterred and the bones laid here. They told her it was to beg for a good year, a gift to the winter solstice and a promise to love and cherish those around.

It was a pretty confusing philosophy, but who was she to say?

"What happens if you don't have any bones to add?"

"There are always bones somewhere. There are bird bones, at least."

The tomb had been swept clean in the previous days; all the old bones used to make a tower on the cliff. It wasn't very tall; most bones were picked and gone each year. As she watched, one of the locals dumped a box full of bones, and children scrabbled to spread them around.

It was chilly by the tomb. Jackie was warmed by the exercise of getting there, but felt her cheeks burning red in the cold. The air was stiller than usual, almost heavy, with a scent of the winter berries that grew wild all over the island. The sky was clear, which caused great excitement amongst the two-hundred-strong crowd (many of whom sipped from flasks, causing a mood of warm cheer to rise).

Many of them wore masks. Some adapted from the ones worn on Halloween, with fur and feathers added. Some carved from large tree roots.

The crowd whistled and called out. Maria played to the crowd, standing at the entrance as if expecting to be chosen, with her head bowed, her arms folded in front of her. She said, "Only a pure person can go inside." Someone called out, "I fucked you six days ago, Maria Martin," and the crowd laughed. Maria took a bow.

The one chosen to enter was pressed forward. Jackie noticed that no one jostled her, or begged to replace her. It was another from the tour group, a nondescript woman with mousy hair and fat ankles. She'd left her bacon on the side of the plate but devoured all the pastries placed in front of her.

She stood now, peering into the tomb. She wasn't a tall woman but still, the space would be tight.

"In you go!" Nigel said. With his brush he painted symbols on either cheek (utter bullshit, he'd tell Jackie later) and held her hand as she entered the tomb. It was two minutes to twelve, and there was a hush as the weak winter sun's rays beamed down on them, touching the tomb. Nigel pulled aside the rough-hewn door cover with the help of two of the men.

A small flock of birds fluttered out, spinning wildly as if lost and confused, then taking off into the distance. "No one knows how they get in there, but they nest every year, have done for decades," Nigel said. "They'll help her choose the Beauty, later. Amazing to watch."

A cheer arose, and people took drinks and called out good wishes to each other, as the woman climbed through. Even as she did, she was momentarily forgotten, as she must have been all her life. There was a countdown from ten. The sun was bright enough overhead, and silence fell as it reached the aperture.

At that moment, dozens more birds flew out through the aperture and the small door. They swirled around over the heads of the observers, calling, squawking and whistling, and they unleashed a hail of shit, almost like snow, Jackie thought. The crowd laughed and shielded their heads but at least half of them were hit, causing hilarity and the sharing of tissues.

Jackie thought she heard sobbing. This happened, she was told. People touched by the light felt their emotions take over. Birds fluttered overhead, one or two swooping back in through the window. The woman inside squealed.

Nigel helped her out. She had been crying, her face wet, her eyes squeezed tight. She opened them when she heard the cheers, but she whispered, "I can't see! I can't!"

Someone helped her to the road and drove her to the restaurant. She would spend the night in the place they called the Bone Shed, a very comfortable cabin with no windows, good heat, all the food and drink she would want. It was the place people went to die, but they didn't expect the woman to do so. Bones of previous years, those not stacked in a tower, were used here, placed around the window and the door for protection. Birds landed on the roof and settled there, singing and shaking their wings out, preparing for rest. Their birdsong filled the air; Jackie realised she'd not heard it on the island until now. She had noticed this small building but assumed it housed the generator or something equally useful but boring.

Jackie stood looking at her long shadow, playing with it as you do, dancing without thinking, waving at herself. She liked her shadow long like this. Nigel danced with her.

"That was pretty creepy," she said.

"It gets less creepy every year. The more you understand it, I guess. You'll understand the importance of the Beauty, too." He kissed her cheek. "How important she is to us."

Jackie felt her heart ache at the wanting. She sat alone eating her picnic lunch, enjoying the sounds of appreciation coming from all those who'd paid for a box.

Back at the restaurant, with the evening meal already on the fire, Jackie spent time looking at the history presented in photos, documents, and newspaper articles on the walls of the restaurant. She'd not really taken an interest before but now felt a sense of obligation in it. The floor itself was one giant mapping of a network of passages no longer in existence, linking tombs discovered and undiscovered. Some had been dug out, others left filled with the dirt of the ages.

"Aren't you Jackie Baker?" someone said. One of the tour group, chewing on a sandwich. He stood beside her, staring at her chest.

"What gave it away?" she said, hands on hips. She was wearing her *The History Cook Off* T-shirt; she'd never hide from it. "And how's the food?"

"Food is brilliant! Bloody brilliant. And I love you. You're such a bitch," the man said. Jackie gave a bow then continued making her way around the restaurant, learning the history of the island and the tomb. There were newspaper articles, personal letters, telegrams and photographs, all mounted in frames made from wood that grew on the island.

The tomb was over five thousand years old, and had sat covered for most of those years. The island was uninhabited until a religious group set up base there, at which time the tomb mounds were discovered when workers were digging up stones.

There was a painting of this; a mound of grass-covered dirt, with the sun's rays blessing it. Around the base stood men, women and children, dressed in heavy clothing, hands held as they encircled the mound. Birds filled the sky, and the painting was named *The Coming of the Wrens*. No one entered the tomb; they wouldn't even have considered it.

Time passed, and a forest grew around the mound. This was seen as an act of God, and the trees were left to grow until the 1950s, when there was a mouse plague on the island and the forest was cleared in an attempt to eradicate them. There was a newspaper story about this; proud photos of mounds of mice, and news that they had been skinned and turned into trousers. Jackie thought of Nigel's soft pants and wondered how old they were.

Two brothers unearthed the entrance to the tomb. There were no human remains, not even bones, left in there, although there were clear indentations of where the bodies must have rested. Instead, piles of small birds nested, the squawk and anxious call of them leading the men to investigate. They discovered, through a yearlong observation, that the sun illuminated the interior at noon on winter solstice. It changed them both. One was the architect, the man who built both the restaurant and his large house on the hill. Both buildings had a massive fireplace, almost as big as the walls themselves, to stave off the cold. He had not been in the tomb when the light entered; that was his brother, who was once a promising artist. He was blinded by the light, unprepared. The articles quoted him saying "I will never be the same. I experienced something last experienced thousands of years ago. I have been given this gift." While his sight was restored, his art changed. His brother built him the house on the cliff so he could look out, capture distance, because all he wanted to do was draw close examinations, which disturbed all around him. He would lay dead birds on a table outside and draw the progression of their decay, with the insects featuring large and fearsome.

When he died, they discovered a tunnel under his house that went nowhere. It was lined with human skeletons, hundreds of years old. No one ever understood how or why he'd moved and hidden them.

Some of the furniture in the rooms was made of yule log remainders, and Jackie thought perhaps she could detect a slight smell of burning. It was a very comforting scent, somehow.

Jackie looked at the bone shed. There was a glow from within, a small fire keeping the woman warm. She made up a plate of food, good food, and she walked over there. It couldn't hurt, surely? She sang to herself, softly but clearly, hoping the strains would reach the woman's ears. Jackie could have been a singer if she wasn't a chef; her voice was good. The birds were quiet, although one or two circled constantly as if keeping watch.

Jackie knocked gently on the door and opened it a crack. She slid the tray of food in there, saying, "Just a little snack. We need to care for each other and I thought of you here, you must be hungry."

"Thank you," the woman said. "A beautiful thing." Jackie could hear a small murmuring. It was like the fire was singing – but no; it was the birds, calling down the small chimney. "I don't think

I'll sleep tonight," the woman said, but she wasn't complaining. She was flushed, excited.

"Sweet dreams," Jackie said.

The morning was cold. Jackie wore a fake fur coat that sat up around her ears. It was white, fluffy, looking almost like bubbles. She looked in the mirror and felt confident; it would be her. It had to be her. The woman would make a choice and it would be her. "Come on!" Maria said. "Let's go!"

The announcement would be made at the bone shed, the moment the woman emerged. Everyone was given mugs of mulled wine and they traipsed out into the cold.

Nigel knocked gently at the door. "Are you okay? Are you ready to come out? We have mulled wine."

She emerged, her hair mussed, her clothing awry. She smiled and surveyed the crowd. "I've had such a lovely sleep," she said. "And such beautiful dreams. I am truly blessed." Someone gave her a coat when she shivered. "I'm blessed," she said again. She'd been told what she needed to do. She turned her head from side to side, seeking. Jackie stood tall, her coat glowing in the morning light, her smile broad, her eyes bright and clear. The birds had long since woken and flew in beautiful patterns, calling, singing, drawing attention to themselves.

The woman walked in the opposite direction from Jackie though, certain, definite, the birds flying overhead, and she placed her hand on the shoulder of the young beauty who'd arrived the day before. The birds flew in a circle, their song beautiful, uplifting, as if applauding her choice. As if pretending they hadn't led her all the way. The crowd cheered; *of course, of course,* Jackie heard. That made her furious; how dare they say that? How dare they?

Still, she called out "brava" as others did, and joined them all as they took the walk back to the tomb. The day of winter solstice was almost over and they needed to do one more thing to ensure a good year. They would mark this turning of the year and look forward to the warmer days, the flowers of spring, the joy of an island summer. If they got this wrong, there could be consequences – and had been, in the past.

Jackie was certain they'd got it wrong. She was the Beauty, surely?

She wondered if she was ugly.

Maria said, "Maybe next year?" which was kind of her.

"Maybe they'll change their minds," Jackie said, but Maria shook her head.

"Too much bad luck if they think they're wrong. And anyway..." She didn't finish, but it was clear she thought the right choice had been made.

Nigel said, "It should have been you. I don't get it. I mean, the birds made the choice and it is only to be confirmed, but you knew that, right?"

She hadn't, not really.

"They've always said the birds choose someone related to the original Missie Wren. Who the hell knows, ay? Anyway," he said. He handed her a mug of mulled wine. "Get that into yer." Jackie would ask him who Missie Wren was later.

The sun was setting as they arrived, and they all cast elongated shadows.

At the tomb, the Beauty, who was as gracious in her win as the winner of *The History Cook Off* had been, stood where she was asked. Her shadow cast long towards the sea, and it was the young men who gathered bones from around the tomb and built a form around her shadow, a line of bones.

They sang a song, then, the lyrics handed around in printed booklets, about cold spells, cracked pipes, cold water. About the beauty of warmth, of good meals, of hot water. "Bubbles to my nose in my bubble bath and it's warm until the supper's ready," Jackie sang at the top of her lungs, showing them what a good sport she was.

Back at the restaurant, the fire was lit. In the second fireplace, never used, a yule log sat. It was hundreds of years old, they said, and chalked with the figure of a man. There was almost nothing Jackie believed of what she was told; they seemed to make stories up to suit themselves, fit to purpose, depending on whether they wanted to seduce or frighten.

People gathered there (at least, those who'd prepaid. The others went home to cheese on toast and soup) and they drank and sang as the meal was served. The Beauty made the most of it, showing off, happily carried around on the shoulders of men, laughing and squealing like a little piggy. She wore a halter dress made out of an old apron, showing off perfectly formed arms. Jackie muttered to Maria, "What, she's a chef now?"

Staff served up Jackie's BBQ feast, filling the tables with

platters of meat, vegetables, fresh-cooked bread, and salads.

Like any group of people who have prepaid for food, they appreciated it and they ate like pigs, piling up their plates so often most of them needed to sprawl out on the window seats, unable to sit up properly anymore. The window seats were one of the most glorious elements of the restaurant, built deep into the walls and surrounded by the same window squares that made up the roof. On this ice-cold night, they sat with rugs and thick coats, enjoying the clear view outside.

Nigel had made a pastry sculpture. It was the Beauty, and Maria, seeing it, laughed. She was helping with the caramel syrup but lost her attention, pouring it over her own hand. Jackie was sure it wasn't her fault; she hadn't wished this on Maria, surely? Surely that laughter, that mocking, was meant to be kind? Still, Maria was burnt badly and could only instruct for the next few days. She would need help. Jackie couldn't be bothered. It wasn't her job to do that.

Xmas. December 25. The Feast.

Jackie prepared her *Gravé* of Small Birds. She tried not to look at the Beauty, or to think about what it must be like to be glorified like that. To keep the staff focused, she told gossip from the TV show, and they all shared recipes, as awful or as wonderful as they liked.

On *The History Cook Off* she'd been castigated by viewers for some of her authentic methodology. "Hypocrites, the lot of them. Besides, it was the judges who mattered, and I managed to impress them."

She hadn't even performed the worst she could have prepared, from "taking a red cock that is not too old and beat him to death", or ensuring a calf's mouth was wedged open before death to release the gases. She hadn't sewn living birds into the belly of a living cow. She had plucked a bird alive, though, and that set people off.

She called herself the cook from Cooktown. People call her the Cunt from Cuntown, which always made her laugh.

She gently reminded a staff member that the copper pans should never be used with acid. "It can cause verdigris. There've been whole families poisoned by that shit."

"We can't poison anyone," Adam said. He'd never been happier; Maria needed his help and he was sure she was falling in love with him.

As Adam had suggested, at least two dozen birds had broken their necks trying to fly through the glass of the restaurant. Jackie had the staff collect them up, warning them to be gentle, not to bruise. They all prepped them, plucking and gutting but not boning. She layered the birds into a large stock pot, to which she added very crisp bacon (provided proudly by Adam), wine, water, pepper, and ginger. She covered it and let it cook on low for the rest of the day. It came out perfectly; the meat tender, falling off the bone, the gravy rich and delicious. Nigel came in for a sample and danced around the room with joy.

"Oh, that's good. That is very bloody good."

The customers agreed.

The day before Christmas Day was one of much preparation. They were partway through their Twelve Feast Days of Christmas (with only a couple of outsiders kindly and patronisingly explaining when the twelve days of Christmas *actually* started) and Jackie was loving it. She wished she had another shot on *The History Cook Off* because she had a gimmick now, a thing that would set her ahead of the others. No one would ever invite her back, though, unless it was a *Villains of the Kitchen* show, which actually sounded okay. While she regretted throwing that pan of boiling oil at the winner, mostly she wished she'd been cleverer about it.

She had the Brennan version of the old French Twelve Days of Christmas pinned to the fridge, like students did when trying to memorise the periodic table.

One Dressed Swan
Two Boiled Cranes
Three Suckling Pigs
Four Savoury Tongue Pies
Five Smothered Rabbits
Six Grape-stuffed Chickens
Seven Savoury Salads
Eight Patina of Fillets of Hare
Nine Poor Man's Pies
Ten Quaking Puddings
Eleven Milk Fed Snails
Twelve Tiny Birds Cooked in their own Bone *Gravé*

Maria was up and about. She whistled quietly and said to herself, "Herby day, herby day, hunting for herby day." Her hand was bandaged but she had strong painkillers, so was feeling fine.

"I'm awake!" Jackie said, sitting up, smiling. "I'm up and at 'em."

They had a quick staff breakfast (flash-fried mushrooms tossed with leftovers from the night before, wrapped in a thin omelette). The feeling was good, all of them in warm gear, gloves in pockets in case there were thorns and brambles as they went herb hunting.

"And broken glass," Nigel said. He was the one who'd lived there the longest and as Head Chef, he'd lead them on their way.

No one really knew who had turned the ruined village into a herb garden, or if it had just happened. It was only a small village; a tiny church, five houses, a small pub that was a converted barn. You could ride the whole island in a couple of hours, and perhaps meet most of the inhabitants on the way.

All the buildings had fallen into disrepair. It was clear it had once been a cared-for place; from what remained of the brightly painted walls, to the broken bird baths, to the rotten picket fences, it was obvious that once people took pride in living here. Now, piles of bricks lay at broken walls, windows stood smashed, tattered curtains flapping and everywhere, *everywhere*, grew herbs. Parsley, alexanders, borage, chervil, coriander, dill, fennel, mint, thyme, garlic, leek, onion, shallot, hyssop, rosemary, rue, sage, savory, sweet marjoram, radish.

Jackie breathed deep. Any decay was long since gone, what remained was gloriously fresh scent of the herbs. She had a very good sense of smell, something the judges had commented on. She cringed now to remember the exchange.

"You mean I smell good? Are you flirting with me?" she'd said. She couldn't bear to think about it. The humiliation made her want to scream.

The herbs had completely overrun the village. The horse's drinking trough was filled with oregano and thyme, the play equipment covered with parsley and mint. It was quite beautiful.

"What happened here?" she asked. There were bird feathers throughout, some decorative, some apparently random, and piles of oyster shells.

Nigel said, "Every time I feel down, I come here. For the ingredients, but also as a reminder that even as something ends, something new can begin. This place is left as a different reminder, though. If ya wanna hear the story?"

Some of them had heard it but were happy to hear it again.

"This was once a thriving village. If we followed that old path down to the coastline, we'd see other houses, huts, there's even an old Jaguar someone brought over on the ferry. The men worked hard, the women too, and it was a community that cared for each other. Children came and went, stayed for life or left for the city. They celebrated solstice like we do, but with more dancing. There weren't too many new people who joined them, but every now and then someone would appear as if by God's hand, and some would fit in and stay, and others would do damage and leave.

"Missie Wren did more damage than you can imagine. She was the most beautiful creature anyone had ever seen. She knocked all the men, and the boys too, for six, as if she mesmerised them with her beauty. She took up residence in the house on the cliff, where our richest family welcomed her.

"She was a relative, they said, but no one quite knew how. Then men stopped working, every last lazy bastard one of them, spending their days watching her, their nights dreaming about her. Everything fell into disarray."

He took a breath. "It's an old story. Told all different ways. What I believe is, Missie Wren led the men into the sea to drown them. All the women fronting up to her and shouting, 'Feck off! Leave us alone, you witch!'

"She climbed on a boat and these men fought to climb on too, pushing out from shore with boys clinging to the side, all of them thinking they might be the one to make a life with this beauty, at least for a night.

"But that boat sank, out at sea. Twenty-two men lost that day, and from the shore what did they see, all those left behind? That beauty transforming into a wren and flying back to the island, only to lay shit as far as she could lay it.

"The wailing cries of the women, the calls of the drowning men, all became one resounding note that shook the foundations of the small church until it collapsed on itself."

"This is why they used to kill every wren they saw, and why Wren Day means so much. Our Beauties are kind and good, to balance out the evil. One of our first was the architect's daughter and no sweeter woman ever trod the earth. She was a chef herself, you know. The Twelve Meals of Christmas came from her. I never saw her, but they say she was like an angel, a floating beautiful creature. We don't kill those small birds anymore," he said, "unless we are going to cook and eat them."

The Beauty said, "Wrens are a beautiful bird," and they all agreed with this annoyingly obvious statement. She floated around, picking flowers, sniffing herbs, as if casting a magic spell on all of them.

"They started a new village, built from scratch, on the other side of the island."

This was the modern, thriving village where Jackie had arrived just before Halloween.

"Winter is a cruel beauty." This was the Beauty again and Jackie wasn't alone in finding her annoying, surely.

"So now we have our Beauty, queen for a year," said Nigel. Quietly, he said, "Sorry, Jackie! We all thought it would be you. But solstice tells the truth, I guess."

"The fact that the woman who chose her knows her is part of it. I mean, they are friends on the mainland, so..." Jackie said, and that was true, although it was the birds that chose. She wanted to be Beauty, be Queen for a year, be the one. The one adored and admired.

She tasted the herbs. Gathered more, filled with envy and rage. Angry at the woman who'd made the choice as well as that so-called Beauty, shallow as she was.

Food prep that night included checking on her snails. They were fed on milk, wine must, and wheat, forced out of their shells by the removal of a membrane and kept in milk which needed to be changed almost hourly. They'd get so fat they wouldn't be able to get back in their shells.

She and the team boned six dozen quail, telling stories to keep themselves from being too bored in this repetitive task that needed a lot of attention.

⌒

Nigel was frantic with the work, but took time to decorate the tables. He was an artist at heart. He'd ordered beautiful sycamore slabs and had painted them himself with wrens. They would walk out the door at an outrageous price; he said that if people were willing to pay, they could afford to pay. He laid out painted bones and feathers, surprisingly beautiful. And he'd made a large ice sculpture, which sat outside the door. It was a bird, mouth open, and inside were small figures. If you looked closely enough, you would see they were making love. Jackie couldn't see their faces.

The dining room was packed for the Christmas Eve dinner, and then Jackie was up until one in the morning, finalising preparations for the next day.

The patrons drifted in from around 11 a.m. on Christmas Day. Many wore new clothes, smelt of new perfume, carried new bags or phones or toys. Jackie and the other staff had all exchanged small gifts. She had received a marvellous slab of rock salt. "From our own shore," she was told, but didn't believe it.

The Beauty sulked in the corner. Jackie took her a glass of champagne with orange juice and a plate of fruit toast. "Having a nice Christmas Day?"

"Not really. I wish I was back home. My friends had a big

party last night and my boyfriend was going to take me to his parent's house. They are so rich, you wouldn't believe it!"

"But you came here! And look at you, the most beautiful girl on the island."

Dessert arrived then, a glorious bombe Alaska, played in by one of the staff on a banjo, to great cheers and applause. Jackie loved these moments, when people were full of her food and pleased with her. The sweets were devoured, then more wine, dessert wine, port, cheese, chocolate. No one was unhappy with the fare, no one felt they'd paid too much. There was a lot of flirting and going off in pairs as night fell, and dancing, and wild behaviour. The staff joined in, with most of the dishes done, the kitchen almost clean. They'd finish that in the morning. For now, they enjoyed themselves, including a high-voiced blonde woman customer, good for her age, wild on drink. She made her play for one of the younger workers, who Jackie thought had the sexiest eyes on the island.

The Beauty danced beautifully, casting a magic spell over everyone, all those interested thinking they might be the one. Even Nigel (or perhaps not "even". Perhaps he'd wanted this all along) followed her with his eyes, tipping beer down his throat, still watching.

And proof of the Beauty's true self; she chose him. She knew Jackie liked him (she must have known) and she chose him. He flashed Jackie a look. She shrugged; she wasn't going to show him she cared. She took up a bottle of rum and worked on it, watching them all, feeling herself growing fat with fury.

She watched as the Beauty led Nigel outside. He was stumbling, stupid with drink. They rugged up in thick coats, warm hats, and Jackie wondered how any sex could possibly happen.

She followed them, unnoticed, to the house on the top of the cliff. She watched, unblinking, as Nigel tried to fuck the girl and she rebuffed him, laughing. He wasn't even bothered; he glanced at his watch as he walked away, neatened his hair. Does Jackie imagine this, that he practised the word "Jackie" in his mouth, smiling? That he thought, *oh well, Jackie will fuck me, no worries?*

Jackie stayed where she was. She imagined the Beauty transformed into a wren and flying away. Her long sleeves, her long hair, like wings and feathers. Imagined that Beauty was a bird. Imagined that Beauty could fly.

"Beauty over age," the girl called out. "Although I'm sure he'll like you again once I'm gone."

"You're supposed to stay."

"As if!" the girl said. That was it for Jackie; she stormed forward and pushed the girl, again, and again, and again, until she went over the cliff.

Jackie arrived back at the restaurant flushed, excited. She covered up her heightened mood by talking about her family, to show how beloved she was. She said, "It's already past Christmas in Australia. I wonder if Uncle Jeff has vomited in the pot plant yet."

That got them in, and she told them about her big family, their rambling beach house. "I'm the second oldest. I left to see the world and to learn to cook more than big one-pot meals. I left the day I realised steak could be tender, not stringy. And veggies a meal all their own, not slop on the side. That things have flavour, not just substance. I left to learn in the kitchens of the world. Somehow ended up on a TV show. Maybe I left broken hearts everywhere, me, the girl next door."

All the while she waited, waited for someone to come with news.

Wren Day. December 26.

Once she was in bed, Jackie could let go. Maria was off with somebody, maybe Adam, and hopefully would stay all night with them, but Jackie didn't want to sob, didn't want anyone to hear. Her whole body shook, as if she was going into shock. At the same time she felt excited, wondering what would happen the next day. She wanted to be up early to get breakfast on. It was the last of the twelve days, after which most of the tourists would leave. The Beauty's tour group would be gone and with them, all memory of her. Jackie would have to decide what to do, stay or go. She loved it on the island and felt as if she'd found some good people.

She wondered what the day would hold, what she would need to do.

A beam of early morning light struck Jackie; she woke alert and bright as if she'd had a good night's sleep. The bird call seemed quieter than previous days, but still musical and beautiful. You never heard birds like that in the city.

Humming to herself, she dressed and pulled on her thick coat and warm boots. Her breath frosted in the air, which was good. Maria had stayed out all night and so hadn't insisted on the heating. Heating was bad for the complexion.

Walking to the restaurant, she saw children chasing birds, throwing stones, their parents laughing and, it seemed, morning drinking, sharing a flask of something.

In the restaurant, staff were drinking as well, getting stuck into mimosas and Bloody Marys.

"You spend this day drunk or stoned," Nigel said. He handed her a Bloody Mary, potent as fuck, which she discovered on first sip.

She was sure they were tricking her, faking the drinking and would do so until she was drunk and silly. She wondered which of the men would try to take her home. Had they drawn straws? She threw back half her Bloody Mary and held out her glass for a top up.

"Good days from here on," Nigel said.

Maria and Adam arrived together, leaning on each other, Maria looking peaceful and actually happy.

Some of the tourists were already gone, so there were fewer diners. As Jackie began cooking a black pudding, Nigel took the utensils from her hands.

"You should take a break. You look all in."

"Cooking is resting for me," she said. "I love cooking! Love feeding people." She paused. "You can't eat me, though."

"Gross!" Maria said. Her hair was pulled into a high messy ponytail which Adam must have done for her. She looked tired but content. She grabbed a croissant to eat, checked the coffee machine.

"Sometimes I think you just work here for the free food," Nigel said, handing her a coffee and the brandy bottle. "Let's get breakfast done and the lunches made and then we can do some serious drinking."

During breakfast prep, a young boy stood in the doorway of the kitchen until Jackie noticed him.

"It's the Beauty," he said. "I found her all smashed up and ugly." He mooshed his face to demonstrate. The staff all clamoured. "They're taking her body to the mainland. She's so ugly now," he said, "but you're not."

Jackie knew he pointed to her even as she pretended disinterest. In the heart she felt victory and vindication. "You're the one," the boy said.

I've won, she thought. She said, "Do we need a new Beauty, or can we consider it done?"

"Not done! The poor girl was taken in a terrible accident. That can't be the end of it."

Jackie dressed herself in a sweet, pale blue dress. It was fitted around the waist, showed off her bust, flowing nicely, sheer, to above the knee. In the sunlight it was transparent and she stood, and she heard the silence, could feel it like a blessed gift.

Nigel was making a sculpture out of butter, a beautiful winged creature. As she watched, he wiped off the Beauty's face and carved Jackie's instead. That was something, all right.

He told her more about Wren Day.

"A long while ago, they used to actually catch the wrens and beat them black and blue. The more dead birds, the better the year. The wrens disappeared for a long time after that, which people blamed on the clearing of so many trees on the island. For the houses, for the restaurant. You know. Progress. But the birds were smart enough not to come to a place where they'd be beaten black and blue."

"I should box your ears black and blue. It is Boxing Day," she said. She'd heard a comedian say this once, but it was funny then. Now it just sounded stupid. "The wrens are back now, anyway. So what does the Beauty do? What do I do?" she asked.

"That Missie Wren was so beautiful, none of the men would work and all the ground lay fallow. She was so beautiful in the light, though. You won't need to do much. Just being so lovely does the job."

Outside, someone threw leftovers out onto the lawn. Dozens of birds fluttered down to feast. Still no seagulls; she hadn't seen a single one.

Jackie wondered when the fuss and attention would start, when she would be feted. "I better get ready, what do I wear?"

"You look perfect," Nigel said.

⁓

Before noon, they walked in a large group to the tomb. They tried to carry Jackie, but it felt ridiculous, and she laughed so hard they had to put her down. Around the tomb, a great debris of bird feathers, eggs, bodies and bones. More had appeared overnight. Underneath that, a layer of spiders and other insects, curled up in balls.

The wailing cries of the women, the calls of the men mimicking the drowned, it was like one long mournful note that shook her to her core. She shivered.

"It's going to be cold," Nigel whispered, his lips touching her ear, giving her goosebumps. "But I can't wait."

He helped strip her naked and then he painted her black and blue. She was aroused by this, so much so she wanted to grab him right there, have him up against the wall, but he kept painting, stroking, painting, stroking. The sun was warmer and brighter than it should be, casting long shadows.

She had never felt more beautiful, not even when one of the judges on the show had said, "You're gorgeous, but you're a bitch."

Nigel dug a grave for the small birds in the shape of the Beauty they had made from bones, and they buried a mound of tiny bodies. She saw he was crying and wondered why he was so moved. Adam said, "His wife was a beauty. He cries every year over her."

Even then, she didn't think. It didn't seem possible. His wife had died, but that was an accident. "How did his wife die?" she whispered to Adam.

"Choked on a bone," he said. "It's what happens when someone cheats. Nigel adored her, which counts for a lot, but the birds didn't choose anyone that year. They didn't want a Beauty at all. And yet there she was."

When the time came Jackie lay down in the bone shadow. She felt the cold earth creep into her bones, let her form fill out the shadow space. Fitting into the other girl's shadow. She felt beaks poking into her; he had buried them so shallow.

Everyone moved the bones until they sat snug around her. She had come to cook; because she was asked. She'd come because she'd lost when she should have won, and because she loved to cook, and this was a lifetime opportunity. She'd found friends here; Maria, and Adam, and Nigel. She trusted them.

She was frightened though. Would they burn her like a yule log? They'd give her some kind of drug, and she'd dream of warmth, of travelling in the sun aboard a beautiful golden horse. Or they'd bury her in the tomb, leave her there a year until her bones waited for the sunlight to enter. She'd watched them sweep the bones out; that was last year's Beauty, wasn't it? And that would be her.

She tried to sit up, shivering, freezing now, wanting to run. Nigel helped her up and held her to him, pressing her hard against his fur jacket. She could feel the buttons, feel his breath. He said, "I'm going to warm you up, my love. You will feel beautiful inside and out. This is going to feel so good." She loved that he believed she deserved to be the Beauty. She *did* deserve it, she *was* the Beauty. He said, "You really are the Beauty, the real deal."

"What would happen if I wasn't?"

"You are."

Someone gave her a coat to wear, nothing underneath, and she thought she'd die from the pleasure of it. Her feet were like ice and Nigel picked her up, tucking her feet under his arm. He seemed huge, enormous, so much bigger than she was. She felt small and light, a feathery breath on her cheeks, her hair fallen loose from the braid.

If he threw her in the air, she thought she would fly.

He didn't, though. There was a terrible squawking, a harsh rattling and chattering, a snapping of beaks of a thousand birds, the sky absolutely blackened, and they attacked him, pecking and screeching, drawing blood, until he dropped her and ran (everybody ran, looking back with surprise, *this isn't supposed to happen, is she not the true Beauty?*).

And the wrens had no mercy.

END

I stumbled across the wonderful Newgrange monument while searching for winter solstice traditions. I loved the way the tomb was designed to light up only at winter solstice, and that it had been hidden from human eyes for thousands of years. I wanted to capture the food celebrations of Christmas time, and found an old French version of the Twelve Days of Christmas, which listed things like "A Good Stuffing Without Bones."

For the recipes, I used a series of books by Maggie Black, "Food History and Recipes". It was the chapter "Flesh-Day Dishes" that really inspired me!

THE VISITATION

Jeffrey Ford

F ROM sunrise on the day of Christmas Eve to sundown on the day after Christmas, if a stranger comes to your door seeking shelter and assistance, you are compelled to help them. There is a moral prerogative to offer aid all year long, but on the three days mentioned, doing so could very well save your life. As in the biblical story of Sodom, sometimes the strangers aren't lost souls but angels operating in secret on a mission from heaven, testing your charity, your humanity, your spirituality. These are the Angels of Accord. If you act with generosity toward them in their indigent disguise, they will shower you and your family with grace and wealth.

On the other hand, whatever amount of negativity you feel in relation to helping the stranger, that amount of negativity— no more, nor less—will fall back upon you. Supposedly, there are those who, when tested, died as a result of their lack of charity. At the very least, things can go terribly wrong and a darkness might swallow your life. It is said that the belief and practice of what was called by old timers Heimsuchung, or "Visitation," originated in those areas of Northern Germany where small groups of Vikings had settled. Before being assimilated by a Christian splinter group, transformed into a story of angels and Christ's reward and revenge, the holiday practice began back in pre-history, in the age of Odin, a sleek creature of an idea of natural community that leaped out of the forest and mated with human imagination.

A belief in the Visitation, though not very popular even in the old country, somehow smuggled itself among the Amish and Mennonites voyaging to the New World on the *Charming Nancy* in 1736. There was a handful of the sect known as the Church of the Angels of Accord—bible-centric beliefs with a few appropriated folk beliefs disguised in Christian trappings. The supposed impetus for Christ's test of the faithful is the fact that his parents were denied any shelter or kindness in the events leading up to his birth. They tried for lodging everywhere, but were turned away, and had to settle for their child, Son of the Living God, being born in a manger, with a bed of straw and animal attendants.

There were enough members of the Church of the Angels of Accord who eventually made the journey to America to create three towns. These were situated in south-western Ohio; the largest one, and the one still in existence, is Threadwell. The other two towns, Bashville and Solantri, both grew old and empty— folks moved off to bigger places like Cleveland and Columbus and Springfield—and then they just rotted and fell apart.

If you can find old books from as late as the 1930s about Christmas in Ohio, the belief in the Visitation might be mentioned.

There was one book—*Strangers* by Esther Grant, from Golden Peacock Press, 1945, a compilation of these types of encounters with secret angels sent to test humanity. The last known or suspected encounter with one of the Angels of Accord was only a couple of years ago. It took place in the farmland on the outskirts of Threadwell.

It was during a blizzard, on Christmas Eve. The temperature dove and the wind whipped, but inside the farmhouse, colored lights were strung upon a tree and around the fireplace mantle in the living room. The house was otherwise dark, upstairs and in the cellar and back in the kitchen and dining room. Jill sat on a rocker and Owen sat on a small couch, between them was a marble-topped coffee table. To her left, and his right, there was a large window that looked out to the road, one hundred yards away.

They watched the snow drive down from the west, watched the drifts form in the blue-gray light of late afternoon, drinking whiskey sours and reminiscing about the ghosts of Christmas past, all the old relatives and their antics. Owen was about to tell a story about Aunt Bob, when he paused and said, "Do you hear a knocking noise?" Jill listened hard and said, "Yeah, I hear it. Very faint." He set his drink down and got up. "Who the hell could this be?" he said as he headed through the foyer to the front door.

Out on the porch he found an old man, dressed in a t-shirt and jeans and a pair of boots, no socks. No winter coat, but a long army blanket that he wore like a cape. Its skirt dragged across the snow, frozen solid. The man's eyebrows, mustache, beard, and hair had turned to ice. He said nothing. His teeth chattered and every breath was a cloud. Owen took one look at the stranger and backed up, closing the door quickly. The old man shuffled forward but the latch clicked shut in his face.

Jill was in the foyer behind Owen. "Who is that?" she asked.

"You know that bum in town, the one who hangs out around the Circle K, panhandling money for beer? I see him sleeping in the laundromat sometimes."

"That guy's a creep," she said. "Tell him to beat it."

Owen thought for a moment and then shook his head. "I can't do that."

"Why not?" she asked. A moment passed and she added, "OK, I'll tell him."

"No," he said and held up a hand. "Remember the Heimsuchung."

"The what?"

"From my religion."

"You don't have a religion. I haven't seen you in a church since we were married."

"Well, not *my* religion," he said. "It was my grandmother's grandmother's, the Church of the Angels of Accord. You can't turn people away on Christmas Eve."

"I've never known you to believe in any religious whim-wham," she said.

"It's not the religious angle, it's that my grandmother seriously warned me about this when I was young. It was in her room of seashells. We were staring out the window at the snow coming down through dusk. She made me promise never to turn away a stranger on the three days of Christmas. I'm gonna let him in."

She shook her head and exhaled in exasperation. "As soon as the storm ends, you're taking him back to town to the homeless shelter."

"OK," he said and went to the door.

A few minutes later, Owen and the stranger sat at the kitchen table. The man from town had Jill's couch blanket wrapped around him. His army blanket had been peeled off and thrown in the washer. He was shivering and what teeth he had were clicking together in an aggressive, annoying rhythm. Steam rose off him as the frost from his hair and beard evaporated. Jill made coffee, and side-eyed his filthy clothes and his droopy eyes and big ears. She was certain he wasn't right in the head. When she handed him a hot cup, he grunted and she stared over at Owen, who shrugged.

"What's your name?" she asked.

He sat silently, moments passed, and then he straightened in the chair and spoke in a high-pitched voice, quietly but deliberately. "My name is Macin Buren. I am 107 years old." Owen raised his eyebrows. It was obvious the man was no more than mid-sixties. Jill laughed. "You look pretty good for 107."

"I know," he said. He drank the coffee quickly and seemed to thaw before their eyes. Every so often, the stranger emitted a sound like a nearly inaudible pop, sometimes a run like a string of pearls. At first, Jill thought she was projecting her negativity onto the stranger, and that she hadn't heard a fart or smelled the odor that permeated the kitchen like a memory of low tide. Only when she caught Owen's expression did she realize it was all really happening and she turned away to gag.

"How'd you get here to our door, Mr. Buren? On Christmas Eve, in a blizzard no less?"

Macin looked over at Owen and said, "Did I tell you that I'm 107? Do I look it?"

"I wouldn't say that you're the picture of youth, but you're definitely no 107," said Owen and laughed as if the whole thing was a joke everyone was in on. An instant later, he could see he'd been mistaken. The stranger was not laughing, and Jill wore an expression that let him know she'd known all along the old man wasn't kidding.

"What's your secret, Mr. Buren?" Jill asked.

"I have the ability to exhale my death. I summon it together, a dark cloud, in my solar plexus and then I siphon it off into the atmosphere as I move through my day. I titrate it so that it doesn't pollute but vanishes. If I wanted to, I could put out a fog of death. I try to keep it within legal limits. My practiced exhalations make it undetectable to most humans."

"And so you stay ahead of your age by exuding your death as it accumulates within you?" asked Owen.

"Eventually it'll catch me. Thank you for taking me in. I'd have frozen in the storm. No matter how fast I leeched off my death, I could never have overcome the spell of the blizzard. I'm still trying to regulate my breathing in order to keep my exhaust at tolerable levels."

"What if you can't?" Jill asked.

"Build up. It's not good for anyone. If I put out too much, you'll begin to see it like a faint orange dust falling from my lips. If it sneaks out the back hatch, after achieving a certain level, you'll hear those ejections like the sound of a trumpet played by cat and the aroma will be a green deliquescence."

"My wife wants to know if it will affect our health."

"Probably not," he said and stood up, holding the blanket around him. Owen asked if he needed a bathroom, but Macin shuffled directly to the refrigerator and opened the door. He reached in and grabbed something and turned back around to face the couple, letting the blanket fall to the floor. There was a plastic tub of cream cheese under his arm. He flipped the lid off and reached in to pull out a chunk of the damp white brick. Eating ferociously, he smeared the cheese all over his face and whiskers, wiped his hand on his t-shirt and jeans. Jill got up and left Owen to his angel.

She sat in her rocking chair amid the colored lights in the living room, squinting at the Christmas tree and finishing her whiskey sour. She cursed the hideous weirdo Owen had dragged in and felt the holiday slipping from her grasp. It was their first Christmas with the kids gone, all three moved to their own places, and it was to have been just her and Owen. She stared for a long time at the colored lights, and the orange cat they called Me-Mau came from under the couch and stepped up into her lap. She spoke to it. "It's one thing harboring someone from the storm, but why does it have to be a disturbed dirt-bag?"

Jill had dozed off in front of the Christmas tree by the time Owen came to fetch her for bed. He shook her shoulder gently and sat back on the small couch. She roused and looked around.

"Where is he?" she said.

"I have him back behind the kitchen in Pete's room."

"I hate to think of him in that bed. How about that B.S. about him exhaling his death? I feel like I should constantly be vacuuming."

"I was thinking we should wear masks," he said. "It didn't seem like he was titrating those farts too judiciously."

Jill laughed. "It's horrible. I feel like I can taste a film in my mouth." She lifted her empty whiskey sour glass from the coffee table and spit in it. Leaning back in her chair, she said, "Well, Christmas is shot."

"If he'd stayed out in the storm, he'd be dead," said Owen.

"True." She nodded.

"Listen, if this is actually a visitation and we do a good job, we could be in the money. I say we err on the side of kindness."

"Are you serious? Now, all of a sudden, you believe in this stuff?"

"I got a hunch," he said. "You don't think this guy's off?"

"Of course, he's off."

"Maybe it's because he's an angel. It all kinda fits together," said Owen.

"Kinda is the operative term."

Jill woke and heard him moving in the night, a slow, monotonous plodding. He went through the house, room to room, and when he stopped in their bedroom and stood over the bed, she felt the breeze of his arrival and managed to close her eyes to slits at the last instant. She spied on him standing in silence, an arm's length away, naked and pale. Then he was gone. She waited until she heard him elsewhere in the house before rousing Owen.

"He's all over the fucking place," she said. "I've been listening to him."

"He's probably looking for the bathroom," said Owen.

"I wouldn't go into a dark house without a flashlight and a stick. You don't know what the hell he's into."

"Now you're scaring me," said Owen.

"Maybe he's not a human or an angel. Maybe he's the devil."

"Why are you saying that?"

"So you can see how stupid it sounds."

He got out of bed and went to his dresser where he had a flashlight in the sock drawer. The wooden martial arts baton lay as always across the nightstand. He took it up and headed for the hallway, dim beam leading the way. "Close the door and lock it," he said.

"Give me a password for when you get back."

He called over his shoulder, "Open up."

She'd meant to tell Owen to tell Macin that, if he liked not freezing to death, he should calm down and go to sleep. She closed the door, locked it, and went back to bed. He was gone a long time and, behind the howling of the wind, she heard strange noises sound intermittently from different quarters of the house. Having the covers pulled up over her head didn't help. Eventually, she got out of bed, got dressed, and unscrewed a leg off the small desk bench to use as a club. She left the room and closed the door behind her.

At the top of the stairs, she called Owen's name but there was no answer. The minute she'd stirred from the bed, all the noises stopped. The place was sunk in stillness. She descended slowly, holding tight to the rail and the bench leg. The foyer, where the stairs ended, and the living room and dining room were all dark, but the lights were on in the kitchen. As she moved toward it, she saw a haze as if something was burning on the bottom of the

JEFFREY FORD

oven. It didn't smell like charred steak or cheese. The aroma was dank and mysterious, a stout turd with a hint of rotten meat.

She stepped into the fog, and the fluorescent lights above showed her Owen and Macin at the kitchen table. Her husband was fallen back in his chair, his flesh loose and wrinkled, his eye lids nearly closed, showing only a sliver of white. He was twitching. The stranger leaned forward as if vomiting, silently expelling mouthfuls of orange dust and dark smog. The glowing substance filled the tabletop and was slowly, like in a dream, cascading toward the floor, gathering in Owen's lap.

Jill screamed, trying to wake either of them. She grabbed Owen under the arms and dragged him off the chair toward the door. He was far too heavy for her, though, and she dropped him onto the linoleum after only a few feet. As she struggled, grasping his wrists, to try to pull him clear of Macin's spew, she grew weary and slightly dizzy. She knew it wouldn't be long until she surrendered to the poisonous fog and both of them succumbed to a death meant for Macin.

The thought of this made her angry, and she dropped her husband's arms and lunged for the knife block on the counter. Her left hand wrapped around the handle of the carving knife of the set. She knew it was sharp, as she had sharpened it herself only the previous week. Macin choked and heaved a half dozen times. More dust fell. His eyes opened, as she made her move toward him. He growled in that high-pitched voice and then shrieked when the blade dug into the side of his neck.

She pulled the knife out with all intent of stabbing him again, but the edges of the wound she'd just inflicted rippled like cartoon lips as orange death sifted out down his shoulder. The speed and

332

force of exuded dust increased and whistled like a tea pot. Jill backed up, and as she did the side of Macin's face blew off into a dusty orange blossom in mid-air. The force of it knocked her onto the floor next to Owen, who was starting to come around. She tasted the chalky residue in her mouth. Helping him to his feet, she led the way up to their bedroom on the second floor. They stripped off their clothes in the hallway near the clothes washer, and they each took a shower.

They celebrated Christmas in rubber gloves and masks, lassoing Macin's ankles and wrists and dragging him through the sliding glass door that looked out toward snow-covered fields. Owen wasn't much help. It was like he'd aged ten years and was now in his mid-sixties. His joints hurt and he easily lost his breath. The blizzard was still blowing, albeit not quite as ferociously as earlier, so they only dragged Macin a few yards to the side of the shed. The enormous wound in his head left a streak of glowing orange on the snow. There he lay as the winter buried him in a white mound. Owen watched from the window while Jill swept, vacuumed, and mopped. When all was said and done, night had fallen and they made coffee.

"Pretty amazing how easily you can vacuum up death," said Owen.

"Concentrate," she said. "We're going to have to figure out what to do with that body before the snow starts to melt."

"We should just call the cops."

"And tell them I knifed him in the neck and his head exploded from the release of death dust? Exposure to that thing's made you a little stupid."

"Definitely slowed me down."

That night, they exchanged Christmas gifts and sat together in front of the tree. He gave her a diamond pendant and she gave him a sweatshirt and socks and a book about World War II. They slept that night, but not well. Owen was now worried about the body under the snow, and Jill woke from dreams where she thought she heard something plodding around the house in the dark. The next morning, after breakfast, they went out in the yard. They each grabbed a broom from the shed and swept the snow off Macin's mound. To their relief there was no body. To their horror there was a long white feather.

Owen never recovered from his exposure to Macin's toxins but grew weaker by the month. Jill spent the following Christmas Eve in the hospital next to her husband's death bed. From that day forward, whenever it snowed at the holiday with any ferocity, Jill would hear a banging at the front door. When the dreadful rhythm sounded, she hid in the upstairs hall closet, the carving knife in her left hand. This went on for years.

Finally, when she was as old as Owen had suddenly become, a good-sized snowstorm hit Threadwell on Christmas Eve. Instead of hiding in the closet, Jill sat ready with the carving knife. She wore gray sweatpants and shirt, sneakers, forearm pads and knee pads that her kids had used in sports. Squinting at the lights on the Christmas tree, she sipped a whiskey sour and listened to Bing Crosby on the radio. In the middle of "White Christmas," a knocking sounded at the door. She put down her drink and rose.

She cocked back her knife hand as she turned the knob and pulled the door open. There didn't seem to be anybody there. Just the moaning wind and the blowing snow. She flipped on the outside light and stepped out on the porch to find it was devoid of angels, only littered here and there with snow drifts. She looked around and off into the darkness of the field next to the house. As she turned back to go inside, it hit her from the left and partially knocked the wind out of her. There was a battering storm of wings beating and a sharp set of talons pierced her side and latched onto her rib cage. She cried out. The pain was excruciating and it made her drop the knife.

She went dizzy and faded in and out, but it seemed she was being lifted off the ground and flown through the storm. She could see the occasional lights of farmhouses below. She tried to look up and see if it was Macin that had kidnapped her, but it was too dark. By the time she had come to her senses to try to retaliate or save herself, her captor unhooked the talons and dropped her from the height of a barn roof into a snowbank with straw beneath it. Maneuvering with the wound in her side was difficult on the snow, but she managed to get to her feet. Staggering, freezing cold, her face feeling frostbitten, she made it to the closest farmhouse door.

She banged on the door and leaned against a column on the porch. There was a light on out there and she saw herself in the glass of the storm door. She looked older than she thought she should: pale, tired, sick, and the outfit she had on came across as more than a little crazy. Then the porch light went out, the wooden inside door opened and a light went on. There was a man—bald head, glasses, a green cardigan sweater—standing there looking at her. Next to him was a woman dressed in a white glittery evening gown. She had a martini in her hand and was smoking a cigarette. The man grimaced and shook his head. The woman's nose wrinkled up as if she was smelling shit. The door closed. The light went out.

Jill stood shivering in the freezing dark and wondered if she might be an angel.

 END

I was in a secondhand shop in Mt. Victory, Ohio, and I came across this old book, its cover a light green and embossed with pinecones. Its title was Christmas Past, *and the author was Carol Toppert. If I remember correctly, its publication date was in the early 1940s by a press in Ohio. The idea behind the book was to discover and record Christmas holiday rituals, beliefs and practices, religious or secular, that have either severely faded or completely disappeared. She had gathered the remains of these rituals from around the world and wrote them up for her book.*

Since I live in Ohio, I was drawn to the one about Ohio, especially the town of Threadwell, not far from here. Ms. Toppert laid out possible origins of each folkloric belief, what its antecedents were, and what might have been its offspring. In quite a few instances throughout the book, she'd stop and tell a story about one of the forgotten beliefs, and they were fascinating. In the case of "Visitation," she did not. So, I took it upon myself to set the universe right.

THE LORD OF MISRULE

M. Rickert

E VER since that first year, when I stood staring at the cross atop the Cathedral San Juan Bautista with its gothic façade—white against the night, as if fashioned from snow and ice—I have become a holiday traveler, waiting in long airport lines to gaze out of little windows at a diminishing world, landing in places where no one knows my name.

The cross pierced a star-flecked sky, and I closed my eyes to inhale the sweet perfume of January's bloom in Puerto Rico, something like a prayer forming at my lips but, before I could speak, *It* did.

"Darla, here you are. I've been looking and looking."

Slowly, I turned, and there It was. Scowling up at me from beneath Its paper crown, red hair pierced by blue lights hung like icicles from the trees.

"No," I said. "I won't. Not again."

It stamped Its foot in Its teddy bear slipper, formed Its hands into fists. "Do you remember who I am?"

"Of course I do."

"Say it."

"Lord," I sighed.

"The whole thing."

"Lord of Misrule."

It smiled, or at least Its lips turned in an upward direction. My resolve, that I would die rather than indulge this creature again, diminished with Its every step until the small cold hand slipped into mine, inciting a shiver I camouflaged by squeezing lightly, the way one might do with a beloved child.

"Look."

A children's choir. Their faces luminous. The audience with their backs to us, completely unaware of what stood watching. So absorbed was I in my dread that I did not immediately notice the little girl who had moved away from the assembled crowd until I felt Its icy grip tighten, a vice that stopped my blood before It let go. She was jumping awkwardly, landing in a squat like someone who had just learned how to make it all work, delighted with the process.

How innocent. Blue lights dripping from the banyan trees. The grownups absorbed in watching the carolers. A little girl jumping. A creature, surely not a boy though he maintained that appearance everywhere but the eyes, in paper crown leading her to me, standing in the dark. She looked up then, the little darling, and I watched her face morph from innocence to fear as if, suddenly, even so young, she knew enough to be afraid.

"Come," I said. Kind but firm. When I offered my hand, she took it.

Afterward It said, "Don't blame me. If you didn't try to hide here, little Aliss would still be alive."

It began as a love story.

I met Patrick in the autumn, a "cute meet" as they say, though its impact was more volatile than the descriptor implies. I was biking on Birch Lane, distracted by the soft shower of leaves fluttering down around me, when Patrick opened his car door, which I crashed into. He said it all happened so fast it was as if I had fallen from the sky to land at his feet, a jumble of legs and arms and skirt, the flowers that had been in my basket, a pot of orange mums, shattered into clogs of dirt and blossoms.

In spite of my affinity for cottagecore, evidenced by my old-fashioned fender bicycle with its wicker basket, I did wear a helmet. Nonetheless, a bored policewoman transported me to the hospital where I was diagnosed as "scratched and bruised and fine."

I didn't expect to find Patrick, who I'd last seen texting by the side of the road, in the lobby, but there he was, hunched in a chair, hands gripped to form a massive fist, head bowed. Looking so forlorn that my best friend, Libby, who I had called to pick me up, later said she thought he was grieving.

But when he saw me, he stood up to apologize and, in short order, asked if he could take me out to dinner sometime, which would have been completely inappropriate except for the fact that I, too, felt that chemistry between us. When I agreed, his smile illuminated the freckles on his broad face. I walked out of the hospital into the darkening day, a sky bruised with gray clouds, wondering at the way life turns.

It wasn't long before we were a couple, laughing at each other's corny humor and forming the sort of private system of communication I once found annoying in others, where either of us could say a single word, "clam," for instance, that would set us into a fit of giggles.

You understand. We were happy. And, in spite of our shared penchant for behavior which might have been described as juvenile (which I might have described that way, were I the outsider, as Libby was) the giggles, and tickles, the popcorn fights and the like, the sex was something else. Many times, I wondered about my attraction to what he became in orgasm, his face a rigor mask before he gasped into my throat, "Darla," until the time he said something else.

"Shalia."

"Who?"

Well, of course we'd had other lovers but, unlike me, he had been in a long-term relationship. Shalia, he insisted, was entirely in his past. Except for this one thing.

"Turns out I have a son," he said.

What? Was there anything else I didn't know? Why the big secret?

"No secret," he said. "Not from me, at least. She's a vindictive person, Darla. I didn't even know she was pregnant when we broke up. She never told me, and then she moved out of state. He's five years old and I only just found out about him. Here's the good thing. She's quite ill. Well, that's not good, obviously, but it turns out that the idea of leaving him to be raised by her mother is even more objectionable than leaving him with me. If that happens. Who knows? She might recover. Either way, she has some regrets. She wants us to get to know each other. And of course I want to know him. He'll be at the farm."

"For Christmas, you mean?"

"The Solstice. Remember? We celebrate Solstice in my family. Please say you'll come."

How could I not agree? I'd been hearing about this idyll, nestled in the driftwood region of Wisconsin, since our first date. The farm was where Patrick spent his childhood summers capturing fireflies in mason jars capped with lids to use as bedside lanterns. A charming picture until it came out how, after neglecting to make air holes, he dumped their tiny corpses on the lawn in the morning, laughing when I recoiled at this detail.

"Come on, Darla," he said. "I was a child. You can't hold that against me. I bet there are regrettable things you did when you were too young to understand the ramifications. That's what childhood is all about, isn't it, learning the limits of behavior?"

I couldn't disagree. My mind reeled with uncomfortable associations. How many times had I guided one of my kindergartners from conduct that, within the adult world, would have been considered psychotic?

I asked myself this very question (though it was really more assertion than inquiry) on that last day before vacation, as I stood beneath paper snowflakes dangling from the ceiling, watching Aaron Marekily, in his red sweater vest and green bowtie, pummel Lisa Rogilin with a plastic Santa Claus because, Aaron said, Lisa had stomped on his candy cane.

The evidence, a crush of red and white on Lisa's shoe, seemed indisputable even as she insisted she hadn't done it. But I had learned, long ago, that litigation is not always the best course for justice. Instead, I told both of them to apologize. Aaron, whose outburst was completely out of character, easily acquiesced. Lisa took a bit more cajoling.

"Say you're sorry," I ordered, "and I won't tell your mother about this."

She apologized glumly and without any trace of sincerity, but even an insincere apology is better than none. Later, I watched as they hugged goodbye. Admittedly, Lisa's hold seemed tighter and longer than necessary, more clutch than embrace, but I was pleased nonetheless. The small, innocent transgression would not follow her into all her Christmases as evidence of an unforgivable nature.

The children gone, I collected the presents they'd given me and packed the leftover sweets into Tupperware to bring with me to the farm, pausing to watch the snowflakes fall outside the classroom window. I had a long drive ahead of me. Patrick had left earlier in the week to spend some one-on-one time with his son before the house was filled with revelers. I imagined the party was already in full swing as I inched my Toyota out of the parking lot, empty but for Gerald the janitor's truck with its cheerful wreath hung lopsided from the grille.

"Are you sure you can't take off a few days early?" Patrick had asked. "Or at least stay longer?"

"I wish," I said. "I really do. But... if... maybe..."

"What? Did you think of a way?"

I shook my head. What I'd thought of was that, with proper notice, I might be able to arrange a substitute next year—but we weren't at that point yet. Talk of a shared future had not bridged more than a few months. In fact, so focused had we been on the Solstice, I realized going over it in my head as I merged onto the highway, that any plans made for after the twenty-fourth, when I would drive back to celebrate with my parents, were vague. Relentlessly optimistic, I still held onto a small hope Patrick and his son would accept my invitation to spend Christmas with me at my parents' house. After all, what child wouldn't want two Christmases? Because honestly, that's what it seemed like to me. Christmas one and Christmas two. It wasn't something I said directly, but I must have betrayed my sentiments because Patrick remarked, with the first hint of annoyance I'd detected in our relationship, "It isn't just Christmas with a different name, you know. You are only going to be there for a small portion of the Solstice tide as it is. I wish you would take it seriously."

The Solstice tide, I had learned, encompassed the seventeen-day period from December twentieth to January sixth, a daunting amount of time to spend with strangers, even in the company of the man I loved.

Besides, the truth was, I didn't want to miss my family celebration. Not even for Patrick or his son would I give up the Banner Family Christmas chili, and hot chocolate with real whipped cream, and black-and-white movie night, my mother's fruit cake (a treat much-maligned in holiday movies, but thoroughly enjoyed in our house) the mess of wrapping paper and ribbon, the mess of us. It made me wonder, briefly, if I really cared about Patrick the way I thought I did, or was merely comforted by the idea after worrying for so long that there was something wrong with me that did not allow love.

The highway, cleared by constant traffic, felt less treacherous than the roads had been. Never a confident driver, I decided not to add to my anxiety by thinking about our little holiday conflict, focusing instead on how much I enjoyed the car heat and the carols on the radio. I relaxed for that first hour and a half in the gingerbread-scented space until GPS notified me of an exit I immediately feared I wouldn't find, imagining myself lost, driving off into a trajectory from which there would be no escape.

There are so many ways to be lost, aren't there? People said I "lost" my sister, even as I stood by her casket. Yet, there she was. I had to look quite hard to see the scar beneath her bangs and the artful application of corpse make up, the small wound above eyes that opened, in my dreams, black as coal.

"Here, I am," I whispered, peering through the falling snow at the road barely revealed by headlights. "I fell in love. I think. And I'm on the way to meet the kid that might be my stepson. Maybe dreams do come true. For me, at least."

What possessed me to laugh the way I did? It didn't sound like joy, more a guffaw or jeer. Like somewhere, deep inside, I didn't believe myself.

Finally I saw golden squares of light, windows lit against the storm, the farmhouse on a snowy hill like a scene scratched out of oblivion. I slowed to traverse the long, bumpy driveway, aware of the threat of ice beneath my tires, convincing myself that the trepidation I felt was only a natural response to my situation. Yet, when finally parked among the other cars, I sat considering a house with long, dark snakelike figures draped across porch railings and beneath windows, as if it was being consumed by boa constrictors, before I saw it right; swags of evergreen boughs, probably lovely in daylight. The mind can play tricks.

Not sure how to proceed, having arrived late to this family celebration, I decided to leave my suitcase, but reached into the backseat for the Tupperware filled with treats I'd salvaged to share, as well as a bottle of wine entirely chosen for its Krampus label. I walked carefully up the snowy stairs to knock beneath a large wreath laden with real fruit. When the door swung open it took me a moment to figure out that I needed to look down to find my greeter, a little boy sporting a gold paper crown atop his red curls, bathrobe cinched tight at his waist, a crest of some kind over his heart. I took all this in at a quick glance, startled by his face which, in spite of the bow-shaped mouth and button nose, bore a surly expression hardly expected on one so young.

"Who are you?" he said, his tone surprisingly bossy. "Why are you late?"

But before I could answer, the little imp raised his hand, palm out.

"Do you know who I am?"

Dear God, I thought, I hope not.

"Speak. Yes or no."

"No." With a quick glance at the cheerfully decorated room (garlands, candles, and even a tree, I wasn't sure there would be one) and seeing no one else there to mind, I added, "I am not sure I care to."

"I am the Lord of Misrule."

"Is that right?"

"Sir."

"Excuse me?"

"From now on, you must address me as Sir."

It was all I could do not to roll my eyes. Where was everybody? What had Patrick been thinking to leave me to this troubled child?

"Well, do you want a cookie?" I asked, and when his brows lowered, "Sir?"

"Yes, please," he said, sounding suddenly very much like an ordinary five-year-old.

I handed him the Tupperware. Let him at it, I thought. I wasn't going to worry about managing his behavior when clearly he'd been allowed free rein long before my arrival.

He ran off with it, as if worried I might change my mind, clomping up the gaily decorated stairs in his little teddy bear slippers, pausing halfway to shout, "Everyone is released. I release you all," and suddenly the space was filled with people emerging from closets and other rooms, dressed in bright-colored clothes, wearing ivy crowns and mistletoe boutonnieres, scotch plaid taffeta and velvet greens. Out of this festive midst came Patrick, who wrapped me in his arms as tightly as if we'd been separated for years.

"Darla. You made it. You're here."

"Patrick, why didn't you tell me this was a costume party?" I whispered.

"But it isn't," he said, and before I could clarify we were interrupted by a Dickensian man, his portly belly protruding from beneath his vest, an uncle of some kind whose handlebar moustache brushed my face when he kissed me on the cheek, and an auntie—there were so many aunties—who exchanged my cheap bottle of merlot for a mug of hot mulled wine, followed by a pretty cousin who brought me a plate loaded with goose, potatoes roasted in fat, bread stuffing, brandied cranberries, and maple sugar squash.

For a while, at least, I was able to forget the unfortunate Lord of Misrule who, it seemed, could be vanquished by nothing more potent than sugar. I didn't see him again until later, when we were gathered outside by the bonfire. Patrick stood behind me, arms wrapped around my waist, leaning down to kiss my face and neck, sometimes executed with tiny bites, which was something new between us when, through the flames, I saw a flash of gold bright crown, a scowling face.

I cannot explain what overcame me; some terrible, selfish, territorial behavior. I smirked at the child then turned to Patrick. Lips to lips, tongue to tongue, his hand moved to my breast. Even now I remember the scorched feeling of us before we were ordered apart by a child's voice, distant at first, muffled by the revelry until, upon hearing a command in the expanding silence, I realized it had been repeated several times.

"No touching allowed. No touching allowed. This party is over," he said. "Go home."

Were there smiles and sideways glances? Yes, there were, but everyone did as ordered. In twenty minutes, most of the guests were gone, the population reduced to those spending the night. Back inside, I watched, in horror, as Patrick allowed himself to be bossed around by his five-year-old son, told what food to throw in the trash, what to save, which candles to keep lit, which to blow out, a litany of orders delivered without reason or wisdom.

At last, the wild child yawned, curled into a damask chair by the hearth, closed his eyes and fell asleep, crown askew on his head.

"Patrick," I hissed. "You can't let this behavior continue."

"You don't understand," he whispered. "You didn't see him before. This has been good for him. He's so much happier than he was when he first arrived. I know he's going overboard, but that's not at all unusual on the Lord of Misrule's first day, no matter what the age."

"The first day?" I asked. "How long does this last?"

"Until Twelfth Night. Epiphany," Patrick said, carefully lifting the boy to cradle in his arms.

The crown fell softly to the floor. I bent to pick it up and saw the child watching me, all trace of fascism wiped from his little face. A dimpled hand reached out. I gave him the crown which he took with a sleepy smile as his lids fluttered shut again.

How very horrible I had been. I was shocked by my attitude, dismayed to see how Patrick looked at me. I followed them up the stairs, lugging my small suitcase. More than once my bag clomped loudly against the inconsistent risers. Every time it happened, I saw Patrick's back flex though he did not turn to look, as if he had decided he could not expect much from me, pointing at our room when we reached the landing before continuing down the hallway to tuck his son into bed.

In spite of our bumpy start, I felt optimistic when Patrick entered the room, but never before had I seen him so glum, so cold. When I reached for him in the dark, the only response was the squeak of old springs as he shifted further away and rather quickly, too quickly I felt, his breathing altered. He was pretending to be asleep.

Well, I had tricks for that, but when I began to crawl under the old quilt, Patrick rolled onto his side, turning his back to me and I realized I was in trouble. I stayed there to try to work it out. All my life I had tried to be a better person, and yet I disappointed everyone, even Libby, who recently invited me to meet her at the Java House for our annual gift exchange, then proceeded to relay her grievances.

"I don't just want to be your fill-in friend," she said, and pushed up the rim of her purple-framed glasses which, too large for her small face, made her look like an owl. "Ever since you met him, it's all about Patrick."

I'd been so annoyed with her jealousy but, curled into a fetal roll, my face pressed against my lover's cold back, I reconsidered. After all, look at me. Jealous of a child.

It was then I decided to explain myself to Patrick. From within my warm cocoon, I told him about my sister. When he finally moved, turning toward me, I guessed I was welcome to sit beside him. Instead, I remained wrapped in the comfort of my dark place.

"It was an accident," I said. Yes, I had intended to hit Ella over the head with the flashlight, but I didn't know the blow would be fatal. When she collapsed to the floor, I was in such a state of shock, they later said, that I simply sat beside her to play with the doll we fought over, which is where my mother found me.

"It's messed up," I said. "But my parents didn't want people to think I was some kind of child murderer. So they put Ella in the garden. Called the cops. Said she was missing. They rubbed dirt on the soles of her shoes, her knees and the palms of her hands to make it look like it happened out there. They wiped the flashlight clean then dropped it in the roses. My father must have left it outside they said, after searching for night crawlers.

She wasn't found for hours. Even when it started raining again, we had to pretend we didn't know she was in the mud. No one ever blamed me. My parents did go through a hard time, the police always suspect the parents first, but they moved on from them and then just moved on.

"I know it's messed up, and I am grateful they did it. Otherwise, my life would be impossible. I mean how could I have escaped that past? A child murderer? I wouldn't be a teacher, that's for sure. But how will I ever find redemption? It's like I'm locked in a place with no forgiveness.

"I can tell you are disappointed in me. It's just... when I see a child acting out of control, it comes back. They don't know how much damage they can do. And I don't want what happened to me to happen to anyone else."

When I felt his hand on my back, I crawled up to him in the dark, and when we kissed, I realized I had never before been kissed so completely.

So this is love, I thought, this victorious feeling.

But the next morning I awoke alone in that strange bed to the severe light of morning after a snowstorm, the scent of coffee and cinnamon wafting from below. I took a quick shower in the hallway bathroom, the water cold before I was done (the charm of old houses never seems to infect its plumbing) before joining everyone in a bright kitchen bedecked with crimson ribbons, populated by a half dozen aunts and uncles. Patrick stood over the boy balanced on a stool, stirring something in a pan on the stove. Hot chocolate, it turned out. The child did not look up when I gave Patrick a good morning kiss; he just kept stirring and stirring. I noticed he was not wearing his crown.

There was a good deal of banter between the adults, most of which I had trouble keeping track of, allusions to past holidays and the health of people I never met. Someone's gout had gotten worse, and someone else had a gallbladder taken out. I smiled for a while, pretending affection for their stories, but when it became clear no one was paying any attention to me, let my face relax, and helped myself to a muffin, which was quite good, studded with chocolate chips and spiced with cardamom. By the time I was finished, the others had departed to attend to whatever strange preoccupations called them, leaving the three of us with our hot chocolate. Patrick drank his plain, but the child and I opted for whipped cream, a shared frivolity I hoped boded well for us.

That day was filled with the wonderful activities I had always dreamed of. Sled riding! Making snowmen! Warming our cold feet by the fire, an uncle snoring in the chair. Plates of sweets passed about as though none of us need fear eating too much. Dinner was a winter picnic served by the revived bonfire, after which we returned to the parlor to drink mulled wine and eat sugar plums, all our faces lit with the golden light of flames that cast dark shadows on the walls and made the wooden floors look as if they bore dangerous pits. It was then that my high spirits lowered with a somber realization.

"You haven't left me alone with him all day," I whispered to Patrick whose arm was draped across my shoulder as we sat side-by-side on the pink couch. "You don't trust me."

"What? Don't be ridiculous," Patrick said, but he spoke like an actor reading the words without comprehension. "What's stopping you? Not me."

He was right. Yet, in that overheated atmosphere by the hearth, I couldn't shake the feeling of something altered, insubstantial as smoke and as choking if I didn't find a way to alleviate it. I nearly leapt off the couch to plop on the rug beside the child, uncrowned all that day, who had been nothing but sweet and good except for a small period when he'd been ornery in the perfectly normal manner of any five-year-old who'd stayed up too late the night before.

I didn't ask if I could join him, the sort of silly ploy adults do to make children think they are being treated like equals. Every child knows they are not equal to adult power. I simply picked up the white crayon and began coloring. I saw his dimpled hand pause for a moment over the page before he continued. We were quite close, our shoulders nearly touching while we colored, and I thought maybe things would be all right, after all.

But the truth is, once you do something like that, like what I did to my sister, there's no path back to innocence. No matter how desperately I collected sweetness in my life: the fairy lights strung throughout my apartment, the assorted teapots, the old quilts, the braided rugs, the children... all the children, I always suspected my life was, at its core, corrupt.

That night, when Patrick came to bed, he mumbled something about how tired he was, then turned his back on me. It was late but I knew it wasn't the hour, or the snow that shone with blue tint beyond the old glass that caused the chill between us. Patrick, who could be so forgiving of his own obnoxious child, could not forgive me for the child I once was.

I shouldn't have told him.

The moon shone through the lace curtains, creating a pattern of flakes across the coverlet and walls, a shadow world so close to our own that I stared at until my eyes burned.

I was awakened, that next morning, by the Lord of Misrule bursting into the room, crown lopsided on his head.

"Pancakes!" he ordered. "I want pancakes."

Laughing, Patrick lunged away from my reach to scoop up the interloper who grinned wickedly at me over his father's shoulder as they left the room.

So began the grand pantomime, that holiday tradition I knew well from my own family celebrations, where we all pretended to like each other, to be happy, to be good.

"I'll be right there," I called cheerfully, though no one had asked. I decided to join the festivities in the comfort of the robe I had bought just for the occasion, red—meant to convey holiday cheer in public places and sexy lady in private quarters— pausing to assess its effect in the old mirror propped against the wall, surprised to discover my countenance betrayed a haggard heart. Red lipstick then, and an enthusiastic hair brushing, a dab of evergreen oil behind each wrist. I took broad strides down the long narrow hallway, the robe flaring out in a most dramatic fashion behind me as I descended the stairs, an effect sadly wasted.

I retied the robe's loosening belt on my way into the kitchen where Patrick and the child were absorbed in laughter. I stood awkwardly watching the happy tableau I would never be a part of.

"I know," Patrick said, a hitch of space between each word when I caught his eye before turning his attention to ladling batter onto the griddle. "It's an ornament!"

It was an ordinary round pancake. If he'd asked, I would have shown him how to make a snowman, or a Santa Claus, but he didn't ask, and the Lord of Misrule cheered as if something tremendous had been accomplished before turning to me with his charmingly flour-speckled face.

"No pancakes for you!"

Pretending it didn't bother me at all to be treated so rudely, I poured a bowl of cereal. Completely ridiculous. Insulting, really.

"Where is everyone this morning?" I asked.

"I told them all to go away."

I glanced at Patrick, hoping to see at least a hint of disapproval but he just smiled. "They went into town," he said.

"I can send you away too if I want."

"Yes you can," I said and then, realizing my tone betrayed my disgust, added, "Sir."

He looked at me. For a moment a mere child with flour freckles and maple syrup sparkling his lips who liked being called "Sir."

"Please Sir, what happens next?" I asked. "After breakfast?"

"Fire," the Lord of Misrule shouted. "Fire, fire, fire!"

"Oh, I don't know," Patrick sighed. "That's a lot of work."

"Not so much," I said. "There's a good start out there already."

I noticed, from the corner of my eye, how the little Lord had gone still, watching this exchange.

"Are you sure it's what you want?" Patrick asked the child, who wilted slightly under his father's less-than-enthusiastic response.

"Of course it's what he wants," I rushed in, smiling at the child, my partner against adversity. "Don't you remember who he is?"

Patrick looked at the boy. "My son," he said with the tone of voice I remembered, the one he once used to call me his Darla-darling.

I smiled as if nothing could have made me happier in all the wintery world than to have lost my lover's affection to the disagreeable child currently picking his nose at the table.

"A fire it is," I said, surprised at how harsh I sounded.

The little Lord removed the exploratory finger to point it at his father. "Fire, fire, fire," he shouted. "I command it!"

Patrick gave me a look. Well, I wasn't the one who had insisted on maintaining this rule. It broke my heart a little bit, the mortality of us.

"Darla."

I saw it in his eyes. He knew too. We were done.

"I've had a change of plans," I said. "I'm going to leave today."

A brief shadow crossed his face but when he nodded a second later, his expression held the softness of relief.

"No, you can't go," the little Lord cried.

"You'll have a wonderful time with your father," I said. "And all your aunts and uncles if you quit sending them away."

He appeared to consider this, even as he pouted to charming effect.

"Darla has to go home. You can come help me rekindle the fire."

He shook his head no, the crown tottering on his head.

"I want to stay with her. You go."

Patrick's countenance crumpled with annoyance. Now he knew what it was like to be on the other side of the little tyrant's affection.

"It's ok. I don't have to leave right away."

"If you're sure," Patrick said, addressing the boy who responded by reaching across the table for my hand. I squeezed slightly, staring into his solemn eyes. How different things might have been had we met in another season. Perhaps it was just as well, though, this glimpse into Patrick's ineffective parenting style. The thought of living under this child, any child's, rule was a nightmare.

"You go," I said to Patrick as if I were the one wearing a crown. "We'll join you in a while."

Patrick hesitated but finally left, stomping up the stairs to change his clothes and, not long after, stomping down again and out the front door.

Alone at last with my little nemesis, I looked at the messy kitchen, drips of pancake batter congealing on the countertops and stove, dirty dishes in the sink and on the table, the maple syrup with the cap off, the butter gouged with a tiny knife. I knew I should tidy up. Had I planned to stay, I certainly would have done so. Instead, I asked the Lord of Misrule what we should do next and, after thinking about it for a moment, he decreed we run through the house screaming, which I thought a terrific idea, in keeping with my mood. We commenced immediately, screaming through rooms, up and down the stairs, down hallways and through the kitchen, until our throats were hoarse and the child's complexion quite red. We were collapsed on the rug by the tree when Patrick returned to announce that the fire was ready. Without complaint, the child left with his father to change into outdoor attire.

I knew I should change too, pack my things, leave, but everything was so lovely. So lovely and so temporary. In spite of the pleasures of that last hour, I would never come back to this magical place. I wanted to enjoy every last moment of it. So I remained, allowing myself to pretend it was my house and my tree decorated with glass ornaments, candied cherries and strings of popcorn, still there when father and son came down the stairs and stood side-by-side watching me.

"What's wrong with her?"

"Nothing," Patrick said.

"I'm just doing a little daydreaming."

"Is she coming with us?"

"Well, she has to leave."

"I can come out for a little while," I said.

The child smiled so kindly at me, I wondered if I was making a terrible mistake but then Patrick patted his son's bare head and, though he'd spent the entire day before without the crown, the discovery of this absence incited panic.

"I need my crown. Where's my crown?" he cried.

We searched throughout the house in all its dark corners and mothball-scented closets, even in the pantry where I lingered longer than necessary, admiring the shelves of jewel-colored jellies, boxes of chocolate covered cherries, tins which, when opened, revealed assorted cookies, inhaling the scent of cinnamon, cloves, sugar, and peppermint, wondering how I could possibly give all that up until reminded by a scream that the crown must be found. We looked beneath the couch and on the stairs, we lifted carpet corners, sneezing at the dust. Exhausted, we found ourselves in the kitchen again, lit by the flickering glow of Yule fire which, Patrick said, needed attendance. He explained to the weeping boy how sometimes lost things are found when we stop looking for them, a concept I suspected far too complicated for one so young, but the child wiped his eyes and, after confirming I would say goodbye before my departure, left with his father.

I wondered, as I packed and dressed, if perhaps in spite of my enchantment with the idea of it, I wasn't suited for love. My relief at leaving was far more prominent than any grief over the end of my romance. Certainly that was something to ponder, and I would do so on my long ride home, I thought, absentmindedly looking around the room as I pulled the zipper of my small suitcase closed, and that's when I spied a glimmer of gold behind the open bedroom door.

I picked up the crown, flattened it out with my hand, briefly considered packing it in my bag, this object of my torment. But no, as bad as I had been, I was better than that. Instead, I decided to return the thing to its grieving owner. It was only as I walked across the yard that I plopped it on my head, smiling through the fog of smoke, wondering how long it would take for either of them to notice. I meant it to be funny.

But the boy's scream stopped me in my tracks, stunned that someone so small could emit such a large noise, that someone so unharmed could keen as if grievously wounded. Though our union since this day has been one of terror, I have never seen the little Lord possessed of a fiercer face, blurred by the shimmer of a blazing fire. I think now it was at this moment the boy became the monster, as if within that strange solstice space, when the sun stands still, horror arrived before its reason. A sort of Christmas miracle, or its opposite.

Everything happened quickly. The boy screamed and raised his arms, his little fingers curled like claws. I reached for the crown, but a gust of wind plucked it from my hand and it swirled, golden in the dismal smoke, and the little Lord, surely old enough to know better—but who has not lost their good sense in grief—reached for it. I saw him reaching and Patrick too. In my memory I reach as well, though it makes no sense from where I stood. What could I possibly have grasped from my position where the crown spun away from me towards the boy, standing on tiptoe reaching, reaching, reaching until he fell forward?

Not wanted at the funeral, I picture it in black and white, like an old movie still. White the snow, dark the grave, Patrick and all the aunts and uncles in somber attire. Though none of that is true. Winter's dead must wait for the ground to thaw before they are buried, but the season lingered as if the earth was not eager to claim such a disagreeable child. When the snow began to melt, I thought the worst part was past, but a cold rain fell and the temperature dropped again. Tree limbs broke under the weight of ice and the power lines gave out. I lit candles, and wept by the shivering flames for the terrible damage of my life, once sticking my finger into the fire, thinking, what? That I could be absolved through pain? Of course it didn't work, and the next day, when I buttoned my coat, I felt the shame of my ridiculous hope for redemption. If it hadn't been obvious before, it should have been obvious then. I could not escape the unforgivable things I'd done, any more than I could escape myself.

The temperature crept up once more. The crocus poked purple and yellow through the dirt. I began to enjoy my bike rides again. In the unbearable heat of summer, I finally felt this terrible thing dissipate. After all, who lives a life without damage? To be human is to harm, I cheerfully reasoned while eating a chocolate chip mint ice cream cone, licking the sweet drops from my fingers. By September, when I opened my classroom to a new group of five-year-olds, I believed I'd found peace.

But when the first snow fell, I felt the flakes—so pretty, so ominous—land like stones in my heart.

I tried oh, how I tried, to be a good teacher. I could do nothing for the dead, but at least could be kind to the living, I thought, gazing at all the small faces turned up to me with trust. Once, in a fit of some kind, I told Erica—my problem child that year, there was one in every class—how I, too, had done terrible things, but she only stared at me without compassion, relieved when I sent her away to play.

It seemed that the more I tried to make things right, the worse things became. By December it was obvious that I had lost control. Never before did I have a class that fought so much, bickering over the crayons and the toys and whose foot touched whose knee when they sat on the rug for story time while I watched the falling snow that pounded my heart.

I tried to make it up with the best Christmas party ever, but the frosting failed and the "cookie" houses (made from graham crackers) collapsed under the weight of candy. The children didn't seem to mind. They eagerly ate the chocolate tiles, lemon stick lamp posts, and coconut snow, and left at the end of the day with smeared green and red grins like lopsided harlequins. I wondered if I had it wrong for so long. Maybe the children didn't need me to teach them how to be good, maybe all they needed was to be loved the way they were, with uncontrolled grievances and desires. Wild.

It took quite a while to clean up the apocalypse they left behind. Most of the sweets were unsalvageable, though I was able to collect some cookies into a Tupperware container I set on top of the box filled with gifts, telling myself how happy I was that I didn't have to drive to the farm. What a horrible ride that had been, I thought. How nice to only travel the short distance to my apartment where I ate decapitated gingerbread men and drank wine while opening presents from the children.

Whenever I thought about Patrick or his son or the bonfire, I took another sip. Who cared if I got drunk? I wasn't hurting anyone. A glass unicorn, a Santa mug, a bottle of Shalimar, a box of chocolates, the children gave me lovely things. The final gift was small and square, neatly wrapped, topped with a silver bow. I couldn't remember who had given it to me; there was no card, no name written on the wrapping. This sort of thing had happened before and I had always been able to identify the giver eventually. The package weighed hardly anything. I guessed it to be an ornament, and I was right, though that's not why I gasped when I pulled it out by its copper cord, a gold crown spinning rainbows of Christmas tree light.

By the time I crawled into bed, everything was spinning. I closed my eyes against the dizziness, thinking I couldn't possibly sleep, though I did, awoken to a pale light seeping through the dark, the Lord of Misrule, his crown restored, standing at the foot of my bed.

"I've been looking for you," he said.

"It was an accident. The wind took it from my hand. I did not throw it into the fire."

"I want you to come run and scream with me."

"I can't. You're... You need to go to the light."

"You have to do what I say."

"Or what?"

And suddenly I burned. I burned as if on fire, though I saw no flames, nor smoke, I tell you I burned and the scream that tore through my throat burned too. There is a place where the body is lost to pain, and I promise, you do not want to go there.

It ended quite suddenly. I inspected my hands, my arms, my legs. How could something that hurt so much leave no scar?

"It only stops," he said. "When I say so. Get up now. We're going for a walk."

Of course I did not want to do so, but I also dared not disagree. I slipped into my boots and zipped my coat over my pajamas. Roused out of bed in the night, I had no way of knowing his intentions, even imagining this was a long goodbye, a last visit to the world for one who died too young, an opportunity for me to help this troubled child find his way. It didn't take long however, before I grew weary of the relentless flakes of ice that stung my face, and the exhaustion of following the whims of this non-whimsical creature.

Finally, I inquired what we were looking for. Was it the light, I asked. Because I clearly saw a glimmer of gold on the horizon, dawn I realized.

"Where are the other kids?"

"What kids? What do you mean?"

"I want someone to play with," he said.

"They're sleeping. And besides..." But he was no longer paying attention to me. He stood quite still. Like a cat eyeing its prey. I tracked his gaze to a small figure trudging through the snow, carrying a shovel over his shoulder.

"Petey," I said.

"Who?"

"He shovels people's sidewalks for money so he can buy Christmas gifts for his family. I used to be his teacher. He's too old for you. He must be nine or ten now."

But the obstinate creature was already moving forward, so I followed.

Petey looked at me with eyes like stars, glittering flakes stuck to his long lashes.

"Hey, Miss Dora. Do you want me to take care of your sidewalk?"

"Use the shovel," the Lord of Misrule commanded.

"No," I said. But as soon as I felt the burn, I wanted only to save myself. "Can I see your shovel, Petey? Just for a second?"

He looked puzzled. I smiled reassuringly, and held out my hand.

How swift the mortal blow, how brief innocence, how quickly the dead rise from bloody corpse to stare with black accusing eyes. How they run and scream through the air like gusts of wind, terrifying shadows devoid of life.

I spent that day in bed, wondering how I would explain myself. Who would believe I was not the reason for the horrible thing I'd done? I canceled my plans to spend Christmas with my parents, disappointed when they didn't seem to mind, hoping they would ask if something had happened. *Has it happened again,* I wished to be asked, but never was. I had to accept how inadequate they were. How different would things have been had they stood by my innocence instead of harboring my guilt? I decided to spend the next Christmas far away from everyone I knew and hidden from the Lord of Misrule, in Puerto Rico where I stared at that cross on the eve of Three King's Day, thinking I had made a successful escape, but It found me. It finds me everywhere.

"Where do they go?" I once asked. "Why do you need so many?"

"They only stay a while," It said.

"This could all be over, if you just follow them."

"No!" It said. "Don't you get it? I don't want it to be over!"

I have eaten rice balls in Taiwan, inhaled the perfumed incense of the ancestors, seen the bonfires on Mount Fuji, watched the ship burn in Edinburgh, and been charmed by the Yule lads peeking mischievously from dark corners in Reykjavik where, later, I wept beneath the Northern lights. The children come with me because I know how to convey warm authority. They skip, they jump, they fall into the snow to make angels, they follow us to the basement to die in the dust. We know how to make it look like a family member did it, or it was an accident. We know how to make bodies disappear, never to be found. After all these years, all these different locations, no one has even begun to suspect a connection. I doubt anyone ever will. Just last week, one of my students told me a story about the Christmas angel who travels with a child that wears a crown, visiting good girls and boys.

"Who told you this?" I asked, but she skipped away without answering and I decided to accept it as a gift, this legend we have become.

All my little horror wants is a single night of laughter carved from whatever darkness holds it the other hours of a year, just one night to run beneath the stars, spin in the snow, pluck blossoms from their stems, scream in joy. For one night, the most wondrous terrible night of all, I can give this comfort to a creature trapped between worlds and, for just a while before I wash the blood by morning light, I watch the children play, listening to the glorious sound of laughter ring through the air and, like a morsel tossed to this wretched traveler by my cruel king, I am forgiven.

E N D

I began looking for an idea in my usual way, paging through books of myths, sitting by a YouTube fire, listening to Bach. It began to snow, and the solar candles on my windowsill flickered on. I am sure I dozed in the cozy atmosphere, what happened next only the dream of a mind searching for horror. When I awoke, a small boy wearing a paper crown stood by my chair. I thought he was a gift of sorts. I smiled. He smiled too, then extended his hand, and I felt my death in his reach, burning. It burns still.

NO LIGHT, NO LIGHT

Gemma Files

*T*HERE *is fire under the ice, always: fire and venom, poison, lava, gas; salt blood, eggs and sperm and bone-fragments, a million foetal, fossilized monsters. And lies, also—above all, below all, lies.*

Everything about *me is a lie.*

Lying, I discovered long ago, is a sort of magic. You tell the truth in advance, and make it so, changing other people's timetables for your own; you reframe a story from your own perspective, occult it, change the narrative, make it your own. I've done this since I began to talk, long after my parents thought me likely to—began with a full sentence (factual rather than fictional, at the time), then kept on going. I made words my weapons, my tools, my trade. I clothed myself in a suit of lies and made my way out into a liar's world, already equipped—apparently from birth—to tell exactly how far the version of reality we socially agree to agree upon might be stretched before thinning, let alone before breaking: lied my way through school, from bed to bed, into and out of trouble. Faked my way into and out of things, learned on the job, fell on my feet time and time again. Charm was part of it, yes; I'm not unattractive, though flexible to a fault. Trustworthy, under the right circumstance. Or at least consistent.

You can't simply make *things be the way you say they are, Thomas,* my mother told me, once, after some formative debacle; *some truths are simply* the *truth.* To which I begged to differ, not that I felt it right to do so to her sweet, slightly sad face.

All truths are negotiable, mother, I might have replied, had I truly wished to hurt her. *Even when we don't want them to be.*

Solstice, the point in the year where the sun appears to stand still, reaching either its highest or lowest point in the sky. Winter is said to start with one, on December 21 or 22, which marks the shortest day of the year—once backdated by Christians all the way to December 13, the feast of virgin martyr St. Lucy, upon the theme of whose truncated holiday John Donne once wrote his famous "Nocturnal": *...let me call/ This hour her vigil, and her eve, since this/ Both the year's, and the day's deep midnight is.*

The Vikings, meanwhile, called the same period Yol, from which our word Yule probably evolved. Not Christmas, not originally, but rather the resonance of a far longer darkness to come, a climax both mythic and terminal. Fimbulwinter, Vargavinter—that's what the sagas call it, the dusk before true night falls. Three successive winters when snow blows from all directions, and summer never comes; innumerable wars follow, the sun's death, the end of worlds. A harsh time, a black time. A time when the wind bites like wolf-teeth.

"Who ever thought we'd look back on the idea of Ragnarök with nostalgia one day, eh, Tom?" Dr. Gríma Kjellson asked me, as we mapped rising temperatures together by the infamous Lakagígar fissure's side. Ice was already softening on Vatnajökull, after all; the shelves were falling both north and south, meltwater rising. Grant applications aside, we both knew we were really there to find out how long we had, then try—*try*—to figure out a way to extend it.

Just science pitted against itself, from one end of the thermometer to the other. As things get hotter, they start to split, to fall apart; holes form, and things once lost are revealed, crawling up toward the surface. Our plan was simple, hopefully too much so to fail: set one disaster to catch another.

"Who indeed?" I replied, meeting his smile with one of my own, equally thin and pointed.

Jokes being all we had to offer, you see, even in the face of certain extinction. Since we knew ourselves abandoned, though not—as yet—by whom.

Throughout my life, I used to have this particular sort of dream, this string of dreams that almost seemed to feed into each other, the way you'll dream about a place over and over, some place you've never really been. Not in real life, waking life. But every time you do, you recognize it, even though it doesn't exist.

I mean… you have to *assume* it doesn't really exist, yes? Or hope so, perhaps.

The place I'm thinking of—I always just called it Coldhame, like Cold Home but with the words run together in compound metaphor, a sort of homemade Anglo-Saxon kenning: "Bone-house" for body, "battle-light" for sword. So "cold" because it couldn't be anything else, snow-crusted and mainly level, but with rocks here and there, gray further off, black closer up. A snowy sky, too, clouds swollen and overhanging; gray wavering light, maybe some fog in the distance, or steam. Hard to see where the horizon lay, if there was one. The shadows of cliffs, or mountains. Maybe glaciers. Mountains covered in ice. And "home" just as much, somehow—instinctually, inexplicably. Because it belonged to me, and I to it.

Sometimes I'd come walking into the Coldhame dream from one direction, sometimes from another. Sometimes I'd just find myself there, suddenly; realize I'd slipped from lying with my eyes closed and trying to breathe slowly, deeply, relax myself part by part until I could go from trying to sleep to simply—*being* asleep, my eyes open again, seeing this landscape inside my skull, this movie projected on the backside of my shut lids. No sense of time-lag, just here, then there. A done deal.

I knew it *was* cold, but I seldom felt it. Maybe because I was wearing dream clothes, all kitted up for survival hiking. Maybe because it didn't matter. I could see my breath, but only when I thought about it. I kept my eyes on the ground, mainly, because I already knew what everything else looked like, after a while. These black fields could be tricky; unstable, untrustworthy. Sometimes the snow lay over scree and your feet would start to slide, especially if you walked too fast. Sometimes the earth gave way entirely.

Much like the time my father phoned me at boarding school to tell me my mother had died—almost exactly that same sudden lurch and shudder, that gravitational spasm. Predicted but never quite believed; the impossible, proven. Unless he was lying. But why would he be?

Because he did, that's why, so often I'd gotten used to simply assuming it: a habit, a game, his job. Because he was, at base— much like me—a bloody liar.

(Not that time, though.)

A slip and a fall, short or long, into darkness. Because there was always a hole under the ice of Coldhame, somewhere—I entered each dream well aware it was there, though I never could tell exactly where, no matter how slowly I moved, how wide I kept my eyes as I scanned the stony dirt. How carefully I struggled to tell cracks from tracks.

Never could tell where the edge was, no. Not until I was right down in it.

These days, after briefly lying myself into the army and then lying myself back out again before any potential charges could stick, I am currently deep in study to eventually become what's known as a vulcanologist: "Vulcan" after the god, the Roman name for Hephaestus, whose forge made all the Greek pantheon's best toys and weapons. He was dwarfish and ugly, crippled too, because his mother Hera disliked the sight of him so much she threw him out of Olympus as a baby, determined to start over.

Of course, next time 'round she got a complete psychopath—
Ares, god of war, a bully who also happened to be a coward—but
at least *that* one was handsome. Which I suppose explains why
when Hephaestus married Aphrodite, the goddess of desire, the
two of them cheated on him with each other.

I don't have any of those problems, thankfully, amongst my
many; an only child, not straight and not married, either. Much
preferring to swipe right on my own Greek gods, meet them
on neutral ground, then leave while they're in the shower and
block their accounts, after. Unless they're useful for more than
sex, that is.

Gríma advised me once that switching my store of archetypes
to those derived from Norse mythology would probably suit
me far better, given how little distinction Scandinavians tend
to make between their deities and their monsters. *Loki is a god
as well, Tom,* he said, *but also a Jötunn; god of the Jötnar, one
might even argue, since he constitutes their main representative
amongst the Aesir. Though the Jötnar themselves would disagree,
if you asked them.*

I'd looked Loki up, by then; you do that, when you're fucking
a guy from Iceland. And he certainly did remind me of myself, at
least in archetype—chaotic and impulsive, quick to plaster pleasant
fictions over his own mistakes in hopes he could fix things before
anyone noticed, gambling the lie wouldn't prove impossible to
deliver upon. Attracted to whatever finds him attractive, changing
himself to match it and settling into the imitation only to tire of
the game long before his partners do, doomed to remain ever
unsatisfied. Apt to turn on a dime and burn things down from the
bottom up, often by setting himself on fire.

Sorcerer, seer, insult comic of the Viking age; he called his fellow gods out on their shit and got away with it, until he didn't. Husband of monsters, father of monsters—*mother* of monsters, in his female form. An enviable ability, even by today's standards of gender-fluidity.

It only makes sense there's a god of lies, even if he comes from a culture I wasn't born into. If there wasn't, I might well have found myself compelled to invent one.

Going by most myths, Loki rarely represents anyone else's interests particularly well, I pointed out, *be they Jötnar, Aesir, or otherwise. Or so I've gathered.*

Which makes him your perfect role model, doesn't it? Gríma replied. *Much better than Vulcan, anyhow.*

Ah. But enough about *me.*

The moment I got off the plane in Reykjavik, it had already occurred to me I might just be headed into Coldhame territory. Not that one necessarily expects to stumble across an imaginary landscape outside the confines of one's brain, but—then again. Perhaps we all spend far more time doing that, on an unconscious level, than we actually think we do.

The team I was joining—Gríma's team—already camped close to Lakagígar, whose hundred and thirty-plus vents bisect the mountain of Laki in the western part of Vatnajökull National Park, not far from Kirkjubæjarklaustur in southern Iceland. It was here, over 1783 to 1785 CE, that a series of violent eruptions caused forty-two billion tons of basalt lava and clouds of sulfur dioxide and hydrofluoric acid to vent from both the fissure itself and from Grímsvötn, the volcano that spawned it. Fluorine gas later joined the party, eight million tons' worth, spewing what came to be called the "Laki haze" across Europe.

The consequences for Iceland were severe. Nearly a quarter of the human population died of starvation, along with eighty percent of all sheep, fifty percent of all cattle and fifty percent of all horses. Dental and skeletal fluorosis ran rampant. In Reverend Jón Steingrímsson's "fire sermon" of July 20th, 1783, he described the situation in horrific detail: "This past week, and the two prior to it, more poison fell from the sky than words can describe: ash, volcanic hairs, rain full of sulfur and saltpeter, all of it mixed with sand. The snouts, nostrils, and feet of livestock grazing or walking on the grass turned bright yellow and raw. All water went tepid and light blue in color and gravel slides turned grey. All the earth's plants burned, withered and turned grey, one after another, as the fire increased and neared the settlements."

Nor did the devastation stop there. As the gas moved through Europe, fog hung heavy and the sun shone blood-colored. Thunderstorms multiplied, spewing hailstones so big they killed livestock; there was widespread panic and flooding as volcanic winter descended. Those who inhaled the gas directly suffocated on their own internal soft tissues, which swelled as sulfur dioxide reacted with the moisture in their lungs, turning into sulfuric acid.

The only "good thing" about the disaster—the detail upon which Gríma built his theory that the rapid recent shrinkage of the Vatnajökull glacier might signal an incipient fresh eruption from both Lakagígar and Grímsvötn, one potentially violent enough to cause yet another fissure—was that the original event *did* manage to lower global temperature all over the Northern

Hemisphere, eventually producing England's own Year Without a Summer. "Not to mention the general, eh, Malthusian fallout," Gríma added, with typical Icelandic fatalism, the sort you can trace right on back to the Sagas themselves: *There is no need to look, it is just as you think; the leg is off.*

"Does the university know you're planning to re-poison your own country, in order to stave off climate change a few more years?" I asked him. "I mean... do they even believe in the concept?"

"Of course, they're not Americans. Besides which, I'm not *planning* on it."

"But you do admit that might be the result," adding, as he shrugged, "and they're willing to sign off on it?"

"Tom, please, do you really think I'd ask them to? This is why *you're* here, my friend."

Gríma and I had met under... interesting circumstances, which is often how I make most of the contacts I *don't* end up deleting. As smart as he was charming, he was ever-so-slightly taller than myself, long-haired and as muscular as one of those giant cats who drew the Norse goddess Freya's war-wagon; like Freya, his passions ran high. Love *and* war. The sort of gorgeous ecoterrorist fully willing to kill some to save most, extend the year's longest night a year or so in order to soothe our planet's fever with a healing fimbul-solstice, no matter the literal fallout. If they tried him for it afterwards, at least he knew he'd look good on television.

I was—*am*—of a far colder turn of mind, which he openly appreciated, when many don't. Sadly, I've never been immune to that sort of flattery.

Our plan was to drill down and take core samples, send heat-sensing pinhole cameras in on filaments as far as we could without them melting, then use ground-penetrating radar to map out as much of the rest as possible. See if the fissure actually *was* forming cracks that might bloom into new vents; see if any of those pre-vent cracks looked hot(ter than usual). Though, with volcanic activity, the "safe" range of heat involved is often somewhat hard to reckon.

On the Reykjanes peninsula, the Iceland Deep Drilling Project almost reached five thousand meters in search of geothermal energy, supercritical water transformed by heat and pressure into something beyond either a liquid or a gas, a five-hundred-degree form of steam. We, on the other hand, were only seeking to map out sub-ice volcanic action—tuyas, tinder—without penetrating the sort of mafic dike swarms that mimic oceanic crust fissures, at least until we felt we had to.

"What if the vents don't *want* to erupt, though?" a younger team member ventured. "In time to do us any good, I mean."

Gríma and I traded glances.

"Those charges I got you from my army contacts might come in handy, at that point, I'd suppose," I said, to which he nodded gravely.

"Tom is correct, sadly, Margrét," he explained. "Since if science has taught us anything, it's that we cannot trust nature to do the right thing on command—no more than nature, in her turn, can trust *us* to."

"Gods and monsters," I found myself murmuring, not quite under my breath. And Gríma nodded once more.

"Since all gods *are* monsters," he agreed.

On day two we broke ground; by day four we were down far enough to sink the cameras and start mapping. On day seven, Thursday/ Thor's Day, we found an interesting deviation, a shadowy area that seemed to involve up to three vents at once, tangled like a knot of plaque-crusted veins hiding beneath an obese man's ventricle. A potential heart attack waiting to happen.

"I could always widen the hole with a few micro-charges," I suggested. "Shear off a bit of shelf and break it down, let it melt in the steam, see what bubbles up. So to speak."

Gríma let his brows tangle and and hike, just slightly. "I love when you talk dirty," he murmured, after carefully making sure poor little Margrét was looking elsewhere.

So that was Friday sorted.

The charges went off a treat, revealing something unexpected— rivulets of extremophile life that glowed and fluttered in water- currents hot enough to cook at a touch, glowing "microbes" large enough to see with the naked eye, fungi sprouting from thin seams of rock poised above lava like groping, twisting tubers, blind yellow insects clinging to half-molten shelling. None of us had ever seen anything like it.

"This is odd," Gríma announced, unnecessarily. "Don't you think?"

"Couldn't not, really."

"Will it interfere with the next stage?"

I studied the fissure. "Can't see it doing so," I said, finally. "Still room on one side to lower down another round of charges. Of course, they'll probably collapse the grotto beyond saving." I shot him a sidelong look. "Margrét's not the only one who'd object to doing that so soon. Before getting a good chunk of fauna samples, anyhow."

"Can't blame her. Strikes me as a shameful waste myself." But Gríma's sigh sounded more like he was sad about not really being upset than anything else. "So I suppose we'd better take the time to do that now. Before anybody has the chance."

"Good," I agreed, and we did.

It was late when we retired, but anticipation kept us sharp.

"You know that Loki is supposed to be imprisoned beneath a volcano, the tales say," Gríma murmured, as we shared the comfortably tight fit of his extra-large sleeping bag. "For killing Baldr, the light-god, and refusing to mourn him afterwards."

There was more to the story, of course; there always is. When the Norns foretold Baldr's death, his mother Frigga traveled the world begging each creature individually to promise not to let him die... except the mistletoe, which she considered far too weak and young to be any sort of threat. But Loki, who disapproved of anyone cheating wyrd except himself, made an arrow out of one of its twigs. When the rest of the Norse gods stood around Baldr in a circle trying to wound him with various weapons and laughing at the way nothing hurt him, Loki slipped this arrow into the hand of the god Hod, who had been blinded in battle. Hod threw it, only to hear a horrified hush as the twig lodged in Baldr's throat, killing him instantly. And though many suspected Loki had disguised himself as the Jötunn woman who would not weep over Baldr's grave, in order to doom him to the dread hall of his own daughter Hela, no one would ever have known the full depth of his guilt if he hadn't gotten drunk and started telling all the other gods how stupid they were, years afterwards.

"Thor caught Loki in a net of Loki's own devising," Gríma continued, gripping my wrists, playing at pinning me down further than I already was. "And Odin All-Father sentenced Loki to be bound to a rock beneath a mountain with ropes made from the guts of his own son by Sigyn, his Aesir wife. There he would lie forever with a snake dripping venom on his face, writhing so hard the earth around him cracked and threw off hot vapors."

"Under this mountain, or somewhere else?" I asked him, licking along his sweaty neck.

"Under every mountain, maybe. Every volcano. He is a god, still."

"Oh yes. And not forever either, really."

"No, only until Ragnarök. Ragnarök, or until he is found and escapes, whichever comes first."

We rutted against each other until the heat inside matched the cold outside, then fell asleep.

In the army, I considered my particular role that of the person who'd actually do those things everyone else around me knew just as well as I did had to be done, even if they weren't willing to risk getting caught doing them. I'm not sure how I thought this would pay off for me, in the end; better than it did, if no worse. They relied on me to be the bastard, and then they got rid of me—this is the way it works, almost always. The part I seem born to play.

Tom as tempter, as agent for ill change. Tom, who says: "That's a terrible idea... of course I'm in." Tom, who—when co-conspirators point out that no one who knows the full plan will ever go along with it—tends to suggest: "Then *lie* to them."

You poison everything you touch, son, and that's the sad fact of it, my former commanding officer told me, right before I was decommissioned. *You contaminate; spread like the clap, no matter where your prick's pointed. Bloody hell, you're Covid in a suit.*

To which I replied: *You mean, I make everything I touch more like me.*

Which is true enough, so far as it goes. Though I can't shift my own shape, regrettably, I do know more than a bit about how to convince others they can alter theirs—what cracks they can get through, what holes they can fit, if they only try their best.

Exactly, what they're capable of—what we all are, if we're willing to admit it.

That night I had the Coldhame dream at last, as I'd somewhat known I would. The only thing that surprised me was how long it had taken to percolate, given the last week's events.

It came upon me more oddly than usual, though it didn't seem so in the moment: On memory's tale, sliding from lived experience to impossibility within an oneiric eye-blink. It began with an impromptu parking-lot rave I'd attended while still in grammar school, all the almost-adults and adults crushed around me far too drunk to tell a tall, equally drunk thirteen-year-old from someone they should legally worry over making passes at. Cradled in the reeking smell of hash, beer and gasoline, I danced wildly, flailing into prospective fights and flirting with anyone willing to flirt back. Until, without warning or explanation, my mother was suddenly there, and I screamed at her to leave me alone—for once being outright honest about how much I hated... well, everything, really, aside from her. Which I know she found hard to distinguish, at the time.

In real life, I turned and ran, trying not to hear her crying behind me, and in the dream the parking lot's cracked asphalt turned to steaming black gravel underneath my feet, then to snow-swathed rock; the sky went steely pale, humid summer flashing to arid, freezing wind. Adult once more, I half clambered, half ran down an ever-steepening slope, not slowing even when the chasm finally opened before me.

Didn't feel as though I fell, but I went down hard nonetheless, too fast for climbing, or even rappelling. My gloves and boots juddered over the crevasse walls, sliding farther down and faster, darkness collecting around me 'til there was nothing but blind black everywhere, feeling my descent in the pit of my stomach. After which it stopped short, the way falls in dreams always do, and I spasmed through the sort of shock people used to fear would actually kill—or wake—you. This did neither, however, so I sat up, looking around.

It felt real: air almost too heavy to breathe, cold and old and dusty; palms skinned sore, grains of rock shoved in under my nails, deep enough to hurt. It looked like the kind of cavern one might find at this depth, if I'd somehow managed to get past the thermophile grotto and the charges we'd hung just beneath it. Granite walls cracked apart by tectonic force and smoothed out by trickling water too deep to freeze, alive with drips splashing into puddles, lit only by glowing stains of lichen. I searched the ceiling for the crevasse I must have fallen through, couldn't find it, then scanned slowly down through the walls' dark places, squinting for a way out. Columns resolved themselves, with effort; cracks and holes, holes and cracks, bulging outwards, retreating inwards. Forming shapes, one of which… moved.

"Christ!" I leaped back, then caught myself; scrabbled over the rock floor and finally got close enough to make the shape out properly: a naked man taller than me, than Gríma, mane of hair equally filthy and its color impossible to see in the faint light. He lay propped up against the wall's base, head slack, though I could see his chest moving. Ribs stood out gaunt beneath lean muscle.

I drew breath. The sound came out sharp, enough so to rouse him; his eyes cracked open.

"*Water*," he husked.

Or seemed to. Not in English, and it wasn't as if I spoke Icelandic, or… whatever this was, something coarser, older. Far older. Yet I understood, immediately—simply *knew*, the same way I knew Coldhame, knew myself. Knew what lie to tell and when, to who. As if he—we—

(shared a common tongue)

I scooped up some from a nearby pool, burning my own skin to trickle it between his lips, both cracked so deep they seemed almost scarred. As if they'd been sewn together once, then ripped free.

At length he held up a hand. His wrists were chafed bloody.

"When?" he whispered.

I told him the date, watching his eyes widen. They were pale enough to throw back the lichen-light, a blue so pure it almost read as white. "Soon," he breathed, and scrambled to his feet with startling speed. "Come. Follow."

He led me to a crack of shadow between folds of granite, a passage I'd never have seen without his help, and before I knew it we were hurrying down a lightless hallway, our feet slapping the stone and raising eerie echoes that rang long distances into the dark.

"What happened?" I called after him, struggling to keep up. "How'd you get down here? Who *are* you, anyway?"

"No time!" he shouted back. His voice was clear and high now, almost girlish. "Touch the stone, think on what you feel! And run—run, run, *run!*"

His footsteps accelerated. I stumbled and let myself fall against the wall, palms flat upon the rock—and froze, sucking in a gasp. The stone buzzed against my skin, almost stinging. A low thrum filled my ears, like the deepest, largest bass string in the world tightened to the edge of snapping. Every cell in me knew what that meant, even before my brain processed the signals and gave them their oh-so-bland English name: *Imminent tectonic event.*

"Hell," I breathed, bursting into the fastest sprint I could manage 'til the slope became a climb, a clamber, spider-swarming through my own blood up the same walls my companion treated like a ladder. Calling up after him, as I did: "Wait, please wait! Wait, *wait* for me, *please—*"

At which point something exploded, filling the entire narrow world with heat too bright to bear.

⌒

A dream, still a dream. Or was it?

What else could it be?

This is the wyrd which cannot be unspun, a voice said, deep inside me—a man's voice, a woman's voice, my own voice, my own. *I bring it to birth, because I must; my malice, my pride. My revenge. Squatting here centuries-long in this fissure waiting to be found, and now you find me... you, who are a splinter of myself, disguised in human flesh; oh, this is loreful, this is correct. This is where my lying-in must begin, here, in the flame's bright heart.*

Birth, I repeated, or thought I did. *Birth of what?*

Gods and monsters, of course, came the answer, a sly smile in every syllable; *you* know *you know it, kinsman. Monsters to kill the gods, then become the gods. The beginning of the end, the beginning IN the end. The beginning.*

Ragnarök.

A hand in mine, reaching down, pulling me bodily up past fungi and insects, stalactites of salt and crystal, old bones and runestones, fluorine blooms, coiling corpse-wax blossoms. That strange face grinning down at me with yellow eyes and blue pointed teeth, hair like red flaming horns, "he" turning into "she" and back again, old to young, young to old, human to inhuman. The wall opening fractal around us, forming a spiral staircase; the hole melting around and beneath us, changing, always changing. That hand in mine sprouted tattoos that spread upwards and downwards along my own limbs in turn, the snaky ridges that united us becoming ever-darker and more complex, calcifying, growing scabs, digging in, becoming scars. Snakes and wolves and scales. Its nails grew and bent backwards, spaded and subdivided, became claws that popped off to embed themselves in the fissure's walls. The fungi puffed up, released spores that turned into gas, suffocating me, making me hallucinate; I spit phlegm and blood, drooled bits of tissue, hearing again that voice which crooned, sympathetically, seeing my distress:

Oh yes, I forget, after all these years, so long away from humans. You really are such delicate creatures—and credulous, too, if I recall. Though probably not you.

The hand in mine getting larger, rougher-skinned, blue-gray and stony. Above me, that face (male once more), a foxy fall of hair sloped down across half of it; he pushed it back to reveal naked bone, fossil-teeth in double rows, one glowing, rheumy, sunken corpse's eye. A shadowy wolf padding in to join us from some parallel tunnel, a giant snake-tail stretching to grate behind us, venom dripping down like boil-off like to scald me, brand me, blind me. And Loki

(for who else? Who else *could* it be?)

(no one else)

Loki, himself, always getting bigger, brighter, hotter, almost too painful to hold on to, not that he let me pull away. His red hair gathering together into a single spiraling horn, ridged like an ibex's, growing so far back it dug into his own skull, drawing blood. And always moving up faster, faster, faster as we rose straight up through the explosion's heart, thermite charges paused between microseconds, their very sparks flinching apart to let us travel through them—

Up into his embrace, his arms closing 'round me trap-tight, a pair of jaws. His scarred lips on mine, snake-teeth biting in, a thousand years' worth of swallowed venom venting headlong down my throat. Telling me somehow, as it did:

*The Naglfar sets sail now, rescuer, that ship made from spite and
dead men's fingernails. My children rejoin me, hungry for heart's-
flesh. Soon they will swallow the moon and sun, breathe poison across
Midgard's skin. Then the cold will come, forever, and this world will
shrink back to its beginnings: a rot bred from my ancestor's bones, a
rim of rime, a crack with darkness above, darkness below, darkness
everywhere. And then, at long last, I shall count myself satisfied.*

But will you? I wonder.

Will I? Will you, *Thomas? Willing shadow, avatar, long-lost
descendant? Bastard offspring?*

Oh, I doubt it.

And I wake, buried in snow, the camp borne away by lava; wake
alone, Gríma no doubt long gone as well, his ashes up-blown to
hang black-burnt on the eruption's tree like Odin's corpse from
Yggdrasil's branches, a sacrifice, himself to himself. Wake blind
and coughing, stripped back to my innermost core, with all my
falsehoods peeled away in the face of a stinging yellow storm, a
sulfurous rain, a phosphorescent overhung cloud of unknowing
that turns the long night bright.

Hearing my dream-god's voice ever in my ear, deep-purring:
*This way, Tom the Liar; stumble away on your jaundiced feet,
down to the shore, just where the ice is breaking. Watch how the
world-serpent rises at last to meet us from his planet-wrapped
coils, breaking surface with a wrench, a hiss—open your raw eyes
wide and see how they shine, my dear one, the keratinous scales
of our vessel's hull, so twisted and broken, where they've grown to
full length after burial!*

Here comes my half-faced daughter, my berserk second son, his wolfskin trailing. My Jötunn and my Aesir wives, who held the bowl so long between them, keeping the serpent's venom from my face. Who never deserted me entirely, no matter how I cursed them for my own mistakes. Let me introduce you: Angrboda, Tom; Tom, Sigyn. Hela. Fenrir, Nari, and Nali. We are family now— you, I and they—if only for the service you have given me. Brothers in blood yet unshed.

The ship is here, so step on board. Help me wield the wyrd with which I'll scratch my fellow gods' faces away from the firmament, bringing an old world down to birth a new. And if we die in the doing so, what of it? All stories live on, for good or ill; all lies become truths if they only last long enough.

No fiction powerful enough to trick a whole world into hanging poisonous green leaves from a plant once used to make the arrow that killed the god of light and forgiveness up to steal kisses beneath can ever be quite forgotten.

And is it only telling me what it thinks I want to hear, this voice? Probably, yes.

Almost certainly.

(I would.)

E N D

Climate change, Loki (always Loki), vulcanology, and the lure of human trickster meeting ur-Trickster were my primary inspirations for this piece. I'd been working on it for quite a while, but the final piece was the idea of extending the longest night of the year as long as possible. Oh yeah, and I also love apocalypses that stay true to the word's original meaning (an opening, not an ending), which makes Ragnarök my favourite. Blame the D'Aulaires Book of Norse Gods and Giants.

AFTER WORDS

John Langan

THREE

AFTERWARD, they lay next to one another, chests heaving, hearts pounding.

"Wow," he said at last.

"Not so bad for a couple of forty-somethings," she said.

Outside the window, open due to the mild winter, a seagull cawed. A breeze smelling of the shore pushed at the curtains. The trio of candles positioned around the bedroom flickered. Shadows shifted on the walls and ceiling, across their skin.

"Thank God Julian wasn't home," he said.

"Benefits of having a kid with a driver's license and a large friend group."

"Yeah, you wouldn't have wanted him to hear his mother saying those kinds of things."

"I'm sure he's heard worse. This is the age of the internet. Pornhub and the rest."

"True. No doubt he knows more at his age than I do now."

"Oh, you do all right," she said, moving her hand.

He inhaled.

"Although." Her hand stopped.

"What?"

"I thought you seemed a tad... distracted."

"Distracted?" he said. Now he moved his hand.

She sighed.

"Does this feel distracted?" His hand stopped.

"Oh, you devil. I'm not saying I wasn't satisfied. It's just... I felt as if part of you wasn't there. At the beginning, at least."

He was silent.

"What is it?"

"It's the date."

"The date? It's December 21st. Shortest day of the year. Christmas is almost here. Are you thinking about what Santa's gonna bring you?"

"Something else. Someone else, really."

"Okay." She paused. "Is it a woman?"

"Yes," he said, but added quickly, "from a long time ago. High school. The last time I saw her was thirty years ago today."

"She must've made quite an impression, if your mind was on her while your dick was in my mouth."

"She did," he said, "but not in that way. I mean, yes, we had sex. We had a lot of sex—"

"Was she your first?"

"No, there was a girl before her. Gayle. In the bathroom stalls in the boys' room after school. When I was fifteen. I told you about her."

"You did."

"I—forget it. You're right, I shouldn't have been thinking about her. Let's talk about something else."

"Oh no," she said. "My curiosity has been aroused. It needs to be satisfied."

"Couldn't I satisfy something else?"

"Let's see how things go. Here's some encouragement."

"Ahh."

"Now. Tell me a story."

"Well. Ahh."

"Is this too distracting? Should I stop?"

"No," he said. "No. Let me see. All right.

"Her name was Maria Granza. I met her when I was a junior. She was a sophomore. Although she was only ten months younger. Not a year. She made a big deal of that. Oh. Oh my."

"Speaking of big deals."

"You're an evil woman."

"It's why you love me."

"True."

"Ahem. She was ten months younger."

"Yes."

"How did the two of you get together?"

"Through my junior prom date. Heidi. They were friends. After Heidi and I parted ways—amicably—Maria was waiting."

"That was fast."

"I guess. It didn't seem like it at the time. Actually, that's not true. I knew it was soon—too soon. But I didn't want to be alone, you know? I had gotten used to having a girlfriend, to being seen with a girlfriend. Teenage insecurity, I suppose."

"Combined with teenage hormones."

"Her boobs were incredible."

"Very nice. Very classy."

"Hey—hormonal teenager, remember?"

"Little has changed, apparently."

"Ahh. Oh, you know just what to do."

"Do I?"

"Yes. You do. But."

"But what?"

"Maybe just—maybe slow down a little? At this rate..."

"You're gonna blow your top?"

"Yeah."

"Trying to conserve your precious bodily fluids?"

"Trying to make this last."

"All right. How's this?"

"Fine—great."

"Continue with the story. You dated this girl after the junior prom one."

"Her family lived in a... I'm not even sure how to describe it. It was like this compound in the middle of Poughkeepsie. There was a massive, three-story house where her grandparents stayed with one of her uncles and his family. White siding, black trim, with a big porch on the front; although no one used the front door. You went behind, to where there was a large yard. Directly across the yard from you was a smaller house—much smaller, a cottage really. Yellow with white, very ornate trim. Completely different style from the main house. An aunt lived there. I think she was the grandmother's cousin, but everyone called her Aunt Georgia. Older woman. Then, opposite the main house was a trailer, double-wide, also white with black trim. This was where Maria lived with her older brother, Giordano. I mean, like ten years older. He was her legal guardian. Something had happened to their parents; I never learned exactly what. All I knew was, they were dead.

"In the center of the houses, there was an in-ground pool. It was huge, had a diving board and everything. And a grill, a restaurant-grade gas grill at one corner of the concrete apron around it. Funny, I think that was what impressed me the most. My dad had a little charcoal grill he'd bring out of the back shed on the Fourth of July. Used to take forever to get going. My brother and I would compete at squirting lighter fluid onto it. We said it was to help the charcoal heat, but honestly, we loved the way it would make a sheet of fire shoot up from the grill."

"What a pair of pyromaniacs you were."

"The hot dogs and hamburgers had a slight gasoline flavor."

"How delicious."

"The grounds were full of plants, succulents. Lemon and lime trees in giant pots. I remember thinking the winters were too cold for citrus trees, but Maria said her family knew how to take care of them. Which, obviously, they did. It was what they had done in the old country, somewhere in Italy. I don't remember the name of it. Benevento? Is that a place? Anyway. Looking at all the vegetation, it seemed obvious they knew what they were doing. I never found out what their business was, what allowed them to own such a large property in the middle of a city, even a city like Poughkeepsie. They had a competitor across the river in Highland, but I couldn't tell you what they were competing over."

"The place made quite an impression on you."

"You've seen my parents' house. This was, yeah, this was something else."

"You spent a lot of time there."

"I did. Our first date, we were supposed to go out for ice cream. To Friendly's. Which we did, but only after we'd had sex."

"Some first date."

"Understand, I had no intention of sleeping with her. Well, not so soon. Bouquet of flowers in hand, I knocked on the trailer door. All right, it was nothing impressive, a half-dozen carnations, but still. Maria invited me to come in while she finished getting ready. She said she was looking for a pair of earrings. She liked jewelry, wore a lot of it. Necklaces, bracelets, anklets; each of her ears had multiple piercings. She wore toe rings, which I had never seen before. Some of the stuff was nice, expensive looking. Some of it looked handmade. She spent what I thought was an inordinate amount of time coordinating her jewelry, matching necklaces to bracelets and so on. I couldn't always understand her choices, why she couldn't wear these earrings with that anklet, why she had to combine those particular toe rings. There was a system, she said. She would explain it to me one day. She never did."

"I'm curious: what did she look like? So far, I know she had great tits and liked to accessorize."

"Tall. Not the same height as me, but not too far off. Five ten, say. Curvy, yeah. She used to complain about being fat, but she wasn't. She was proportioned classically. Like Marilyn Monroe, as opposed to the cocaine chic of the time. Her face was round, and she wore a pair of oversized round glasses, which emphasized how round it was. She was always squinting, as if her glasses were the wrong prescription. She kept her hair short, spiked on top, very eighties New Wave. She dressed… eclectically, I guess you would say. Lots of thrift store finds. Vintage concert t's with ankle-length skirts. Men's dress shirts with pencil skirts. Dresses, lots of dresses. She loved dresses with bright floral prints. She wore sneakers with pretty much everything. Back Keds, usually. Her feet were small, dainty, even. The one thing she didn't skimp on was underwear. The bras and panties she wore were nicer than anything I'd ever seen in the windows of the Victoria's Secret in the mall. Very fine material, all lacy. Imported from Italy, special-ordered for her. By her grandmother, which seemed a little on the strange side to me, but what did I know?"

"Let me guess: she was an artist."

"Actually, she was interested in science, chemistry and physics, the more math-heavy stuff. Calculus, too."

"Huh. So: she invites you into her home and the next thing you know, the two of you are naked."

"Just about. She stepped into my arms and said something to the effect of, 'Well, I guess we should get this over with.' I assumed she was talking about our first kiss. She was, but a whole lot more than that, too."

"Your lucky night."

"Yeah. To be honest, I was a little freaked out. None of the other girls I had been with had been as… direct."

"Oh, how young and innocent you were. It's kind of sweet to imagine."

"Unlike now, when I'm old and corrupt?"

"Older, yes, but still pretty innocent."

"Innocent?" His hand moved.

She gasped.

He shifted his hips. "Not to interrupt the story, but I really think we need to do something about this."

"Come on, then."

TWO

Afterward, they lay next to one another, chests heaving, hearts pounding. Outside the window, open due to the mild winter, a train rumbled in the distance. A breeze smelling of the cows across the road rattled the venetian blind. The half-dozen candles positioned around the bedroom flickered. Shadows shifted on the walls and ceiling, across their skin.

"How long has it been since we did that?" he said at last.

"I can't see the clock, but I'm gonna guess an hour. Maybe an hour and a half."

"No—I mean twice in one night."

"Ah. I don't know. B.C., I want to say; although I can't believe it's been that long."

"It can't be Before Child. I mean, Julian's eighteen."

"Before Children," she said. "The girls are twelve."

"What?"

"The girls are twelve. Hard as it is to believe."

"No—I—"

"Alison and Nadia? The twins?"

"I—"

"What's wrong?"

"It's—"

"Are you all right?"

"Fine," he said in a long exhalation. "I'm fine."

"Really?"

"Yes."

"Because for a minute there, you looked like you were having a stroke."

"A stroke?"

"It could happen. We're not as young as we used to be."

"I did not have a stroke."

"Okay. If you say so."

"I do."

"Because it was either a stroke, or I killed you with sex."

He laughed. "That is my preferred means of death."

"Yeah, well, it isn't mine, so don't do it again."

"I won't," he said. "It was—you know what it was like? Do you remember when I saw the neurologist, went through all those tests? The EEG, the CAT scan? What was it? Five years ago?"

"More like ten. And yes, I remember. I had three small kids I was afraid wouldn't have a father."

"The... event that brought me to the doctor in the first place— driving over the mountain to work and suddenly having no idea where I was, where I was going, where I was coming from—this was like that."

"You had no idea where you were?"

"My life—it was as if my life had fallen apart, crumbled into a million tiny pieces, and I couldn't tell how any of them fit together."

"Sounds terrifying. Also, like you need a return visit to the neurologist."

"I'm fine."

"What you just described does not sound fine."

"Okay," he said. "Okay. First thing tomorrow morning, I'll make an appointment."

"Good. Thank you."

"You're welcome."

"Do you remember where you were in your story? Or do you not want to talk about it anymore?"

"I guess. I mean, yes, I do remember. And that depends on whether you want to hear the rest of it."

"Yeah. I like to picture teenage you, all hormonal and horny."

"You're more secure than I am."

"Oh? You don't want to hear about my adventures with Big Dan Anders? Got me through senior year of high school."

"Ugh. The thing is, sex was such a big part of it. You have to understand, my friends and I would joke about books like *The Joy of Sex* and the *Kama Sutra*. I snuck glances at both in the back of the local Waldenbooks."

"You must have been blushing *so* hard."

"I was red as a traffic light. I was positive one of the staff would say something to me."

"'See anything you like?'"

"More like, 'Get the hell out here, you filthy degenerate.'"

"They probably dealt with much worse than a self-conscious kid sneaking a peek at a couple of racy books."

"No doubt. In fact, I know they did. I was friends with a guy who worked at Brentano's, which was kind of an upmarket

Waldenbooks. They might've been owned by the same company. I think. It was in the Poughkeepsie Galleria, which was the local upmarket mall. Anyway, the store had these long magazine racks beside the register. The dirty magazines—*Playboy, Penthouse, Hustler*—were located on the highest shelf of the racks. To ensure no kids got into them, of course, but also to embarrass any adults wanting to buy them. There was this one old guy, though, who used to come in once a week. Hunched over, shuffling his feet, trembling madly. Smoker's skin, creased and leathery, kind of yellow. No matter the weather, he wore the same tired trench coat."

"Uh-oh."

"Yes and no. So, every week, the guy makes his way into the store. Circles around the register to the adult magazines, reaches up, and grabs one of them. They all came in plastic wrappers. He tears it off. Which you aren't supposed to do, but none of the employees wants to confront him. The old guy starts paging through the magazine. By now, he's shaking like mad, like he's having a seizure. The magazine is jumping in his hands, the pages flapping together. At some point, the centerfold falls open, and he turns the magazine to have a look; although it and he are shaking so badly, it's hard to believe he can see Miss Whoever. This goes on for a while, all the booksellers doing their best not to look at him, until the old man folds the centerfold back into the magazine—poorly—stuffs it in among the other dirty magazines, and leaves."

"No one ever said anything to him? The manager?"

"Eventually, someone did. Not my friend, but one of his coworkers, an older woman who used to do an hysterical impression of the guy. I saw her once at a party. The woman finally confronted the old guy and said, 'Sir, I'm sorry, but the magazines are not for reading in the store.' Well, the old guy turns to her, and he's furious, face contorted with rage, and he says, 'I'm looking for my *daughter!*'"

She burst into laughter, through which she said, "Really?"

"Hand to God."

"What did the woman do?"

"I don't think she did anything. At least, not that she said."

"Do you know if he ever returned?"

"Or did he move on to another bookstore?"

"Yeah," she said.

"Don't know. Funny: I thought about writing a song about him. It was gonna be a mock-ballad about his quest to find his daughter every month in the pages of a whole bookshelf's worth of porno mags. Maybe I should give it another look. I could try it out this weekend, at the marina."

"What do you mean?"

"I—"

"Honey?"

"Oh my god."

"What? What is it? What's wrong?"

"I think you're right. About me seeing a doctor."

"What happened?"

"How long has it been since I played guitar?"

"Fifteen years? Since Julian was a toddler."

"Right. Which was when I realized I wasn't getting anywhere with music, sold my gear, and went to work for IBM."

"Uh-huh."

"While I was telling you about the old man, I was certain I was still a musician. I had a job as a session player at a studio in Brooklyn. I commuted there from our house on the Jersey shore. I went on tour a few times with different singers. I played most Saturdays at the seafood restaurant at the local marina."

"Okay..."

"None of which is true, I know. But it felt real. It felt like my life. Our life. I could tell you anecdotes about working with Dylan. About touring with Sheryl Crow. About filling in for a track on the last Lord Huron album. And our house: it wasn't on the shore, exactly, it was a few streets away, near a public park with big old trees. I played at the Fourth of July and Labor Day celebrations there, once with the guys from the Smithereens. When the wind blew, you could smell the ocean."

"Sounds like quite the fantasy."

"It is—was. I don't know. I'm afraid I'm having a psychotic break."

"Do you know who I am?"

"Yes."

"The kids?"

"All three of them, yes."

"You said you work for IBM."

"Management."

"Do you remember where we live?"

"Not the Jersey shore. Though we vacationed there a few times, when the kids were younger. Point Pleasant, right? The girls were obsessed with the miniature golf course. There was the restaurant with all the ceramic pigs."

"Right."

"But we don't live there. We talked about it once, pretty seriously. We decided it made more sense to stay where we were, to keep building the life we'd already started on. In Pawling," he added.

"You aren't having a psychotic break."

"Oh? What makes you say that?"

"If you were, I wouldn't expect you to be able to distinguish between fantasy and reality. You recognize the difference, which makes me think it's something else. Maybe connected to your bout of amnesia."

"Is that what we're calling it? Amnesia?"

"Sounds better than a stroke."

"Ouch."

"Maybe one thing triggered another—the momentary blankness released a hidden fantasy."

"Can that happen?"

"We'll ask the neurologist."

"Yeah. I guess we will."

"Are you all right? Do you want to get dressed?"

"No," he said. "I mean, how often do we have a chance to be alone like this? It's still a few hours until Julian returns, and the girls—"

"Are at their sleepover."

"I remembered."

"Just in case."

"The girls are at their sleepover, so let's enjoy one another's company."

"I thought we'd done that already. Twice."

"Yes, well, I was regaling you with a tale from my misspent youth."

"'Dear *Penthouse*, I never thought it would happen to me.'"

"Very funny. Kind of true, though. We were talking about the *Kama Sutra*, weren't we?"

"And *The Joy of Sex*. And your guilty perusal of them in the back of the bookstore."

"Maria had both of them in the bookcase next to her bed. Along with books on tantric sex, Kundalini yoga, and lucid dreaming. She knew her way around them. Our first time was fairly vanilla, but afterwards..."

"She took you through the table of contents?"

"You could put it that way. The summer after junior year—this was when I saw her the most—I was in possession of a driver's license and a car, a little red Hyundai Excel, five speeds and four cylinders. I had a job waiting tables at the Palace diner, only a few blocks northwest of her house. As long as I was approximately on time, my parents didn't pay too much attention to my comings and goings, and I took advantage of their relaxed attitude to fit in a lot of kinky sex."

"Like what?"

"I don't want to upset you."

"I'll tell you if you do."

"There were positions modeled on the way certain animals did it. The bull, the elephant, the tiger. There were others drawn from Hindu lore. A few were pretty athletic. It wasn't always the most comfortable sex, but I didn't care. As far as I was concerned, trying to do it standing up against a wall was better than not doing it at all."

"Who could argue with such logic?"

"The longer we were together, the more elaborate things became. We would tie up one another with long silk scarves. I had to use very specific knots. She would paint symbols all over the two of us. She used gold paint, which glittered in the light but was a bitch to scrub off in the shower. One time, I thought I had washed all of it away, only to have my mom ask what that was on my cheek."

"Oh God. What did you say?"

"I told her Maria had been teasing me and had dabbed some of her makeup on my face."

"Did she believe you?"

"She did. She said it looked nice, wanted to know if I knew the brand."

"What did you tell her? 'Fornication?' 'Kink?' 'Youthful Debauchery?'"

"I said I didn't know the name."

"Probably just as well," she said. "Not to interrupt your erotic reverie, but what brought the relationship to an end? I can't imagine you would have broken up with the Queen of the *Kama Sutra.*"

"She got sick. Very sick. It was the beginning of November. She was out of school for a week. I called, but she didn't say much, only that she was ill and didn't want me over. My feelings were a little hurt, but I wasn't especially keen on catching whatever had laid her up. I stayed away."

"Your dick must have appreciated the break."

"Kind of? You might not believe it, but sometimes, all the sex became a tad monotonous."

"Poor you."

"I know, I know. But there were other things I wanted to do, too. Go to the movies, maybe, or go for a walk. Or just hang out and talk. To be fair, I could've said no, but I kept my mouth shut."

"Lest your well of sin go dry."

"Yeah. Turns out, I shouldn't have worried. When Maria returned to school, our sexual odyssey reached its end."

"Because of her sickness?"

"Uh-huh. She came back on a Tuesday. Monday night, she called and asked me to pick her up the next morning. I had been driving her to and from school most days since the new term had started."

"A chauffeur with benefits."

"We were late for first period on a handful of occasions."

"You hate doing it in the morning."

"I wasn't at my best."

"Did you have any gold paint on you when you walked into school?"

"Once, yes."

"Good grief. What was your excuse this time?"

"I mumbled something about an art project and ran to the boys' bathroom."

"Honestly."

"All of that was in the past, now."

"What was wrong with her? Cancer?"

"No," he said. "Or I should say, I'm not sure. When I saw her the next day, she was dressed entirely in black: long-sleeved man's dress shirt, ankle length skirt. And a veil, which she had pinned to her hair and draped over her face. It was transparent, with all these tiny black beads sewn into it. It must've been like looking through constellations of black stars. Before I could say anything—before I could do anything more than hug her—she told me she was on a strict timetable. There were thirty-three days left for her to complete the Great Work we had begun. Until the winter solstice. Doing so would require all her attention, so no more sex."

"The Great Work?"

"Yeah. I asked her what she meant. She said—well, she said a lot of things, so many, we were late for school, again. The gist of it was—you remember I mentioned the guy in Highland? The competition to her family's business?"

"Whose exact nature we never established," she said, "but yes, I do."

"This rival had done something to her. She used an Italian phrase, *meso un semo nero,* which translates, 'placed a black seed.'"

"He placed a black seed in her? What does that mean, exactly? He poisoned her?"

"No. It wasn't anything as direct. She was speaking in symbolic terms; although there was a physical dimension to what had happened. I'm not explaining it very well. This man had conveyed some kind of... information to her, and the information was toxic, was eating away at her life, which was its purpose."

"Sounds as if he cast an evil spell on her, a curse."

"Yes, it does."

"Why her, though? Wouldn't it have made more sense for the guy to target his actual rivals, like her uncle or grandfather?"

"She said they were too well protected. Also, that it hurt them more to see her suffering. I don't know. Whatever the cause, in order to defeat the information—the curse—Maria first had to generate a huge amount of energy."

"Let me guess: sex energy?"

"Sex energy. Our exertions had allowed her to access certain centers of energy—like chakras, but not exactly. The scarves and body paint had helped."

"Naturally. Or supernaturally."

"These semi-chakras allowed her to keep the worst effects of the black seed at bay, and to plan her Great Work."

"Which was?"

"She called it a Catapult. Something—a process to propel her free of the curse's range."

"I don't understand."

"Neither did I. She did her best to explain it to me. Several times. The problem was, I couldn't tell what I was supposed to take as fact, and what was metaphor. One time, she said to me, 'It's all true, and it's all symbolic.' Not terribly helpful. The gist of it was, the only way to be free of the black seed was for her to be hurled away from it very fast and very far. 'Imagine you were on a dying planet,' she said, 'like Superman on Krypton.' Just as the infant Superman needed his parents' rocket to blast him off to Earth, she needed the Great Work to shoot her out of her collapsing life. 'To where?' I asked her. 'Someplace far away,' she said. 'Someplace new.'"

"Sounds like a lot to deal with."

"You can say that again. Everything she said to me was through the black veil, with its tiny black beads. There were times I was one hundred percent certain I was the victim of an incredibly elaborate practical joke. There were other times I was sure everything was in preparation for dumping me. Still other times, I was certain she was seriously ill and dying, the black seed just a way for her to speak about something she couldn't bear to face head-on."

"Did you talk to anyone else about what was going on?"

"Not really. A couple of times, I started to, to my guy friends, but I couldn't come up with the words for it. I absolutely couldn't talk to my mom and dad. We had a pretty good relationship—better than most of my friends had with their parents—but what was I going to say? 'My girlfriend is sick, maybe dying, and the reason I think so is we've stopped having crazy sex every day?' My folks weren't *that* progressive. I don't know. Even now, after all the years I've had to turn it over in my mind, I feel like, the more I say, the less clear I make everything."

"It's okay."

"The final thirty-three days, we spent a lot of our time together in silence. Maria covered her kitchen table with giant sheets of white paper and filled every square inch of them with writing, math stuff, long chains of equations I didn't understand. They were mixed in with drawings of what looked like astrological charts. I sat on her living room couch doing homework or reading, listening to the squeak of the marker on the paper. At random moments, her brother, Giordano—you remember I said she lived with him—walked into the kitchen and stood beside the table, watching as she worked. Every now and again, he would point at something, a number or symbol. Maria would grunt and amend it. Prior to this, he had not been especially talkative, but now he looked through me, as if I wasn't sitting right there in front of him. I mentioned the decline in his attitude toward me to Maria, but she brushed it off. Her labors on the sheets consumed all her attention. Honestly, I don't know why she kept going to school, because in class after class, all she did was jot down complex equations. I thought about asking her, but I was afraid it would give the impression I didn't want to see her."

"Did you?"

"Yes. I was—I had feelings for her. Strong feelings. I'm not sure I was in love with her, exactly—not in the way I am with you. I could have been, though, if the situation was less... whatever it was. However I would describe my emotions toward Maria, I felt them deeply. Plus," he added, "if she was in as bad a way as she said she was, she should have been resting, conserving her strength, not carrying on as if everything was normal."

"You stopped having sex. From the sounds of it, that must have saved a considerable amount of strength."

"Very funny."

"How did she look? Aside from the veil and what not. Could you tell she was sick?"

"Not really. When I would hug her, she felt about the same. The only..."

"What?"

"It shows how much stress I was under. A couple of times, as she was working on her Spirit Map, which was what she called the tabletop project, and I was reading on the couch, I saw her out of the top of my vision, and she was blurry."

"What do you mean?"

"Blurry. Out of focus. I looked up, straight at her, and for the barest of moments, a half second, less, she was still blurred. Then she wasn't. I assumed there was something wrong with my vision, maybe my eyes were dry from so much reading and this had affected them, but I wasn't convinced. I mentioned it to Maria, but she ignored me."

"Could've been stress."

"Possibly. The problem is, only she was out of focus. If what happened had been stress-induced, you would have expected everything to be blurry. At least, I would."

"The brain is weird. Could be, she was the source of your anxiety, so your brain blotted her out to give you a break, if just for a half second."

"I suppose."

"So we've arrived at day thirty-three. The last time you saw her. Or, I assume we reached it. Did anything else happen before that?"

"Sort of."

"Meaning?"

"Maybe a week before our final night together, I got it into my head I was going to drive across the bridge to Highland and confront the man who was the cause of all this, Mr. *Semo Nero*. I had floated this idea to Maria a few times, only to have her shoot me down. He was too dangerous, she said. I wouldn't be able to do anything to help her, and I would likely end up in the same situation as she was, without anyone to help me. I said, 'Not even you?' She said, 'I won't be there.'

"Maria didn't want me going to Highland, but Giordano was fine with it. At least, he wrote down the man's address for me. I told him not to say anything to Maria. He snorted and walked away.

"The place wasn't hard to find. I crossed the bridge, went north a mile, and turned onto a side street. The house was on the left a little ways along, maybe half a mile. It was massive, a red brick beast three stories tall, with a cupola rising another story above that. A porch wrapped around the ground floor, but it was difficult to see because there was a wall of trees in the way. Bushes, actually, holly and rhododendron, grown to tree-size. Everything was dusted with snow. It was like looking at a picture from the end of the eighteen-hundreds. There was no clear path to the porch, no walkway or front steps visible. There could have been, and I just couldn't see them. As far as I could tell, I would have to leave my car, clamber over a low stone wall in front of the bushes, and try to maneuver between the holly and the rhododendron, all the while knocking snow onto myself. Reaching the porch was not something I was going to do in a hurry. Nor was exiting the place—I want to say, escaping it—if things went bad, if Mr. Black Seed turned violent.

"I couldn't even pull over to the side of the street to study the grounds and weigh my options. Instead of a shoulder, the asphalt dropped to a deep ditch, intended for storm water, fatal to the axle of a car. I sat in the street, hazards on, foot on the brake, looking at the obstacles in my path and attempting to work out the best way to deal with them. It was like one of those logic problems they give you in high school: 'You have two chickens and a goat on one side of a stream; there's a fox on the opposite shore. Your boat can transport only one animal at a time. How do you get all the animals to the other side safely?' Or something. I don't know. I was never very good at those kinds of problems."

"Sounds like you didn't talk to the black seed guy."

"No," he said, "I did not. My window was starting to fog—the defroster in the car wasn't very good—so I rolled my window down to get a clearer look through the bushes. A man was standing on the front porch. Prior to that moment, I hadn't noticed him, but I hadn't seen him coming out of the house, either. He was tall, somewhere in the neighborhood of seven feet, and thin, skeletally so. White, white skin, toadstool white. He was dressed in evening wear, black jacket with tails, gray striped vest and trousers, white dress shirt with a gray cravat."

"Was this him?"

"I don't think so. I suppose he could have been *Semo Nero*. It just didn't feel like it. He was glaring at me, his eyes burning with pure, naked hostility. Despite the distance, the wall of vegetation between us, the emotion blew over me like a jet from a flamethrower. I actually tried to duck, as if a stream of fire were shooting at me, but the seatbelt held me in place. I'm pretty sure he had been waiting for me to see him, because the minute I did, he *leapt* off the porch. I mean, this was some standing jump. It carried him into the thick of the holly and rhododendron. The leaves snagged his nice clothes, the branches pushed against him; he didn't care. He fought his way through them, leaning forward, his long legs lifting high, his elbows out. It was like watching a great bird, a prehistoric monster that would have eaten small animals in a single gulp. Snow dropped on him in clumps and showers. The whole time, his eyes remained locked on me. From mildly irritated at not being able to figure out how to gain access to the house, I was now terrified, lightheaded with fear. The holly was tearing the man's clothes and skin, the rhododendron snarling his legs, and he kept coming.

"I lifted my foot from the brake, killed the hazards, and dropped the car into gear. There wasn't time or space enough to three-point back the way I came, so straight-ahead it was. The road led downhill to the river in a series of sharp curves and steep straightaways. At the height of summer, in the brightest daylight, I would have taken it slowly. Now, I raced it as if the Devil himself was after me. There were patches of ice all the way to the end, most small enough to shimmy the tires as they passed over them, a couple large enough to wobble the entire car and make me certain I was on the verge of shooting right off into the trees. I never thought of myself as an especially skilled driver—still don't—but I couldn't have been too bad, because I made it to the bottom of the hill with both the car and myself intact. I turned right and sped alongside the waterfront, next to the train tracks there. A freight train was rolling north in an endless procession of container cars. To the right a short distance on, a road ran back uphill. I swung onto it. Ridiculous as it sounds, I kept my eyes peeled for whoever the guy had been. I swear, I half-expected him to come crashing out of the woods and throw himself onto the windshield. You can imagine, I was back across the river as fast as I could."

"Weird. I wonder who he was?"

"Know what's funny? The next time I saw Giordano, the following day, he asked me about the visit. 'Did you make your trip?' he said, utterly deadpan, but I swear to you, the fucker knew exactly what he sent me into."

"Of course he did. You'd already been warned not to go, by Maria. You ignored her."

"I—"

"Yes?"

"I guess you're right."

"You guess."

"You're right; you're right."

"Thank you. Now let's hear the rest of your story."

"The last time I saw Maria was December 21st. Winter solstice. This year, it fell on a Saturday. My parents were out of town for the weekend, at someone's kid's wedding. I was working an early shift at the diner. I figured I'd stop over at Maria's for a couple of hours on the way home, maybe watch a movie with her if she felt like it, maybe sit with her if she didn't. The last few days, she'd reached the end of working on her Spirit Map. Instead, she spent our time together sitting cross-legged on her bed, hands resting palm-up on her knees, staring through her veil at a point I could not identify. I asked her what she was doing. She said, 'Preparing.' Sometimes, she would take a break from her preparation and we'd put on the TV or listen to music. Those moments, I could almost fool myself into believing everything was fine, was going to be fine. Always in the back of my mind, though, was a clock, counting down the days until whatever was supposed to happen, the conclusion to the Great Work, broke over us.

"Here we were, down to hours. I didn't think anything of it at the time, but it amazes me how much I was living with. I wasn't the only one: everyone I knew was shouldering enormous burdens. It makes me wonder what's going on with Julian or the girls that we don't know about. We've tried to be open with them, accepting, you-can-tell-me-anything-and-I-won't-freak-out parents. Ask my folks, though, and they would tell you they were the same way with me. They would swear to it. And I would be willing to bet hard cash everything we've talked about would shock them so deeply, so profoundly, they wouldn't know what to do with themselves."

"Oh, I've never had any doubts the kids have lives apart from us. How could they not?"

"This far apart?"

"Maybe not, but who knows? I'll admit, I would hope they'd come to us if the situation became as... complicated as it had for you, and I would be worried to find out they hadn't, but this is something you do when you're a kid, isn't it? You think you can handle the world in ways your mom and dad can't. You're convinced you understand things—you have a grasp on them your parents don't. Sometimes you're right. Would your parents have helped you? Would they have been able to?"

"Honestly, it's difficult to believe they could have. Still makes me feel bad."

"Which is okay."

"Yeah. All right. I had clocked out at the diner and was driving to Maria's. This was, I don't know, six thirty, seven o'clock. On my way through Poughkeepsie, everything seemed so dark, as if the night were somehow thicker. Probably because I was aware it was the solstice, which never meant too much to me previously: it was something the DJ would mention on the radio, or the science teacher would ask about, the answer to a trivia question. With Maria's fixation on it the past weeks, the date had overshadowed Christmas, reduced it to an afterthought. And you know how big Christmas is for my family, so you can appreciate what a statement like that means. The strings of lights people had wound around the trees and bushes in front of their houses, the large plastic Santas and Frostys glowing on the doorsteps, the decorated trees shining through their living room windows, all seemed impossibly far away, stars burning in a distant galaxy. I felt sad, melancholy the way I sometimes do at the holidays, except this time, it was more acute, piercing. I didn't know what was about to happen to Maria, to the two of us, but it was hard to believe something wasn't on its way.

"When I knocked on her door—"

"She was already gone."

"Exactly the opposite: she was very much there, and she was very much naked."

"Oh?"

"Yes. She was hiding behind the door when she opened it. I saw candles first, dozens of them, set all around the living room. The air smelled of hot wax and a spice I couldn't identify, like incense, but not exactly. Little pieces of paper hung from the ceiling on pieces of thread so fine it was invisible. I thought they were Christmas decorations, then I saw they were black, cut to the shape of stars. What living room furniture there was, mainly the couch and easy chair, had been pushed to the side. A coffee table had been moved, too. In the center of the space cleared, Maria's Spirit Map had been laid on top of the carpet. A sound was coming from somewhere—I assumed it was music, although the volume was so low I wasn't sure. I felt the sound as much as heard it, a deep stuttering bass line thumping against my eyes and throat.

"I was already confused, and when Maria closed the door and I turned to her, my confusion dropped into something else."

"From what you said, I think I can guess where it dropped to."

"Well sure, only not right away. At first I was... stupefied. Maria wasn't just naked, she had decorated her body more elaborately than ever, used her skin as the canvas on which she painted sweeping lines and designs, letters from alphabets new and old, symbols from astronomy and astrology, figures geometric and fanciful, all in gold paint which caught the candles' glow and made her appear covered in shining light. In the fiery depths of those decorations, I saw myself reflected in part and in whole, every version of me wearing the same, dumbfounded expression."

"How did she look? I mean, could you tell she was sick?"

"It didn't seem like it, but the way the paint was glowing on her made it difficult to know. The brightness of the decorations obscured the unpainted skin. She didn't act sick. In no time at all, she had me out of my clothes and was pushing me gently backward, toward where the Spirit Map lay. By this point, I had found my voice and was using it to ask questions: Was she okay? Was this all right? Hadn't she said we were done having sex? She didn't answer. Instead, she ran her left hand up my cock. I was already rock hard, my dick bouncing a little with my pulse, which was pounding. Maria knelt before me and took me in her mouth. It's a miracle I didn't come right then and there. She slid her lips off me and raised her right hand to my dick. She was holding something between her thumb and index finger, a large, metallic ring. She placed it around the head of my cock and slid it all the way down to the base. The fit was snug, but not painful. Or not too painful. Once the ring was secure, she lifted a slender black cord from the floor and carefully but firmly tied it around the top of my balls. This was considerably less comfortable, but before I could complain too much, she lowered me onto the Spirit Map and climbed on top of me.

"Did I mention she was no longer wearing the veil? Instead, her face was painted with more symbols and designs. The Spirit Map crackled underneath us as we moved. The entire time, she was talking, words mixed with sighs and groans. I couldn't understand most of what she was saying; it was so soft, it blended with the music playing, the mix of low notes. She reached a shuddering climax right away, then rolled us over and I was on top, her legs out and high, her arms up over her head. The Spirit Map rustled and shifted against the carpet. Candlelight highlighted the jagged outlines of the black stars overhead. Maria continued speaking. I couldn't tell, but I had the impression she was looking past me, to the pieces of paper.

"She came again. We shifted positions. To doggie style? Reverse cowgirl? I can't recall the exact order. We ran through—I won't say all of the *Kama Sutra*, but we hit the highlights. I was on the verge of coming for I don't know how long. It felt like hours. Every last millimeter of my cock was alight with sensation. It was difficult to keep any thought in my head. At one point, I gazed up at the paper stars and it was as if I was staring at a field of stars, at strange, black constellations. Maria did not stop speaking, though her voice was growing hoarse. I could hear her words. She was talking about me. I was going to the future, she said. I was going into tomorrow, and tomorrow, and tomorrow, into all the tomorrows. I was going for her. I was going to have a life. I was going to college. I was going to travel. I was going to marry and to have children. I was going to live, and what I was going to live was going to be for her. All of it was going to be for her. She was going to step into what I lived and it would be hers. There was more, but that was the gist of it.

"Finally, she pushed me off her long enough to untie the string around my balls and remove the cock ring. She pressed me down onto the Spirit Map, by this point all kinds of crumpled and torn, and lowered herself onto me. In the five or six seconds before I came, I had the distinct impression the low music which thrummed against my naked skin was in fact the sound of the black stars overhead. Then I came. The orgasm thundered through me, not the usual series of spasms, but a long rush that went on and on, carrying all of me with it. You know how, every so often, I'll say, 'That was a baby-maker?' This would have made triplets. For I can't tell you how long, I went blank, my mind wiped clean by pleasure. I think I was shouting. I must have been. The funny thing is, I had the sense what I was shouting and the music of the stars were one and the same. Maria was—I want to say she was calling out, but I don't know what.

"My heart was still pounding when she stood and padded away; to use the bathroom, I assumed. While I lay waiting for her return, I dozed, swept to unconsciousness by the endorphins swimming in my blood. I had plenty of questions remaining, but I was happy to let their answers wait.

"The next thing I knew, the lights switched on and someone was yelling at me. I sat up and was confronted by the sight of Giordano and a much older woman—Aunt Georgia, I remembered. They were standing in the doorway, and they were not happy. In fact, enraged might be a better word to describe them. Their faces were red, outraged, and they were shouting in a mix of English and Italian."

"Oh my God."

"Yeah. Giordano charged inside, gesticulating madly. The two of them were dressed up, him in a black suit with a white shirt, her in a black dress. As Giordano was making his way around the couch, I was scrambling to haul on my jeans and sneakers. With my right sneaker on and my left half-off, I swept up the remainder of my clothes and made a break for it, vaulting the couch and brushing past Aunt Georgia, who cast a string of invective into the night after me."

"Oh my God." She was laughing. "I'm sorry. That's terrible."

"It was freezing, is what it was. I was attempting to drive away as fast as I could and finish dressing myself at the same time. I was positive some passing cop would pull me over and ticket the hell out of me."

"For what?"

"Driving while unclothed—I don't know. All the way home, my heart was in my throat. Thank God my parents were away. For the next week, I lived in dread the phone would ring, my mother would answer, and Giordano would ask her if she knew what her son had been up to with his baby sister."

"On the living room floor, no less."

"Indeed."

"Would your mom have believed him?"

"Who knows? I didn't want to find out."

"Big brother never called, though, did he?"

"He did not. Nor did Maria. I didn't dare dial her number, in case Giordano picked up. We were on Christmas break, so I couldn't see her at school. On the way to and from work, I drove past her family compound, but I saw signs of no one, let alone her. Christmas Day was pretty miserable, as was New

Year's. My parents knew something had happened between my girlfriend and me, but for once had the good sense not to ask too many questions. I brooded, and I moped, and at the end of vacation went as far as to lift the receiver from its cradle and punch in the first three digits of her number. I hesitated over the fourth and lost my nerve. The next day, I went straight to school. Maria was absent. I can't recall how I learned she had been withdrawn."

"That was it? The End?"

"For a couple of weeks, I fantasized about driving over one last time, forcing a confrontation, learning exactly what had happened to her. I pictured Giordano and Aunt Georgia keeping Maria confined to her room, Rapunzel in Poughkeepsie. But I was afraid she was completely comfortable with the current state of affairs. If she truly wanted to, I couldn't believe she wouldn't have found some means of contacting me, even by letter. So yeah, it was the end. Not with a bang but a whimper, as the poem goes."

"More like a bang than a whimper, I'd say."

"Anyway. This is why I'm always a bit distracted when the winter solstice rolls around. In that made-up life where I'm a musician, I probably would have written a song about the whole affair. Maybe more than one. A couple of years ago, I searched for Maria on social media—I'm pretty sure it was on the 21st, or a day or two later. I never found anything."

"It's all so sad. Here was this poor girl dealing with... something awful, and she constructs an elaborate fantasy in which she has the agency she must have craved desperately. She draws you into it, because you're sweet and kind and decent—"

"Don't forget, good in the sack."

"I was coming to that. She tangles you up in her delusion and you don't know what you're supposed to do."

"You don't think there was anything to it?"

"What? To her being a witch? Would she have been a witch? Someone using magic, anyway."

"Sure. Casting a spell."

"A spell requiring months and months of enthusiastic fucking. Followed by another month of less enthusiastic celibacy. Then the grand finale. I don't know. I can't imagine how something like that would work. Not to mention, its purpose. She wanted to step into your life? What would that mean for the person she was replacing? Would she erase them? Could she afford for them to remain alive somewhere? Could she count on them not being able to remember the years you had spent together, or on them dismissing any fugitive memories as merely vivid dreams? She couldn't, could she? The risk would be too great. She would have to remove them from existence, excise them down to the last molecule. It's the kind of wish a kid would make, without worrying about the implications."

"Suppose she thought about the implications?"

"But went ahead, anyway? Someone that clear-eyed—that deliberate—that ruthless—would be fearsome. Frightening. Instead of very, very sad. But I don't want to talk about this anymore."

"What do you want to talk about?"

"You tell a pretty good dirty story, mister."

"You think so?"

"Worked on me."

"You don't say?"

"I do say."

"There's one problem."

"Oh?"

"I'm pretty sure twice in one night is my limit. The perils of age."

"I don't know about that. Hang on a moment..." She rolled toward the nightstand on her side of the bed. The drawer rasped. A plastic cap snapped open. Liquid squelched. She rolled back toward him. "Move a bit."

"How—like this?"

"A little more. That's good. Hold still. This stuff is a little cold."

"What are you—"

"Shh."

"Wha—hey."

"Shh."

"You're—"

"There."

"Ahh. Wha—oh. Ohhh."

"Uh-huh."

"Oh. Oh my—"

"That's right."

"Where—ahh."

"There we go."

"Where—where did you learn how to do this?"

"Better Homes and Gardens."

"Ohh. Oh my dear. Oh, I do love you."

"And my wicked ways?"

"And—oh—your dexterous fingers."

"Want to give it a try?"

"Uh-huh."

"Come on, then."

ONE

Afterward, they lay next to one another, chests heaving, hearts pounding. Outside the window, open due to the mild winter, a train sounded its horn as it rolled out of the station on its way to Grand Central. A breeze smelling of lemons belled the drapes. The dozen candles positioned around the bedroom flickered. Shadows shifted on the walls and ceiling, across their skin.

"Oh," he said. "Three times—how long has it been—I mean, I must have been a teenager. Maybe in my twenties."

"Don't sell yourself short," she said. "It wasn't too long ago. Remember the trip to Benevento for our twenty-fifth? The miserable hotel we booked?"

"Too much Strega," he said. "I seem to recall joking about the powers of the witches' milk. Not to mention, the hangover the day after."

"Worth it, though."

"Yeah."

"How about next year? The big three-oh. Have you given any thought to where you'd like to go?"

"Not really. Back to Italy?"

"Possibly."

"Would we take the kids? Who would watch them if we didn't?"

"Julian'll be almost twenty," she said. "He's fairly self-sufficient as it is. The girls think they can take care of themselves, but they could stay in the big house with Giordano and Griselda."

"They—wait. Who?"

"Giordano and Griselda. My brother and his wife."

"Your—"

"Brother. And his wife."

"I—"

"What? You what?"

"It's—I—"

"Are you all right?"

"No. No—I—"

"You what? What's wrong?"

"I—"

"Talk to me."

"Fine," he said in a long exhalation. "I'm... fine."

"Are you sure?"

"I think so, yeah."

"Because for a minute there, it looked like you were having a stroke."

"A stroke?"

"Or a seizure. I don't know."

"No. It wasn't a seizure. Or a stroke."

"How do you know?"

"I don't. I mean, I'm not a doctor. It didn't feel like a stroke— like how I've read a stroke is supposed to feel. Or a seizure."

"What did it feel like?"

"Do you remember when I saw the neurologist, went through all the tests? What was it? Five years ago?"

"More like ten. And yes, I remember: I had three small children I was afraid wouldn't have a father. It was after our trip to Scotland."

"Right. You wanted to see that place..."

"Renfrew's Keep."

"Yes."

"You had your... episode there."

"This was more like that. For an instant, I had no idea who I was, who you were, what any of this was. It was as if my life had shattered into millions of pieces and I had no idea how they fit together."

"Sounds terrifying."

"It was. Sad, too."

"Sad?"

"In that moment, I had a sense of incredible loss, which was somehow connected to the terror, part of it."

"Also sounds like you need a return visit to the neurologist."

"I'm fine."

"What you described does not sound fine."

"Okay," he said. "Okay. I'll make an appointment with Dr. Satyamurthy. Might be hard to get in to see her during the holidays, though."

"Just as long as you make the appointment. I came a long way for you, remember."

"I do. Thirty years later, I have not forgotten."

"You haven't, have you? Let's see if you can still recite the poem I wrote for you when they let me out of the hospital and we finally saw each other again."

"You think I don't know it?"

"Show me you do."

"I will. In English," he added. "My Italian is atrocious."

"English will do."

"All right.

> *For you, I have come—*
> *I have leapt over Death—*
> *I have broken Time and repaired it—*
> *You have prepared a meal for me, a great feast*
> *With many dishes and many flavors—*
> *I eat it all, suck the last*
> *Juice from the last lemon—*
> *I move the stars,*
> *I make new constellations for you.*

"Well?"

"Not bad."

"What was that?"

"What?"

"I thought—for a second there, I thought I heard something— someone. Screaming, maybe. Far away."

"I didn't hear anything. It's probably nothing."

"If you say so."

"I do," Maria said.

For Fiona

E N D

"After Words" was inspired by Philip Roth's novel, Deception, *which is written as a series of dialogues between two people*

engaged in an adulterous affair. (There's probably a little of the end of Faulkner's Light in August—*also written as pillow talk— in the story, too.) I've been thinking about how I might use such a narrative setup for a while now, but it wasn't until* Christmas and Other Horrors *that I found the right fit. In my experience, Christmas stories tend to skimp on the erotic, let alone the out- and-out sexual, perhaps because of the focus on a virgin birth. The idea of a holiday story centered on the pleasures of the flesh tickled my fancy. Given the story's magical concerns, I thought it made sense to focus on the solstice, as a kind of hinge point in the year where spells and the like might be more effective. The weird constellations? They probably have their origin in my first reading of Rilke's* Duino Elegies. *And it occurs to me that this story is in some way in dialogue with my earlier story, "Outside the House, Watching for Crows." Oh, and the butler? Yeah, that's who you think it is.*

ACKNOWLEDGMENTS

THANK you to my editor George Sandison and his team at Titan, and to my agent Merrilee Heifetz.

ABOUT THE AUTHORS

NADIA BULKIN is the author of the short story collection *She Said Destroy*. She has been nominated for the Shirley Jackson Award five times. She grew up in Jakarta, Indonesia with her Javanese father and American mother, before relocating to Lincoln, Nebraska. She has two political science degrees and lives in Washington, D.C.

TERRY DOWLING has been called "Australia's finest writer of horror" by *Locus* magazine. The *Year's Best Fantasy and Horror* series featured more horror stories by Dowling in its twenty-one-year run than any other writer. Dowling is author of *Basic Black: Tales of Appropriate Fear* (International Horror Guild Award winner for Best Collection 2007), *An Intimate Knowledge of the Night, Blackwater Days*, and *The Night Shop: Tales for the Lonely Hours*. His homepage can be found at www.terrydowling.com.

TANANARIVE DUE is an American Book Award and NAACP Image Award-winning author who was an executive producer on *Horror Noire: A History of Black Horror* for Shudder. She teaches Afrofuturism and Black Horror at UCLA. She and her husband, science fiction author Steven Barnes, co-wrote an episode for Season 2 of *The Twilight Zone* for Paramount Plus and Monkeypaw Productions. Due is the author of several novels and two short story collections: *Ghost Summer: Stories* and *The Wishing Pool and Other Stories*. She is also co-author of a civil rights memoir, *Freedom in the Family: A Mother-Daughter Memoir of the Fight for Civil Rights* (with her late mother, Patricia Stephens Due). In 2013, she received a Lifetime Achievement Award in the Fine Arts from the Congressional Black Caucus Foundation.

Formerly a film critic, journalist, screenwriter and teacher, GEMMA FILES has been an award-winning horror author since 1999. She has published four collections of short work, three collections of speculative poetry, a Weird Western trilogy, a story cycle and a standalone novel (*Experimental Film*, which won the 2015 Shirley Jackson Award for Best Novel and the 2016 Sunburst Award for Best Adult Novel). Her collection, *In This Endlessness, Our End*, won the 2021 Bram Stoker Award for Superior Achievement in a Fiction Collection, another is just out from Trepidatio—*Dark is Better*—and another is forthcoming.

JEFFREY FORD is the author of the novels *The Physiognomy, Memoranda, The Beyond, The Portrait of Mrs. Charbuque, The Girl in the Glass, The Cosmology of the Wider World, The Shadow*

Year, The Twilight Pariah, Ahab's Return, and *Out of Body.* His short story collections are *The Fantasy Writer's Assistant, The Empire of Ice Cream, The Drowned Life, Crackpot Palace, A Natural History of Hell, The Best of Jeffrey Ford,* and *Big Dark Hole.* Ford's fiction has appeared in numerous magazines and anthologies from Tor.com to *Magazine of Fantasy and Science Fiction* to *The Oxford Book of American Short Stories.*

CHRISTOPHER GOLDEN is the *New York Times* bestselling author of such novels as *Road of Bones, All Hallows, Ararat,* and *Snowblind.* With Mike Mignola, he is the co-creator of the Outerverse comic book universe, including such series as *Baltimore* and *Joe Golem: Occult Detective.* He has also written for film, television, and video games. He was born and raised in Massachusetts. His work has been nominated for the British Fantasy Award, the Eisner Award, and multiple Shirley Jackson Awards. Golden has been nominated for the Bram Stoker Award ten times in eight different categories, and won twice.

GLEN HIRSHBERG's novels include *The Snowman's Children, Infinity Dreams, The Book of Bunk,* and the *Motherless Children* trilogy. He is also the author of five widely praised story collections: *The Two Sams, American Morons, The Janus Tree, The Ones Who Are Waving,* and *Tell Me When I Disappear.* Hirshberg is a three-time International Horror Guild Award Winner, five-time World Fantasy Award finalist, and he won the Shirley Jackson Award for the novelette "The Janus Tree." Check out his Substack at https://glenhirshberg.substack.com/. He lives with his family and cats in the Pacific Northwest.

STEPHEN GRAHAM JONES is the *New York Times* bestselling author of nearly thirty novels and collections, and there are some novellas and comic books in there as well. Most recent are *Earthdivers* and *Don't Fear the Reaper.* Coming soon is *I Was a Teenage Slasher.* Stephen lives and teaches in Boulder, Colorado.

RICHARD KADREY is the *New York Times* bestselling author of the Sandman Slim series. *Sandman Slim* was included in Amazon's "100 Science Fiction & Fantasy Books to Read in a Lifetime," and is in development as a feature film. Some of Kadrey's other books include *King Bullet, The Pale House Devil, The Dead Take the A Train* (with Cassandra Khaw), and *Butcher Bird.* He's written for film and comics, including *Heavy Metal, Lucifer,* and *Hellblazer.*

ALMA KATSU is the multiple Stoker-nominated author of eight books, including three historical horror novels (*The Hunger, The Deep,* and *The Fervor*). She's also written two spy novels to memorialize her long career in intelligence. You can find out more at almakatsubooks.com.

USA Today bestselling author CASSANDRA KHAW is an award-winning game writer whose short fiction can be found in places like *The Magazine of Fantasy and Science Fiction,* Tor.com, and *The Year's Best Fantasy and Science Fiction.* Their novella *Nothing but Blackened Teeth* was a Bram Stoker, World Fantasy, Shirley Jackson, and British Fantasy Award finalist.

JOHN LANGAN is the author of two novels and five collections of stories. For his work, he has received the Bram Stoker and

This Is Horror Awards. He is one of the founders of the Shirley Jackson Awards and serves on its Board of Advisors. He lives in New York, Mid-Hudson Valley with his family and certainly not too many books.

Josh Malerman is the *New York Times* bestselling author of *Bird Box* and *Daphne*. He's also one of two singer/songwriters for the Michigan band the High Strung. He lives in Michigan with the artist/musician Allison Laakko.

Nick Mamatas is the author of several novels, including *The Second Shooter* and *I Am Providence*. His short fiction has appeared in *Best American Mystery Stories*, Tor.com, *Weird Tales*, *Asimov's Science Fiction* and many other venues. Mamatas is also an anthologist; his most recent title is *Wonder and Glory Forever: Awe-Inspiring Lovecraftian Fiction*. His fiction and editorial work have variously been nominated for the Hugo, Bram Stoker, Shirley Jackson, Locus, and World Fantasy awards. Forthcoming is his first critical monograph, *The Way to Higher Ground: Anarchism and Daoism in the Work of Ursula K. Le Guin*.

New York Times bestselling novelist Garth Nix has been a full-time writer since 2001, but has also worked as a literary agent, marketing consultant, book editor, book publicist, book sales representative, bookseller, and as a part-time soldier in the Australian Army Reserve. He has written many books, including the Old Kingdom series beginning with *Sabriel*, the Keys to the Kingdom series, *The Left-Handed Booksellers of London*, and others. He also writes short fiction, with over sixty stories published. More than six million copies of his books have been sold around the world and his work has been translated into 42 languages.

BENJAMIN PERCY is the author of seven novels—most recently *The Sky Vault* (William Morrow)—three story collections, including *Suicide Woods*—and a book of essays, *Thrill Me*, which is widely taught in creative writing classrooms. He writes *Wolverine, X-Force,* and *Ghost Rider* for Marvel Comics. He co-wrote the film *Summering*, which debuted at the Sundance Film Festival in 2022. His work has been published in *GQ, Esquire, Time,* the *New York Times,* the *Wall Street Journal, Men's Journal,* the *Paris Review, Cemetery Dance,* and *Ellery Queen Mystery Magazine.*

MARY RICKERT has worked as kindergarten teacher, coffee shop barista, Disneyland balloon vendor, and personnel assistant in Sequoia National Park. She is the winner of the Locus Award, Crawford Award, World Fantasy Award, and Shirley Jackson Award. She has published three short story collections, and two novels. Her most recent novel, *The Shipbuilder of Bellfairie,* was published by Undertow Publications. Her novella, *Lucky Girl, How I Became a Horror Writer: A Krampus Story* was published in 2022.

Shirley Jackson award-winner KAARON WARREN has published five novels and seven short story collections. She's sold over two hundred short stories to publications big and small around the world and has appeared in Ellen Datlow's *Year's Best* anthologies. Her novel *The Grief Hole* won all three Australian genre awards.

She has lived in Melbourne, Sydney, Fiji, and Canberra, and her most recent novella is *The Deathplace Set*. She won the inaugural AsylumFest Ghost Story Telling Competition in 2022.

ABOUT THE EDITOR

ELLEN DATLOW has been editing science fiction, fantasy, and horror short fiction for forty years as fiction editor of *Omni Magazine*, and editor of *Event Horizon* and *SciFiction*. She currently acquires short stories and novellas for Tor.com. In addition, she has edited around one hundred science fiction, fantasy, and horror anthologies, including the annual *The Best Horror of the Year* series, and most recently *Echoes: The Saga Anthology of Ghost Stories, Final Cuts: New Tales of Hollywood Horror and Other Spectacles, Body Shocks: Extreme Tales of Body Horror,* and *When Things Get Dark: Stories Inspired by Shirley Jackson.*

She's won multiple World Fantasy Awards, Locus Awards, Hugo Awards, Bram Stoker Awards, International Horror Guild Awards, Shirley Jackson Awards, the Splatterpunk Award, the This is Horror! Award, and the 2012 Il Posto Nero Black Spot Award for Excellence as Best Foreign Editor. Datlow was named recipient of the 2007 Karl Edward Wagner Award, given at the British Fantasy Convention for "outstanding contribution to the genre," was honored with the Life Achievement Award by the Horror Writers Association in acknowledgment of superior achievement over an entire career, and honored with the World Fantasy Life Achievement Award at the 2014 World Fantasy Convention.

She lives in New York and co-hosts the monthly Fantastic Fiction Reading Series at KGB Bar. More information can be found at www.datlow.com, on Facebook, and on Twitter as @EllenDatlow. She's owned by two cats.

WHEN THINGS GET DARK: STORIES INSPIRED BY SHIRLEY JACKSON

By Ellen Datlow

Chilling, human, poignant and strange, Shirley Jackson's stories have inspired a generation of writers and readers This anthology, edited by legendary horror editor Ellen Datlow, brings together today's leading horror writers to offer their own personal tribute to the work of Shirley Jackson.

Featuring:

Joyce Carol Oates
Josh Malerman
Carmen Maria Machado
Paul Tremblay
Richard Kadrey
Stephen Graham Jones
Elizabeth Hand
Kelly Link
Cassandra Khaw
Karen Heuler
Benjamin Percy
John Langan
Laird Barron
Jeffrey Ford
M. Rickert
Seanan McGuire
Gemma Files
Genevieve Valentine

IN THESE HALLOWED HALLS: A DARK ACADEMIA ANTHOLOGY

By Marie O'Regan and Paul Kane

In these stories, dear student, retribution visits a lothario lecturer; the sinister truth is revealed about a missing professor; a forsaken lover uses a séance for revenge; an obsession blooms about a possible illicit affair; two graduates exhume the secrets of a reclusive scholar; horrors are uncovered in an obscure academic department; five hopeful initiates must complete a murderous task and much more!

Featuring brand-new stories from:

Olivie Blake
M.L. Rio
David Bell
Susie Yang
Layne Fargo
J.T. Ellison
James Tate Hill
Kelly Andrew
Phoebe Wynne
Kate Weinberg
Helen Grant
Tori Bovalino

TITANBOOKS.COM

For more fantastic fiction, author events,
exclusive excerpts, competitions, limited editions and more

VISIT OUR WEBSITE
titanbooks.com

LIKE US ON FACEBOOK
facebook.com/titanbooks

FOLLOW US ON TWITTER AND INSTAGRAM
@TitanBooks

EMAIL US
readerfeedback@titanemail.com